HARD
AS ICE

HARD
AS ICE

RAVEN
SCOTT

Kensington Publishing Corp.

http://www.kensingtonbooks.com

DAFINA BOOKS are published by

Kensington Publishing Corp.
119 West 40th Street
New York, NY 10018

All Kensington Titles, Imprints, and Distributed Lines are available at special quantity discounts for bulk purchases for sales promotions, premiums, fund-raising, and educational or institutional use. Special book excerpts or customized printings can also be created to fit specific needs. For details, write or phone the office of the Kensington special sales manager: Kensington Publishing Corp., 119 West 40th Street, New York, NY 10018, attn: Special Sales Department, Phone: 1-800-221-2647.

Dafina and the Dafina logo Reg. U.S. Pat. & TM Off.

ISBN-13: 978-1-61773-539-4
ISBN-10: 1-61773-539-6
First Kensington Mass Market Edition: August 2015

eISBN-13: 978-1-61773-540-0
eISBN-10: 1-61773-540-X
First Kensington Electronic Edition: August 2015

10 9 8 7 6 5 4 3 2 1

Printed in the United States of America

To my husband, Scott Henderson—
thank you for your love and support,
and for always making me laugh.

Chapter 1

"How's your first assignment so far, Ice?"

The teasing question came through the video connection from one of the large-panel screen monitors set up around the room. It was from Lucas Johnson, his friend and business partner.

"Well, it's been twenty hours and I haven't been shot yet," Evan replied. "But it's still early."

Lucas laughed.

"Looks like you'll have to get used to the slower pace of civilian work. You might not be under fire for a few days in."

Evan shifted his stance and felt the pull of tight scar tissue in his thigh. The bullet wound was a souvenir from his final CIA mission in Azerbaijan eight months ago. It had been a long road to recovery, including an early retirement from government service. Now, he was a managing partner with Fortis, a full-solution security firm, along with his best friend, Lucas Johnson, and their third partner, Sam Mackenzie. They had a team of twenty-two specialized field agents, technicians, and operations analysts with experience from all branches of elite government service.

As Lucas mentioned, this Boston assignment was Evan's first with Fortis. He was leading a team of three agents on the ground to solve a multimillion-dollar jewelry heist, and recover the assets within a matter of weeks.

"I'll do my best not to get bored," Evan retorted with a hint of a smile.

"Looks like you guys are set up there?"

"Yeah. The additional surveillance is up and running through the building," Evan confirmed. "Michael and Raymond are on-site since early this morning to start the investigation," Evan replied, referring to two of the Fortis agents working on the ground for the mission.

Lucas nodded. His high-definition screen was so sharp, he could have been standing right next to Evan instead of over five hundred miles away in Virginia.

"Yup, we have the images from the Worthington building coming through here, now. When are you going in?" asked Lucas.

Evan checked the time. It was eleven forty-five in the morning. According to their client, Edward Worthington, the key subject usually took lunch at twelve-thirty each day, and had no appointments in her calendar for that afternoon.

"I'm headed to the auction house in a few minutes. I should make first contact before one o'clock," he confirmed.

"Okay. I've assigned two of our analysts here to do the preliminary research on the other employees.

I've sent you what we have so far on James," Lucas explained.

"Got it. I'll review on my cell phone, and give you an update later."

They ended the video call. Evan did a final check on the surveillance equipment. He and his team were based in two hotel suites in downtown Boston, several blocks from their client's offices. One suite served as Evan's temporary residence while in the city as part of his cover, and his three agents were staying in the connected room. In there, two powerful six-core CPUs were connected to four forty-two inch LED flat-screen monitors set up around the living room, creating a control center. Evan looked around the various live feeds, all showing a different view of the Worthington business offices, the large art gallery in the front, and the warehouse in the back. It was a quiet day, with only four employees on the corporate floor, and three in the gallery and warehouse. His gaze landed on the image of Nia James, his target subject, as she sat behind her office desk reviewing several documents. He watched her for a few moments, until his cell phone rang.

"Yeah," he answered briskly, noting it was his third agent, Tony Donellio, assigned to local reconnaissance.

"Hey, Ice, I'm at her apartment." Evan clenched his jaw at the nickname. It was a remnant from his time in the CIA. Though he had left the agency, the Fortis team insisted on using it. That was mostly because Lucas chose to forget his real name.

"Good, do a full search and wire the place up so we have eyes throughout. Then, you're searching the security guard's place, right?" Evan asked.

"Yeah," confirmed Tony. "His shift at Worthington

doesn't start until six tonight, but our intel says he's usually at the gym by three o'clock in the afternoon. I'll be there by about one-thirty to have a look around the area."

"Good. He's the weak link. With nothing of use captured on the Worthington surveillance videos, and no signs of forced entry, there's no way he wasn't involved in the heist. Raymond and Michael are interviewing him tomorrow, but we need to find something on him to use as leverage. I'll meet you back at control later this afternoon."

"Got it," confirmed Tony.

Evan hung up and checked the time again. With one more hard glance at the subject, he checked the clip of his Glock and slid it smoothly in the small belt holster secured against the right side of his back. He added his suit jacket before leaving the hotel room.

In the lobby, the concierge gave him a friendly nod.

"How are you doing, Mr. DaCosta?" asked the middle-aged man, well dressed in a tailored suit.

"I'm good, Carlos. How are you?" Evan replied smoothly.

"Very good, sir. Shall I get your car for you?"

"Please."

Carlos waived at one of the valet attendants to request Evan's car to be brought around.

Worthington was an easy enough walk into the center of downtown, but Evan's cover required the image of wealth and prestige, and that didn't include a brisk walk in balmy May weather. His leased car, a sleek black Bentley, was brought to the front door within a few moments, and Evan smoothly made his way through the streets of Boston.

The Worthington Gallery and Auction House was a small chain owned by Edward Worthington. It had expanded from a single storefront operation based in Connecticut into a national player in the world of arts, jewelry, and estate auctioning over the last twenty years. They now had five locations across the country, a solid reputation, record sales, and plans to expand into Europe. All of that was now in jeopardy. Two nights ago, their Boston office was robbed in a meticulously executed jewelry heist. The thieves managed to enter the warehouse undetected and break into a digital safe, all while bypassing the state-of-the art surveillance and security system.

The stolen jewelry included a white diamond necklace with a rare 13.16 carat pear-shaped red diamond in the center, known as the Crimson Amazon. The piece was scheduled to be exhibited around the world prior to the auction at the end of August. According to appraisals and expert opinion, that necklace alone should fetch over twenty-five million dollars. Along with a broader collection of rare and high-end jewelry pieces, the summer event was now anticipated to be one of the highest-value auctions in years, certainly the biggest in Worthington's history. It would put the company solidly on the map as a major North American player.

Within twelve hours of discovering the robbery, Edward Worthington hired Fortis. Evan and his team of highly trained protection and asset recovery specialists now had under six weeks to find the thieves and recover the jewels intact. As with most of Fortis's assignments, confidentiality and discretion were critical. If Worthington's clients or anyone in the industry discovered this massive breach in security, the auction house would be ruined. Which meant police involvement was not the preferred option at this stage. Fortis had the skills and resources in security, surveillance, investigations, and threat neutralization to quickly and stealthily deliver services to their high-end clients, all without the bureaucratic restrictions of law enforcement.

Evan arrived at the Worthington offices at a few minutes to one o'clock. He parked on the street in a spot where he could see the storefront. With a few moments to spare, he took out his phone to review the file Lucas had sent. Most of it was old information provided by the client in their initial meeting. It confirmed that other than the owner, only one employee knew when the Crimson Amazon necklace had been delivered, and only one had the combination to the safe: Nia James, the managing director. The digital copy of her employee identification photo showed a young woman with a rectangular face and sculpted cheekbones. Her hair was pulled back into a sleek ponytail, accentuating the feline angle of her dark eyes.

Evan scrolled through the other documents to see if there was anything new or revealing about her. Twenty-six years old, valid driver's license, no passport. Born and raised in Detroit, moved to Boston eight years ago to attend college as a part-time student. Worked as a waitress, then graduated four years ago with a B.A. in Business. Senior sales manager at a jewelry store before being hired at Worthington eleven months ago. Clean criminal record, except for a sealed juvenile file.

A tire squeal and a honked horn caught Evan's attention. He looked up to assess the situation and it was easy to see the distraction to drivers nearby. The object of his surveillance was crossing the street at the intersection in front of his car. Nia James walked with a straight, proud posture, her chin held high with bold confidence. She wore a dark skirt-suit, tailored to fit her lithe body like a fine wool wrap. Her lean legs were coppery brown, naked and elongated by high-heeled shoes in a glossy burgundy leather. Their extravagant cost was evident in the telltale red soles. Half her face was covered with oversize sunglasses and her lips were coated in a rich ruby color that accentuated their shapely fullness.

The lunchtime traffic was pretty busy, yet cars slowed as the men driving them did double takes, or stared openly. Even guys walking nearby turned to appreciate the view of her figure, both coming and going. Evan would have found the show amusing, except it uncovered a complication he hadn't anticipated. Nia James was far more attractive in real life than her identification photos suggested. She walked with a smooth, sexy sway that told him she was very aware of her effect on men and was comfortable working it.

If his instincts were correct, and they usually were, he would have to adjust their plan accordingly.

Evan opened the driver's door to the black Bentley convertible just as she passed in front. He slowly unfurled his tall frame to exit the car, fully aware of the impression he made: rich, powerful, young. It was an image designed to capture the attention of an opportunist, and one he's used successfully many times as a covert operative. And like most women, Nia James responded. It was subtle, only with a slight tilt of her head in his direction, but it was enough. First goal accomplished.

She entered the premises, and Evan was only a few

steps behind. The Worthington's offices occupied the first two floors of the historical building. He had the architectural specs well mapped in his head. On the first floor, there was an art gallery and antiquities dealership, selling a wide variety of valuable collectibles on consignment. The business offices were on the second level in an open loft space, accessed from the main floor by a wide, curving staircase. The warehouse and secure storage was is the rear of the building, with a delivery bay backing onto an alley.

Evan stepped through the front doors into the large gallery with twenty-two-foot-high ceilings. The walls were lined with framed art of various types and sizes. The center space had glass display cabinets and sleek tufted white leather benches. He could easily see Nia standing near the rear of the room, next to a reception counter that was manned by another employee. But he started a slow walk around the room, stopping occasionally to admire one of the many drawings, paintings, and photographs. He also knew the moment his target left the area through the door to the warehouse.

"Hi there?"

Evan turned to find a young girl walking toward him. She was twenty-one years old, with a bright smile and even brighter blond hair. And he already knew she was the gallery receptionist and office administrator, Emma Sterling.

"Is there anything I can help you with?" she continued, stopping next to him.

He smiled back.

"I hope so," he stated. "I would like to get some information about your auction services."

"No problem," she replied smoothly. "Are you looking to buy or sell?"

"Sell."

"All right. I'll introduce you to our managing director, Nia. She'll be able to evaluate your needs."

The young girl turned away a little, and pressed a button on a discreet earpiece. She spoke in soft tones for a few seconds before clicking it again and facing him again.

"Nia will be with us shortly. Can I get you something to drink?"

"Sure, some water would be great."

"Sparkling or flat?"

"Hmmm, flat is fine."

"No problem, Mr. . . . ?" She raised a brow and smiled even bigger.

"Evan. Evan DaCosta."

"Great, Mr. DaCosta. Nia will be here shortly."

He nodded and she walked away.

About a minute later, Evan watched Nia James cross the room with the same smooth, sensuous gait he witnessed earlier. He found himself anxious to see her up close, feel how potent her attractiveness was. Not that he would be affected, of course. He'd seen her type too many times over the years to be fooled by the artifice. And glammed-up women weren't really his type. He preferred the outdoorsy, active women who didn't take hours to get ready. The girl next door.

Yet as this woman, their prime suspect in a ballsy jewelry heist, stopped in front of him, Evan stopped breathing.

"Mr. DaCosta," she stated in a sultry voice, her hand

extended. "I'm Nia James. I understand that you'd like to hear more about our auction services?"

She looked up to meet his eyes squarely. Hers were a warm brown, with speckles of copper and honey. Evan cleared his throat, matching her firm handshake. Tiny sparks sizzled up his forearm.

"Nice to meet you, Miss James. I was told Worthington would be able to help with an estate auction?"

They were interrupted before she could respond.

"Here you go, Mr. DaCosta," stated the receptionist as she handed him a chilled bottle of fancy imported spring water.

"Thank you. And it's Evan, please. Mr. DaCosta was my father."

Emma giggled, flipping back her silky blond hair. Evan thought he caught Nia roll her eyes, but it was the tiniest movement, and her pleasant, polite smile didn't waver.

"Thanks, Emma," added Nia. The young girl nodded and walked away.

"Yes, we handle estate sales," continued Nia smoothly. "Depending on what items are involved, we could provide support for an on-site event, as part of a larger auction, or here through our consignment sales. We've also done several successful online auctions if that's something you're interested in."

Evan nodded, taking a small sip of his drink.

"I haven't given it much thought, to be honest. My father died last year, and left me his collection."

"I'm very sorry to hear that," she immediately replied. Her eyes softened, causing Evan to pause. He wasn't expecting authentic empathy. *She's really good.*

"Why don't you come up to my office, and we can go over some of the details?"

He looked at his watch.

"I have a meeting shortly, so I can't stay now. But I can come by again later today. Is six o'clock too late?"

"I'm afraid it is. We close at five."

"That's unfortunate. I have to sort things out as soon as possible. I don't have much time available over the next few weeks before I head back home to Virginia, and Worthington comes very highly recommended."

"I'm sure we can arrange something," Nia offered.

"Good. If you don't mind meeting after hours, I'm staying at the Harbor Hotel. Why don't I make us dinner reservations tonight for six o'clock?"

It wasn't a question, and he could see that Nia was genuinely surprised.

"Mr. DaCosta—"

"Evan, please."

"Evan, that's not necessary."

"Sure it is. If you need to work late to meet me, the least I can do is feed you," he dismissed her qualms while pulling a business card out of his inside jacket pocket. "My cell phone number is on there, and my assistant's."

"But—"

Evan's phone rang, interrupting additional protests.

"Sorry, I have to take this. See you at six," he told her with a nod, then turned to walk briskly across the gallery floor. "Tony, what do you have?"

"The security guard is on the move," the agent stated. "He's on foot, carrying a duffel bag and looks pretty agitated."

"Did he make you?" Evan asked. He was now outside and getting into his car.

"Negative. I just arrived when he burst out of the back entrance of his building. Something spooked him and it wasn't me. I'd bet my paycheck that he's skipping town."

"Follow him," instructed Evan as he revved the engine. "I've got your location and I'm on my way."

He hung up the phone, then pulled the Bentley smoothly out into traffic, headed toward the Boston neighborhood of Dorchester.

Chapter 2

"Wow, he was hot!"

Nia gave Emma an exasperated glance. They were back at the reception desk in the rear of the gallery.

"You think every rich guy who walks in here is hot," Nia replied.

"Not like *that*. I haven't seen anything that yummy in a long time. Rich or not," Emma surmised. "It's just an observation. I'm not interested or anything. I'm seeing someone."

Nia raised an eyebrow but didn't bother to respond. She didn't have time for idle chitchat about men or relationships.

"Has the courier arrived yet?" she asked instead, changing the subject.

"Yup, here you go."

Emma handed her a bundle of envelopes and parcels.

"Thanks," Nia added

"Oh, and Edward's going to be here at about two o'clock this afternoon. Are you still available to meet with him?" Emma asked.

"Of course. My calendar is up to date, so just book whatever time he needs."

Emma nodded, and Nia turned to make her way through the spacious gallery and up the stairs to her office on the second floor. She placed the packages on the desk before shrugging off her suit jacket to drape it over her chair. Once seated, she eased off her shoes and wiggled her toes to stimulate circulation. Her feet were throbbing. As much as she cherished her shoe collection, it was a love/hate relationship.

Thinking about the upcoming meeting with her boss, Edward Worthington, Nia logged into her laptop to double-check her e-mails and schedule for the rest of the afternoon. As suggested, Emma had booked ninety minutes for them to meet in Worthington's office. It was going to be a difficult conversation, and she could not afford to be distracted by any other tasks due by the end of the day. So, she had just over an hour to get as much work done as possible.

But, first things first. Evan DaCosta appeared to be a very viable potential client. She needed to do some research on him and his family to prepare for their meeting that evening. As she launched an Internet name search, Nia nibbled on the side of her cheek, thinking about their brief conversation. It was common for her and the other account managers on her sales team to conduct meetings outside of the office. Their clients were some of the wealthiest in the northeastern United States, which meant they were often very busy and very demanding. Supporting their needs meant being available wherever and whenever they had time.

But Evan DaCosta's suggestion for a dinner meeting had still caught her off guard. Well, it was less of a suggestion and more of a command. And her hesitation had nothing to do with how viable his business could be. While Nia would not admit it to Emma, "hot" was just one way to describe him. Gorgeous, delicious, and sexy as hell also came to mind.

Many of their clients wore Savile Row tailored suits, handmade Italian leather shoes, and Patek Philippe watches. It was her job to notice those types of details as part of the sales assessment process. But none of those things had anything to do with her first impressions of Evan DaCosta as she walked toward him in the gallery. In fact, sales potential was the last thing on her mind. Nia's first thought had been that he was a spectacular male specimen, and it was too bad he was wearing so many layers. He was something north of six feet tall, with broad, tight shoulders that tapered into a lean torso. Her keen eye suspected the real prize was under his very expensive wrapping. Now, the thought of a dinner meeting at his hotel just heightened the inappropriate desire to peel off his clothes.

She let out a deep breath, and tried to focus on the task at hand. While her physical reaction to him as a man was completely human, now was not the time to indulge in fantasies. In the end, Evan DaCosta was no different from any other potential client and she had a job to do, while she still had one.

The Internet search results provided a couple of pages of useful information, mostly about the late Santos DaCosta. Up to his death last year, Santos was the founder and CEO of DaCosta Solutions, a major U.S. military defense contractor based in McLean, Virginia. One site had his obituary, noting that he was born and raised in Brazil where his family owned a coffee plantation. There he met and married his African-American wife Cecile Rothman while her father was the U.S. ambassador to Brazil. They moved to the U.S. soon after, settling in the D.C. area.

Another page had a picture of Santos and Cecile at a charity event a couple of years ago. Evan looked like a blend of both. He had the imposing size, rich hazelnut skin, and wavy hair of his father, but dark eyes and sensuous lips of his mother.

Nia continued to build an account file on the DaCosta family. There were some details about Evan as an only child, working overseas for his father's company, and his appointment as the new CEO at DaCosta Solutions four months ago. There was little about his personal life. Not that she was looking.

Once she was satisfied with her research, she moved on to the various other things that needed to be done in her workday. The biggest focus was the preparation for the upcoming jewelry auction in August and the various exhibits scheduled in the weeks prior. Everything still had to be planned, despite the disastrous events on Monday night. So that's what she would do until Edward told her differently.

When the meeting with her boss was only a few minutes away, Nia took a few quiet moments to try to calm her nerves. But it was hard. At moments like this, it was so easy to relive the sense of panic and disbelief when she opened the safe on Tuesday morning and found it empty, the Crimson Amazon necklace gone, along with half a dozen other pieces of jewelry. Even now, over eighteen hours later, Nia was still in disbelief, her heart often racing with dread. Of the nine permanent employees in the Boston office, she and Edward were the only ones who had known the diamond was in the safe, and only they knew the combination, which Edward had updated the Friday prior as an added measure of security.

With no sign of a break-in, or anything suspicious on the surveillance cameras, it was logical to assume it was an inside job. It didn't take much to deduct she would be the first person suspected.

With another deep breath, she slipped on her shoes and walked to the much bigger office only a few feet from hers. Edward was standing behind his desk on the phone. With a slim build and a full head of hair, he was still an attractive man for fifty-five years old. He also had a kind, open face with a personality to match. Though today, his face looked much more tired and haggard than usual. Nia really enjoyed working for him, and only hoped the current situation would not put an end to that.

When he saw her waiting by the doorway, he waved her in, gesturing to the small, round table in the middle of the room. She nodded and walked over to sit in one of four chairs around it.

"How are you doing?" he asked once his call ended.

His eyes showed genuine concern. Nia felt her throat close with the urge to cry. She blinked and tried to smile.

"I'm okay," she replied.

He walked across the room and sat beside her.

"The investigators want to meet with you tomorrow morning to review everything that happened on Monday afternoon and Tuesday when you came in," he continued.

"Okay, but I don't really have much else to contribute."

"I know, but these guys are professionals. They're

hoping you'll remember something more during the conversation."

"You mean the interrogation," she stated, trying really hard not to sound resentful.

Edward shrugged with one shoulder. After working together for almost a year, he was used to her blunt honesty.

"It can't be helped, Nia. Yes, it might be uncomfortable, but I've hired them to solve this problem as quickly as possible. So they're going to take the straightest route to the answers."

"I know. Of course I'll cooperate," she conceded, feeling a little childish. "Are you sure this is the best approach, Edward? Shouldn't we just call the police and the insurance company? For all we know, they've already taken the pieces out of the country. It's safe to assume they'll be broken down and sold as loose stones."

Edward let out a deep breath and ran both hands through his gray-streaked brown hair.

"From what I've been told, Fortis is the best at finding things. This is what they do. If there is any chance to get the pieces back intact, I have to try. But, if we don't have any answers back by the end of the week, then I might have to pull the plug on the whole thing."

Nia nodded. It seemed pretty unlikely that anything could be solved within the next couple days. She had been in the jewelry industry long enough to know this was the work of professional and well-funded thieves. They weren't waiting around to be found with the goods.

"In the meantime, it's business as usual," Edward continued. "Let's look at last month's numbers."

They spent the remainder of the meeting reviewing

the sales results from her team. As managing director for the Boston office, Nia was responsible for the overall revenue. She had four sales managers under her, all who secured new and repeat clients to sell and buy valuable inventory. Her team also included two sales coordinators who provided support for the various events scheduled every week. All the other support functions were managed by the operations manager, Chris Morton; Emma; and temporary warehouse staff when needed. It was a small team. But as the newest Worthington location, the costs needed to be kept low until they started to make a profit. If the August auction was half as successful as anticipated, it would guarantee their profitability by the end of the year. It was just one more thing that was at risk.

Nia was back in her office just after four o'clock. By the time she finally went through the stack of courier deliveries and responded to various phone and e-mail messages, it was after five. There was no time to stop at home before the meeting with Evan DaCosta. She pulled a mirror out of her desk drawer to have a look at how her makeup was holding up. With some blotting to her nose, and the reapplication of her lipstick, she'd be okay. Her skirt was a little crushed, but it couldn't be helped. With her jacket on, it would have to do.

The hotel was only a five- or ten-minute cab ride from the office, so she continued working for another half hour. That left enough time to pack up her large purse with her laptop, power cable, and cell phone before she locked up her office and freshened up in the bathroom. Everyone else on her sales team was already gone for the night.

Down in the gallery, Emma and Chris Morton where near the main doors, locking things up.

"Hey Chris," Nia said politely.

"Hey," he replied, pausing to look back at her. "Have you met with those security consultants yet?" he asked.

Nia looked at him speculatively. Chris was a few years older than her, maybe in his early thirties. He was a decent-looking guy, with dark hair and hazel eyes. Many of the women in the office thought he was charming, including Emma. But Nia didn't see it. He was nice enough, but just didn't seem to know when to take no for an answer.

"Not yet. I have a meeting with them tomorrow morning," she confirmed.

"Me too. I just don't get why Edward is looking at a new security system. The one we have is barely a year old."

Nia shrugged. That was the memo that Edward has sent to the rest of the employees yesterday. That he was bringing in a security consulting firm to review their current system and protocols, then make recommendations for improvement.

"I guess you can't be too careful," Nia suggested.

Chris smiled back.

"I'm meeting them tomorrow too," inserted Emma, looking between Nia and Chris.

"Well, I'm sure it will be fine. Have a good night, guys," added Nia before pushing through the front doors.

Outside, she flagged down a taxi and arrived at her destination with a few minutes to spare. The Boston Harbor was a swanky, five-star waterfront hotel. Nia had been there a few other times over the years for sale conferences and charity events. The food was always fantastic.

At the entrance of the main restaurant, she approached the hostess.

"Hi, ma'am, will you be dining alone or with a party?" the young woman asked.

"Hi, I'm meeting Mr. Evan DaCosta. I believe he has reservations?" Nia replied, questioningly.

The hostess smiled brightly.

"Miss James, I presume?"

Nia blinked.

"Yes."

"Wonderful. Mr. DaCosta is running a few minutes late. He asked that you meet him in his hotel room. Oliver will escort you upstairs," she told Nia, gesturing to a bellhop standing nearby.

Nia opened her mouth to object, looking back and forth between the two polite and eager hotel employees, but closed it instead. They wouldn't have any answers to her questions.

"Thank you," she stated instead.

In her head, she was thinking there was no way she was going up to that hotel room! Sure, Google had confirmed his identity, but it couldn't guarantee that he wasn't a serial rapist or murderer. Now, she wished she had satisfied her curiosity and done more digging into his life.

"Right this way, ma'am," urged the bellhop as he walked farther into the lobby and toward the elevators.

"Would you mind giving me a minute to make a quick phone call?" she asked, bringing them to a stop.

"Certainly," he replied, then walked a few steps away to give her some privacy.

Nia reached into her purse and pulled out the business card she had tucked into the inside pocket earlier that afternoon. She had no idea what she was going to say to Mr. DaCosta to cancel the meeting, but that was exactly what she was going to do. Or would have done, if he had answered his phone. But he didn't. Instead, it went to voice mail. She hung up and let out a deep breath. Then she dialed his assistant's number.

"Evan DaCosta's office, Sandra speaking. How can I help you?"

"Yes, hi. My name is Nia James. I have a six o'clock appointment with Mr. DaCosta."

"Yes, Miss James. Are you at the hotel? Did you get the message at the restaurant?" the woman asked.

"Yes, I'm downstairs. But—"

"Good! We'll see you in his room shortly."

And the line went dead. *Really?!*

"Is everything okay, ma'am?" asked the bellhop.

Well, if Nia took Evan's assistant literally, it sounded like they were both in his room. Her well-earned street-wise instincts told her something was still fishy. But, it now seemed less likely that it was all an elaborate ruse to kill her, or worse.

"Yes, thank you. I'm all set."

The young man nodded politely and gestured for her to follow him. He guided her into the elevators where they exited on an upper floor, then stopped at the end of the hall.

"Here you are, ma'am. Have a great evening."

Then he was gone, without even hinting for a tip.

Nia squared her shoulders, brushed invisible lint off her suit jacket, then knocked. The door was immediately opened by a middle-aged woman in a blue pantsuit. She smiled warmly and opened the door widely.

"Miss James, thank you for being so flexible this evening. I'm Sandra Blake, Evan's assistant."

Nia followed her into the room, her apprehension reduced considerably. Sandra reminded her of the head librarian at the UMass Boston campus library. A stickler for the rules but pretty harmless and motherly otherwise.

"Nice to meet you, Sandra," she replied with a genuine smile. "Is Mr. DaCosta still available? I'm happy to rebook our meeting if needed."

"He's just finishing a call, then he's all yours. We've just had a few delays with a contract negotiation. So it seemed easier for him to meet you here while we wait for the final paperwork to be sent. Why don't you have a seat?"

Nia looked across the very expansive room toward the seating area near the wraparound windows of the corner suite. She also took in the full-size dining area, and the double French doors that must lead into the separate bedroom. It was a beautiful room, decorated with stately pieces, traditional style, and character. Very representative of historical Boston.

"Would you like something to drink?" continued Sandra.

"No, thank you," she replied, perching on the edge of the sofa, placing her tote-size purse on the cushion beside her. "I'm fine for now."

"I'll let Evan know you're here. I'm sure he'll be out shortly."

Sandra went through the French doors, leaving Nia alone in the parlor.

After one minute turned into ten, she couldn't sit idle any longer. Nia walked across the room to look out at the harbor and city-line. Once in front of the windows, she noticed a door that let out onto a large terrace. Without hesitation, she opened the door and stepped outside. The May evening was cool and breezy at such a height, but it was such a spectacular view that Nia lost track of time.

"It's beautiful, isn't it?"

She jumped with surprise before turning to the voice. It was Evan DaCosta, standing near the terrace doors. His jacket and tie were gone, and his crisp white shirt had the sleeves rolled up past his elbows and several buttons undone at the neck. The wind pressed the cotton and fine wool of his clothes against his body, confirmation of her earlier assessment. He was a pretty spectacular male specimen.

"Yes, it is," she finally replied, glad for the distance between them to hide her discomfort. "I'm sorry. I hope you don't mind me coming out here."

He smiled. A slow teasing twist of well-shaped lips.

"Access to the balcony is the least I can offer you after keeping you waiting so long. I should be the one apologizing."

She looked away, back out at the harbor. Funny things were happening in her stomach. Things that had no place at a business meeting.

"Your assistant let me know you were unexpectedly detained. Did everything work out?" she asked politely as she walked toward him.

"Yes, finally. Sandra just left with everything she needs."

Nia smiled back, but it felt stiff. If Sandra was gone, they were alone. In his very impressive hotel room. With his shirt open low enough for her to see the smooth, silky skin of his firm pecs.

"As I told her, I know you have limited time to decide what to do with your father's collection but I'm happy to reschedule for a better time in your schedule," she explained as she brushed by him to reenter the suite.

The scent of his woodsy, amber aftershave teased her nose.

"Nonsense. I'll order dinner in and kill two birds with one stone. What do you feel like eating?" dismissed Evan.

"All right, then," she conceded. "Fish would be fine, whatever they have available."

"Fish it is. Make yourself comfortable."

Nia sat back down on the sofa next to her purse, and watched out of the corner of her eyes as he placed their order through a tablet on the desk near the bedroom.

"White wine?" he asked a few moments later, holding up a chilled bottle.

"Thank you," replied Nia against her better judgment. But something about the man made her feel jumpy, unsettled. Maybe a little wine would help to relax her. It would also be rude to decline.

He sat down on the other side of the couch and handed her a glass of crisp, golden liquid.

"They had sea bass, so I hope that's okay?" She nodded. "Good. Now, let's get to work."

Chapter 3

Five hours earlier, Evan and Tony were converging on Matt Flannigan. The Worthington night-shift security guard was still walking at a rapid pace through the neighborhood streets of Dorchester. With the brim of his baseball hat brim pulled low, he looked around with frequent, sharp glances as though he was worried about being followed.

"He's headed toward you on Bay Street, Ice," advised Tony through the tiny earpiece Evan was wearing.

"There's a subway station about two blocks east," Evan replied as he jogged in that direction. "That has to be where he's headed. Let's take him near the entrance. There'll be enough people around so we don't draw any attention."

"Got it," Tony confirmed.

Two minutes later, Evan spotted the suspect a half a block away, with the other Fortis agent following at a steady but discreet distance.

"Okay, I have eyes," he notified Tony. "I'll get ahead of you so he's cornered. . . . Shit!"

Suddenly, Flannigan ducked between two buildings and disappeared from view. Both Evan and Tony burst into full-speed sprints, determined not to lose their target. Tony turned into the alley first, just as the distinctive sound of two sharp pops went off, echoing faintly against old brick and stone.

"Tony, what do we have?" Evan demanded within paces of the scene, his gun drawn and pointed to the ground. Thankfully, the street was vacant of pedestrians.

"He's down," Tony replied a few seconds later.

Evan ducked between the buildings and ran to where Tony was standing, next to a big dumpster. The body of Matt Flannigan was sprawled out on the pavement, with a bullet wound in his forehead. Evan registered all the details as he took cover to case the immediate area. The shooter could still be in the vicinity, ready to complete his objective. They waited for several minutes, but nothing happened.

"Did you see anything?" he asked Tony, as they both holstered their weapons.

"Nothing specific, just movement at the other side of the alley. Whoever it was knew he would cut through here and was waiting for him."

The men looked down at the body, with the duffel bag still draped across his chest, then back at each other hard for a few seconds with understanding. The killer hadn't tried to take anything. It wasn't a robbery, it was an execution. Which meant Flannigan was nothing but a pawn.

"Check him just in case," Evan instructed before he ran to other end of the alley. A quick but thorough survey of the area didn't produce any additional information. Whoever shot Flannigan was long gone.

By four-thirty, Evan and his team had reconvened for an update in the hotel room that was now their control center. His partners, Lucas and Sam, were joining by video from their headquarters outside of Alexandria, Virginia.

"Why are we changing the plan, Ice?" asked Lucas through the telepresence.

Evan rubbed at his chin, thinking through the new variables discovered today that changed the viability of his original plan for Nia James.

"We built the covert approach to get as close to James as quickly as possible and confirm her involvement in the robbery," Evan explained. "Based on the information Edward provided about her as smart, dedicated, and honest to a fault, and her fairly clean background, we made the logical assumption that if she were involved in the robbery it was likely as an unwilling participant in this heist. Perhaps coerced by a boyfriend, or forced to participate for some other reason. As such, she would be scared, vulnerable, and looking for any way to get out of the mess. So by presenting me as an eager buyer of hot goods, we could see if she would take the bait out of desperation. Her reaction alone would tell us if she was in some way involved."

His team all nodded from their various positions in the room. Tony was standing beside Evan, similar in height and size, but about ten years older. After spending over twenty years with Interpol, he was their expert in stolen commodities. If there was any intel about the heist in the black market, he would find it.

"It's a good plan," Sam stated from his seat beside Lucas in the large conference room at their headquarters.

"It *was* good," Evan countered. "When we had the security guard as our weak link, and could play James and Flannigan off each other until one of them cracked. But someone's taken him out of the equation."

"He was the key," stated Raymond Blunt, their on-site security specialist. He was about the same age as Evan, with a long, wavy head of dirty blond hair that made him look more like a surfer than a former NSA specialist. "There is no way someone inside or outside Worthington got around their video surveillance and the motion sensor technology throughout the gallery and near the safe without his help. Flannigan might have missed the image loop on the security cameras, even though I found it in two minutes, but he couldn't have missed the thirty-minute power disruption to the warehouse sensors. There would have been warnings lighting up his security monitors until they were manually turned off."

"Well, judging by the bullet in his head, he wasn't the thief," Tony added. "He only had a couple of hundred bucks on him. Whoever took him out never even tried to take what he had, so they just wanted to shut him up."

"And we couldn't get to his apartment before the police," Evan explained.

"Flannigan must have made a real mess because his girlfriend got home just after he left and thought they had been robbed," continued Tony. "The cops were still investigating when his body was found. It might be a couple of days before I can get in."

"So, right now, that only leaves James as our prime suspect," summarized Lucas.

Evan crossed his arms across his chest and took a deep breath.

"Except we never considered that she may actually be the thief or a willing accomplice."

"Not seriously, anyway," Tony added, walking up to stand beside Evan. "It didn't make sense at the time. Selling the red diamond was going to make her career in the auction world, and earn her a tidy bonus. So why risk it by stealing the necklace and other pieces?"

"Yup, we agreed, it didn't make sense," Lucas chimed in. "Particularly since she would obviously be the first person under suspicion."

"So that left her as an unwilling accomplice, likely coerced with some serious leverage," finished Evan.

"Assuming she is the inside man, not someone else within Worthington," threw in Sam. "I still think she's too convenient."

"She was the only one with the code to the safe, so we have to put her at the top of this list," stated Michael Thorpe.

He was the last, and youngest member of Evan's team. As a former FBI agent, he was their prime investigator.

They all nodded.

"So, what's changed your thinking, Ice?" Lucas asked again.

"My gut. Now that I've met James, I can't see her as a victim. This woman has her game together, tight."

"You mean, she's sexy as hell?" chuckled Raymond.

The other men grinned knowingly.

"Yeah, she's attractive. But it's more than that. She knows it and she's working it," Evan explained, turning away to pace the room. "Every instinct tells me the desperate victim role just doesn't fit."

"And if she's not an unwilling accomplice, then she's either willingly involved, and smart enough to set it up so she's too obvious a suspect to seriously be considered . . ." Lucas added.

"Or she's not our man," finished Sam.

There was silence as the six men thought it through for a few minutes.

"Tony, are you sure there was nothing significant in her apartment?" Evan asked.

"Nope. It was clean. Lots of expensive clothes and shoes, but nothing to suggest she's in any kind of trouble," he replied.

"Her financials are good. Pretty boring, actually," Raymond added. "She spends a pretty penny on her appearance, between designer stores and spas, but otherwise, she's in the black. There's money in the bank and solid equity in her condo. We can't find anything to suggest money is the motivator here."

"Money is always a motivator," Evan stated, still pacing.

"Or she's just innocent," mumbled Sam, again. He liked to play devil's advocate, and take the opposite side of almost every debate.

"Maybe," whispered Evan.

"We haven't found much to go on with other employees. They all seem fairly normal, no red flags yet," Raymond added.

"It's only been a day and a half, but things are completely quiet underground," Tony stated.

"Which means, whoever stole the jewels likely already had a buyer lined up. If there were hot goods of this value in the black market, someone would be talking about it. It wasn't random or opportunistic. It was meticulously thought out," explained Evan.

"And someone at Worthington had to have provided some of the intel, or did the deed," Michael assessed. "According to Edward, Flannigan wouldn't have known when the jewels were arriving or the code for the safe."

"Exactly," confirmed Evan.

"So, back to the covert operation," Lucas stated. "Ice, you're thinking: If James is clever enough to help plan this whole thing and fool us by putting herself out there as the prime suspect, and if she already has a buyer, she's not going to take the bait of you as a potential buyer for the jewels."

"But, if you're a boyfriend or love interest, she will eventually let something slip," Tony finished.

"From what we know, she's unattached and clearly has a taste for expensive things. What could be better than a wealthy businessman from out of town to sweep her off her feet? Close proximity to her will also give me access to her communications outside of work. It will take a little longer than we thought, but it will work. If she has anything to hide, I will find it," Evan added without smugness. It was a strategy he'd used very successfully on several occasions.

"I guess it's lucky for you that's she's so attractive, Ice," Lucas stated with a wolfish grin. The team could always trust him to insert his sense of humor in almost every situation.

Evan shrugged with a hint of a smile on his lips.

"It's a tough job, boys. But I'm doing it for the mission."

They all laughed.

"Okay, looks like we have a new plan for James," Lucas confirmed. "Edward is giving us until Friday to produce a solid lead, either on the buyer or thief. We can now confirm that Flannigan was the security breach, and I'll update him on our status tomorrow. Ice, we're keeping your covert investigation under wraps for now, even from Edward. It's too vital to risk any exposure."

Evan nodded in agreement before Lucas and Sam

disconnected their video feed. Evan checked his watch and he turned to face his team.

"Okay, I have my assistant from DaCosta Solutions on her way here to play her role," he told them. "Let's turn on the surveillance for the parlor in my suite. I'll keep James waiting for about thirty minutes. Let's see what she does with that free time. Maybe we'll get lucky, and she'll make a very informative phone call."

He then studied the video feed now available for the living area of his suite to understand the scope of the monitoring.

"Okay, showtime," he declared. "Let's connect later tonight to see if we have any progress."

An hour later, Evan was sitting across from Nia James discussing his father's death. The best cover stories were always based on the truth.

"Did he have heart problems?" Nia asked.

Though she held the wineglass as they spoke, she had only taken two sips. But her posture had gradually relaxed over the last fifteen minutes. Where originally she had been perched at the edge of her seat, both feet planted flat, she now had her legs crossed toward him and leaned against the back cushion. Evan could sense that she was still on guard, but no longer ready to bolt.

"No, not that we were aware of. Honestly, if he had experienced anything, I don't think he would have told us. My dad was not one to share the burden."

"That must have been hard on your mom," she surmised.

"Yeah, I suppose. They were together a long time and he traveled a lot for the business. I think they just fell into a routine."

"His sudden death must have been a shock."

He nodded, a frown wrinkling his brow. How had they gotten into such an intimate and honest conversation about his life? His father?

"I'm sure you've seen and heard your share of family drama in the auction business," he replied, shifting direction. "How long have you been doing it?"

"Almost a year," she replied. "I was in retail jewelry before that. And I have seen some pretty interesting situations. Death and divorce doesn't always mix well with money and inheritance."

"Yet they go hand in hand," he murmured.

"Unless you just avoid them," she stated with a teasing grin. "Except money, of course."

Evan laughed. "Of course."

His eyes were drawn to her red-stained lips, and the glossy white of her teeth. She was even prettier when she smiled like that. It was almost wicked. He liked it.

"Is that what you're doing?" he probed.

"What do you mean?" she asked, though she was sharp enough to know exactly what he meant.

"You're not wearing a ring, so I have to assume you're not married. Is that your plan to live forever? Avoid marriage and all its messy complication?"

She raised a brow, and he felt scolded before she even responded. Though he could tell she was still amused.

"I'm not sure that's an appropriate question, Mr. DaCosta. Or a feasible plan."

He laughed again.

"So I'm back to 'Mr. DaCosta,' am I? Well, I'll just have to work my way back to being Evan."

Nia narrowed her eyes dramatically, letting him

know she was onto his flirty game and was not having any of it. She was clearly used to effectively dealing with even the most subtle advances. Evan was suddenly eager to find out what she'd do when he really turned it on.

There was a knock at the door.

"This should be dinner," he stated, standing up. "Why don't we eat the table?"

Two of the hotel waitstaff entered the room to set the table and lay out their meals. Evan watched Nia remove her suit jacket to drape it over the back of the dining chair before she sat down. Underneath, she wore a silk tunic in pale lavender with a draping scoop neck. The feminine color made her skin look soft and silky. He suddenly wished she would undo her hair from the tight ponytail so he could see it flowing around her face and shoulders.

He cleared his throat, uncomfortable with the directions of his thoughts. Then he rationalized them. The more relaxed and comfortable she got, the easier it would be to connect with her. And the faster he would get the intel he needed. *Right?*

Once their meals were ready, Evan escorted the hotel staff to the door with a tip, then joined Nia at the table. He knew the moment he sat kitty-corner to her at the table that she had reinforced her defenses.

"This turned out to be a much better solution, don't you think, Ms. James? A quiet dinner here rather than a loud restaurant? Much more conducive to business," he explained as he topped her wineglass. "I hope the sea bass is to your liking."

"Thank you, I'm sure it will be. I've always found the food at this hotel to be excellent."

They ate silently for a few moments.

"So, what else do you need to know about my father's estate?"

"You said earlier that you live in McLean, Virginia," she confirmed.

"My parents. Or at least my mom does now. I live a little farther south."

Nia nodded, and took a sip of her wine.

"Is that where the collection is? At your parents' home?"

"Most of it. There are some in his office, but I'll see if Sandra can have them transported to the house for you."

"How many pieces?" she asked.

Evan shrugged. He really had no clue. His dad had commented a few years ago that there were over fifty original contemporary paintings, and he'd certainly acquired several more since.

"I'm not sure, but I'd guess over one hundred pieces including painting, sculptures, and other antiquities."

"And you want to sell the full collection? Nothing you want to keep?"

"I'm not really a collector. There may be a couple of things I'll hold on to. Dad has an old mahogany humidor in his office that I've always liked," Evan told her honestly. "He said it was his grandfather's. I'll keep it."

"Once you go through all the items again, I'm sure there are other things you'll want," she assured him with a soft smile.

"So what do you think? Is this something you and your people can manage?" he finally asked.

"I would be happy to, Mr. DaCosta. From what you described, your father certainly has an impressive collection, and it would do well at auction or on consignment.

We've done lots of work in the D.C. area, so I think we have options," she replied.

"Good, then it looks like I've found myself a solution."

"Excellent."

She stood, slipping her jacket back on as though the meeting was over.

"Grab your drink, let's go enjoy the evening view outside and toast our agreement," Evan added, standing also.

He strode to the terrace doors and stepped through, holding it open for her. Nia was a few steps behind, indicating she had hesitated to follow. But she was there, with her face void of expression. He walked beside her to the rails, the evening breeze whipping around them.

"Here's to a lucrative business relationship," Evan declared, raising his wineglass.

"Cheers," she replied, tapping her glass to the rim of his.

They both took a drink, and their eyes met. Hers were filled with an unexpected mix of nervousness and speculation. Then her gaze dropped to his lips, and Evan felt a deep pull at the base of his stomach. She lowered her glass and licked the corner of her mouth. His eyes were instantly drawn to the spot, with a need to trail his tongue across the path hers had taken.

Their eyes met again.

"When will you have the necessary paperwork done?" he asked briskly, his tone deep with guilty arousal. Now was not the time to lose sight of the endgame.

"I should have it ready for you to sign by tomorrow morning."

"Good. Now that we have an agreement, have dinner with me again tomorrow."

She was about to take another sip of her wine, but paused with the glass halfway up to her lips.

"There're really no need, Mr. DaCosta, we can take care of the contract by e-mail."

"I'm not talking about your auction services, Nia," he replied, stretching out her name. "I want to enjoy your company for the evening."

Evan recognized his mistake the moment the words left his lips. Something in the way he said the words made it sound like a proposition, rather than a date, for Christ's sake! Her eyes turned from cautious to stone cold in seconds. Damn, he must be rusty. Thank God the team wasn't able to hear him, he thought to himself.

He instinctively reached out to touch her arm. Nia shrugged it off delicately, stepping back and placing her wineglass down on a small bistro table next to them. Her expression was still polite, but he could feel the anger radiating from her.

"Nia, that's—"

He intended to say that his words had come out wrong. That he didn't mean to imply she was for sale or something. But she cut him off with a chilled tone.

"Mr. DaCosta, thank you for dinner and considering Worthington for your needs. But I'm afraid I can't provide you with the services you are seeking."

As she turned to walk away, he grabbed her arm in a grip firmer than he intended. She pulled back with surprising strength and momentum. Evan reacted, pulling her back toward him. She stumbled in her shoes, landing against his chest. He quickly put down his drink in order to catch her before she fell farther.

"Nia," he stated, looking down at her. Fear now

replaced anger in her brilliant, feline eyes, yet she still tugged at his hold, defiantly.

He didn't think, he didn't strategize, he just kissed her.

She froze against him, but Evan was on autopilot. Her body felt soft and lush in his arms. The scent of her skin teased him, like dark, sweet cherries. He swept his tongue along her lips, wanting to taste more, praying she would open for him. Something dark and primitive was driving him to savor the moment before they both came to their senses.

Her lips parted with a sigh, and Evan deepened the kiss. Nia tentatively brushed his tongue with hers, and sharp tingles of energy swept down his spine. One of them groaned and he felt the vibration in his balls. He pulled her closer, with his arms wrapped solidly around her lithe body, devouring her mouth like a starving man. It was hot, deep, and so intimate that sweat broke out on his forehead.

If the way that Nia was responding to him was any indication of how successful his cover was going to be, Evan should have been elated. After all, he had almost blown it with his thoughtless remark. Yet, all he felt was out of control, like he was drowning and couldn't get enough air. His heart was racing, his body hard and throbbing. And none of it had to do with his cover, his job, or the mission.

Evan let go of her, stepping back so he could cool down. He watched through hooded eyes as she brushed her hand over her lips with a dazed look on her face, as though she was as confused as he was. It made him feel better. Just a little.

"I'm sorry, Nia," he stated.

She straightened her shoulders and faced him squarely.

Whatever she had been thinking was now erased from her face.

"For what exactly, Evan?" she shot back. "For insinuating I'm a commodity available to buy? Or for . . . that?"

She gestured between them with her hands, obviously indicating the kiss. Evan wiped his lips with his finger, certain they were now stained with her red lipstick. There was only a trace of bold color left on hers.

"For the former. Definitely not for the latter."

She just glared at him.

"Nia, I am inviting you to have dinner with me to spend more time with you, get to know you better. That's all. No strings," he clarified.

"Why?"

Evan raised his brows.

"I think we both know why, Nia. I like you. I'm attracted to you, that's why."

"I mean, to what end, Evan?"

He smiled with satisfaction. This woman was not a helpless victim, or easily manipulated. Nia James was just as sharp and strong-willed as he had predicted. He licked his lips deliberately, suggestively, reminding her of how hot they had both been only moments earlier.

"Ms. James, do I have to explain the birds and the bees to you? This can't be the first time you've been asked out on a date?"

She looked away, exasperated with his teasing.

"This isn't a game, Mr. DaCosta. I'm not interested in being played with, nor am I for sale."

Evan nodded. He stepped to her, close enough to enjoy her scent without touching.

"Like I said, I'm attracted to you and I would like to get to know you better. If you're not interested, just say no. But either way, you will still have my business."

Nia looked away briefly to a spot over his shoulder.

"It's late, I have to go," was all she said in response.

He nodded again, feeling awkward.

"All right, I'll walk you out."

As they walked across the terrace, Evan's mind was racing. He'd screwed up. Nothing had gone according to his plan. Instead of wooing her with the promise of a quick liaison, he had let his physical reaction to her mess with his control. Now, their best opportunity to solve the job fast was about to walk out the door.

In the hotel suite, she picked up her purse off the sofa and continued to the front door.

"Nia." She paused with her hand on the door handle, her back to him. "Send me the auction papers in the morning."

She turned to face him then, her shoulders stiff and back straight. Her eyes met his unflinchingly. They were sharp and clear, letting him know that anything further that happened was her decision, including accepting his business. Evan had to admire her balls.

"Good night, Mr. DaCosta."

Chapter 4

Nia was barely aware of the cab ride home from the hotel. Her mind was running in a hundred directions, trying to make sense of the evening. And the kiss.

That kiss was . . . spectacular, on every level. She had felt it from her lips down to her toes, and in every erogenous zone in between. Even now, she clearly remembered the impact, and recrossed her legs to smother the tingle between her thighs. How was it possible for a virtual stranger to light her up like that, with just a kiss?

The situation itself was not all that unique. Men often asked her out, from clients to business associates. Some even propositioned an "arrangement," like she had assumed Evan was doing. They might be married or engaged, but wanted something on the side, from one night to full-on mistress status. It was not uncommon in the world that Nia worked in.

She had learned years ago that the wealthy elite lived by a different set of rules than regular people, and very often had a different moral compass. It usually didn't bother her, and she had developed a knack for effectively turning down the offers. In fact, many of those men had become regular buyers or repeat customers over the years. Of course, some still continued to try getting into her bed. After all, men in general, rich or poor, wanted what they couldn't have.

It was true that Nia did get more than her fair share of offers. Her best friend, Lianne, insisted it wasn't just because she was an attractive woman. Lianne claimed that Nia, with her power suits and killer stilettos, had a high-end dominatrix vibe going on that drove men nuts. They had some sort of primitive urge to break her control or have her control them. The instinct was likely even stronger for powerful and influential men. Nia assumed Lianne, a psychologist, knew what she was talking about. As fascinating as that might be, it didn't matter. Her weakness for expensive clothes had more to do with once being the poor girl in a wealthy school than attracting men. And she wasn't looking for a sugar daddy or husband right now, anyway. She only wanted clients with big wallets or valuable collectibles to sell.

At least, it usually was. Evan DaCosta had caught her eye from the moment he had stepped out of his car in front of Worthington. Something about him got under her skin. Sure, he was good-looking in a clean-cut, Boy Scout sort of way. But it wasn't really about that. From their first meeting in the gallery, he seemed strong and capable. Not that she needed those things. Nia had spent years taking care of herself, and certainly wasn't looking for a man to take over. But she couldn't deny that she was attracted to him.

Now the question was what to do about it.

It was shortly after nine o'clock when the cab dropped her off in front of her two-floor apartment in a South Boston duplex. Once inside, Nia peeled off her clothes upstairs in her bedroom, and headed straight into the bathroom for a long shower. She used the time to wash her hair, and to think. There was so much going on, between the upcoming auction and the investigation into the theft. It was hardly time to start dating someone new.

Or maybe it was exactly what she needed. Maybe a harmless diversion would help her get through the next few weeks. Assuming she didn't get fired, or arrested for a crime she didn't commit. And since Evan was only in Boston for work, why not at least go out for dinner? Standing in front of her foggy bathroom mirror, Nia couldn't think of a good objection.

Decision made, she slathered her skin with body cream and dried her hair straight, before dressing in soft cotton pajamas. Downstairs, with her iPad and a cup of tea, she spent the remainder of the evening listening to music and reading all the web links about Evan DaCosta that she had skipped over earlier. Diversion or not, she still wanted to know exactly who and what she was getting involved with.

Nia headed up to bed at around eleven o'clock. She snuggled under the covers, ready to fall asleep to the drone of the nightly news with her bedroom television on sleep mode.

"In local news, the police have identified the body of the man killed in Dorchester this afternoon," the female news anchor stated. "Matthew Flannigan, a local resident of Dorchester, was shot dead in an alley near the Savin Hill train station. . . ."

Nia bolted up into a sitting position, certain she had heard wrong. But the portrait on the television screen was indeed that of the Worthington security guard. The same security guard who had worked the night shift during a flawlessly executed robbery just forty-eight hours ago.

She flopped back onto her pillow, covering her mouth with both hands while her heart beat fast and hard. First theft, now murder? The people who were behind this were serious. And with over thirty million dollars of irreplaceable jewelry in play, there was likely very little they wouldn't do to get away with it all.

How the hell had she ended up in this middle of this crazy mess?

Nia's mind raced in circles for several hours before she managed to get some restless sleep. Thursday morning, she skipped her usual workout at the gym in order to get into the office before eight o'clock. The investigators had booked two hours with her, starting at nine, so she planned to get as much work as possible done before that, including the contract for Evan.

"Morning, Nia."

She looked up to find one of her sales coordinators, Adam Peterson leaning against her door. He was one of the first hires she had made when she joined the team, and was still one of her favorite employees. He was bright, energetic, and creative, always willing to go above and beyond to get the job done.

"Hi, Adam," Nia replied somberly. "Did you see the news?"

"You mean about Matt? Yeah, I couldn't believe it," Adam replied, stepping closer to her desk and lowering his voice. "Do you think it was random? Like robbery or something?"

Nia nibbled on the side of her bottom lip.

"I don't know," she replied, wishing she didn't have to lie.

"I saw Chris a little while ago and he seems pretty shaken up," Adam continued. "They were good friends."

"Really?" Nia probed.

"I think so. They hung out together on the weekends, and stuff. Emma too."

Nia looked down at her desk, trying to hide the surprise and alarm on her face. His innocent words had planted a seed in her brain that was rapidly growing. There was no doubt in her mind that Matt had been the inside man for the robbery. He must have provided access to the premises. Did Chris know anything about what Matt was into? Emma? Were they also involved?

Even if they were, it didn't explain how they knew the security code for the safe. Only she and Edward knew it.

"I didn't know that," she finally replied softly. "What does Chris think happened?"

"He has no clue. He just said that Matt was a stand-up guy, really easygoing. No one would want to hurt him."

Nia nodded. She wanted to ask more questions, but was concerned Adam would think it was odd. She was usually the last person to stir up office gossip.

"Listen, I have a new client contract that needs to go out this morning," she told him, changing the subject. "Can you take care of it for me? I'll send you all the details."

"That walk-in from yesterday. DaCosta?"

"Yeah, how did you know?"

Adam shrugged.

"Emma," they both said at the same time, then smiled at each other.

"Apparently, he made quite the impression on her," he added.

Nia just shook her head. A receptionist really should be more discreet.

"Anyway, I had a meeting with him yesterday evening and he's agreed to have us take care of his collection."

Adam sat down in the chair in front of her desk.

"What's involved?"

"Mostly art and a few antique artifacts from around the world. He recently inherited his dad's full collection, but only wants to keep a few pieces. So we'll need to do a catalog and appraisal of the items, then recommend the best approach," Nia explained.

"Estimated values?"

"He wasn't sure, but he showed me a couple of pictures of contemporary pieces. One was by Etienne Blanc, and if it's an original, could be worth over five hundred thousand at auction. So, it sounds like a pretty valuable collection, maybe worth several million? But we won't know for sure until it's all appraised."

"Nice," Adam stated, his eyes glittering with excitement.

As an art major at the Boston campus of the University of Massachusetts, this was just the type of account he enjoyed working on.

"The only complication is that Mr. DaCosta is based in Virginia, near D.C., so we'll have to do the work there," she added.

"Are you going to manage it?" he asked.

"I'm not sure. It depends on how things progress with the August auction."

"I can work on it with you," he offered.

Nia nodded.

"That would make it easier," she agreed. "Let's get all

the paperwork done, then we can confirm the details over the next few days."

"Cool. Send me the specifics and I'll take care of it this morning."

"Thanks, Adam. I'll be in a meeting until about eleven o'clock."

"Sure, boss."

Nia smiled as he strode out of her office. There couldn't be more than five to six years between them, but Adam made her feel old.

At eight fifty-eight, Nia left her office to walk to the conference room in the far right end of the loft floor. She had worn her favorite dress, using it like armor to feel more confident and self-assured. It was a black sleeveless sheath with a square neck and white exposed zipper from neck to hem down the back. A thin white belt accentuated her waist, and matched her black-and-white four-inch pumps. A light pink-and-turquoise silk scarf was wrapped loosely around her neck to soften the look and cover her cleavage.

She took a deep breath before pushing open the boardroom doors. There were two men inside standing next to the long, oval table. God, they were big. Almost as big as Evan.

"Ms. James?" one of them asked as they approached her. "I'm Michael Thorpe, a security consultant with Fortis. This is my colleague, Raymond Blunt. Thank you for agreeing to meet with us."

Nia shook both their hands, but remained silent. Though they both seemed professional and cordial, she knew better than to relax. These men were hired to find professional thieves and millions of dollars in jewelry, and they needed to do it fast. Like Edward had reminded her, they were going to take the straightest path to the truth, and unfortunately she was directly in their sight lines and could easily get run over in the process.

"Have a seat, Ms. James, and we'll get started," added Raymond.

She did as he offered, choosing the seat at the head of the table. Raymond sat in the chair to her right, and Michael remained standing behind him.

"Has Mr. Worthington explained the purpose of this meeting?" Michael asked.

"Yes, of course. It's regarding the robbery," she replied, glancing back and forth between them. While Michael looked to be taking the lead on the interview, he seemed like the younger of the two. He had a rich, deep brown skin tone and clean-cut appearance, while his partner was in his early thirties, with fair skin, and long, dark blond hair and goatee, in a more rugged look.

"That's right, ma'am. In order to find the stolen items, we need to determine how the facilities and safe were accessed," continued Michael.

Nia nodded.

"I understand," she stated.

"Good. Then let's get started," he replied. "You are the managing director, correct? The sales team reports to you?"

"Yes."

"So you are familiar with each of the items that were stolen, correct?"

"Yes."

"Good. Can you go through the list provided and tell us who was responsible for each of the accounts?"

Michael asked, while Raymond removed a sheet of paper from a folder and slid it in front of her.

"I'm sure I could, but I already provided all the information to Edward two days ago," Nia replied, recognizing the document she herself had created right after finding the safe empty. "It's all right there."

"Yes, but we'd like to reconfirm all the details from the very beginning. So let's review each of the nine items one by one."

Nia nodded again, but wondered at their tactics. Was it an attempt to shake her with seemingly minor questions? Or did they know something she didn't, and were testing her honesty? Whatever their strategy, it wouldn't work. She had nothing to do with the robbery, so none of their evidence could possibly lead back to her. Could it?

She took her time going through each piece of jewelry, confirming the sales manager and client, including the particulars of the contract to sell the piece in the August auction.

"The Crimson Amazon necklace was mine," Nia stated when they reached the bottom of the list. "I mean, it's my client."

"Is that common in your role? Do you do a lot of sales?" asked Michael, while Raymond continued to take notes.

"I carry a sales quota like the rest of the team, plus responsibility for our overall sales target," she explained. "So I will often bring in my own clients."

"So tell us about the seller. A Mrs. Aubrey Niknam?"

"Yes. I met her at another jewelry auction about a year ago. She's been slowly liquidating her assets after a divorce. The Crimson Amazon necklace was her prized possession. But based on the unfavorable terms of her divorce agreement, she couldn't afford not to sell it. So she approached me earlier in the spring."

"How did she get it? Mr. Worthington mentioned that it had an interesting history?"

"Well, it's a known stone. Red diamonds are very rare, certainly ones that size. The Crimson Amazon was mined in Brazil in 1936 by the DeWeer mining company. It was 23.4 carats uncut, the third largest ever found in the world," explained Nia. She had seen pictures in her gemology books.

"Wow," Michael replied, sitting back in his chair. "How did Mrs. Niknam acquire it?"

In her comfort zone, Nia relaxed a little. She crossed her legs and rested an elbow on the conference table.

"Sometime in the nineteen-fifties, the diamond was bought by someone in the British royal family and made into the current necklace by a custom jeweler. Then, in 1954, the wife of Mohammed Al-Fayed received the necklace as a wedding gift from her brother, a wealthy Saudi arms dealer. Dodi Fayed was her only child, so he inherited the necklace when she died in the eighties. It was sold privately to Mrs. Niknam by Dodi's estate a couple of years after his death."

"Did you know about the necklace when you met Mrs. Niknam?"

"Not at first. But I found it in my research. In the media frenzy after the deaths of Dodi and Princess Diana, there were pictures of her wearing the necklace within the months prior, along with speculation that Dodi had given it to her. So there was some interest in the auction gemology world when it was sold to an American socialite in 1999."

There was a pause as the two men looked at her speculatively. Nia sat straighter again, feeling as though they were reading her. Had she said something incriminating? How was that possible? It was all true.

"You must have been pretty excited by the discovery, right, Nia?" Raymond asked, breaking his silence. "Connecting with the owner of such a rare piece of jewelry?"

She turned to him, now smelling where they were going.

"Sure I was. It's a great story connected to a stunning gem. But that's the auction business. It's not just the jewelry or art that holds value; it's the background. The artists, the owners, the historical significance. That's what we sell."

The men looked at each other, then went back to their questions, asking her to walk through how and when she signed the agreement with Aubrey Niknam, and the final delivery of the necklace to Worthington that Monday.

"Why did you take possession so early? The auction isn't for almost three months," Michael asked.

"Since it's one of the biggest and most brilliant red diamonds in the world, we've set up a series of charity-based exhibits around the world over the six weeks prior to the auction. It's a great way to attract more buyers for the final sale. The first exhibit is in New York around Independence Day, so we needed the time prior to that to complete the marketing strategy and catalog."

"Is that normal?"

"Not for Worthington. We haven't done an auction this big before. But it's more and more common with the big firms."

"Mr. Worthington is concerned that the theft of these items will ruin his business, even though he has the insurance to cover the loss," said Michael as he stood up and walked behind her.

"I don't know if it would completely shut us down," she responded in a quiet voice. "But it will be pretty bad. It's not the money, it's the brand damage. Like I said, it's not the items themselves that we sell, it's the history and the connection to significant people and events. A Rolex watch or Davidoff humidor is a collectible, it will retain its value over time. But one once owned by Mandela or Walt Disney is irreplaceable. Not all of the items we manage are like the Crimson Amazon, but our customers and the industry need to trust that significant items are safe in our possession. Otherwise, we might as well run a flea market."

Michael returned to her line of vision with a smirk on his face from her sarcastic quip.

"And what about you, Nia. You're fairly new in the auction world. What would this do to your career?" he questioned.

She shrugged.

"The lost commission would put a dent in my retirement plans, for sure."

Raymond laughed.

"I don't really know," she continued, looking Michael in the eye. "I guess it depends on whether I'm found to be responsible in any way."

"Are you responsible?" he shot back.

"No. Not intentionally, anyway," replied Nia, honestly. "I've gone through all the details over and over again to make sure I did everything I was supposed to. Trust me, I've thought of little else since Tuesday morning. But I don't know of anything I did that left the safe vulnerable."

Michael nodded.

"Where were you on Monday night, Ms. James?" he asked smoothly.

Nia knew it was a reasonable question for them to ask, but it still made her heart pound.

"I was at home."

"All night?" Michael probed.

"Pretty much. I worked until after seven o'clock, then got home before eight o'clock."

"You didn't stop anywhere after work? Meet anyone?"

Nia blinked.

"I stopped at the drugstore near the house," she added.

"Did you meet anyone? Or is there anyone who can confirm you were at home all night?"

She let out a deep breath. There was no way around it.

"No, no one."

Both men looked at her hard for several seconds. She tried not to fidget under their inspection.

"Let's talk a little bit about the other employees here. We know that Edward had changed the safe combination on Friday evening before the jewels arrived, and only shared it with you. Did anyone else know the jewels were arriving?"

"Sure," she quickly replied. "The account managers for the other jewels had brought in their clients' pieces in the week prior. Edward only changed the combination because of the Crimson Amazon. Taking possession of a twenty-five-million-dollar necklace makes you a little extra cautious, right? But no one else knew it was arriving on Monday afternoon. It came by private delivery directly to me."

Michael nodded, sitting back down beside her.

"Okay. Now tell me about the other Worthington employees, starting with your people."

She took a deep breath and provided as much information as she could about the rest of the team. It wasn't much, beyond the specific roles and responsibilities.

"Tara Silver is the most senior account manager. She was hired directly by Edward before the Boston location opened, so she was already here when I started. She's a solid performer with an extensive client list. The earrings she brought in for the auction put her over target for her sales quota this year."

"And where was Ms. Silver when the Crimson Amazon necklace was delivered?" Michael asked.

"We had a standard team meeting Monday morning from eight-thirty to ten o'clock, then she left the office soon after to visit clients, and was gone for the rest of the day," Nia recalled. "So had Cain Abbott and John English. Mimi Rodrigues was on vacation. She's not back until Monday."

"That's all of your sales team?" clarified Michael. "Tell me about each of them."

"Well, Cain and Mimi joined about the same time. I hired them about nine months ago. They both have good sales experience. Cain is doing a little better, but Mimi has enough on her plate to have a good year, I think," she summarized. "John only started three months ago, so he's still getting his feet wet. He had four lower-value pieces of the jewelry from the auction collection."

"And your other two employees, Nancy Copeland and Adam Peterson?"

"They're our sales coordinators. They help with client contracts, event planning, and other admin things."

"Were they also aware of items purchased for the auction?" Michael asked while his partner kept writing.

"Of course, they drew up the contracts," she explained.

"Did they know when the red diamond was arriving?"

Nia was about to say no right away, but stopped. Michael noted her hesitation with raised eyebrows, and sat back in his chair. Nancy had been assigned to the Niknam account. Nia stared at the conference-room wall, thinking through all the conversations and e-mails that had been exchanged about the Crimson Amazon. Had she let something slip?

"No," she finally stated. "I'm sure of it."

Michael gave one nod, then stood up.

"You've told us about everyone's job. What can you tell us about them personally?" he asked, walking slowing behind her desk.

"What do you mean?" she asked.

"What you know about the lives of your employees, Ms. James? Are they single, do they have children, hobbies?" he elaborated, looked down at her. "Is anyone struggling with anything that would suggest they could be involved in stealing from the company?"

She had no idea what to say. While she had a strong team and they worked well together, Nia didn't know much about their personal lives beyond the basics.

"You're asking me if I know who was involved in the theft? Of course not!" stated Nia.

"I just want to know a little more about them than their job title. Unless there is a reason you're being vague."

The formidable agent was now standing with his feet planted wide, and arms crossed. The interview was no longer cordial.

"I'll tell you what I know, but I really can't add very much," she explained evenly.

"And why is that?"

"Because I don't get involved with my team beyond work. That's why. Office gossip is destructive, and I don't allow anyone to participate in it," Nia advised him. "So, I can only tell you the facts I know. Tara is a newlywed. She got married in March. Cain and Nancy are both married. Cain has a son and Nancy has three teenage kids. I can't remember if it's two boys and one girl, or the other way around."

Michael watched her hard with lowered brows. Nia tried not to bite the side of her cheek with nervousness.

"Adam and John are both single, I think, and Mimi has a boyfriend."

His brows lowered farther.

"I don't know what else to tell you," she added, feeling pressured and annoyed. "They have lunch together sometimes when they are in the office. And they all go to the bar across the street with others in the office on Fridays after work for drinks. But I can't see how that helps your investigation."

Michael didn't react to her sassy comment. Instead, he took the slow path behind her chair, back to the other side of her chair.

"How well do you know Chris Morton and his team?"

She shrugged.

"I won't have much to add there either, unfortunately," she admitted. "Chris started with Tara when the office opened. He's the operations manager, so he has Emma Sterling reporting to him. She's the receptionist and handles any walk-in sales for the gallery."

Michael stopped again, refolding his arms. Nia shrugged with frustration.

"I don't socialize with any of them," she insisted again. "Emma seems to come from a big family. She's always talking about brothers and sisters and cousins. And I think she's dating someone."

"And Mr. Morton?" he probed.

Nia sighed. There wasn't much to add there either.

"He's divorced, no kids that I'm aware of. He's really into sports. I think he even plays basketball for some kind of city league."

There was a few seconds of silence.

"Ms. James, I don't think I have to outline the seriousness of your situation," declared Michael, before he went ahead and did just that. "You are the only person other than Mr. Worthington who knew when a twenty-five-million-dollar diamond arrived here. And the only other person to know the security code to a very secure safe, surrounded by motion sensors and in a building with comprehensive video surveillance. This is not the time for polite discretion."

"I'm perfectly aware of what's going on here, and how this looks," she shot back coldly. "I don't have any more information to give you. If I did, I promise you I would."

"What about the rest of Morton's team. He manages the three security guards and the warehouse staff?" added Michael.

"Yes. The security guards work shifts through an agency, but Chris supervises them. We also use laborers in the warehouse, from a staffing company, I think. Chris brings them in hourly when needed. But I don't think we have any in this week."

"And Matt Flannigan? He was the security guard on shift Monday night," Michael stated, and Nia swallowed.

"I'll assume you've seen the news? He was shot to death yesterday. What do you know about him?"

"Not much, really. He was here before me, also. But, he used to have the day shift until a couple of weeks ago," she told him.

"Do you know why he changed shifts?"

"I don't know for sure, but I got the sense from Emma that it was for something personal," Nia explained. "Something about his girlfriend, I think? I'm sure Chris will know the reason."

Michael nodded as he sat back down in his chair.

"I think we both know Matt Flannigan was involved in the robbery, and was killed for his efforts," Michael said in a silky voice. "Did you work with him to steal the jewels?"

"No!" Nia immediately replied.

"Did you give him the security code to the safe?"

"No! I had nothing to do with any of it!" she insisted.

"Well, someone gave the safe code to either Flannigan or another party. Who could have done that other than you?"

Nia couldn't answer. What else could add to her defense? Without proof, it was fruitless.

"I don't know who it was, but it certainly was not me," she finally told him, her throat tight with anger, fear, and frustration.

"Okay, Ms. James. We only have a couple more questions for you. Let's start with last Friday when Edward changed the security code and gave it to you."

Nia went through the details that she was certain Edward has also provided.

The password administration for their digital safe was managed through a secure cloud solution, with a private key encryption code and digital signature validation. It allowed Edward to remotely generate a unique access code to the safe remotely. That Friday, Edward was in town, and gave Nia the new code verbally in her office. She memorized it, with nothing written down anywhere. That was their protocol, though they had only employed it twice in the last eleven months.

Then, Michael asked her to walk them through everything that happened from the time she woke up on Tuesday morning, through opening the empty safe just before noon. There was nothing significant that she could provide.

By the time the interview ended, Nia was exhausted and it was only eleven o'clock in the morning. But at least it was over. As she walked away from the two imposing investigators, Nia felt conflicted emotions of relief and anxiety. While they obviously didn't have enough to prove to Edward that she was involved, it was clear they thought she knew more than she was saying. Nia was smart enough to know someone at Worthington had something to do with the robbery. Her own history had proved the best person to pin something on was often the easiest, whether it was the truth or not. And, once again, all the fingers were pointed at her

Chapter 5

"She's definitely hiding something," Michael stated.

Evan looked at Raymond, and the other man shrugged ambivalently.

Michael and Raymond were back from their interviews with select Worthington employees, and had just debriefed the team in the control room. Other than Nia James, everyone at the gallery was told they were going through a professional review of their security system and protocols.

"Why?" asked Evan.

"She's cagey, walled off. It was odd," explained Michael. "Particularly about the other people at Worthington. Getting even the smallest detail was like pulling teeth. And she got pretty defensive when I pushed a little."

"You think she knows more than she's saying?" Evan probed.

"No doubt. I just can't say what or who about," Michael admitted. "When we asked about everything else to do with the robbery, she was calm, articulate, and responsive. Even while showing concern about the situation and her exposure as the likely suspect. But as soon as we mentioned the other employees, she clammed up."

"Too calm at times?" Raymond threw in.

"Is that what you think?" Evan asked back.

"I don't know. She's just as you pegged her, Ice. Sharp and composed, yet straightforward," Raymond summarized.

"Yeah, and strategically smart," added Michael. "She knows she's the prime suspect, and didn't hide from it. She also didn't try to put the heat on anyone else in the office. We gave her plenty of opportunity. I'm thinking she's betting that the less she gives us, the less we have to poke holes through."

Evan nodded, scratching at the rough stubble on his jawline.

"Well, we haven't found any holes yet," he reminded the agents. "Raymond, your review of all public and private video surveillance we could find from Monday night shows the same time line she stated, correct?"

"Yup, she entered the subway at seven-fourteen that night, exited at the station near her house. Then, the street camera near the drugstore captures her at seven-forty-three. I can't find anything that suggests she left the area after that."

"What about her cell phone activity?" Michael asked.

"Negative. From the video loop and motion sensor override at Worthington, we know the robbery happened between twelve-thirty and one o'clock in the morning," Raymond advised. "But there was no cell phone or data usage outside of her home location after eight o'clock when she claims to have gotten home. And no usage at all after ten-eighteen that night. At least not from the devices we know about. She could have used an untraceable cell phone."

"So, other than access to the safe, there's nothing we've found to confirm her involvement," stated Evan. "Not unless I can find a burner phone on her."

"We have something, Ice," Tony stated from his position at the computer across the room. He had spent the day reviewing the data gathered by Raymond's systems surveillance software, embedded within the Worthington network architecture.

"What?" Evan demanded, joining him.

The other two men followed, standing to the rear.

"James sent an e-mail from her work computer about two hours ago. The response just came back a few minutes ago. It's from a guy named Nigel St. Clair. I can't find any other e-mails to him from her work account, or calls in the phone records from the last six months. But this is what I found on him," Tony explained as he pulled up a mug shot on the screen. "Nigel St. Clair, lives in Watertown. Works as a shift supervisor at a warehousing company there."

Evan let out a deep breath as he looked at the older mug shot of a young man with fair skin, long, dark blond hair, and green eyes. He read the page.

"Three years in Michigan state prison for attempted murder, released early as part of a plea bargain. That was eight years ago."

"Yup. Here's the good part. He was originally from Boston, arrested in Detroit, then moved back here around the same time that James started school at the University of Massachusetts. So, I dug further," Tony explained, pulling up additional computer files. "And found this. They had the same address for five years, until about three years ago. An apartment in Dorchester."

The men looked at each other. Their dead security guard was from Dorchester. While it was the largest Boston neighborhood, it was still a big coincidence.

"Her e-mail to him is pretty cryptic," suggested Evan as they read the message. "Just that she needs to talk to him. Old boyfriend?"

"Makes sense," Tony agreed.

"So, why is she reaching out to him now?" Evan mulled.

"I've sent the info over to the analysts at headquarters. They're going to dig deeper into St. Clair, use his IP address to check for other online communications between them, see where that leads."

"Doesn't she also have a sealed juvie record?" remembered Evan.

"Yeah, we're working on getting the details. She was fifteen at the time. But interestingly, it's from the same year that St. Clair was charged with attempted murder."

"Then they both moved to his hometown within a year of his release from prison. It can't be by chance," mumbled Evan.

"No way," Tony agreed.

"Okay. Find me everything you can on St. Clair's prison associates," demanded Evan. "Three years in state lockup is plenty of time to learn more criminal skills and make long-term friends. We may have just found our connection between Flannigan, James, and the heist."

* * *

Nia stared at the signed contract with Evan DaCosta. It was after four o'clock that afternoon, and she was quickly running out of time to let him know her decision about dinner. After the stress of the investigation on top of work, she should just want to go home to watch mindless television while curled in the fetal position for the evening. But that would only make her feel more helpless and vulnerable. More alone. All feelings she hated.

In comparison, a dinner date with a very attractive man seemed so normal. Isn't that what girls her age should be doing? Going to fancy restaurants, trying to meet the man of her dreams? Or at least that's what Lianne always says. It was just dinner, conversation. It was harmless.

Before she could change her mind, Nia picked up her office phone and called the number on Evan's business card.

"Evan DaCosta," he answered in a deep, blunt tone.

"Mr. DaCosta, it's Nia James."

There was a brief pause.

"Nia," he replied a little softer. "Did everything go okay with the contract? I signed it this morning."

"Yes, it's fine. I have it and we're all good."

"Great. So, what can I do for you?"

Nia wrinkled her nose. He must have known why she was calling, but he obviously wasn't going to make it easy for her.

"Well, it turns out that I am free for dinner this evening. If your offer still stands," she added.

Silence followed. She squeezed her eyes tight, but waited.

"Of course the offer still stands. What time do you finish work?" he asked smoothly.

She tried not to let him hear any sign of her relief.

"I should be done by around five-fifteen, maybe five-thirty?"

"Good. I'll have a car pick you up at five-thirty."

"That's not—"

"Good-bye, Ms. James."

His voice was laced with teasing humor before he promptly cut the line.

"*Really?*" she mumbled to herself, only a little annoyed at his high-handedness. Now that their plans were confirmed, Nia felt lighter, even a little excited.

At a quarter after five, she was in the bathroom freshening up, and once again thankful that she wore her favorite dress. The bathroom door opened as she was reapplying her lipstick.

"Hey, Nia," said Tara Silver, her most senior account manager.

"Hi, Tara. How did the meeting go with Norman Appleby?"

Tara specialized in contemporary art. Her latest client was the senior partner in a national law firm. They were renovating several of their offices in Boston and Connecticut, and had hired Tara to sell their current art collection.

"It went well. I'm pretty stoked," Tara replied as she fluffed her dark brown hair in the mirror. "Some of the pieces are only worth a couple of thousand dollars, not much more than when they were bought back in the nineties. But they also have three original minimalist paintings. I'm sure each of them would fetch at least two to three hundred thousand at auction."

"That's fantastic," Nia replied with a big smile.

"I know! I'm telling you, Nia, this is going to be my year!"

"Well, you're certainly off to a good start."

"Yup! Between the ruby earrings for the summer auction, and this art collection, I'm feeling pretty good."

Nia held her smile, though it dimmed a bit on the inside. As instructed by Edward and the investigators, none of the other Worthington employees knew about the theft as of yet.

Except the person involved.

"Hot date?" Tara added as Nia pulled a brush out of her purse.

"What?"

"Do you have a hot date? You hardly ever wear your hair out."

"Oh. Nothing serious, just dinner," replied Nia cautiously.

"Well, you look great. You always look good, but I really like your hair like that."

Nia accepted the compliment by picking some lint from the paddle brush.

"Okay, I'm off. Enjoy your dinner!" announced Tara, then she was gone, leaving a cloud of the latest Chanel perfume behind.

Nia looked back at herself in the mirror, reflecting on Tara's comments. It was true, her hair was usually pulled back into a tight bun or ponytail during the week. Her makeup was bold and dramatic, creating the desired effect of a woman in charge. Capable, assertive, fierce, and in control. But others had told her the same thing Tara had, men in particular. With her shoulder-length hair out, either straight or loosely curled, she looked softer, younger, and more feminine. *Weak.*

Nia let out a deep breath, and put down the brush. There was no denying it now. She had gotten dressed today hoping to see Evan again, wanting to look good for him. It was an uncomfortable realization that made her heart race with uncertainty. Why was she acting like such a stupid, naïve . . . girl? Wanting the sexy, rich guy to think she was pretty? It was juvenile, and not at all who she was anymore.

She ran her fingers through her hair, now falling in soft waves. Without any hair elastics or products, it was too late to put it up anyway. But, it was time to put a stop to whatever fantasies were brewing in her subconscious. She was not soft or sweet. Not anymore. So if that was what Evan DaCosta was looking for in a woman, he would be sorely disappointed.

Feeling fortified, Nia left the bathroom and went downstairs, pulling on her trench coat on the way. As she reached the landing, she could hear the high-pitched trill of Emma giggling. Nia looked toward the sound and found the tall, broad form of Evan DaCosta, leaning casually against one of the display cases near the front entrance. Hearing her footsteps, he and the receptionist both turned to face her. He said something else to Emma that Nia couldn't hear. The young girl blushed, and Nia felt the pinch of annoyance in her chest.

"There she is," he said louder, as he walked forward to meet Nia.

"I'm sorry, I thought you were sending a car?" she questioned.

He smiled, that slow, predatory grin she was becoming used to.

"My meetings ended a little early. And this was too important an assignment to delegate," he replied, stopping in front of her.

She felt the heat of his gaze as he looked her over in a long, deliberate glance. The beat of her heart increased measurably. But Nia forced herself to remain poised, seemingly unfazed by his perusal. When his eyes finally met hers again, she raised a brow.

"You approve?" she asked, sarcastically.

The grin widened, revealing beautifully white teeth, and the hint of dimples.

"I do." He stepped closer so their bodies brushed, bent his head, and pressed a soft, light kiss on the spot right beside her lips. "Thank you for joining me for dinner."

His nearness was messing with her composure, but Nia managed to produce a small smile in response.

"All set?" he asked, pressing a warm hand to the base of her spine.

She nodded.

"Good evening, Emma," Evan stated, his gaze still fixed on Nia.

"Bye, Mr. DaCosta, bye, Nia," the girl replied in her usual bright, bubbly voice.

"'Night, Emma," Nia replied politely.

His car was parked on the street a half-block away. They were silent for the walk. He opened the passenger door for her before sliding behind the wheel. The powerful engine roared with a low, deep rumble, then they were on their way.

"How was your day?" Evan asked a few moments later.

It was such a mundane question that it caught Nia by surprise. She knew the appropriate response should be to say "fine" with a smile, then ask him the same. But she always preferred honesty.

"Not good," she replied bluntly, looking out the passenger window at the passing city.

"Why, what happened?" he asked.

"Just work stuff." God, it would be nice to talk to someone about the crap she was in. "It will resolve itself eventually," she added instead.

"Well, then we have to make sure we take your mind off it all this evening."

She looked over at him with a grateful smile.

"Do you enjoy what you do?" Evan asked a moment later.

"Sales? It's okay, I guess. A means to an end, really," she stated.

"What end?"

"Life," she retorted with a chuckle. "Life is expensive."

He threw her a smile then refocused on the road by pulling up to a valet parking booth in the trendy area near Fenway Park.

"I'm told this place has the best seafood in the city," Evan told her as he walked through the doors of the elegant restaurant. Nia knew the place well, and was aware that it usually took weeks to get a reservation. The hostess led them to their table at the back of the room, near a blazing fireplace. Nia handed the woman her coat and soft scarf before they were seated.

"So, Evan, how was your day?" She emphasized his

name, teasingly confirming that this meal was not a business meeting. It was a date, and she was feeling pretty good about it.

He grinned, flashing the dimple. It should be a sin for a man to look so appealing.

"It was all right. But much better now," he replied. "In case it wasn't obvious, you look beautiful this evening."

Nia opened her mouth to give a sarcastic, dismissive remark. But she met his eyes, and her brain stopped working. There it was, written plainly in the clench of his jaw and intensity of his gaze. He wanted her and he wanted her to know it. Nia licked her top lip, her mouth suddenly dry.

Their waiter interrupted them at that moment to take their orders. Nia chose the ahi tuna and Evan ordered the prime rib. He also ordered a bottle of Australian pinot noir.

"So, Nia James," Evan stated as they took their first sips of the light wine. "If you didn't need a job as a means to an end, what would you be doing?"

"As a new client, I probably should tell you that sales is my life. That there is nothing else I would rather do as a career, right?" she replied with a pout of her lips.

"Well, I'm not your client tonight. I'm your date, trying to get to know you better," he replied.

"In that case, I'd have to think about it a little. But my client should know that I'm very good at what I do."

Evan smiled, clearly amused.

"He knows."

Nia nodded, satisfied. Then she contemplated his question. The instinctive response was there, but it took her a few moments to acknowledge it and find the words. It had been years since she had given it any serious thought.

"I would write songs," she finally stated.

He paused with his glass halfway to his mouth, and Nia took pleasure in her ability to catch him off guard. It also felt good to say the words out loud.

"Really?" he queried.

"That surprises you," she surmised.

Evan put down his wine and leaned forward.

"Are you good at it?" he questioned.

"I used to be. But I haven't written anything in a long time."

"Why not?"

Great question. One she wasn't ready to answer honestly to Evan or herself. It had too much to do with her fear of feeling exposed, naked. Vulnerable. Instead, she shrugged dismissively.

"Life," she quipped.

"Life," repeated Evan, but his eyes said he knew a little about what she wasn't saying.

"What about you, Evan?" Nia returned. "Do you enjoy your work?"

He generously allowed the change in direction. As their meals arrived, he talked about working for his father's company in various functions overseas until his father's death last year. Then he became the acting CEO.

"Why acting? It's your family's company. It would seem you'd be the obvious choice," she asked, spearing the final slice of tuna, grilled rare to perfection.

"It was my suggestion to the board. I wasn't sure I was the right choice, to be honest. I have a few other business interests that need to be sorted," he explained.

"So I asked for an eighteen-month interim period to decide."

"Have you ever wanted to do anything else?" Nia asked.

"No, not really. I was raised to believe that the most important thing a man could do was protect his family and his country, and to ensure justice is served. That's why my father started his company. So it's an honor to continue his legacy."

"That's great."

Evan nodded, though he seemed a little embarrassed by his passionate declaration.

"Come, let's go for a walk," he suggested.

Chapter 6

Within a few minutes, the check was paid and Evan was helping Nia into her trench coat. It was almost eight o'clock and the air outside had chilled a bit as the sun was starting to set. Without thought, he laced his fingers through hers and started a leisurely stroll down the busy downtown street.

Evan was familiar with the neighborhood, and remembered a small café a few blocks down the way. It seemed like a good spot to sit for a bit and have coffee, maybe share a dessert. As they continued walking in silence, he studied their dinner conversation in his head, trying to determine his next move. It was uncomfortable to realize that the evening was feeling less and less like an assignment.

Damn, she was gorgeous. That dress was made for her body, teasing him to unzip the back like a candy wrapper. Even now, side by side in silence, he felt her energy. The touch of their skin created a low hum of arousal at the base of his spine, messing with his breathing. As though testing him, Nia brushed her thumb along his wrist and his traitorous cock twitched.

But that was chemistry, biology, male instinct.

Evan knew it was a complication that could work to his advantage on the case if he was smart about it. It wasn't the real problem.

Evan looked over at her profile, noting she was deep in thought. He wondered what she was mulling over. Their conversation? Or the investigation at work? He immediately wanted to say something funny, to see that wicked smile return to her lips. Watch the lights sparkle in those sexy, feline eyes.

He liked her. That was the problem, and it was ridiculously unprofessional. Everything they knew so far about the burglary pointed to her as an inside man. And the circumstantial evidence was mounting by the day. There was nothing about her he should like.

"Coffee?" he suggested as they approached the café.

"Sure," Nia replied.

He opened the door for her. It was a quaint Brazilian shop. Evan made a habit of finding similar spots in almost every city he visited. With his ancestral roots in a coffee plantation, it was an indulgence from his upbringing that he never gave up.

At the counter, he ordered an espresso, and Nia asked for a latte. Evan then talked her into trying a small chocolate cake ball called a *brigadeiro*. They took a seat near the window with a view of the street. Samba music played softly in the background.

"This is a nice place," she noted as they enjoyed their purchases.

"Yeah, I found it the last time I was in town," Evan replied.

"Are you in Boston often?"

"A few times over the last year. Not much prior to that. We have a few partners and subcontractor firms based here."

"How long are you here for this visit?"

He knew what she was asking. How long would this thing between them likely last. Evan couldn't tell what answer she was hoping for. His instincts said she wasn't really looking for a long-term commitment, from him or any other man. He wondered why a gorgeous, sensual woman would choose to be unattached.

"That depends," he replied cryptically.

"On?" probed Nia.

"On you."

"Why?"

Evan smiled. She was always so direct. He liked it.

"I think you know why, Nia. You intrigue me, and I enjoy your company. I want to see if there is anything more between us."

Her eyes never wavered from his, but he could see her mind working.

"I'm not going to sleep with you," she finally stated, calmly sipping her coffee.

He laughed.

"This isn't really the appropriate time or place, Ms. James, but I'm glad you're thinking about it."

She glared at him, but he could tell there was a smile struggling to break free.

"I mean, I'm not looking for a casual thing right now," she clarified.

"Good. Neither am I. What are you looking for?" Evan quizzed.

Nia looked away, clearly surprised by his response.

"I don't know," she finally replied.

"Okay. Let me know when you've decided. In the meantime, I'd like to continue seeing you. Whether you sleep with me or not," he told her. "I don't think we'd do much sleeping anyway."

That did make her chuckle, a warm, bubbly sound that did funny things to the area behind his ribcage. *Shit*, he was in trouble.

They stayed at the café for another half-hour or so, chatting about Boston and the areas he had seen in his last few visits. Nia confirmed that she had always lived in the South Boston area or in nearby Dorchester since arriving in the city to attend the nearby University of Massachusetts campus.

"Do you have family in the city?" Evan asked as they walked back to the restaurant to get the car.

Nia shook her head.

"Nope, just me. Most of my relatives still live in Detroit," she explained.

"Any siblings?" She shook her head again to say no. "Something we have in common," he mused.

"Yeah, I guess. But I stayed with my aunt and a bunch of cousins often. So, it didn't feel that way growing up."

"Where were your parents?"

There was a heavy pause for a few moments.

"It's a long story," Nia finally stated.

"I'd like to hear it," Evan assured her.

She looked up at him with a wistful smile.

"Maybe another time."

He let it go. Clearly, there was something significant there, but he'd have to wait for another opportunity to uncover it. He made a mental note to have Lucas and the team dig around. Then, he immediately felt an uncomfortable pang of guilt. *Christ!* Becoming a civilian had completely messed with his balls.

Once back in his car, Nia gave him directions to her apartment about ten miles outside of the downtown core. He used the time to ask her mundane questions about her life, like what she did with her free time.

"Typical stuff, I guess," she told him.

"Like what?" insisted Evan. "Lacrosse? Yoga? Fishing?"

She burst out laughing, followed by a snort. It made her laugh harder, cover her mouth with embarrassment. He found it hard to keep his eyes on the road. Evan glanced repeatedly at her with a goofy grin on his face. She was just stunning.

"No lacrosse. I did try yoga a few times, but it's too slow for me," she revealed once calmed. "Kickboxing is my thing."

"Really," he replied. "I can see that."

"You can? Why?" probed Nia, sounding suspicious.

Evan smiled, wondering if she was girl enough to be pushing for a compliment.

"You're obviously very fit. Strong."

She looked out the window.

"What else do you like to do?"

"I used to fish when I was a kid, back in Michigan with my cousins. But it's not my pastime these days," she told him. "I like watching movies."

She peeked up at him as though confessing a deep, dark secret.

"Hmmm. That sounds intriguing. What kind of movies?"

His cheeky grin made it very clear exactly what he was thinking.

"In your dreams," Nia shot back. But she was smiling.

"Exactly!"

They both laughed.

"So, are you going to tell me what kind of movies? Or should I just go with what works for me?" he continued.

He could feel her hesitation. It was clear she wasn't used to revealing private things about herself.

"All kinds, really. Big action movies for sure. Corny romantic comedies."

Evan raised his eyebrows in surprise.

"You're a romantic!"

"Not particularly, no," she immediately rebuffed. "But movies are fantasy, escapism, right? So the idea of a soul mate, or love at first sight works on screen because it's not reality."

"You don't believe in love?"

"Whether it truly exists or not, it doesn't solve everything. It's not unconditional and ever-enduring. Not like in *Pretty Woman* or *When a Man Loves a Woman.*"

She looked at him, waiting for Evan to respond. He thought about the unaffectionate marriage his parents had, and his failed engagement that had ended over three years ago. While he was long over the confusion and disappointment, it hadn't encouraged a belief in ever-enduring love.

"Don't you agree?" Nia probed when he didn't comment.

He chose the easy way out.

"You're probably right, but a man can only dream."

Nia laughed out loud.

"What?" he demanded.

"Sorry, I just can't see you as a dreamer."

He shot her a look to express how offended he was. She just shook her head, not at all swayed.

"Okay, Ms. James. Looks like I just have to show you my soft, sensitive side."

She snorted again, then covered her mouth, her eyes wide with embarrassment. Evan laughed until she also burst into giggles.

All too soon, he pulled the car into a parking spot in front of a four-floor semi-detached duplex on a residential street. He stepped out of the car to open the passenger door for her.

"Thank you for dinner," Nia murmured softly once she was standing in front of him.

"You're welcome. But I still have to get you to your door," Evan teased.

She looked around, almost self-consciously as though people might have been watching them.

"That's not necessary. I'm right there," she countered, gesturing to her apartment.

Evan didn't respond. He just took her hand and started walking toward the front door.

"What about your car? Aren't you worried about it?" she insisted.

He shrugged. "It's insured. Why? This looks like a pretty nice neighborhood."

"It is nice. Just not *that* nice."

She unlocked the building entrance, and they both entered a small common area.

"Okay, this is me," she announced, stopping in front of the first-floor apartment door.

"Do you live in the hallway?" he asked, pursing his lips.

Nia narrowed her eyes before turning away to unbolt the lock with her key. Evan used that moment to quickly pull his iPhone out and disable the video and voice surveillance Tony had installed in her apartment the day before, using the mobile interface application. The team didn't need to see all the details of his covert work. Then, he followed her inside the unit, closing the door behind him.

"This is nice," commented Evan as he looked around. He could see through the main living area to the back of the room. The space had been recently renovated into a modern, open area, but still had lots of the early twentieth-century architectural character.

"Thanks," mumbled Nia. She hadn't moved more than two steps into the apartment.

"I don't suppose you're inviting me to stay for a nightcap?" he couldn't resist asking.

"No, I'm not," she bluntly replied.

"Fair enough. Now that I've completed my gentlemanly duties and escorted you into the safety of your home, I suppose I should go," Evan continued.

He stepped forward, entering her personal space. Nia held firm, only lifting her chin so that she could still meet his eyes. They were so close that her soft, floral scent teased his senses.

"Thank you for going out with me tonight," he stated, similar to her statement when they arrived.

Her gaze dipped to his lips, and Evan felt it like a stroke against his skin.

His plan had been to wine and dine her, get her to see the benefits of dating him. In his experience as a covert agent, shared interests or a physical attraction was a bonus in these situations, but not essential. After all, it was an assignment, a job, a means to an end. It wasn't personal.

Yet, as he leaned down, anticipating the moment when his lips would meet hers, everything about Nia James felt intense, intimate, and very, very personal. His heart pounded hard and slow as time seemed suspended. Until he finally kissed her with the lightest, softest brush. It was pure electricity. Another taste, and Evan was lost in her. Gentle pecks quickly turned long and sweeping, then deep, hot, and wet. At some point, Evan cupped her face with one hand, and delved his fingers into her hair with the other.

She was so delicious, so responsive.

He was on autopilot, running his lips along her jawline and down her neck. Nia groaned when he nipped the taut tendon then sucked at her flesh. His arousal pulsed, threatening to bust through his zipper. His mouth was back on hers, sucking on her tongue as he slowly pulled up the narrow skirt of her dress until it was bunched around her waist.

"Delicious," mumbled Evan as he grasped the soft curves of her bottom in his big hands.

"Wait," she whispered, breaking their kiss.

He rested his forehead against hers. The sound of their labored breathing filled the space. Evan squeezed her round flesh again, then swept one hand over the front of her panties. Her hips flexed from the touch.

"Nia," he breathed. His intention had been to tease her a little with a few hot kisses, maybe some innocent touches. But now, in the moment, whatever he had planned didn't seem to matter. His hunger for her was quickly consuming him.

He slid his middle finger along the seam of her sweet folds. She sucked in a sharp breath. Evan pressed harder, gently swiping her clit through the soft silk.

"I want to make you come."

He felt her shake her head, even as her body quivered.

"Yes," Evan urged, brushing aside her underwear. He couldn't remember wanting anything more.

With patient attention, he stroked and teased her flesh until she was slick and wet. Every moan she uttered drove him nuts, urged him to give her the ultimate pleasure. Evan could feel her body tighten as she drifted closer to climax.

"Look at me," he demanded as he slid two fingers into her tight wetness.

The heated arousal on her face almost unmanned him. Her hooded eyes burned with intensity, and those full red lips were pouted with abandon. Evan felt a primal need to watch her come in his arms while chanting his name. He stroked his fingers into her slick core while sliding over her clit in slow, small circles with his thumb.

"Oh God," groaned Nia, holding his gaze. She now clutched his shoulders.

"Yeah," Evan urged.

He increased the speed, narrowed the circle, worked his fingers deeper.

"Yes, like that . . . That's it . . ." she stammered.

He wanted to kiss her so badly, but was held captive by their visual link. Her beautiful face was flushed with passion. She now bit her bottom lip, attempting to suppress a litany of soft, kitteny moans. It was the sexiest sound he'd ever heard. He was throbbing with need. Damn, he wanted her.

"Evan," Nia whispered urgently.

Her eyes widened with surprise and her body tightened. Then, she fell apart in his arms, her deep moans echoing around the room. Her hot sheath clenched around his thrusting fingers as her body shuttered uncontrollably. Evan read every sensation in her eyes. It was so intense, yet deeply humbling. He hardly remembered to breathe in case he missed a moment of it.

"So beautiful," he murmured in a deep, husky voice, stroking her slick flesh as she descended from the peak with tiny shivers.

Finally, she closed her eyes, throwing her head back with a deep sigh. Evan lowered his head to kiss and suck on her neck. There was a strong urge to mark her skin, tag her with his brand. But he resisted. It was too crazy.

"Well. That was unexpected," she finally stated in a low, lazy voice.

He smiled. She really did have a great sense of humor. But it did very little to cool his raging arousal. Only distance and time could do that.

Evan continued to run his lips teasingly along her neck and shoulders as he slowly straightened her underwear and pulled down her dress. As much as he wanted to bury himself inside her sweetness, it wasn't the right timing. Tonight needed to be about her. Anything else was too soon.

"I'm not sure if that's an insult or a compliment," he replied quietly.

She shrugged, refusing to stroke his ego. Evan laughed out loud, then covered her mouth in a long, deep kiss, but pulled back before he lost his head again.

"I guess I should quit while I'm ahead. Good night, Nia," he stated. "Sweet dreams."

He left through her apartment door before she could respond.

Chapter 7

Feeling frustrated and conflicted, Evan called Lucas on his way to the hotel from Nia's place.

"I'm on my way back to the control room," he had told his friend through the Bluetooth phone connection. His tone was calm and controlled, with no hint of the sexual frustration churning in his stomach.

"How did it go?" Lucas asked.

"As planned, more or less. She's pretty tight-lipped and guarded, but I made some progress in the romance," Evan told him honestly. "Anything new on that St. Clair character?"

"Yeah, we sent Raymond more info. They've been in touch, sporadically over the last three years. He has a girlfriend who he lives with in Watertown. But there is no doubt that the history between him and James goes back to Detroit," explained Lucas. "There's also something odd about his release from prison. His attempted murder conviction was reduced to only three years as part of a plea-bargain deal."

"For snitching?" asked Evan. It was common enough in prison for inmates to provide valuable info to the D.A.'s office in exchange for a reduced sentence.

"Maybe. The team is looking into it."

"Anything underground on the heist?"

"Nothing concrete, but Tony's got a bite from an Interpol contact in New York. Don't know if it's connected, but I think we should send him there tomorrow to check it out."

"Okay, I'll confirm with the team at our debrief," Evan agreed. "Then we'll need to land on a plan of attack for the weekend."

"What are you thinking?"

"I got close to James tonight. I think we should continue the momentum. I'm going to take her away for the weekend," suggested Evan, the idea taking shape as he spoke. "The Clements are having a charity event on Saturday night in the Vineyard."

"As in your ex-fiancée's parents, the Clements? Is that a good idea?" quizzed Lucas.

"You know Mikayla and I parted on good terms. It won't be a problem," Evan dismissed. "At the very least, it will cement my cover. Mikayla and her parents only know me as an executive for DaCosta Solutions, and the new CEO."

"Do you think James will go?" asked Lucas with skepticism. "There's a lot going on in her life right now. From how you and the team have described her, she hardly sounds like the type to take off in the middle of it all."

"But it might be exactly what she needs. Between the Fortis investigation and the police looking into Flannigan's murder, a weekend out of town could be enticing. It might even get her to relax her guard and reach out to her contacts."

"And you'd be close enough to witness every move she makes," continued Lucas.

"Exactly," Evan confirmed, but with more certainty than he felt.

While he had no doubt he could do the job impartially, the sharp attraction he felt for Nia James made him uneasy. It was not something he'd dealt with before in the many CIA operations in his career. Would more contact and intimacy make it better or worse?

"We don't have the luxury of time, so it's our best option," agreed Lucas. "I'll give Worthington what we have so far tomorrow, which may satisfy him. We have lots of circumstantial stuff, but we need a solid lead within a few days or we'll have missed a critical window."

"Agreed. I'll give you an update on our plan in the morning," Evan stated.

The two men hung up as Evan reached the hotel parking garage. Upstairs, he went to his suite rather than join the team in the other room. His body was still humming with pent up sexual tension that he hoped could be cured by a cold shower. Fifteen minutes later, under the spray of chilling water, he was still hard and aching. It didn't help that the sight of Nia James coming in his arms was vividly burned in his brain, interfering with all other rational thought. Evan cursed out loud, and finally shut off the shower tap. He needed to get his head out of his ass, and fast, he thought while toweling off and dressing in worn jeans and a T-shirt.

It was close to eleven o'clock before he went through to the control room, feeling slightly more in charge of his mind and body. The team needed to debrief for the day and finalize the short-term game plan.

* * *

After a restless night, Nia started the day feeling pretty optimistic about life. It could have been the relaxing night out, or the aftermath of a heart-stopping orgasm. Either way, she chose not to analyze it too much. Considering everything going on at work, and the precarious situation she was in, the diversion felt too good not to just ride with it.

As usual during most days of the week, she was up by six o'clock in the morning, at the gym before seven, then showered and dressed after kickboxing class by eight-fifteen. It was a short subway ride into downtown, and she was at the gallery about twenty minutes later.

By midmorning, Nia was knee-deep in work with only the occasional thought of when or if she would next hear from Evan DaCosta. Her cell phone rang, and she immediately thought it might be him.

"Hey, little girl."

Nia felt a small pang of disappointment when she immediately recognized the voice of her stepbrother, Nigel. Then she remembered why he was calling. It was because of her e-mail.

"Hey, Nigel. Everything okay?" she asked. "How is life in the suburbs?"

"It's all right. I just finished my shift at work," he explained. "What's going on, Nee?"

Nia looked around her office. The door was already closed but she swung around in her chair so her back faced the entrance, and lowered her voice.

"I need your help, Nigel," she whispered.

"What's wrong?"

"I know it's been a long time since you were inside, and we both cut ourselves off from some of the people we grew up with. But, do you know anyone who's still in the game?"

"What exactly are we talking about here, Nee?"

She looked around again.

"I can't go into too much detail. But there was a robbery in our warehouse. It was professional, Nigel. I mean, clean. They got away with millions in jewels."

"Shit!" he muttered.

"I know. But it gets worse. The security guard on duty that night was shot dead in Dorchester yesterday. And I was the only one with the combo to the safe, other than my boss."

"Damn it, Nee. Are they looking at you for it?" he asked. They both knew the way these things worked.

"Yeah, as much as they can without real proof. But only because my boss is more interested in getting the stuff back than calling the cops. But if they don't find who's really responsible soon, it's all going to point in my direction," she explained. "I can't just wait around for that to happen, Nigel. I didn't go through everything in my life and come so far to be falsely accused, again. Not going to happen!"

The words hung between them, heavy and choking with truth.

"Okay. Let me see what I can find out. But, Nee, I don't want you to call anyone else about this, okay? This is not the time to be reacquainting with anyone from the old hood."

"I know. I won't. I wouldn't even know where to begin," she muttered. "I just wish I didn't have to involve you, but I don't know what else to do."

"I'd be pissed if you hadn't, little girl."

Nia smiled at the protective affection in his voice.

"How's Angie?"

Angela was his girlfriend, a schoolteacher working in their town.

"She's good. She asked about you the other day," Nigel revealed.

"Sure she did. Making sure you wouldn't see me anytime soon, I bet."

He chuckled, unable to deny there was some truth to the statement.

"It's not that bad anymore, Nee. She'll come round eventually."

Nia barked out a sarcastic laugh.

"When's that exactly? It's been over three years since she convinced you to move to another area code, and she still thinks we're secretly in love. It's ridiculous. We barely talk anymore."

"I know. Maybe if you gained fifty pounds and lost your hair, she'd feel better about our relationship," he quipped. It was an old topic of debate between them.

"Yeah, well, she's going to be waiting forever."

She could tell he was smiling. At times like this, she really missed his friendship.

"Look, give me a couple of days to do some digging. I'll get back to you on Monday or Tuesday."

"Okay, but don't send anything to my work e-mail. Just call me on my cell phone. I can't be too careful around here."

"You got it, little girl."

"Thanks, Nigel."

"Anytime."

Nia hung up, then spent a few minutes indulging in memories. Though she had always thought of Nigel as her stepbrother, he really wasn't. Like many other times through her childhood, her mom had hooked up with his dad for a few years when Nia was around eleven. Nigel grew up with his mom in Boston, but he had spent several summers with them in Detroit. She remembered the first time he'd shown up at their doorstep on a Friday evening, with a duffel bag over his shoulder after a long string of train rides. Their parents were out at a party for the night, so only Nia was there to greet him. At sixteen, Nigel St. Clair had seemed so big and mature to her. Like the older brother she had always wanted. The image was magnified by how pissed he was that Nia had been left alone for the night, in a pretty rough, crime-ridden neighborhood.

Nigel had spent four summers with them, and the bond between him and Nia became stronger each time. Then, by the end of that last visit, their parents were broken up, and Nia's life was about to be altered forever. The only person who had cared at that time was Nigel, and it had cost him three years upstate.

Her musings were interrupted by Adam as he opened her office door to poke his head in.

"Do you have a sec, boss?" he asked.

"Sure, what's up?"

Nia took the opportunity to stretch her legs. She stood up from her office chair and walked across the room.

"I'm working with Nancy on the engagement activities through June, and I want to add that new DaCosta contract. Do you have any more details?" he asked.

"Nothing confirmed yet. Mr. DaCosta didn't mention a specific timetable. But let's go through what's booked already and I can propose some times to him."

"Okay," Adam agreed as they walked through the office toward his cubicle. "His stuff is in Virginia, right?

So we'll need a local appraiser? Or will one of us be doing it?"

"We'll see. I think you and I can probably do the cataloging. Then we can decide on the appraiser once we know what we're dealing with. Mr. DaCosta said his dad dabbled in a lot of different things."

Adam did a poor job of hiding his smirk. Nia only had to raise a questioning brow. He immediately cleared his throat and straightened his expression. But he didn't divulge what exactly he had found so funny.

"What?" she finally demanded.

"Nothing," he quickly replied, trying hard to look innocent. "It's just that Emma mentioned that you had gone out on a date with Mr. DaCosta yesterday."

"And?" Nia questioned, not bothering to deny it. With the speed that news traveled in the office, even the temporary warehouse staff were probably already talking about it.

"Uhmm, nothing." There was a pause. "It's just that it's so unusual for you to accept a date with a client, that's all. From anyone, actually. I don't think you've ever even mentioned a boyfriend."

Nia let Adam ramble. He was only asking what others would, though probably not to her directly. That would defeat the purpose of juicy gossip.

"Anyway, according to Emma, he's pretty good-looking. Evan DaCosta, I mean. In which case, good for you!"

Her patient silence and blank facial expression finally got through to him. Adam let out a deep sigh of frustration and turned back to his computer.

"What does your schedule look like for the next few weeks?" she continued, as though the topic of her dating life had never been introduced.

They spent the next thirty minutes looking at their current client commitments in order to determine when the team could complete the cataloging and appraisals for Evan. It was pretty clear that the only viable window for her to travel to Virginia would be in the next two weeks. Otherwise, it would have to wait until later in the summer. Or someone else on the team would need to manage it.

Nia went back to her office knowing that she would have to call Evan today and discuss the options. After last night, it felt strange for their first conversation to be business-related. It was even more awkward that she had to be the one to call. Would it look like she was chasing him, eager for a repeat performance, using work as an excuse?

This was why she never dated anyone related to work. Too many added complications.

By late afternoon, she couldn't procrastinate any longer. Nia picked up her desk phone and started dialing, but paused as her cell phone also rang. Hoping it was Evan, she quickly answered. Instead, it was her best friend, Lianne Bloom.

"Are we still on for tonight?" Lianne asked after a quick hello.

Nia bit the inside of her cheek, trying to think of a good excuse. Lianne's fiancé, Eddie, had his brother in town for a couple of weeks. Lianne had made plans for Nia to join them for a night out. It wasn't a double date or anything since Eddie's brother, Kevin, had a girlfriend back in Seattle. But Nia still hesitated. She wasn't really in the mood to hang out as part of a group.

"Please don't cancel, Nia. I found this place downtown that has a live band playing tonight. You can't leave me with the boys by myself!" pleaded Lianne. "If you're not there, they'll just insist on going to a bar and I'll be stuck watching baseball all night or something."

That did sound like hell, so Nia caved.

"Okay, okay, I'll go," she conceded.

"Yes! I'm thinking seven o'clock for dinner?" suggested Lianne.

"Sure. I'm going to go home and change, but that should be fine."

"Do you want us to pick you up?"

"No, that's okay," Nia replied. "I'll just grab a cab."

"Okay, I'll send you a text with the address. See you later!"

Nia barely had time to say good-bye before her phone was beeping with another call.

"Hello?" she quickly answered.

"Hi, Nia, it's Evan."

She sat back in her chair, trying to regain her composure.

"Hi, Evan," she managed to reply smoothly. "How are you?"

Geez, that sounded so formal. She could almost see his teasing grin, mocking her.

"I'm fine. How are you?"

It was her turn to grin.

"I'm good, thank you," she returned.

"Did you sleep well?" His tone lowered a bit, making his words sound more suggestive than they should have. Heat warmed her cheeks.

"I did, actually."

"Good," he stated. "I didn't sleep at all, in case you're wondering."

Nia smiled harder, enjoying his flirting more than she should.

"Really? That's unfortunate. What do you think caused that?"

"I was feeling a bit tense for some reason," Evan surmised, his voice smooth as silk.

"Hmmm. Tension is very bad for you, Evan. You should do something about that."

"Yeah, that's what I was thinking. What are you doing this evening?"

Nia couldn't stop grinning.

"I have plans, unfortunately," she told him.

"Any chance you can change them?" he probed. "I'll make it worth your while."

She squeezed her eyes tightly shut, really tempted to accept his offer.

"Sorry, I can't. I just confirmed them with a friend."

He cleared his throat, and Nia waited for him to respond.

"There is something to be said for a good workout at the gym, I guess," he stated.

Nia paused for a moment, hoping he would suggest another opportunity to get together. The silence became awkward.

"I'm glad you called anyway," she added.

"And why is that?" Evan drawled.

"We need to start work on your collection," she explained in her best professional voice, as devoid of flirtation as possible. "I need to sit down with you to look at the options for when we can do a complete inventory, followed by the appraisals. Once those two processes are complete, then I can advise on the best strategy to auction off the collection."

"Okay, let's do that tomorrow," he stipulated.

"Tomorrow? It's Saturday," Nia reminded him.

"Exactly. So plenty of time to discuss it. I have a

charity event to attend at the Vineyard. You can come with me. We'll drive, take our time," he added.

"What? Martha's Vineyard?" she stammered. "Isn't that a little far?"

"Only just a couple hours' drive. It's Memorial Day weekend. We'll stay the night, drive back Sunday. Or even on Monday if you'd like."

"Evan, I . . ."

"No expectations, Nia, other than your company. My family has a house there, plenty of room."

"You have a house there," she repeated, feeling both surprised and overwhelmed by the offer.

"Just a little summer cottage," he humbly clarified. "Come with me, Mia. I was going to fly in just for the party, but I would much prefer to make a weekend of it with you. And there will be plenty of time to discuss my contract."

Nia squeezed her eyes tight, trying to think of a response. It would be so easy to say yes, to rush off for the weekend with the hot guy she'd just met. And they would very likely end up in bed together. The physical attraction they shared was undeniable. But self-preservation and life experience were both screaming in the background that it was too good to be true. He was too good to be real.

"I don't think I can go, Evan. I have a commitment tomorrow that I can't break," she finally told him.

He was not dissuaded.

"What time?"

"Nine-thirty," she replied, weakly.

"In the morning? For how long?"

"About two hours," estimated Nia. It was technically only an hour, but she felt the need to make it sound more time-consuming.

"Perfect. I'll pick you up at one o'clock, then we'll have a late lunch in Cape Cod. Unless you have other plans for the weekend. Or don't you want to go?" Evan suggested when she didn't respond right away.

She couldn't lie, even though it would have been better for her well-being to do so.

"No, no other plans. You just caught me off guard, that's all," she explained. "It sounds like a great trip."

"So, you'll join me?"

With a deep breath and eyes scrunched, Nia went with her desire.

"Yes, I'll go. But, only for one night."

Chapter 8

Evan had always approached surveillance with analytical detachment. Early in his career with the agency, it was effective training on reading people and surroundings to predict behavior and all possible outcomes. Later, in the field and as part of the CIA Protective Services, his instincts became razor-sharp. There were countless files where the smallest observations effectively foiled plots, apprehended suspects, and saved lives. Even his final mission in the Protective Services division was completed successfully. Despite taking a bullet in the leg from the assailant, Evan had still managed to save the ambassador to the United States from an assassination attempt in Azerbaijan near the Iranian border. His injury was unfortunate, but was also a calculated and necessary risk in the situation.

Today, as he and Raymond tailed Nia's taxi into downtown Boston on Friday evening, he didn't feel sharp or detached. His thigh muscle throbbed from the intense workout he'd gone through that afternoon. Evan rubbed at the tight scar tissue, trying to relieve the ache. Eight months after the shooting, he only had lingering pain when he pushed his body beyond

normal endurance. It was an acceptable amount of
discomfort considering the original prognosis had been
permanent disability. The bullet hit him from close
proximity and punctured a main artery, tore up his
quadriceps, and chipped the femur bone. In the chaos
after the shooting, the priority had been to get the ambassador safely out of the vicinity without causing an
international incident. It was several hours before Evan
could seek proper medical attention, resulting in massive blood loss followed by a deep infection.

Five months and two surgeries later, there had
been minimal improvement to the mobility in his leg.
Evan was unwilling to accept that he would be forever
crippled. He politely retired from the CIA and returned home to move on with his life, determined to at
least walk without a limp again. The first thing he did
was start private sessions of physical therapy, the second
was to reach out to his good friend, Lucas Johnson.

The two men had met in Washington, D.C., early in
their government careers. They worked together on a
lengthy bank fraud case with ties to Eastern European
organized crime, and quickly became close friends.
Over the years, while Evan was home in Virginia between assignments, they often talked about starting a
private agency together, providing elite asset recovery,
corporate security, and personal protection services
beyond what local police could offer.

Four years ago, when Lucas wanted to launch the
company, Evan wasn't quite ready to leave the CIA.
Instead, Evan offered to be an investor and silent partner. With the strength of the DaCosta name in the
military security and defense industry, they would have
quick access and credibility to a very niche client list.

Fortis was born. Evan provided seed money from his

trust fund, Lucas managed the operations, only needing to consult with Evan on major decisions. One of which was the opportunity to extend their partnership to include Samuel Mackenzie, a former British MI5 agent whom Lucas had worked with in the Secret Service. After meeting the burly Scot, Evan was fully supportive. It was a smart investment. The agency quickly grew into a successful organization with few competitors in North America.

Evan's attention returned to the present as the cab they were following stopped at the curb a half a block ahead. He parked the nondescript black SUV he was driving a short distance back. He and Raymond watched Nia exit her cab and walk into a small bar. Raymond then quickly installed a small earpiece and prepared to follow her in.

As planned, Tony was in New York for a couple of days, looking into the lead that had surfaced yesterday. There was an Interpol informant, known only as Spencer, who ran a well-respected art and antiquities dealership in Manhattan. The word in Tony's network was that Spencer was the man to talk to about high-end stolen goods in any major city on the East Coast.

Before he left, Tony had managed to get into the dead security guard's apartment while his girlfriend was out. Unfortunately, Flannigan had been too smart to leave anything incriminating or relevant there.

Now, with Tony out of town, the team was a man down and had to make do with someone Nia had met before. In casual clothes and a baseball cap, it was unlikely that she would still recognize Raymond as one of the Fortis investigators, if she saw him.

"Let's get a picture of everyone she talks to," Evan instructed, repeating their surveillance plan. "I want to hear about every move she makes. And make sure she doesn't spot you."

"Got it."

Raymond exited the car and casually followed Nia. His voice came through to Evan's earpiece about three minutes later.

"Okay, I have her. She's just joined a guy at a table in the back of the room. They hugged," Raymond described.

Evan clenched his jaw, the only physical reaction to the instinctive annoyance he felt. He knew it was ridiculous. He should feel good, this man could be the break they were looking for, a tangible lead into who Nia is working with, if in fact she's involved in the robbery.

"I've just sent the image," continued Raymond. "This would be a good place for a meeting. It's small, a little dark, music playing but not too loud for conversation. But they're laughing now. It looks more like a date than business, to me."

"It could be," Evan replied, in a neutral tone. "She only said she had plans with a friend. Let's see if Lucas can find anything on the guy with his new facial recognition toy."

"Okay, looks like a foursome," Raymond quickly added. "Another couple has joined them, bringing a round of drinks. More hugging, laughing. Pics on the way."

"Got 'em," replied Evan a few moments later. "Sit tight until I hear back from Lucas."

"No problem. There's a live performance that's about to start. I'll just chill out with a beer and enjoy the show."

Within a couple of minutes, they had Nia's associates confirmed: Lianne Bloom, registered psychotherapist, engaged to Edward "Eddie" Thompson, financial analyst, brother to Kevin Thompson, veterinarian. The latter was visiting Boston from Seattle, according to a social media post. Not one police arrest or known illegal association among them.

"Wow, it's a real who's who of the criminal underground," quipped Raymond. "How do you want to play this, Ice?"

"Let's keep watch, just in case," Evan instructed. It wouldn't be the first time he'd seen a clever criminal operate in plain sight.

But the rest of the evening went by without any notable activity. The group of four left the club together, and Nia was dropped off at home before eleven o'clock.

"The music was pretty good," Raymond stated as they drove back to the Harbor Hotel.

Evan only raised an eyebrow.

"Seriously, it's pretty hard to find a nice place with live music these days," the agent added. "It's called Moody's, and I pulled up their website. Turns out they have a few locations on the East Coast, including Arlington. I'm going to have to check it out. Impress the ladies."

Evan was saved from responding when a call came in from Lucas.

"Ice, when will you be back at the room?" he asked through the speakerphone.

"In about five minutes. Why?" Evan replied, on edge.

"We got something from the sealed juvenile record on James. It was a burglary charge. Call me when you're in the control room and I'll give you what I know."

Twenty minutes later, the ground team was in the middle of a debate. Lucas's intel revealed that Nia

James had been attending a prestigious private high school in Bloomfield, Michigan, on scholarship. In the middle of her junior year, she was accused of trying to steal diamond earrings from the home of a schoolmate. Six months later, the charges were dropped by the victim, but not before Nia lost her scholarship and was expelled from the school.

"That's it, boys. The evidence against James just keeps stacking up," Raymond stated.

"No wonder she was so cagey in the interview," added Michael. "A prior burglary charge. Even if she was just fifteen and the charges were dropped."

"It's still a fact we can't ignore," contended Raymond. "Millions of dollars in rare jewels as motive, the access to the safe for opportunity, and now a previous arrest for theft. Of diamonds, no less. Then add recent communication with the ex-con?"

"Nigel St. Clair," stated Evan.

"She's the only viable suspect, guys. We've got zippo on anyone else in the company," Raymond reminded them.

"Can't argue with that," Michael agreed.

Evan turned from the spot he had been planted, near the window with a view of the glittering harbor, ignoring the disappointment that had settled low in his stomach.

"We continue the plan with James as the prime suspect," he instructed. "I'll trail her to the appointment she has in the morning, then I'll keep a close eye on her for the weekend. Tony will be back Sunday from New York, so let's use the next few days to get all the answers we need. Either James will slip up, or we need to confirm the buyer and locate the money trail."

The other two men nodded in agreement, then

broke up to pack it in for the night. Evan entered his suite. His body was exhausted, but his mind was racing. For the first time in his professional career, he couldn't trust his instincts and it was frustrating.

Like Michael and Raymond, Evan could not dispute the evidence stacking up against Nia. All logical reasoning told him she had to be involved in some way. His initial assessment was still accurate; she was not a woman who could easily be pressured or coerced into anything. So the same logic would indicate she was dangerously manipulative and conniving. An unscrupulous thief, callously using her femininity to dupe the men around her, including Edward Worthington. And maybe even capable of planning the murder of an accomplice.

Unfortunately, other than logic and common sense, nothing Evan had observed about Nia James in the last three days suggested she could be willingly involved in the high-stakes game of grand larceny and assassination. When he was with her, pretending to start a hot love affair, nothing between them felt like she was guilty. If he was really honest about it, their time together hardly felt like working a case. It felt like a man wanting a woman in the most natural way. And that was just fucked up.

And there was no doubt he wanted her. Even now, knowing what was in her juvenile file, seeing her out with another man, Evan was anticipating their weekend together. She triggered something in him that he didn't understand. A physical attraction that was unlike anything he'd experienced before. It was uncomfortable and unnerving. And Evan knew he had to get it under control. He had two days in close proximity in which to do that, and uncover whatever secrets Nia James was still hiding.

Evan spent another couple of hours packing a weekend bag and reviewing the various files and reports they had gathered on the case to date before catching a few hours of exhausted sleep. He was up at six o'clock Saturday morning to join the team for a workout in the well-equipped hotel gym. By eight o'clock, he was inside the black SUV, watching Nia's front door. Thirty minutes later, she walked out of her apartment dressed casually in narrow fitted jeans, a light jacket over a T-shirt, and flat shoes. Her thick hair was still in the usual ponytail, but without the professional clothes, stiletto heels, and blood-red lipstick, she appeared younger, less untouchable.

He watched as she walked in the direction of the nearest subway station. Evan stepped out of the truck to follow her on foot. For the next fifteen minutes, he stayed within visual range, but well hidden by the other transit passengers. Wearing track pants, a hoodie, and running shoes, he looked like every other guy headed to the gym. His holstered gun was concealed under the baggy sweat clothes. Nia exited the subway in Dorchester, just south of downtown Boston. Evan's senses were on high alert. This neighborhood seemed to be at the epicenter of the suspects involved in the robbery. Whatever Nia was doing there had to be related.

She walked another three blocks, head held high, with no sign of concern for the rough characters gathering at front stoops or the drunks hanging out in front of the closed liquor store. She was focused on her destination, with a strong, determined stride. Evan almost wondered what would happen if someone tried to mess with her. He remembered her firm body, and comment about kickboxing. His money would be on Nia doing some serious damage.

Finally, she turned to enter a small community center. It was five minutes before nine o'clock. Evan sped up his pace so that he wouldn't lose sight of her inside the building. He cautiously opened the front door, but found the center hall in front of him empty.

"Excuse me, mister." Evan turned to find a young girl standing behind him. "I need to get in or I'll be late for my class."

She was tall and reed-thin, with dark hair and ivory, freckled skin. He figured she wasn't more than eleven.

"Class on a Saturday? That sucks," he commented while opening the door for her.

"It's not school," she shot back, like he was an idiot. "It's music."

Then she was off running down the hall, stepping into the last doorway on the right.

Evan looked around again. The rest of the building seemed empty. He slowly made his way down the corridor, cautiously checking each of the rooms along the way. He was halfway to the end when he heard Nia's laugh. It sounded natural and genuine. There was also the trilling giggle of a girl. Cautiously, he crept forward toward the doorway the girl had entered.

"Okay, enough silliness. Let's get started," he heard Nia state. "How much practicing did you do this week?"

He peeked in to find the two females seated beside each other on a bench in front of a full-size piano with their backs to him.

"Three hours?" the girl replied, hesitantly.

"Three? Meghan, you were supposed to do at least forty-five minutes a day," Nia scolded.

"I know, Nia. I tried, but my brothers were making too much noise in the house, and my mom got mad."

"Okay. But it means that we'll just have to work harder on Saturdays."

"I know. I can do that."

"Good. So show me what you've been working on. Let's start with the number six sonata."

Evan stepped back from view, but listened. The young girl started playing a classical song. He knew very little about the piano, but it seemed like a complicated composition. She struggled a little in places, but she did pretty good overall.

"Not bad!" Nia announced. "It's coming along, Meghan. Let's try the beginning part again, focusing on the rhythmic groups."

He stayed by the door, listening to the lesson and keeping an eye out for any suspicious activity. A security guard walked by, nodding at Evan, but otherwise, the place was empty.

"Okay, lesson over. What do you want to hear?"

There was more girlish giggling.

"You know what song, Nia."

"Really! Katy Perry again?"

"Please? You do it so good!"

"Oh all right," Nia replied, making it sound like a big effort.

Evan smiled to himself, liking this side of her. Then she started playing one of those songs that were popular on the radio. He stood straighter, his skin prickled with goose bumps. It was incredible how she re-created the melody. He wanted to close his eyes and fully experience it. But Evan was on a job, doing surveillance, uncovering the truth.

When she reached the chorus, Nia's voice came in slowly, almost as though she didn't realize she was singing. Even to his uneducated ear, she was a very good singer, with a rich, clear voice filled with passion and honesty. Evan felt disappointed when the performance ended. The silence after was so empty.

"Okay, it's time for you to go, Meghan."

Evan checked his watch. It was only ten o'clock. She had told him her appointment was for two hours. Did she have another lesson?

"I know. Thanks, Nia."

He quickly took cover around the corner at the end of the hall. Their voices carried into the corridor as they said good-bye. There were more girlish giggles and both pairs of steps retreated toward the main entrance. Evan stayed hidden, but took a quick glance into the hall to see what was going on. The young girl was now holding a man's hand, and Nia was talking to him. They were too far away for Evan to hear the conversation. He took out his phone and took a picture, just before the girl and the man left. Evan listened to Nia's return to the room with the piano, then stayed concealed to see what came next. His right hand lingered near the handle of his Glock, just in case.

Fifteen minutes later, no one else arrived to meet Nia. Instead, she was still at the piano playing various songs, strung together back to back. She was practicing.

Evan crept up to the doorway to check her status, then casually strode out of the building. Once outside, he pulled out his cell phone.

"Raymond."

"Hey, Ice, any intel?"

"I followed her to a community center in Dorchester. As promising as that sounds, I don't think I got anything useful to the case, unfortunately," Evan replied in an annoyed tone. "Listen, were there any other sources of income when we looked at James's finances?"

"Nope, just what she made at Worthington, and a small investment portfolio. Why?"

Evan walked to a secure spot where he could still see the entrance to the community center.

"Well, it looks like she tutors music, or something," he told Raymond, then gave him a quick summary of what he had observed.

"Maybe she's paid in cash?" suggested Raymond. "Let me see what I can find online. What's the name of the center?"

They had their answer with a few search results.

"She volunteers music lessons in a program for underprivileged kids, Ice," Raymond confirmed, and Evan pinched the bridge of his nose. "It doesn't have her name on the website or anything. It just says that the center has a volunteer program that runs on the weekends. So it's the only thing that makes sense. She's a fucking philanthropist."

"Tell me about it," Evan spat. It was hardly the picture of the coldhearted, scheming vamp involved in a daring jewelry theft. The facts on this assignment were becoming more confusing by the moment.

"I'm sending you a picture I took. I'm not sure you'll be able to get anything off it, but she was talking to a man for a few minutes. Looked like a relative of the student she was tutoring. Maybe the father, or something. But let's check him out anyway."

"Sure thing, Ice," Raymond confirmed before they hung up.

A few minutes later, the front door of the center opened and Nia walked out, bouncing down the front stairs with extra enthusiasm. Evan watched her progress, his brows furrowed by one perplexing question: Who was the real Nia James?

Chapter 9

Evan parked his car in front of Nia's apartment at one o'clock. The street was busy with activity as kids played outside and pedestrians headed to their various local destinations. As he stepped out of the Bentley, he could feel their eyes measuring him up. Even in dark jeans, a golf shirt, and leather loafers, it was obvious he was out of place in this modest, middle-class neighborhood.

Nia stepped out of her apartment door before he made it halfway up the front walkway, suggesting she had been watching for his arrival. He noted that she had changed out of her earlier clothes into a soft blue dress and a denim jacket. She carried a large tote bag, which Evan quickly took out of her hands.

"You're on time," he teased, leading her back to the car.

Her eyes snapped with defensiveness.

"You didn't expect me to be?"

He shrugged, enjoying her fiery energy. It had to take time for her to look that good.

"It's a woman's right, isn't it?"

"Well, not this woman," she mumbled.

"Hey, I'm not complaining," Evan explained, grinning back boyishly.

He opened the passenger door for her, then put her bag in the backseat. The neighborhood eyes continued to follow them.

"How was your morning? You had an appointment, you said?" he asked, pulling away from the curb.

"It was good," Nia replied, simply.

Sensing her pensive mood, Evan didn't pry. She was definitely the type to become stubbornly evasive if pushed.

"Should I put on some music?" he asked, turning on the radio. It was preset to a twenty-four-hour news channel.

"Sure."

"Anything in particular?"

"I'm easy, anything is fine," she replied, looking out her door window at the passing cityscape.

It was clear from her posture and tone that she had a barrier up. Evan flipped through the radio stations, landing on one that played the top hits list. Any insights into her musical talents would have to wait for a better time. They continued the drive in easy silence, only interrupted by the occasional question from Evan about her comfort with the temperature in the car, or her seat position.

"I realized when I was packing that I should have asked you more about this thing tonight," Nia finally stated.

They were about thirty miles south of Boston, but still an hour or so away from Cape Cod.

"I wasn't sure exactly what to bring," she admitted.

"I'm sure whatever you have will be fine," he advised. "What kind of event is it?"

"It's a charity thing, for adult literacy," explained

Evan. "The Clements manage the foundation and they're old family friends. Every year over the Memorial Day weekend, they launch their summer fundraising calendar with a barbecue at their beach house."

"Oh, so it's casual?" she asked, surprised.

"Well, maybe the term *barbecue* is a little misleading," he surmised with a smile. "I haven't gone in a few years, but I remember it being more like a cocktail party than backyard cookout."

"Okay."

He looked over at her profile. She seemed concerned.

"We'll have plenty of time after we have lunch. We could do a little shopping if you need to," Evan offered.

Nia looked up at him, surprise and relief written all over her face.

"That would be great, if you're sure it's okay."

"Of course," he assured her.

"Well, I won't take long. There are a couple of stores that should have something."

"Take as long as you'd like, Nia. Have you been to the Cape before?"

"A few times, for client meetings. I've always wanted to go for a weekend away, it's so pretty. But just never managed to plan it," she admitted.

"Why don't we spend the day there tomorrow before we return to Boston?" suggested Evan.

She smiled softly. It touched that spot behind his ribcage.

"That sounds nice."

He kept the conversation alive by talking about the various sites and activities they could see and do in the area. The rest of the drive went by quickly until they arrived in the town of Falmouth in the Upper Cape. Evan drove into the commercial center, now bursting with tourists for the long weekend. He parked the car within walking distance of restaurants and retail shops.

"Are you hungry?" he asked, helping Nia out of the car.

"Starving!" she declared.

He laughed at her dramatics.

"You should have said," he admonished. "We could have stopped earlier."

"Don't worry, I'll survive."

"Well, let's hurry just in case."

Evan took her hand in his and they walked a couple of blocks to a restaurant he knew well. It was built sometime in the 1950s and hadn't changed much since.

"My parents and I always stopped here for lunch on our way to the Vineyard when I was young," he explained as they looked through the menu. "The food is great. Everything is fresh and local."

"It does look really good," she agreed. "I know I'm supposed to choose seafood while here, but I have a craving for a burger."

They placed their orders, and Evan took the opportunity to ask a few seemingly innocent questions.

"How was last night? Were your other plans enjoyable?"

Nia raised an eyebrow, but her lips twitched.

"My evening was good, thanks," she replied. "I joined some friends at a bar downtown for open mic night."

"Really? One of them is a musician?" he asked casually.

"No. We were just listening. The guys wanted to go to a sports bar, so we compromised."

"Guys?"

Her brows went up again.

"Are you jealous, Mr. DaCosta?" she teased.

Evan flashed a charming smile.

"I don't get jealous, Ms. James," he clarified in deep, slow tone. "Should I be?"

"Hardly," Nia dismissed. "They were just friends."

"Do you have a lot of male friends?"

"No. Only a few acquaintances, really," she clarified, looking away.

"What about girlfriends? Are you one of those women who only travel in packs?"

Nia rolled her eyes.

"Hardly. I never understood that."

"What?" he probed.

"You know. People with a zillion friends. It must be so exhausting."

Evan chuckled at her exaggeration.

"So you're a loner?"

"I like my own company, if that's what you mean. I'm an only child, remember?" she reminded him with a shrug. "I know lots of people, but I only have a small number of real friends. People that I trust completely. That's all you really need, right?"

Evan nodded in support.

"What about family?" he asked. "Don't they count?"

"I don't know. I'm not very close to mine."

"Why not?"

She looked over his shoulder with a faraway expression on her face.

"We just have a different way of looking at the world. I love them, but I wouldn't say they have my back no matter what," she explained softly. "But you can't choose your family, right?"

Their meals arrived just then, interrupting the sensitive moment. They ate in silence.

"Come, let's go shopping," he stated as he paid their tab.

Outside, they walked hand in hand down the busy, historical streets until Nia pointed to one of the boutiques she knew. Inside, she slowly walked through the collection, stopping to touch a few things here and there.

From the world of international espionage, Evan was more familiar with women's clothing than he could explain. He quickly noticed several dresses that he knew would drape her body to perfection. But Evan feigned disinterest like the average civilian man would and casually went to the sales counter.

"Can I help you?" asked the middle-aged woman behind the desk.

"Yes. I would like to arrange payment for whatever the pretty lady would like to purchase," he requested, pulling out his personal credit card and handing it over.

"No problem, sir," she replied with an eager smile.

"Maybe the yellow dress near the window? But, let's keep it between you and me," he added with a wink.

"No worries, Mr. DaCosta, I'll take care of it."

He watched Nia pull out a few items while the saleswoman wrote down his information then handed back the card.

"How are you making out?" he asked Nia as she stood in front of a full-length mirror, holding up a black cocktail dress.

"All right, I think," she replied.

"Good. I'm going to run over to the liquor store down the street. They carry vintage wines and liquors and George Clement has a thing for single malt scotch.

I'll be back in about twenty minutes?" suggested Evan, checking his watch.

"Okay. I should be done by then."

As he exited the shop, he could see the sales rep talking to Nia, and pointing to the garment he suggested. Inside the liquor store, he called Raymond to provide a status update.

"How's Tony doing in New York?" he asked as he walked through the aisles of rare and expensive bottles.

"He checked in a couple of hours ago. It's not good."

Evan paused.

"His lead, Spencer, has gone underground and no one seems to know where to find him," Raymond explained.

"Damn it!" Evan exclaimed. "Any more details on what kind information he might have?"

"Negative. Tony's going to stake him out for a couple of days, in case he resurfaces."

"Okay. I'll check in again tonight. But send me a text if there are any new developments."

"You got it," Raymond confirmed.

"What about the picture I sent you this morning? Were you able to identify the guy?"

"Not immediately. It was too blurry. But I have one of the analyst at headquarters working on it. It will take a few days, but we're trying digital image enhancement software."

"What about video feeds? Anything in the area we can use to cross-reference his identity?"

"No, it a pretty rough neighborhood. If there are any cameras in the immediate vicinity, they're not linked to any online network," explained Raymond. "Beyond that, every other guy on the street is wearing jeans and a white T-shirt."

"Okay, thanks, Raymond. Keep me posted."

"No problem, Ice."

When Evan returned to the clothing boutique, Nia was waiting outside, looking in the store window next door. The glossy garment bag she now carried gave no hint to which dress was the final purchase. They walked through the streets of Cape Cod for a little while before returning to the car for the rest of the trip to his house on Martha's Vineyard.

Almost three hours later, Evan was standing in the kitchen of his family's beach house when she walked into the room wearing the yellow dress of his choice. He could not have pictured her looking more stunning. The silk dress was simple in design. Sleeveless, with a boat neck and side gathering at the waist, the flared skirt fell to her midthigh. The buttery color made her dark-honey skin glow. The fluid fabric draped her body sensuously, revealing more curves than it hid. As his wayward body hardened with heavy desire, he considered that the black dress might have been a better choice. At least for his sanity.

"Is this okay?" she finally asked as the silence and his staring became awkward. "The salesperson insisted it was the best choice. But the color is a little paler than I usually choose. I have another dress that I brought with me, but it's probably too casual."

"No," he finally responded, walking toward her. "No, it's beautiful."

He smoothly pulled her into his arms and kissed

her. The moment his lips touched hers, he realized how much he had craved her taste. He delved deeply into her mouth, indulging in the sweet wetness, and two days suddenly felt like an eternity. What was wrong with him?

"You look beautiful, Nia," he told her softly when they finally came up for air. "Maybe I can get a little jealous. I don't want anyone else's eyes on you but mine."

Her silky hair now fell to her shoulders in soft waves. She tucked a section behind her ears and turned away from him.

"Please, I'm sure I'll hardly be noticed," she surmised, clearly uncomfortable with his compliments. Her tone suggested she might actually believe her statement. Evan found her reaction puzzling. How could the unflappable woman who stopped traffic and was facing investigative interrogations head-on not know how incredibly stunning she was?

"Give me five minutes to finish getting ready?"

She was gone before he could respond, returning quickly wearing delicate high-heeled sandals, a cashmere pashmina around her shoulders, and a small clutch purse in her hand. Her lips glistened with soft pink lip gloss. Evan felt guilty fascination.

The Clements cottage was only about three miles down the beach in the village of Chilmark at the southwest end of the island, but a ten-minute drive through the rural roads. The house sat at the end of a long, winding, private road under the canopy of old oak trees. As they got closer, there was a line of cars parked along the shoulder, and a couple of valet attendants to assist guests if preferred. Evan tossed over the car keys to one of the young men and slipped the claim ticket into the inside pocket of his light gray blazer. Then he escorted Nia into the house, his arm wrapped possessively around her waist.

There was no sign of her earlier vulnerability. She walked with the same air of confidence he'd first noticed, shoulders back and head high. Evan could feel the slinky undulation of her hips against the palm of his hand. He was tempted to walk behind her just to enjoy the show, but liked the feel of his hands on her body too much.

"Before we go in, I should tell you a little about the Clements," Evan stated in a low voice. "They're not just old family friends. I was engaged to their daughter, Mikayla, for a little bit."

Evan felt Nia's back stiffen.

"Okay," she replied, stretching out the word to suggest more information would be appreciated.

"We broke up over three years ago, and it's all good. But I just thought you should know in case someone brings it up," he added.

She looked at him, perhaps to ask questions, but they were now inside the wide front entrance of the house.

"Evan! You made it," exclaimed Mrs. Elaine Stone-Clement as she approached them. "It's so good to see you."

He hugged the older woman who had always been like a second mom to him. She was glamorous and youthful in her late forties with the warm brown skin of her face still smooth of wrinkles.

"Shame on you for not staying in touch more," she scolded when they stepped apart. "But you look great. You're fully recovered, I take it?"

He could feel Nia's questioning gaze on his face.

"Almost as good as new," Evan confirmed. "Nia, this is Elaine Stone-Clement, chairman of the Clement Literacy Foundation. Elaine, this is Nia James."

The two women shook hands and exchanged pleasantries.

"Where is George? I brought him something," he asked, holding up a generous bottle of Glenfiddich, a forty-year-old scotch.

"Oh, he's going to kiss you. He's outside somewhere pretending he's doing some of the cooking," Elaine teased. "Leave Nia with me, I'll get her something to drink."

Evan glanced down to make sure Nia was okay with that. She smiled back agreeably.

"I'll be back shortly," he promised.

"Take your time," Nia urged, cool as a cucumber.

As Evan walked away, he heard Elaine asking Nia about her drink preference. He knew she was in good hands.

On the way out to the back of the house, he passed several people he had not seen in years, but knew well as part of the Vineyard summer community and through his social network in the D.C. and Virginia area. As suggested, George Clement was in the vicinity of the state-of-the-art outdoor kitchen, but there was a hired chef working behind the grill. The older man was about the same height as Evan, but with a girth that suggested he was less active than in the past and dealing with some stress. Unlike his wife, he looked every bit his fifty years. His curly hair was now fully gray and his coppery skin was creased with frown lines.

"Son!" the older man exclaimed with genuine delight. "Elaine said you might join us this year."

The two men hugged.

"I brought you something," Evan announced when they parted.

The founder and chairman of the board of a powerful media conglomerate beamed like a schoolboy. He took the bottle of scotch in both hands, clearly touched by the thoughtfulness.

"Oh, Evan. You've outdone yourself. We have to toast a glass later this evening," insisted George.

"Absolutely."

"So, how are you doing, son? We haven't seen you since you came back injured from overseas. How's the leg healing?" George asked.

"It's pretty good. Still a little sore at times but nothing too serious."

"As I live and breathe! Evan DaCosta gracing us with his presence in our humble home?"

Evan grinned, recognizing that saucy tongue anywhere. He turned around to find the petite and very pretty Mikayla Stone-Clement with her hands planted on her slender hips.

"You're on your own, kid," chuckled George, and he made a quick escape.

His daughter clearly had a bone to pick with Evan, and the wise man wanted no part of it.

"Hi, Mikayla," Evan stated, a little sheepishly. He knew exactly what was coming.

"Hi to you, too. You could have just returned my phone calls seven months ago, Evan. No need to come all the way to the Vineyard on my account," she drawled sarcastically.

"Sorry about that. Things were a little crazy at the time," he explained, lamely.

"Yeah, I know! You were shot. I get it. That's why I called," pressed Mikayla, clearly not ready to let it go.

"I just wanted to make sure you were okay, Evan. I was worried about you. Your poor mom was in bits."

"I know, I know. I'm sorry. I should have called you long before now."

His acknowledgment seemed to take some of the wind out of her sails. She straightened and stepped close.

"Damn right you should have. But you seem good. Healthy. So I suppose I have to forgive you."

She opened her arms and they hugged.

"It was just such a shock to find out you got injured in the middle of a conflict somewhere in the Middle East," Mikayla mused when they parted. "I know DaCosta does work in some high-risk places, but I just never considered that as an executive for the company, you might be in danger."

"I'm not usually. It was a fluke, really. Wrong place at the wrong time, that's all," explained Evan.

His CIA cover identity had always been under the broad reach of DaCosta Solutions as a U.S. defense contractor. Even his mother thought he had spent the last ten years working for the family business, managing their overseas operations. The only person who had known the truth was his father, and only because of his high-level security clearance.

"When you didn't call me back, I wondered if maybe you were still angry with me," she added when they stepped apart.

"You know that's not true," he insisted. "I was never angry."

She shrugged.

"Well, I'm glad you've recovered well," she declared. "So, I met your girlfriend. Nia?"

Evan looked down at his ex-fiancée, waiting for the rest of her commentary.

"She's . . . not really your type, Evan."

"Really? And why is that?" he replied evenly, though he felt irritated by the suggestion.

Mikayla shrugged again.

"You know what I mean. She's stunning, really. Sexy. Junior can't seem to take his eyes off her. But I always thought you preferred women who are more natural, unadorned, that's all."

"This might come as a surprise, Mikayla, but you're not the complete definition of my type. Every red-blooded man is attracted to sexy," he advised in a cool tone.

Her eyes shot sparks at him.

"That was cruel."

"Yes it was. And you're being catty and jealous. Which you really have no right to be. In case you forgot, you broke up with me, three weeks before our wedding day."

His words were a matter of fact, with no anger or resentment in them. She looked away, but Evan could tell that he had hit home. The two of them had known each other for most of their lives, going from childhood friends to dating before getting engaged. Their relationship had always been based on genuine affection and honesty.

"You're right, I am jealous. Not because you're moving on, Evan. Honestly, I want you to be happy more than anything," she admitted, her eyes still downcast. "But damn it, did you have to choose someone who's everything I'm not? It's a little petty, don't you think?"

Evan smiled, glad the mood had lightened. He always hated fighting with Mikayla.

"Believe it or not, you guys are more alike than you would think," he stated, realizing at that moment how true the statement was. They were both smart and confident, and with a certain relentless drive that he respected.

"Yeah, well it's definitely not our cup size, I'll tell you that," she quipped, looking down at her very adequate B cups.

"No, it's not," confirmed Evan, knowing that Nia's curves were likely in the generous D range. Then he laughed as Mikayla slapped him on the shoulder. "And I can confirm that Nia is very natural."

"Now my ego is so bruised that I need a drink," she declared dramatically. "And you need to find your girlfriend before my brother proposes to her and starts a feud."

She hooked her elbow into the bend of his and they walked back into the house together.

Chapter 10

Nia stood beside a makeshift bar table, sipping her drink and looking around the large, open family room. She nodded politely at strangers, and smiled at the odd passing comment. But her thoughts were elsewhere. They were back in Boston with the drama that had become her life.

The robbery was still unsolved and the jewels still unrecovered. She was still the prime suspect, and time was running out for her to escape this crazy situation.

Nia also thought back to the visit from Nigel at the community center that morning. He had first told Nia about the volunteer music program over four years ago when his niece, Meghan, wanted to learn to play the piano. When they had shared an apartment together for the five years after they had moved to Boston, he would often pick up Meghan after the lessons to take her for ice cream. But this was the first time he'd come by since he had moved to Watertown with Angela.

"How are you doing?" he had asked quietly.

He was average height, a couple of inches taller than her. His thin face appeared casual but his green eyes were intensely serious. Nia had let out a deep breath, unprepared for the discussion.

"Have you heard anything?" she had asked, not wanting to say anything more specific.

"No, not yet. I've put out some feelers though," he had promised. "But the last thing I need is any attention around something like this."

"I know. I'm sorry to pull you into it, Nigel," she had insisted.

"Don't be. Who else are you going to call, right?" he had teased, with a small twist of his lips. "But remember what I said, Nia. Don't talk to anyone else about this, okay? A job like this was done by professionals. They won't hesitate to shut people up."

Nia had swallowed, thinking about Matt Flannigan. She completely understood what was at stake.

"I won't," she had promised.

"Keep your head down, and stay out of it. I'll call you in a couple of days with any info."

She had nodded before they had parted. Now, her only hope was that Fortis would find some evidence to prove her innocence, or that Nigel would uncover something from their network that would help prove who Matt Flannigan had been working with.

"You don't have anything to worry about. They finished a long time ago."

Nia refocused on the party, and glanced over at the young man now standing beside her. Elaine Stone-Clement had introduced him as her son, George Jr., and he seemed to be restocking the drinks table. She looked in the direction he had indicated with his head, to see the two people embracing outside.

"Who?" Nia asked innocently, glancing back at him.

"Evan and my sister. They broke up years ago,"

Junior explained. "It was pretty scandalous at the time, only a few weeks before their wedding date. Mom and Dad were so disappointed, so was Evan's family. But everyone survived."

Nia smiled politely, digesting the information and trying to figure out what it all meant. Judging by the warm welcome Evan had received, he was still close to the whole family, including his ex. She took another sip of her drink.

George Jr. continued to look at her with obvious interest. He seemed like a decent enough guy. Tall and lean, with a rich red-brown skin tone, he was fairly attractive in an easygoing, frat-boy kind of way. So young.

"So, how long have you known Evan?" he finally asked.

"Not long," she replied simply. It hardly seemed possible that they had met less than four days ago.

"What do you do, Junior?" countered Nia before he could pry further. Almost everyone preferred to talk about themselves when given the opportunity.

"I just finished law school. So I'm preparing for the bar exam," he declared.

"Wow, that's impressive. Have you decided what field?" she asked.

He told her something, but Nia was distracted by Evan and his ex-fiancée walking arm in arm toward them.

"Okay, Junior. Leave poor Nia alone and stop talking her ear off," Mikayla stated when she and Evan were in hearing distance.

Nia turned to face them with a friendly smile, careful not to show any sign of discomfort over the situation. She had met both the Stone-Clement children when

Elaine had introduced them earlier. At the time, Nia had thought the pretty and petite girl seemed genuine and sincere in welcoming her to the event. But now, she couldn't help questioning if that were really the case.

Evan walked over to Nia and wrapped his arm around the back of her waist, pulling her close so their hips brushed.

"You okay?" he asked attentively.

"Yup. Junior's been keeping me company," she replied.

Nia hadn't intended to play it like that, but the words just came out, sounding very flirtatous. It wasn't really in her nature to play mind games. She felt rather than saw Evan's reaction and his hand tightened on her hip.

"Has he," mumbled Evan in a deep, silky tone.

"Hey, I'm a gentleman like that," the younger man added, jokingly.

"There's plenty of food outside. You guys should go and eat before it's all gone," Mikayla suggested.

Nia got the sense that the other woman was very aware of the tension in the air.

"Good suggestion," agreed Evan.

Nia glanced over at him as they walked through the spacious home and out the back door. It was impossible to read his expression. Outside, there was a large buffet table set up under the covered patio, laden with a wide selection of dishes. Evan handed her a plate that they filled with food.

"Come, let's sit out in the sun," he suggested, leading her to a seating area away from the house and closer to the beach. "It's not too cool is it?"

"No, it nice out here," Nia affirmed.

It was close to seven-thirty in the evening, and the

sun was making a brilliant descent into the western horizon.

While they ate, Nia looked between the expansive backyard space and the magnificent ocean view. Despite the years she spent living in the wealthy Bloomfield area of Detroit and working with affluent clients in Boston, she still found it hard to comprehend this level of extravagant wealth. How the hell can this mansion be called a cottage? And it was not much bigger than the "beach house" that Evan's family owned.

She recalled the feeling that swept over her as they arrived on Martha's Vineyard earlier that afternoon by car ferry. As they drove out of the busy port area and into the rural countryside, they passed numerous picturesque farms and estate properties. But she was still incredulous when Evan drove them up to the five-bedroom, four-thousand-square-foot property sitting on two acres and with its own private beach. Of course, she hadn't said anything. Her sense of pride required that she be complimentary about the beautiful house, but act like she regularly spent weekends away at multimillion-dollar vacation homes.

It wasn't that Nia felt out of place or insecure in that environment or around the wealthy. She'd overcome that years ago. They were essentially the same as anyone else; worth no more or less than average people, but with a moral compass that was sometimes compromised by their warped view of the world. They used people and situations to suit their needs, with little regard for the carnage left in their wake. Nia just didn't want to get sucked into the destructive vortex often created by the rich and powerful. She knew from experience that it could chew you up and spit you out as garbage.

Which brought her thoughts back to Evan. He was

chatting with another couple sitting near them. Nia had known exactly what world he came from the day he'd walked into the gallery. Yet, she had let her attraction to him blind her. She agreed to go out with him despite the significance of his lifestyle and wealth. Now, after meeting the pretty socialite he'd loved enough to almost marry, and being surrounded by corporate executives and influential people, Nia could hardly ignore all the reasons why dating Evan DaCosta would never develop into something more.

It was too bad. She really liked him, and the things he did to her body. But Nia was a realist. At least she would have this weekend to remember.

Once all daylight was gone, the party had moved inside to start the fundraising activities. Evan stayed next to Nia, either holding her hand or with an arm around her shoulder as they looked at the various items available for the silent auction. It felt like he was staking his claim, but she didn't mind it at all. The constant contact created a secret intimacy that suggested more was to come.

"Do you see anything you like?" he asked at the table covered with jewelry.

"No, don't usually wear much," she told him. Even now, she only wore a vintage Cartier watch.

He smiled down at her.

"That's a little ironic, isn't it?" he asked.

"I know," she agreed with a shrug. "I have a few pieces that I love and were worth the investment at the time I bought them. But otherwise, I'm just not into the costume stuff."

Evan brushed a finger along the side of her face, his eyes glittering intently.

"You don't need it. You're beautiful enough without

any adornment," he mumbled deeply. "I think we've put in the required time here. Are you ready to go?"

Her knees went a little weak.

"Yeah, sure. Let me just run to the bathroom. Where is it?"

He leaned forward, so he was whispering right into her ear. His lips brushed her skin. She shivered.

"Down the hall, before you get to the kitchen. Do you want me to go with you? To make sure you don't get lost, of course."

Nia swallowed, so tempted to accept his offer.

"No, I'll be okay."

"Hurry back."

He stepped away, leaving her breathless with anticipation.

She found the bathroom easily enough and used the facilities as quickly as possible. Mikayla stopped her on the way back.

"Are you enjoying the evening?" she asked Nia with a bright smile.

"I am, thank you," responded Nia, equally as friendly. "It's gotten pretty busy in here over the last little bit. I think you guys will do pretty well with the auction."

"I hope so," Mikayla sighed.

There was a pause as they both looked over to Evan, now waiting for Nia at the end of the hallway, and he was looking back. "He really likes you."

Nia glanced over at Mikayla with surprise.

"It's obvious that he can't keep his hands off you. I'm glad. He's a great guy. The best I know. He deserves a partner who can make him happy," added the petite woman. "It was nice to meet you, Nia."

She walked away, disappearing into the crowd, leaving Nia somewhat speechless.

"Everything okay?" asked Evan as he approached her.

"Yeah, it's fine."

"Good. All set?"

Nia nodded.

"I just need to get my wrap," she explained.

Within a few minutes, they were on the way back to his place. Evan drove the powerful car a little faster than he should, with the windows down and the warm evening breeze whipping through. Nia appreciated the fresh air, despite the havoc done to her hair. By the time they pulled to a stop in front of the DaCosta cottage, her heart was racing with adrenaline and anticipation.

He opened the passenger door for her, and took her hand to help her out. Then he pulled her close so her body was flush with his. The hard length of his arousal branded her lower torso. He was telling her what he wanted, asking if she was ready. Nia was a big girl. She knew what this moment meant and she knew what she wanted, both now and for the future. Evan DaCosta was only for now, and she intended to take full advantage of the moment.

"Let's go inside," she suggested.

His grip around her waist tightened, then he took her hand and led her into the house.

"Do you need anything? Something to drink?" Evan asked as they walked through the dark house.

"No, thank you."

They continued past the kitchen and dining room, toward the wing of bedrooms along the left side of the cottage. Past the room he'd given her to use, and into the one beside it. Filtered light spilled into the space from outside, illuminating the king-size bed, dresser, and a leather wingback chair near the window.

As Nia looked around, Evan shrugged off his blazer

and tossed it on the bench at the end of the bed. He then undid the cufflinks to his shirt, and placed them on top of the dresser. She remained rooted in the center of the spacious bedroom, watching as he slowly unbuttoned his cotton shirt. He shrugged it off, dropping it to the floor, and walked to her. Nia stared openly at the impressive expanse of Evan's bare torso. Whatever she had imagined he would look like naked was nowhere near as incredible as the real thing. He was all carved muscle, with an eight-pack of sculpted abdominals. Not an ounce of loose fat anywhere.

When he reached her, Evan gently took her purse out of her hand and added it to the dresser. He took her hand in his.

"Come," he whispered, leading her over to the window, pulling off her cashmere wrap so it fell to the ground along the way.

Evan sat down at the edge of the large leather chair, leaving her standing in front of him between the spread of his knees. His hands slid under the skirt of her dress and up her bare thighs.

"You've been driving me nuts all evening," he mumbled in a deep, sexy voice. His eyes roamed over the length of her torso.

"Really?" she challenged, looking down at him and admiring the flex and folds of sinewy muscles. "And how did I do that?"

He looked up and flashed a smile with a hint of dimples.

"Oh, I think you know exactly how. This dress should be illegal."

She looked down at her body, clad in pale yellow silk. It did display her curves well. Even now, her hardened nipples were clearly visible through the delicate fabric.

"I think it's my new favorite," she teased.

"Take it off," urged Evan.

His fingers teased at the space between her thighs, causing her to gasp.

Nia reached up and unhooked the clasp at the back of her neck, and lowered the zipper along the side of her waist. With a sweeping motion, she took hold of the skirt and pulled the dress off over her head. Evan took it from her hands and tossed it in the direction of the bench. She was left in only a minuscule thong and a sheer demi bra the color of dark ivory.

"Jesus, Nia, you're so beautiful," he whispered.

Nia felt it. She felt sexy and powerful. Desired and in control. It was liberating. She leaned forward, bending at the waist until she was able to kiss him. She started softly, teasing him with gentle brushes and light licks of her tongue. Evan seemed content to let her go at her own pace. Until she swept her tongue into his mouth, and twirled it around his.

With a groan, he grasped her naked bottom and pulled her high on his thighs with her knees straddling him. The kiss became deep, wet, and intense. Evan flexed his hips, brushing the rigid length of his erection between her thighs. Nia forgot about who was in charge, and got swept away by the flush of arousal. She clutched his shoulders and met his thrust. He swore thickly, trailing his lips down the side of her neck, over her collarbone and to the top of her breast.

"Yes," she urged, leaning back to watch him.

He grazed his tongue over a nipple through her bra, then swirled around the peaked nub. Wetness pooled in her panties. He did the same to the other breast, until Nia was singing with a soft litany of moans. She wanted more, needed his mouth on her skin.

She leaned back on her knees and pulled down her bra strap, freeing her generous mounds from the lacy cups.

"Nia," Evan growled before sucking a thick firm tip into his mouth.

"Ahh, yeah," she sighed. As he tugged harder, her moans got louder. The temperature in the room went up several degrees.

"Condom," he mumbled a few moments later.

"Where?" Nia gasped, her brain barely functioning.

"In my bag, beside the chair."

It took another few seconds before she found the strength to pull away from his wicked lips. She slowly unfurled from her straddled position to stand in front of him. God, he was a beautiful sight, half naked and fully aroused. The way he licked his lips suggested he liked what he was seeing also. Feeling inspired, she unhooked her bra, and threw it aside, but left on the panties and high-heeled sandals. She then bent over suggestively, reaching into his leather weekend bag to pull out a square packet.

"You're killing me," muttered Evan, his fists gripping the arms of the chair.

She smiled wickedly, really liking his reaction.

"Really? Are you feeling tense again, Evan?" she teased, tossing him the condom.

"You have no idea," he growled back.

"Well, let me see how I can help."

Rather than returning to his lap, Nia remained standing, but leaned forward to trail her fingers over his chest and down the ripples of his stomach. He sucked in a breath, demonstrating the impact of her touch. Encouraged, Nia continued her play by unbuckling his belt, and undoing the button to his pants. Next was the zipper, until only the cotton shorts covered his arousal. She looked into his eyes to find them hot and fixed on her every move.

"Nia," he pleaded, telling her what he craved.

Holding his gaze, she stroked his hard length. Evan clenched his jaw. Almost in slow motion, Nia slipped her fingers under the band of his boxers, pulling back the elastic revealing the smooth tip of his penis. She tugged farther until his thick erection sprung free. God, he was incredible!

Nia knelt down in front of the chair to take him into her hands. He felt like hot silk. She stroked her hands along his length, loving the way his body quivered from her touch.

"Jesus," he hissed.

Then she bent forward to lick his head, swirling her tongue around the firm edge. Evan moaned a curse, running one of his hands into her hair. She sucked the wide tip into her mouth and he threw back his head with a deep growl. Nia was aching in her core, hungry for his touch, but really wanting to give him this unique pleasure. She slowly sucked in as much of his length as she could take.

"Nia, baby," he whispered tightly. "Christ! I can't . . ."

Increasing the rhythm, she tightened her lips to stroke over his pulsing arousal as he hit the back of her throat. She wanted to make him come apart in her mouth, but Evan had other plans.

He gently pulled himself away, and had her back into his lap. Within seconds, he was encased in the condom and lifting her up by the hips. Nia closed her eyes in anticipation.

"Look at me, Nia," he demanded, brushing aside the thin barrier of her thong.

She opened her lids, meeting his heated gaze as he

slowly lowered her onto his shaft, working into her slowly until he was buried to the hilt. Neither of them seemed to breathe as her body adjusted to his tight fit. The sensation was incredible, overwhelming.

"Evan," Nia begged, rotating her hips against his, demanding more.

"Ready?" he asked, teeth clenched hard.

"Yes," she whispered.

He started slowly, gently, warming her to his size. Every penetration triggered electricity. Then, as his strokes became deeper, faster, they both got lost in the rhythm. Their bodies moved together in a wild, unrestrained gallop. Their skin became damp with sweat, and their guttural sounds echoed in the room. Their eyes remained locked, creating a link that seemed to connect their souls. Nia lost all awareness of her surroundings; she could only feel the clawing frustration of building arousal that had spread through her whole body. It was growing and mounting until she thought she would die if it didn't peak.

Suddenly, Evan slowed his thrust, and brushed his fingers over her swollen clit. Nia shivered, on the verge of coming. He thrust hard, deep, and rubbed her bud just so. That was it. She finally closed her eyes as her body tightened like a bow, then fell to pieces in a long, pulsing orgasm.

When she finally collapsed against him, boneless and sated, Evan was still stroking into her, slow and deep. He brushed a hand along her cheek, cupping her face tenderly before leaning forward to kiss her deeply.

"Hold on," he whispered, taking the curves of her behind in his hands.

Nia gripped the arms of the chair as he took her hard and deep. Watching him stroking into her, climbing toward his own climax, was the most erotic thing she had ever seen. He chanted her name, completely lost in his passion. It had her slick and tingling all over again. Then he slowed his pace, opening his eyes to look between their bodies. His expression was hungry, urgent as he made a final thrust, his body shuddering in climax.

Chapter 11

Evan slipped stealthily out from under the sheets and off the bed. He glanced over at Nia's sleeping form, naked with her head nestled in a feather pillow. Her hair was curly and damp from their second time together in the shower, and her breathing was slow and deep. He crept over to his walk-in closet to pull on a pair of athletic shorts. Back in the bedroom, he paused near the door for another minute to ensure she hadn't sensed his departure. Satisfied that Nia would remain asleep, he strode out of the room, her small clutch purse almost hidden in one hand and a small LED flashlight in the other.

In the dark spare bedroom, Evan went into the attached bathroom and closed the door before he turned on the flashlight and opened her purse. With quick efficiency, he memorized exactly how every item was placed, then dumped it all on the counter. There wasn't much, only a bejeweled clam-style mirror, a face powder compact, a tube of lipgloss, and her cell phone. Her driver's license and a credit card were tucked into a small inside pocket. Evan examined each item to ensure they were what they seemed to be. There was nothing unusual.

The cell phone turned out to be equally as innocent. It was her registered iPhone. Evan reviewed the contact list, text messages, and e-mail but found nothing unusual or remotely suspicious. While there was a private e-mail account configured on the phone, there were only a few messages from her bank and several high-end retail stores. The bulk of her messages went to her work account, and appeared synced with the corporate server.

There was also nothing noteworthy in the account before or after the night of the robbery.

Evan repacked her purse so it looked undisturbed, then went back into the spare bedroom. Her travel bag was on a chair next to the bed, and he noted a few items of clothing hanging in the closet. He went through all her things with the same thorough efficiency. *Nothing*.

A few minutes later, he was outside the house in a secure spot to call the control center. It was after eleven o'clock.

"Ice, everything good?" Raymond asked.

"Yeah, unfortunately. I got nothing in my search here. She doesn't have a burner phone on her."

"If she's been using one, it doesn't make sense that she would leave Boston without it," Raymond mused. "But I'll have Michael check out her apartment tomorrow, just in case."

"I agree with you," stated Evan, rubbing an agitated hand across his forehead. "If there's no burner, we have no proof she was at the scene of the robbery. Everything proves her alibi of being at home for the night."

"She didn't have to be there to be involved. Maybe

she just provided the info to Flannigan, and he did the rest?" suggested Raymond.

"Maybe. But how's she communicating with her contacts? Flannigan's dead, so who's she working with now? Who's running the show? Who had possession of the jewels, and how is Nia going to get paid?" questioned Evan. "We're missing something."

Both men were silent for several seconds, until Evan swore.

"The man at the Dorchester community center," he stated in a deep tone. "He's the only one she's met in person other than her friends and people at work. We need to know who he is and fast."

"We're working on it, Ice. But I don't think we'll get anything."

"Damn it!" he exclaimed under his breath. "What about the charity organization, or the community center? Can we find out who the student is through them? The girl's name was Meghan, and she has to be registered somewhere. The man was holding the girl's hand, so I'm betting he's a relative of some kind."

"I'll see what I can find," Raymond confirmed. "By the way, Tony finally pinned down that contact in New York: Spencer."

"Nice!" uttered Evan with relief. "Any more info?"

"Not yet. They're meeting tomorrow morning."

"Good. I'll have James back in Boston sometime in the evening. We can regroup at the control center."

"Sure thing, Ice."

"Okay, thanks Raymond. I'll call in again around noon, but send me whatever you find before then."

Moments later, Evan crept back into his bedroom. Nia was still sound asleep, curled into a tight ball. He returned the small purse to the top of the dresser and slid back into bed. Nia groaned softly and turned toward him as though seeking out his body heat. Then, she snuggled against his left side until her head was cushioned on his chest. Evan moved his arm out of the way before it became trapped beneath her and folded it so the back of his head rested in his palm. It helped him in the effort to resist the urge to pull her closer into his arms. Partly so he didn't disturb her, but mostly because he needed to get a grip on reality, fast.

An hour later, it was well after midnight, and Evan still couldn't fall asleep. His mind was too busy trying to compartmentalize what was happening to him. In the quiet of the night, it became impossible to ignore the conflict between his rational thinking and natural instinct. He had to face the disturbing fact that at some point between arriving at the Clements party and the moment Nia fell asleep, he had managed to forget she was an assignment. It was the only explanation for the sense of complete physical satisfaction that had settled over him after their first time together. And their second time. That was a hard fact for Evan to swallow, since it went against everything he had been trained to accomplish as a field agent in the CIA. And it betrayed his sense of justice and dedication to his job.

Evan took a deep, frustrated breath. He didn't have to close his eyes to recall the vivid memory of Nia naked and lush, flushed from orgasm, her dark honey skin slick with perspiration. It was an intensely primal and erotic image, and one he was already itching to experience again. Christ, she did something to him. She sparked a hunger and excitement that no other woman ever had. Including Mikayla.

It was an unacceptable situation.

He shifted in the bed, careful not to wake Nia up.

She sighed softly in her sleep and snuggled into his neck. Evan brushed aside some of her hair. It was still a little damp and curly from their second round in the shower. Another delicious memory. And a sharp reminder of how far he had crossed the line.

Another hour went by as Evan ran through all versions of the possible outcomes to this assignment as it pertained to Nia. He may have taken her completely, even lost himself a little in her sweet body, but the reality of the situation was inescapable. He and the team would eventually determine her role in the robbery. There was no doubt about that. It was only a matter of time, and there was one unchangeable outcome. As addictive as it was, this thing he was experiencing with Nia was inappropriate and pointless. It was a fact he needed to come to terms with, and quickly.

Sex was one thing. Like many times before, it was a potential part of his cover on this mission from the beginning. But, Evan had no right to feel this softness for her; this affection that caused his stomach to quiver when she smiled at him. It needed to be snuffed out at all costs, before it started to impact his objectivity, and ultimately his ability to do his job.

At some point, Evan finally fell into a light sleep only to wake up shortly after sunup. It was a sunny, clear morning so he quietly headed out for a run along the beach. Pushing hard, he completed the eight-and-a-half-mile route in under an hour. Back inside the house, he grabbed a bottle of water from the fridge and guzzled it while heading to the shower attached to his bedroom. He wasn't surprised that Nia was still sound asleep. It was still fifteen minutes before eight o'clock.

After a long shower, Evan stood in front of the foggy bathroom mirror and looked intently at his reflection.

Somewhere around the six-mile mark, while ocean waves rolled onto the beach, he had achieved some clarity and come to a realization. This heightened interest in Nia had more to do with all the changes in his life over the last year than any real feelings for her. He'd lost his dad, ended his civil service career, and recovered from a crippling injury. It was more than enough upheaval to explain his unusual distraction by a very sensual woman.

But it wasn't real and he had a job to do. A certain amount of intimacy and affection was necessary to the mission. But Evan just needed to be smart by keeping their physical contact to a minimum, and keeping his head focused on the endgame.

Feeling grounded, Evan finished washing up and went back into the bedroom with a towel wrapped around his waist. He found Nia sitting up in the bed cocooned in the thick feather duvet. She looked adorably ruffled and much younger than she should.

"Good morning," he greeted with a soft smile.

She bit the side of her cheek, her eyes roving over his near-naked form.

"Hi. What time is it?" she asked, looking out the window.

"Just after eight. Are you hungry?" Evan asked as he sat next to her at the edge of the bed. "I could make us some breakfast. The kitchen was stocked up yesterday."

The offer seemed to amuse her.

"You cook?" she asked with skepticism.

"I do all right. It won't kill you but to be honest, my true talents are in other areas."

Her eyebrows shot up.

"Really? Such as?"

Evan shrugged.

"I'm too humble to brag. It's the type of talent that has to be experienced," he teased.

Nia couldn't hide her smile. It was soft and sultry. Evan felt that familiar, unwanted stirring in the bottom his stomach.

"Well, now that you've piqued my curiosity, you may as well show me."

"I would, but it's quite time-consuming," he replied as he stood up and walked over to his dresser, effectively putting some distance between them. "You'd starve to death before I was done. I can't be responsible for that."

"Or so you're told?" she questioned sarcastically. "So much for humility."

"I'm just telling you like it is."

He heard her shifting on the bed, then the soft steps of feet as she crossed the room. Evan took a deep, silent breath, bracing himself for her approach.

"Why don't I be the judge of this special talent of yours," she stipulated. One of her soft hands slid around his waist to press flat against the lean plane of his stomach. The muscle twitched in reaction.

Evan could feel the silky heat of her naked body as she hovered a breath away. He clenched his jaw, willing himself to stay focused on his strategy. Touching her again would only lead to trouble.

Her hand slipped lower, and she stroked her palm over his now-firm erection. Evan meant to remove her hand, step out of her reach, but his brain was on pause. All function had flooded into his cock, leaving him breathless with anticipation.

"Unless you're all talk," accused Nia in a throaty voice. She quickly pulled off his towel, and wrapped dexterous fingers around his pulsing thrust. It felt insanely good.

"Don't say I didn't warn you," he whispered back, mentally recalculating the risk versus reward of what she was pulling him into.

How would he possibly explain stopping her now, with the obvious evidence of his arousal in her grasp? What harm could one more time with her cause, he reasoned. It was just two people enjoying sex; natural physiology. Nothing more. He could deal with that.

"Duly noted," Nia quipped.

Evan turned around and swiftly lifted her naked body into his arms until her legs wrapped around his waist. He had her back on the bed within seconds.

"Okay, I need silence in order to do my best work. Now lie back and close your eyes."

Nia rolled her eyes, mockingly, but did as he asked.

"I'm curious about how you discovered this talent? Was it by accident, or did it take lots of practice?" she asked with mock seriousness.

"Silence, please! I can't be distracted," Evan demanded.

She pursed her lips. Evan fought the urge to smile, to notice how adorable she looked.

Starting at her feet, he worked his way up her bare legs. Evan stopped at her calves to stroke and massage the firm curve, using his finger tips to lightly tease the back of her knees. Nia squirmed with a gasp. He brushed the sensitive spot again, enjoying the ticklish response and eager to see how else he could make her react.

Slowly, he continued his path up her naked body, occasionally stopping to brush or stroke a particularly intriguing spot. Her belly button was the perfect, sweet innie. Evan dipped his finger in its shallow well. There was a slight valley running up her belly. He trailed his thumb along it, up into the hollow between her breasts.

Her dark, peaked nipples pebbled in response. The hollow above her collarbone had skin that was soft and silky.

She was incredible. All dark honey and milk chocolate with all the right lean dips and generous curves. He couldn't wait to taste her, but forced himself to be patient, take his time.

From his position at the edge of the bed, he spread both hands over the span of her hips and started a firm but gentle massage with the heels of his palms. He went down her legs and up the side of her waist repeatedly, stopped below her breast. Nia started to relax, her body loosening, releasing tension. Evan put extra attention near the top of her thighs, creeping inward to the juncture between. She bit her lip and flexed her hips. Eager to explore her secrets, he trailed his fingers along the silky skin over her pubic bone, waxed bare except for a small strip along her delicate lips.

"Evan," she whispered, her eyes still closed.

"What?" he teased, stroking along the crease of her thighs.

"Please . . ."

"Please, what?" he urged. "Tell me what you want."

Nia sighed.

"I would. But it might distract you."

Evan chuckled. Cheeky girl.

"Fine. I'll just have to do whatever I want," he vowed.

Leaning forward over her body, he swiped one of her nipples with his tongue. She took in a deep breath with a hiss. Evan pulled the tight tip into his mouth, teasing and tweaking it with his lips until she moaned. He did the same with the other nipple. She was so sensitive and responsive, her body taut with mounting pleasure. He sucked harder, and stroked his thumb over the valley between her thighs. She was now dewy and slick.

Evan climbed farther onto the bed until he was on his knees. He spread her legs apart so he could position himself between them. Bending down, he rained light kisses down her stomach, stopping to dip his tongue in the well of her belly button. Nia arched her back. He slid his finger deeper into her wetness, brushing her clit.

She groaned, gripping the sheets beneath her with tight fists.

He loved how unrestrained she was. How hot she felt. He brushed his lips lower until his tongue replaced his fingers, licking her tender bud.

"Oh God," she moaned.

He delved deeper, pressing a little harder, circling the sensitive flesh with the firm tip of his tongue. Her hips bucked, begging him wordlessly. Evan wanted to give her everything. He took his time licking, sucking, stroking every fold of her sweet, satiny flesh. She smelled like soft, sensuous vanilla. Tasted warm and sweet. He wanted more.

Spreading her legs wider, Evan urged her knees to bend upward. She was all his. He stroked into her tight sheath with his thick middle finger. Nia was now panting softly. Christ! She was so hot and tight. He stroked into her again, sucking at her clit with soft pressure. Her body quivered.

"Evan!"

He looked up at her body, loving the flush of her skin, the look of sharp arousal on her face.

"What?" Evan demanded, his voice deep with his own building desire. He added a second finger, pumping into her with increased speed.

"So good!" she panted.

She was so incredibly beautiful like this, creeping closer and closer to orgasm, that he could watch her forever. Every groan from her throat and shiver of her body sent lightning bolts down his spine, tightening his balls until he was close to spontaneous combustion. But he clenched his jaw, holding back his need to be encased in her sweetness. Her pleasure was all that mattered.

Evan returned his focus and his mouth to her feminine bud, finding a rhythm with fingers and tongue that had her moaning and begging for more. There was a moment of tight stillness, then Nia came with hard, shuttering intensity. Her body pulsed around his fingers, slick and molten. God, it felt amazing. He could barely wait for her body to quiet before he was throwing off his towel and rolling on a condom.

Back between her legs, he draped them over his thighs. Her body was dewy with sweat.

"Nia," he whispered.

She slowly opened her eyes, now glassy and sated.

Gripping her hips, Evan slowly stroked into her with his stiff, thick cock. They both groaned. *Delicious.*

He tried to go slow, take his time, give her a chance to get warmed up again. But Evan got lost in her. Again. He forgot about everything but the feel of her tight satin gripping his length like a glove. Being inside Nia was like nothing he'd ever felt before, nothing he thought could exist. It was all-consuming, turning Evan from a man of calculation and control into a primal being that could only feel.

Over and over, he buried himself into her, savoring every stroke yet desperate for completion. Her name dripped off his tongue like a chant until the sharp blades of orgasm dug into the base of his spine. He groaned harshly as the climax ripped through him, robbing his body of all control. Incredibly, he felt Nia's body pulse around him, joining him over the edge, adding to the intensity until he felt weak in the aftermath.

Chapter 12

When he came to his senses, their bodies were entangled with his draped over hers. She was running her fingers up and down his back. He sighed with contentment, lingering in the moment for a long as possible.

"What was that?" Nia finally asked after some time.

Evan knew exactly what she meant, and didn't pretend otherwise. They had shared something unusually intense and connected. Something unique. He really wished it wasn't.

"I'm not sure," he replied honestly.

"Well, you weren't kidding about your talents."

He was so grateful for her sense of humor at that moment, and placed a gentle kiss on her forehead.

"I'm glad I didn't disappoint you."

"No, I'm definitely not disappointed. But I am hungry."

"Hmm. Well, I did try to warn you," Evan mused.

"I'll make you a deal. Why don't I cook and you focus on the other things you do so well," she quipped, wiggling out from under him to sit at the edge of the bed.

"How could I turn down an offer like that?"

Evan rolled onto his back and laced his fingers

across his stomach. That now-familiar sense of sexual contentment still surrounded him, and he held on to it for a few more stolen moments. With his eyes closed, he felt so lazy, he could easily sleep the rest of the morning away. Something he hadn't done since college, except while lying in a hospital bed, knocked out on pain medication and antibiotics.

Something tickled at his ribs. He scratched the spot, instantly awake and alert. Then it brushed around his ear. Evan swatted at it, holding back a smile. He felt the shift in the air as the offending presence approached the side of his head again. With a swift reach, he grabbed Nia's hand by the wrist and pulled her on top of him. She squealed in surprise.

"I thought you were still sleeping," she gasped.

Evan opened one eye to peer at her.

"So you thought you'd take advantage of my vulnerability, huh."

She tugged at her wrist, still trapped in the vise of his loose grip.

"You, vulnerable? *Please!*"

He closed his eyes again.

"I think I've just been insulted." She twisted some more to get her arm free, but Evan held firm. "I did fall asleep. What time is it?"

"Just after nine o'clock," Nia confirmed. "I only came to tell you that breakfast will be ready in about ten minutes. Instead, I'm attacked and held against my will."

"My apologies," he mocked, releasing his hold to gently brush along the soft skin on the inside of her arm. "But you know what they say about sleeping dogs."

She used the opportunity to roll off the bed and stand at the side.

"Oh, so you're a dog. Good to know."

Evan sat up, stretching widely, unconcerned with his nakedness. He could feel her eyes running over him.

"That's not such a bad thing, is it? Loyal, reliable, protective, well trained. So what if I drool a little."

Nia rolled her eyes, and he chuckled.

"Ten minutes if you want a hot breakfast," she stipulated, turning on her feet to walk out of the bedroom, sashaying her sweet ass in a pair of snug jeans.

"Damn, you're bossy in the mornings."

She was gone without responding.

He allowed himself a satisfied smile, and headed into the shower, suddenly famished. A hot breakfast sounded amazing.

When he entered the kitchen a short while later, wearing worn jeans and a T-shirt, Nia was laying out plates of food on the small round table. There was French toast, bacon, and scrambled eggs. The last dish had roasted potatoes, seasoned and crispy on the outside. The delicious smell of brewing Brazilian coffee filled the room. Evan was tempted to rub his eyes to make sure it wasn't a mirage. Jesus! He had hope for toasted bagels, maybe some eggs.

"I hope you're hungry," she stated, grabbing dinner plates and cutlery.

As expected as her lover, Evan pulled her into his arms from behind and snuggling into her neck with a string of kisses.

"Starving," he mumbled, then took the dishes out of her hands to set them on the table.

"Good. I wasn't sure what you'd like, so . . ."

"It looks fantastic, Nia. But you didn't have to go through so much trouble."

She shrugged, as though it was nothing.

"Eat before it gets cold," she instructed.

"Yes, ma'am."

They ate in silence. After the energetic sex and rigorous run, his appetite was at its peak. He finished two full servings without any effort and it was delicious. Nia only shook her head in wonder.

"Coffee?" she finally asked when he sat back in his chair, chewing on the last chunk of potato.

"Hmm," Evan agreed. "I'll get it."

He stood up and took their empty plates over to the sink.

"How do you take it?" he asked, taking out two mugs from the cupboard.

"Just with cream, please."

Evan made their drinks, loading his up with cream and a good spoonful of sugar.

"I hate to get serious, but we should talk," Nia stated as he rejoined her at the table.

She took her cup from him and took a small sip. Evan did the same, then sat back in his chair, his legs extended out in an effort to seem unaffected by her statement. Whatever she wanted to discuss so seriously could not be good. He was suddenly very resentful of a situation in which he might be forced to lie to her further.

"Sure, about what?" he replied, sipping hot brew again.

"You know what. Your father's collection," she clarified, as though there could be nothing else of importance between them. "We need to confirm when my team and I can complete the catalog. Unfortunately, we have a big auction happening in three months, so there's very limited availability. Either we do your work very soon, or we may have to push it out until near the end of the summer."

Evan appeared unfazed, but his mind was analyzing her response. He had anticipated her wanting to ask about the direction of their relationship, what his plans were to see her in the future, or maybe even discuss the unnerving level of intimacy they'd shared. It's what he wanted her to be thinking about as a part of the seduction. That's how she would drop her guard, and share details he needed to solve his mission. Her focus on work and their business agreement was unexpected.

"How soon?" he asked casually.

"Later this week, if not early next? I know that might be challenging, so we can also look at other options. We have several consultants in the D.C. area who could—"

"No," he stated firmly before she could finish the thought. "I want you to do it. Later this week is fine. How long do you need?"

She seemed surprised by his decisive response.

"I think a day should be enough, maybe two at the most."

He nodded.

"We'll go to Virginia on Thursday, stay for a few days. I'll have Sandra make the arrangements. I was intending to fly home for the weekend anyway so you'll have plenty of time."

"Okay," she agreed, somewhat reluctantly.

"Good. Now that we have business taken care of, let's get on the road."

By eleven o'clock in the morning, they were driving across the island. There was an unusual energy between them that Nia couldn't quite put a label on. At first, as they drove in silence, only interrupted by the occasional short discussion, she thought it was just her. The intimate connection they had shared the night before was still fresh in her mind, and she was preoccupied trying to understand it.

She looked over at his profile speculatively. He glanced back. Nia smiled then turned away to stare out the passenger-side window at the beautiful landscape. She could feel his gaze on her occasionally, but she resisted meeting his eyes again. Her nature was to be transparent, ask direct questions, say what was on her mind. Yet this time, Nia held her tongue. She needed time to decide what this weekend really signified for her before taking Evan's intentions into account.

It was a big question. A week ago, Nia would have said maybe it would be nice to date someone regularly. Nothing serious, just a guy to do things with, like see a movie or try a new restaurant. Maybe even attend the occasional work event. In her head, sex was optional in the scenario, not essential. It was hard to find a man who was enjoyable company but also able to stir any chemistry. Pretty much impossible to at this point in her life. The expectation for *great* sex? Unlikely, since as of a week ago, Nia didn't even know what that really meant.

Today, the term *great* was insufficient. Even the word *sex* seemed too simple. Evan DaCosta was a physical and mental experience. Based on her racing heartbeat and nervous tension, he was threatening to become an emotional one as well. Nia was not ready for that.

Somewhere on Cape Cod, as they walked through the Memorial Day weekend crowds, Nia realized that she wasn't the only one who was preoccupied. Evan was polite and charming, even attentive. He held her hand as they strolled around the city, touched her back or arms to keep her close. But he seemed pensive, as though his thoughts were elsewhere. For a moment, she wondered if he were struggling with the same concerns she had about where this weekend could lead, then quickly dismissed it. He was a busy man with a big job. His concerns probably had nothing to do with her at all.

They stayed in the Cape area for an early dinner, then arrived back in Boston shortly after eight o'clock in the evening. Evan parked in front of her place then walked her inside the building, carrying her weekend bag. He stopped in the open doorway of her apartment, placing her bag on a stool in the corner. They faced each other.

"In case I didn't mention it, I'm really glad you joined me for the weekend," stated Evan as he brushed the back of his hand gently along her cheek. "I had a really great time."

Nia let out a deep breath.

"So did I," she replied.

He brushed his finger over her lips, dipping between them.

"The thing is, I really want to kiss you right now."

Unable to hold back her response, she licked the pad of his thumb with her tongue.

"What's stopping you?"

"If I do, I might not be able to leave," he explained without any hint of teasing. "I have an early morning meeting."

Nia knew what he was saying, what he was asking. This was her opportunity to draw a line for herself, put a break on the madness. But she looked into his eyes and read the need he made no attempt to disguise.

"Maybe, you can just stay for a nightcap," she suggested.

"Hmmm," he mumbled. "Since you've twisted my arm."

Evan pulled her into his arms, and kissed her lightly, followed by another series of sweet, gentle pecks. He rested his forehead against hers for a few seconds then stepped away.

"Are we talking coffee, or something stronger?" he asked. She let out a deep, disappointed breath, trying to recoup from the sparks he had lit of in her body with just that brief touch.

"I would love a cup of coffee. But I have some wine if that's what you prefer," she suggested.

"Coffee's good,"

"Okay, give me a minute to unpack, then I'll be right back," Nia told him as she picked up her travel bag. The thought of the beautiful yellow dress getting any more crushed gave her hives.

"Take your time. I'll make the coffee," he replied, already walking into her apartment to seek out the kitchen.

"Okay. There's ground beans is in the cupboard beside the sink," she called after him. It felt pretty strange to have a man strolling through her place.

"I'm sure I can figure it out," he replied back.

Nia went into her bedroom and quickly took everything out of the bag. Most of the items went into the laundry, but she gently hung the new silk dress in the closet.

The garment bag from the Cape Cod boutique was also still in her luggage, folded neatly at the bottom. Nia took it out, removing the sales receipt before tossing the bag in the trash. Then she paused, looking more closely at the slip of paper.

There was an American Express credit card slip attached to the back of the invoice, yet Nia clearly remembered paying for the dress with her Visa. In fact, she didn't even own an Amex card. Puzzled, she looked at the card information, noting the name imprinted on the bottom.

"Evan?" she called as she walked through the living room to the kitchen.

He was on his cell phone, but hung up as she walked toward him.

"The coffee's ready," he stated.

"You know that store where I bought my dress for the charity event on Saturday? The yellow one?" she explained. "I'm looking at the receipt, and there's been some kind of mistake. They charged it to your credit card. How is that even possible?"

Evan put his hands in the pocket of his jeans, his legs spread in a wide stance.

"It wasn't a mistake. I asked them to."

She was still holding up the receipt, but froze at his statement.

"What? Why?"

He shrugged, completely unfazed.

"I wanted to."

Nia looked at the receipt then down at the floor. A flood of annoyance swept over her. She clenched her jaw and turned away, walking over to her computer desks on the other side of the kitchen. There, she removed her checkbook and a pen, taking her time writing out the details of the purchase.

She walked back to him with her back straight, head high, and handed him a signed check. He didn't even look at it.

"Nia," he repeated, now with a dismissive attitude.

It annoyed her even more.

"Take it, Evan."

"What's the big deal? I bought you a dress for the party. It's nothing."

Nia clenched her teeth.

"The big deal is that you had no right."

He folded his arms across his chest and raised his brows sardonically.

"No right?"

"I'm perfectly capable of buying my own clothes, Evan. I'm not looking for a man to do that for me."

"Come on, Nia. It wasn't like that. You were only buying it because I had invited you to the party. So, I didn't want you to be out of pocket," he explained, still confused by her reaction. "It was a gift."

"A nine hundred dollar gift? Seems overly generous for someone you've just met, don't you think?" she sneered, frustrated by his highhanded arrogance.

"What's that supposed to mean?"

"Take the check, Evan."

"No, I won't. You're completely overreacting, Nia," he stated. "I wanted to buy it for you, it's that simple. In fact, I may buy you other things, so you better get used to the idea."

"Well don't! I don't want anything from you, okay? As shocking as this may be, I have no interest in your money or what you can buy with it." She turned away, feeling even more pissed off that he was refusing to let her pay him back. "In fact, I agreed to go out with you in spite of your wealth, not because of it. And now I'm starting to think it was a bad idea."

When he didn't respond right away, Nia faced him again, her arms folded to match his.

"I can't be bought, Evan."

"Nia," he stated in a low voice, his expression icy hard. "You're turning this into something it's not. I paid for the dress because I wanted to, no other reason. Your insinuation of something more sordid is ridiculous and insulting."

She stood firm, as unwilling to back down as he was.

"Take the check," she insisted again, holding out the bank note.

"No. And since you can't return the dress, it looks like you're stuck with it."

Nia wanted to slap the smug arrogance off his face.

"Maybe coffee wasn't a good idea after all," she stated sharply as she walked toward the front door. "Don't you have an early meeting?"

"Nia, come on," he cajoled, clearly exasperated by her response. But when she didn't show any sign of bending, he strode smoothly up to her.

"Good night, Evan," she mumbled, opening the door.

He gripped the back of her head in his palm and pulled her forward into a deep, intense kiss. His lips consumed hers, and his tongue delved into every recess, leaving her breathless. Then she was free and he was striding away, but only after flashing her an arrogant, mocking smile.

Really? Nia let out a deep, annoyed breath and closed the front door with a hard shove. She strode back across her apartment to toss the rejected check on her desk.

What a great end to a romantic getaway, she thought sarcastically. Her intense anger was slowly fading, but maybe it was for the best that Evan had left on such a sour note. His obnoxious wealth was going to be a barrier for them at some point anyway. And, if things didn't improve this week at work, she wouldn't be available for a relationship, casual or otherwise, except with a cellmate named Bertha.

While Nia turned off the coffeepot and got ready to turn in early for bed, Evan was meeting his team in their control center about twenty minutes later. Tony had just returned to Boston ready to provide the team with an update on his meeting with the Interpol contact. Spencer provided some information, but most importantly, he provided a name: Walsh.

"What do we know about this Walsh?" Evan asked.

"Not much," Raymond stated as he pulled up some information on one of the panel screens.

"According to Spencer, if you want something rare and expensive at a deep discount, Walsh can get it," Tony explained.

"And how does he know this?" questioned Evan.

"He was a little cagey on the details, Ice. But when he was in Boston about six months ago, the word in a very small circle was that you could get anything you wanted for the right price."

"So, what does that mean? And what does it have to do with the Worthington robbery?" Michael probed.

"It means anything you can't get legitimately. Drugs, women, guns, contraband. Anything," Tony explained. "According to Spencer, Worthington's acquisition of the red stone was known by anyone who wanted to know about high-value gems."

"So, someone wanted it, and our thieves were just filling an order?" Evan asked.

"Theft by contract," Michael stated. "Makes sense. Buyer commitment up front. You take only what you're paid for. Guaranteed money, less risky than trying to sell the hot items after the fact."

"Exactly. It explains how quiet things have been about it in the black market," added Tony.

"Does he know who this Walsh is, or the name of the buyer?" Evan asked.

"Not specifically," Tony confirmed. "Only that Walsh operates out of some of the top hotels in Boston."

Raymond quickly typed in some more information on his computer and pulled a full screen of data to show the team.

"I've been working on a potential match for this

Walsh character, based on what Spencer provided, using search strings on dealer, suppliers, and known fences in the police database. Assuming that's his real name, we have eighteen matches in the greater Boston area."

He pulled up a string of pictures to represent the results, filling up the large flat-panel screen.

"If we search people named Walsh that work in a downtown hotel, we have thirty-seven," continued Raymond as his fingers flew over the keyboard. "Cross-reference the list, and we have seven."

"Nice," Michael added. "Any of them live in Dorchester?"

Raymond did a quick scan.

"No. That would be too easy," he told them.

"Okay, team. We now have a viable target. A broker who will lead to either the buyer or the thieves. Then ultimately the recovery of the jewels," Evan surmised, his tone sharp with urgency. "In the morning, this will be our immediate priority."

The team moved close, ready for Evan's direction.

"Tony, you'll take James first thing in the morning. It's a holiday, and I want eyes and sound on her at all time. Use the long-range surveillance equipment, and get pictures of anyone she talks to."

The older man nodded.

"Raymond, we'll need you here, looking for any connection between the Worthington employees and our mystery man, Walsh. Michael and I will split up and check out the Walshes on our shortlist."

The other two men acknowledged their assignments.

"I'll meet you guys in the gym at oh-five hundred," he concluded before they packed it in for the night.

Chapter 13

Memorial Day was a mild day with a light breeze and a sunny, cloudless sky. On Friday, Lianne had suggested that the group meet again to spend the day together before Eddie's brother, Kevin, flew back to Seattle. Nia met Lianne, Eddie, and Kevin near her apartment, and they walked to Pleasure Bay Beach. The temperature was in the midsixties, ideal for walking around and a competitive game of Frisbee. They had an early dinner at a pub nearby, before the others left to drop Kevin at the airport for his late flight. Nia was home by nine o'clock.

It didn't take long for her to calm down and acknowledge that Evan was right about the dress. She had overreacted to the situation. Yes, it was presumptuous for him to think she would be okay with him buying her anything, but his rationale made sense. Nia only needed it to go to the charity event he'd invited her to. And since it had been done on the sly, Evan obviously didn't want her to feel obligated to him in any way.

She was going to have to apologize. But her phone had been disappointingly silent all day. While Nia had considered calling Evan several times, her self-control won out. He had started this thing, whatever this thing was, and she wasn't going to chase after him now. Even if her reaction had been a little irrational.

Tuesday morning, Nia was up early for her usual kickboxing class. Then, she was in the office just after eight o'clock, dressed in a gray dress with a matching jacket and navy blue heels. She wanted a few minutes to review the sales forecast before her weekly team meeting, pushed forward a day due to the holiday weekend.

Chris Morton was the first person she saw as she entered the building. He was setting up a display cabinet in the gallery.

"Hey Nia," he said across the room.

"Hey," she replied with a hesitant smile. Usually, she would avoid small talk so early in the day, and just head upstairs to start work. But after everything that happened last week, Nia felt obliged to say something. She walked a little closer to Chris.

"I heard about Matt Flannigan on the news," she stated in a soft voice. "I couldn't believe it."

Chris turned to face her. He looked tired, with dark bags under his eyes.

"Yeah, it's pretty crazy," he agreed.

"You guys were friends, right? Do you know what happened?" she asked, trying to sound casual. This interest in the personal lives of her work associates was completely unlike her. The question sounded awkward and stilted to her ears. But Chris didn't seem to notice.

"No, nothing beyond what the police had released."

"Did he have any family or anything? Somewhere we can send a card or flowers?"

"I don't know. He lived with his girlfriend, but I've only met her once," he replied with a sigh. "I can check with the security company to see if they have her contact information."

"That's a good idea. Let me know," Nia replied.

"Thanks, Nia."

"No problem. Good luck."

She turned away toward the stairs.

"Those security consultants were in over the weekend," added Chris. "They're going to be updating our servers and network protocols. Our systems will probably be offline sometime this week. But I'll send an e-mail to everyone when I have the details."

"Okay, no problem," she replied.

In her office, Nia was preoccupied as she unpacked her laptop and the power cable. She wasn't sure what she expected from the exchange with Chris, but it wasn't to feel sympathy. When Adam had mentioned the friendship between Chris and the security guard, she had immediately been suspicious, wondering if the operations manager was somehow involved in the robbery too. So, while she hadn't expected him to suddenly break down and admit his guilt, she was surprised at how genuinely upset he was about Matt's murder.

If they were partners in the crime, wouldn't Chris be concerned that Matt's role in the robbery would lead back to him? Wouldn't he try to downplay their relationship instead of pursuing contact with Matt's girlfriend? Or maybe he knew that hiding their connection would look suspicious?

Nia didn't have long to mull it over. At eight-thirty, she met her team of six in one of the small boardrooms. Tara, John, and Adam were already seated around the table, chatting. Not surprisingly, they were talking about Matt.

"It's weird not seeing him in the office," Adam expressed.

"Yeah, I know," agreed John. He was a shorter man, slender with a flashy, colorful sense of style. With his legs crossed, his turquois-and-pink striped socks were brightly displayed.

"I'm telling you, it has something to do with all that partying . . . ," added Tara, but she stopped when Nia joined them at the table.

Mimi Rodrigues arrived at the same time, nicely tanned from her weeklong Florida vacation. She was a curvy, petite woman with a big personality and an endless supply of pretty dresses. Nancy and Cain arrived shortly after. The tall, gangly sales coordinator appeared to be lecturing him about disorganized contracts. Cain was a tall, lean man with deep chocolate skin and sparkling white teeth, now clenched in annoyance. Once they were all seated, the meeting got started. It was the start to a busy day with several meetings in and out of the office.

The first was a brief call with Edward after the staff meeting.

"I just got the sales projections you sent, Nia," he started. "They look good."

"Yes, I agree. We'll end May ahead of target," Nia confirmed. There was a short pause.

"I'm glad to hear that, but that's not why I'm calling," Edward continued. "I met with Fortis on Friday. They will continue their investigation."

"They've uncovered something?" she asked, breathless with anticipation.

"I can't share the specifics, of course. But they have some new information, and it's enough to suggest they'll be able to identify the culprits and recover the jewels within the timeline needed."

"That's . . . That's great," she replied, with a gulp. "Am I still a suspect?"

"I'll be honest with you, Nia. They haven't ruled out your involvement," her boss stated reluctantly. "But if I really thought you had anything do with it, I would have fired you on the spot."

"I know," she whispered, trying desperately to hold on to that belief.

"Let's leave them to do their jobs, okay?"

"Okay. Thanks, Edward," she added before they hung up.

Nia tried to be relieved. She still had a job. And if Fortis was still on the case, then maybe the whole mess would be resolved with minimal impact to her. It was a big if. Too big to leave in the hands of a group of people that were still convinced she had a role in the theft.

She closed her office door, then took out her cell phone and called Nigel to see if he had managed to uncover any valuable information.

"I was going to call you later today," he stated right away.

"Why? What did you hear?" she demanded.

"Well, word on the street is that the Flannigan dude was well connected inside the gallery," Nigel stated in a solemn tone.

Nia let out a deep breath. While she wasn't surprised, it was still uncomfortable to have it confirmed.

"Meaning, he was working with someone else here?" she asked.

"Meaning, he knew enough to be dangerous, Nia," he explained.

"Shit," she mumbled. "I can't believe fingers are pointed at me for something like this, but now someone I work with might have set me up to take the fall, Nigel."

"You don't know that," Nigel countered.

"Yeah, I think it's a pretty safe bet," she shot back with a frustrated sigh. "Now I have to be looking over

my shoulder, wondering who it is," she whispered.
"There's only eight other employees here, and six of
them work for me. I had a meeting with them just
this morning. Which of them is planning to reap the
profits while I take the fall for them?"

"Look, Nia, you can't panic about it. Just keep your
head down until it all gets sorted out."

She closed her eyes, feeling overwhelmed by all the
implications.

"What if it doesn't, Nigel? It's grand larceny and
maybe even murder!"

"Trust me, Nee. It will all get resolved. You won't go
down for something you didn't do," he insisted. "But
promise me you won't get involved or talk to anybody
else about this? These people are serious bad dudes.
For thirty million in diamonds, they won't hesitate to
take you out if you get in their way."

"I know," she agreed with a sigh. "I don't have anything of value to say anyway."

"Good. It's better that way."

His words sunk in and Nia paused.

"Nigel, you've told me everything you know, right?"
she asked.

"I've told you everything you need to know. Just trust
me, okay? Keep your head down and your mouth shut,"
he commanded.

"Okay, okay. I get it," she finally conceded.

"I'll call you later in the week to see how you're
doing," Nigel added in a softer tone.

"Thanks, Nigel," she replied, feeling grateful about
the help he was providing her.

They said good-bye and Nia hung up her cell phone.
She sat back in her chair, her brows curled in a frown.
Despite his protests, she couldn't shake the feeling

that Nigel had uncovered more information about the robbery and the jewels than he was sharing with her. Like the value of the stolen gems. Had she told him that their estimated value was thirty million dollars? Her first instinct was to keep pushing him on it, but something in his voice made her hesitate. Maybe it was safer to know as little as possible.

Nia was pulled out of her musing by the notice indicator on her cell phone. It was a text message from Evan DaCosta and she sat up straight at the words.

Have dinner with me tonight.

She smiled a little, welcoming the diversion. After his abrupt departure Sunday night and silence since, Nia had wondered if she had managed to put him off his interest in something personal.

Okay, but I have to work a little late.

How is 6:30? I'll pick you up at your office.

6:30 it is.

Once back to work, Nia's day flew by. She went to meetings from one end of the city to the other in cab rides, finally getting back to the office shortly after four o'clock. At one of her client visits, she had the opportunity to acquire a large nineteenth-century Italian marble statue. Nia had been unable to commit to accepting the piece on consignment for the gallery until she spoke to Chris. The size and weight far exceeded what they usually managed.

Imagining special equipment and extra laborers, she

went into the warehouse to get Chris's opinion. When he wasn't in his office, she looked around, intending to check in a couple of storage areas. On the way, she passed the back door next to the delivery bay and noticed it was left slightly ajar. Nia hesitated, concerned about security. With soft steps, she walked closer, until she heard someone talking in an agitated tone. Still apprehensive, Nia leaned closer, and the words of the one-sided conversation came through the narrow opening of the door

"I'm telling you, Matt's girlfriend must have it, but don't worry about it. I'll find her. I'll get the stuff back. I just need a little more time, that's all."

He turned toward the doorway, and Nia jumped back, then walked away as quickly as possible, embarrassed by the thought of being caught snooping. It wasn't until she was halfway up the stairs that the significance of Chris's words registered.

Evan and the Fortis team had spent the last day and a half tracking down any scent of a broker named Walsh, but they had come up empty.

At five o'clock on Tuesday afternoon, they were back in the control center looking speculatively at the virtual picture board displayed on one of the flat oversized LED screens. It was a visual map of the people they had in their scope. The employee photo of Nia James was still front and center, with the mug shot of Nigel St. Clair on one side, and the picture of Matt Flannigan on the other. There were two squares next to Flannigan; one was blank with only a large question mark in the center and the second one had the name Walsh captured in it.

The other Worthington employees were displayed in a row below.

"We need to rethink the profile of Walsh," Evan stated. "None of the names we short-listed were viable suspects. It was too easy. If we're on the right track, we need to find a real connection. James or someone at Worthington made contact with the broker, either directly, through Flannigan, or through another third party. It's the only way a heist like this could have come together. We just need to find out who and when," Evan summarized.

The team uttered their agreement.

"Let's review all our known variables again to see if we missed anything," Evan decided. "We know there's a low probability that Nia handled the jewels herself. We can't place her at the robbery, and she hasn't been in contact with anyone outside of work."

"Except for her visitor on Saturday at the community center," Raymond stated as he pulled up the picture. "We couldn't get facial recognition off the picture you took. So I took another route. The music student is Meghan McFarlane. She lives with her divorced mom, Julie McFarlane, just a few blocks from the community center. Julie's maiden name is St. Clair. And meet her younger brother, Nigel."

He pulled up a recent picture of the subject, then layered it against the original Michigan mug shot from eleven years ago. The newer picture showed a thinner, more clean-cut man.

"Nicely done, Raymond," Evan commented. "Now we can remove our unknown subject from the list."

The team watched as Raymond updated the virtual picture board by removing the square containing the large question mark.

"But now we still need to connect James to possession of the jewels or a way to get paid for her role in the job," Tony reminded them.

"And, based on the system alerts, Flannigan was on the surveillance video doing his rounds at the time the safe was accessed. So it's unlikely he ever took possession of them," Raymond added.

"Agreed. I did a complete search of his place. There was no money, and no sign of him receiving any payment for his role. So, his job was just to provide access to the warehouse. And we have to assume he was going to get paid after the heist," Tony surmised.

"Explains the timing of his elimination. They tied up a loose end and removed a slice of the pie," concluded Michael.

"By the way, it looks like his girlfriend is now staying with her parents in Worcester, Massachusetts, about an hour away," added Tony. "I guess she was pretty spooked by the whole thing."

"Not surprising," Evan mumbled. "Keep tabs on her. We can't rule anything out at this point."

"What about his friendship with the ops manager and the receptionist? Any meat there?" probed Evan.

"Looks accurate. Morton was visibly upset when we spoke to him on Wednesday. A few other people we talked to confirmed a friendship outside of work," Michael verified. "Even Flannigan's supervisor at the security agency mentioned it. They usually move their people around with various clients to managing shifts, but Morton had requested Flannigan as a regular on their account months ago."

"And he did move from the day to the night shift about a couple of weeks before the robbery," added Raymond.

"Does that make Morton a viable suspect? What do we have on him?" Evan probed.

Raymond pulled up another screen full of personal data on Chris Morton.

"Thirty-two years old, divorced. Worked for Worthington for about five years, and moved to Boston from New Haven a year ago to take the manager role," outlined Raymond. "Rents an apartment in Cambridge. Likes to party quite a bit, with a preference for cocaine on the weekends. His finances are basically paycheck to paycheck. But no sign he's into anything more serious."

Evan crossed his arms across his chest and rocked back on his heels.

"Where was he the night of the robbery?"

"Security cameras and cell phone data put him in the Mission Hill neighborhood until the morning."

"With Emma Sterling," Michael stated with a smirk.

"Yeah, the rumors about their relationship look accurate," agreed Raymond. "They spend a lot of time together outside of the office."

"So, neither of them did the robbery. And neither had access to the safe," concluded Evan. "But the friendship with Flannigan is still a red flag for me . . . I don't like it. Keep digging on Morton and Sterling, just in case. Check out his drug usage and money problems more, there might be a motive for quick cash that Flannigan was exploiting."

"Got it," Raymond acknowledged.

"Is there anyone else at Worthington that looks like a suspect, other than James?" continued Evan.

"We're halfway through the background checks and all communications by the other employees," Raymond advised them. "Everything that's happened in the office or on personal devices going back two months. I haven't seen any flags yet, other than the stuff on Morton," Raymond stated.

"So, that brings us right back to James," Evan stated with a sigh. "But we have to assume that she's working with someone else, other than Flannigan," Evan stated. "Let's go back to St. Clair. Any new activity?"

"None," Raymond confirmed, and he pulled up St. Clair's cell phone records over the last four weeks. "All his communications look pretty consistent. There's the occasional connection to people with some criminal background. But none appear active in the business over the last few years."

"Maybe he's using another way of communicating about the robbery?" Michael suggested. "Unregistered phones, some other off-line method?"

"Then why would Nia call him about it on his registered line?" Evan reasoned. "She would call the burner phone. And he would use that same phone to call her back. It doesn't make sense."

"There's only one logical answer, guys," insisted Tony. "Nia reached out to him for help when she knew she was fingered for the job. She wanted to see if he knew anything about it from his network. It's the only thing that makes sense."

"Maybe," Tony conceded. "But that also suggests she wasn't involved, right? It blows our whole strategy to hell."

"We still don't have enough to draw any concrete conclusion," replied Evan with a sigh. The case was doing his head in. All of their tangible leads still pointed back to Nia, yet none of the specifics confirmed her culpability. But they were getting close, he could feel it. They just needed to uncover a few key facts and the whole thing would come together.

"It's been one week since the heist," he stated. "Assuming Spencer has put us on the right track, we know there is a broker and a buyer. That's confirmed payment as motive. James as our means to get into the safe, and Flannigan provided the opportunity to access the warehouse undetected. Then someone has to, or will deliver the jewels to Walsh. That's our window. If it wasn't James or Flannigan directly, there's a third party at play. We find Walsh, and we find the buyer, the jewels, and the money trail. The money will lead us back to everyone involved."

"Maybe we need to dangle a carrot," Michael suggested. "Like having the new wealthy boyfriend tell James about something that he really wants. Something that he'll pay well to get? If she's in any way connected to Walsh directly, she'll definitely pass on the lead."

Evan smiled broadly, and slapped the young agent on his back.

"I like it!" he agreed. "I'm meeting her for dinner in less than an hour, so I'll think of something to bait our hook."

The team broke up to focus on their individual tasks while Evan went back to his suite to shower and shave off the four days' worth of beard that he'd grown over the long weekend. During a long hot shower, he combed through all the facts they had on the mission. Some were concrete; others were only tied together in loose, flimsy tendrils. And he added the ones he couldn't easily articulate to the team.

Like the fact that the character composite he was building about Nia James just wasn't adding up. From his extensive experience, Evan knew how to read people quickly. He also knew for certain that if it were a woman at the center of this whole scheme, she would fall into a narrow range of profiles. She could be greedy and opportunistic, taking advantage of her position and contacts to make big money. She might be frustrated, angry, or scared about her life situation, and the theft would solve her problems. It could be personal, and stealing from Worthington was the means for revenge, or a reasonable way to right a wrong. Or, perhaps it was for ideology, where stealing the jewels was for the greater good in some way. Whatever it was, the motives weren't always obvious at first, but one or more of them were almost always there. So were the personality and behavior traits associated with those motives.

Nia just didn't demonstrate any that he would expect. Sure, she was reserved and aloof, maybe even secretive. But everything else about her seemed genuine. Instinct told him she was being honest and authentic when they were together, particularly in their intimacy. She wasn't playing him, or using his status and wealth for ulterior motives. Look how pissed she had been about the damn dress.

Or was she? Was his physical attraction to her blocking his objectivity? It was an unpalatable thought. Particularly since the same honed instincts told Evan she was involved in the robbery in some way. He just couldn't piece it together.

Dressed in a dark gray blazer over a crisp white monogrammed shirt and black slacks, Evan left the hotel a few minutes later. He called Lucas from the car on the way.

"Have you had a chance to review our status update?" Evan asked.

"Yeah, Raymond just sent it through," confirmed Lucas.

"I'll bait James tonight, but let's assign a few analysts

to help with the search of the identity of the broker. Walsh is probably not his real name, but there has to be a trail somewhere."

"Do you think she'll take the bait?" his friend asked.

"I don't know," Evan replied honestly.

There was silence for a few minutes. Lucas's brain was like a high-capacity computer, so Evan waited patiently for him to run through his process of data analysis.

"You're questioning whether James is our prime suspect after all," Lucas finally stated.

Evan let out a breath. There was a reason the two men were so close. They had different methods for getting the job done, but ultimately they usually came to the same conclusion.

"I read her wrong from the beginning," Evan acknowledged. "She's not a victim in the plan, but she's not an opportunist either. It's just not in her personality."

"Yeah," agreed Lucas. "I don't know many female cons that spend their weekends volunteering with low-income kids."

"So, what's her role in all this? That's what I can't figure out," Evan admitted. "And it gets even better. Without telling her, I paid for the dress she wore to the Clement party on Saturday. She flipped when she found the receipt with my credit card on it."

"Really?"

"Here I was thinking it would be a romantic thing to do for a woman I'm trying to impress. But instead of appreciating it, she all but accused me of trying to buy her, and insisted I take back the money. She even wrote out the check!"

Lucas whistled. "Wow, that's a first."

"Tell me about it. You'd think I tried to pay her for the night."

"Or maybe you've just lost your charming touch" his friend teased.

"Yeah, maybe."

There was a brief silence.

"Or, one thing has nothing to do with the other, Ice. The better question is: If she's not our suspect, what do you think is going on with her?"

Evan was now parked across the street from Worthington, with about five minutes to spare before he was to meet Nia.

"What do you mean?" he asked Lucas.

"You've said she's a bit cagey, reserved. Like she was hiding something, right?"

"She's definitely not the chatty type at first, that's for sure. I can't say I learned anything about her background that's material to the case, but she relaxed a bit over the weekend."

"How relaxed?"

Evan should have known Lucas would have heard what he wasn't saying.

"Look, the purpose was to get her to lower her guard and provide any insights into what may have happened to the jewels. It worked. If we consider that she may not be actively involved in the robbery, we can redirect our focus and resources."

"Ice, that's not what I'm asking."

"I know what you're getting at, Luc," Evan bit back.

"Look, I know you well enough to know you're struggling with something here. Why did you need me to tell you that James may not be our target?"

"I just needed a second opinion, that's all. You're reading too much into it."

"Don't give me that bullshit, Ice. You've never needed a second opinion in your life," Lucas retorted sarcastically.

"It's under control," Evan shot back, shutting down the conversation. "If she takes the bait on a job for Walsh, it will all be moot anyway. I'll let you know later how it went."

He ended the call abruptly just as the topic of their discussion exited the gallery. Evan stepped out of the car, and Nia acknowledged him right away with an upward nod of her head. She started toward him, crossing the street on a green light. He headed down the block toward the intersection to meet her.

Evan heard the aggressive rev of an engine before he saw the vehicle. The sound, angry and predatory, sent chills down his spine. Instinct and seasoned reflexes had him running across the street between stopped cars as soon as the big, black pickup truck pulled out of the alley beside the gallery. The tires squealed as it picked up speed, racing through the red light and aimed directly toward Nia.

Chapter 14

Everything was in slow motion. Evan watched the scene unfold even as he rushed toward Nia at breakneck speed. Somewhere in the background, he recognized the muffled sounds around him as horns blared and cars braked. He was aware of shouting her name at the top of his lungs.

Yet the only thing he could hear clearly was the rhythm of his rapid breathing and the pounding of his heart. The only thing he could see was the two tons of speeding metal as it whipped by Nia. Then, the image of her crumbled form lying in the road. He was beside her within seconds.

The details of the situation filled his brain. She was unconscious. There was no blood or obvious signs of major physical damage. The truck was speeding away. Other drivers and pedestrians were watching the situation, unsure of what exactly had happened. Several people shouted that the paramedics should be called. Evan heard someone close to him talking to emergency on their cell phone.

He looked back at Nia, his breathing hard and ragged. Her jacket was torn at the shoulder and the heel of her shoe was broken. She looked so fragile. Her lipstick was smudged.

Evan blinked, and the universe rushed forward into real time.

"Nia," Evan whispered, gently touching her face.

She didn't respond. Immediately, he started a slow, thorough inventory of her body, assessing the damage and checking for broken bones. There was nothing obvious. He knew that meant she either moved out of the way in time, perhaps knocked out by her landing on the pavement. Or, the car had hit her dead on in the midsection, in which case the damage was internal and much more worrisome.

The ambulance and police arrived quickly. Instinctively, Evan took on the persona of the average boyfriend. He stepped back so the paramedics could examine and stabilize Nia, and he provided a solid statement to the police, but not so detailed as to raise eyebrows. Within ten minutes, he was riding to the hospital with Nia on a stretcher as the sirens wailed. She was still unconscious.

Evan called Tony to fill him in on the situation. Someone had tried to kill Nia, or at least do some serious damage.

It was amateurish, poorly planned. Opportunistic. The act of someone desperate or scared.

Why? Why now?

The variables raced around in Evan's brain while he held Nia's hand. His thumb brushed the pulse at her wrist, keeping track of the rate despite the beeping machine clipped to her finger.

Someone had targeted Nia, and he hadn't seen it coming.

At the hospital emergency ward, the doctor on call took her right into an exam room, leaving Evan at the counter to fill out whatever patient information he could provide. He completed the forms, listing himself as her boyfriend and her only close contact, with no next of kin. Without her insurance information, he also provided his credit card to cover any costs.

Tony arrived a few minutes later to find Evan standing outside the exam room, legs spread and arms folded.

"Ice, how's she doing?"

"They're still running tests," he replied in a clipped voice, his gaze fixed on her through the glass window.

"Has she come to at all?"

"No."

There was an awkward silence. Evan could feel Tony's stare but ignored it.

"Ice."

Finally, Evan looked back at him. His anger and frustration was hidden behind a granite-hard expression.

"She's going to be all right," the other man assured. "I gave the description of the truck to Raymond. He's trying to locate it through traffic cameras and other surveillance. We'll find it."

Evan nodded, looking back into the exam room. Nia was still motionless, wearing a blue hospital gown and covered with a white sheet. The heart rate machine beeped steadily at regular intervals.

"You're certain it was deliberate? Not some random accident?" Tony asked.

"Positive. They pulled out of the alley beside the gallery and ran the red light to get to her. No way it's a coincidence. It's our guy."

"You're saying it was the thief?" Tony clarified.

"The thief or whoever's our suspect on the inside. They could be one in the same for all we know. For some reason, they want to take Nia out of the equation."

"Why? What's changed in the last week?"

"That's what we need to find out," affirmed Evan, turning to the agent. "I want the team all over it. Let's look through everything she did today, again. Inspect all surveillance and communications we can get our hands on."

"You got it, boss."

"Thanks."

"Do you need anything? Coffee?"

"No, I'm good."

Tony pulled out his cell phone and called the team, relaying the instructions and working out a plan of attack. Evan returned his focus to Nia, resisting the urge to check the time. *How long has she been out?*

Finally, the doctor came back to provide an update on her status and the test results.

"Mr. DaCosta? I'm Dr. Gordon. I've been overseeing the care of Nia James."

"Hi, Doc. How is she doing?"

"Well, she has several abrasions and contusions along the right side of her body, likely due to how she landed on the ground. The good news is that we haven't found any sign that she was hit by the car. X-rays are clear and no fractures that we can find."

Evan let out a deep breath. He felt a sharp sense of relief.

"But she's still unconscious," he stated.

"Yes," the doctor confirmed. "We're concerned she may have also hit her head when she landed causing a concussion, and some swelling. It's still early, so it could also be from the shock of the incident. We're going to watch her closely for the next couple of hours."

Evan nodded.

"Thanks, Doc. Can I go see her now?" he asked.

"Yes, that should be fine."

Now that he knew how Nia was doing and had the team in motion with a plan, Evan was able to turn down the activity in his brain and be in the moment. He sat down in the chair next to her bed, elbows braced on his knees, head hanging low. The reality of what had happened slowly settled, along with a tight knot of dread at the pit of his stomach.

She had almost died. On his watch.

Best-case scenario, she would be in pain for a few days. Worse case? A serious concussion, maybe even a coma. Instead of meeting her at the gallery, being there to protect her, Evan had been on the phone debating her innocence and pretending he had things under control.

Shit! How had he missed the signs that she was vulnerable and could be in danger? Evan had been so busy trying to control his feelings for her that it had clouded his judgment. And he failed Nia because of it. His stomach sunk deeper, twisting painfully until he felt nauseous. Evan now had a clear sense of how he would feel if anything happened to her, and it hit him hard.

When he finally had the courage to look over at her prone shape, she seemed frighteningly still and lifeless. He reached out to stroke her cheek then froze. Evan could have sworn Nia responded, shifting her head slightly in reaction. He held his breath, heart beating loudly, but nothing further happened. Sitting back in the chair, he took her soft hand into his and began the patient wait for her to wake up.

Less than an hour later, her fingers twitched. Evan was deep in thought and the gesture was so slight that he almost missed it. But she moved again and groaned.

He stood up to lean over her bed, squeezing her hand in his.

"Nia? Sweetheart?" whispered Evan.

She blinked, wrinkling her forehead from the effort. "Evan?"

"Yeah, it's me." He was so relieved, he felt lightheaded.

"What happened? Where am I?" she asked, looking around.

"Shhh, it's okay. You're in the hospital."

"What? Why?"

Nia tried to sit up, but Evan gently coaxed her down by the shoulders.

"No, don't move," he urged. "There was an accident. A truck ran the red light while you were crossing the street. You were hurt."

She relaxed back and closed her eyes. Evan roamed his eyes over the length of her body, reevaluating her mobility and checking for signs of other injury.

"How do you feel?" he asked.

"Weird." She slowly reached up and touched her forehead.

"You've been unconscious for a bit," he explained. "Are you in pain?"

Nia wrinkled her face again, but her doctor entered the room followed by one of the nurses.

"Nia, we're glad to see you awake," the physician stated with a satisfied smile. "I'm Dr. Gordon. How are you feeling?"

She looked around the room, as though finally understanding the situation.

"I don't know. A little beat up, I guess. Evan said something about a truck while I was crossing the street. What happened?"

Evan gripped her fingers tighter. He was so relieved

to see her alert and talking, but hated the confusion and fragility on her face.

"Well, we were hoping you could help us with that," the doctor replied. "Do you remember anything, Nia?"

"I'm not sure. I saw you across this street," she explained, looking up into Evan's eyes. "Then I started across the intersection. You called my name and you were running."

Evan nodded, encouraging her to continue.

"That's all I can recall."

"That's good, Nia," stated Dr. Gordon. "The police were concerned it was a hit and run, but your scrapes and bruising suggest you got hurt when you hit the ground, rather than from being hit by the car. So that's good news. We're just going to do another exam to make sure we haven't missed anything."

"I'll be right outside," Evan told her. "Do you need me to call anyone for you?"

She shook her head to say no.

"I'll call my friend Lianne a little later."

"Okay."

He kissed her forehead and left the room.

Outside the door, he looked around feeling a little lost. The nurse had pulled the curtain over the window for privacy so there was nothing to do but wait. Evan walked down the hall where he found a vending machine. Suddenly hungry and thirsty, he bought a sports drink and a protein bar. It was hard to believe it was only after nine o'clock in the evening.

He was back in front of the exam room when his cell phone rang. It was Lucas.

"How's she doing?" his friend asked right away.

"She's awake."

"Good. What's the doctor saying?"

Evan filled him in on the details.

"Well, I have bad news. Raymond tracked the truck heading toward Cambridge, but lost it after that," Lucas confirmed.

"Damn it! Any plates?" growled Evan.

"No."

Evan cursed roughly, his fist clenched tight.

"Tony said you think it was someone at the gallery?".

"We have two viable scenarios," explained Evan. "Either she was involved from the beginning and she's another loose end, like Flannigan. Which means she wasn't the ringleader. Or she's not involved, but discovered something about the robbery that puts the plan at risk. Either way, someone wants her out of the picture."

"By trying to run her over?" Lucas questioned. "Doesn't have the same M.O. as the person that took out the security guard, Ice. That was at least semi-professional. This is amateur hour."

"I agree. They wanted it to look like an accident, but it was sloppy."

"And why now?" continued Lucas. "We're still going through her day to figure that out, but I'm sending you an audio file."

Evan heard a message indicator on the cell phone.

"She definitely spoke with St. Clair on her cell phone in the morning," continued Lucas.

"Anything valuable?" Evan asked.

"From her side of the conversation, it corroborates your second theory," explained Lucas. "Nia called St. Clair after the fact, to see if he could find out anything about the robbery."

"Did he know anything?" Evan asked, rubbing his forehead.

"Hard to say. She's clearly worried that someone in the office was setting her up for the fall," Lucas concluded. "Listen to the audio. I don't think Nia had any involvement in the robbery."

Evan nodded. After everything that had happened in the last twenty-four hours, he wasn't surprised.

"What about Edward? Have we notified him yet? She'll have to be off work for a few days at least," suggested Evan.

"Yeah, Mike called him almost immediately," Lucas confirmed. "We told him that one of our agents was on-site as part of our investigation, and we're looking into any connection to the theft."

"Good."

"Do you need anything"? Lucas added. "Do you want me to come out there? I can take the chopper and be there in a few hours."

"Nah, I'm good. I need you at headquarters tracking down this asshole," replied Evan, running a hand through his hair. "He won't have another opportunity to get her. That, I promise."

"We'll get him, Ice. He's revealed himself and we'll get him."

They hung up soon after. Evan then called the team to give them the update on Nia.

"Mr. DaCosta?"

He turned to find the doctor behind him.

"How is she?" he asked.

"Pretty good, considering. There's no sign of any other injuries so it seems she managed to move out of the way in time."

Evan sucked in a deep breath and dropped his head in relief.

"We're still concerned about the possibility of a concussion, so we'd like to keep her overnight for observation," continued the doctor. "We're moving her to a more comfortable room. But otherwise, she should be fine to leave in the morning."

Both men turned as an orderly pulled Nia's bed out of the exam room and headed down the hall.

"Thank you, Doc. That's very good news," Evan stated as he shook the other man's hand.

They had Nia settled in a hospital room a short while later. Evan managed to talk to her briefly, offering to go to her apartment to grab toiletries and a change of clothes. Tony met him at the hospital to provide a ride to Evan's car, still parked downtown. Evan then stopped by the hotel to pack a bag before driving to Nia's place in South Boston.

When he returned to the hospital, she was asleep. So he settled into a chair with his phone to finally listen to the voice recording of Nia's conversation with St. Clair, caught off their surveillance recordings. Evan clenched his jaw at the worry and fear that was palpable in her voice. After three reviews, he tossed aside his phone in frustration.

Surprisingly, Evan also managed to sleep that night for a few hours, waking at dawn as one of the nurses stopped in for a regular checkup. Evan used the opportunity to wash up a bit, then grab a large cup of coffee.

He was reviewing the various files on the other Worthington employees, sent by Lucas and Tony when Nia woke up. She immediately tried to sit up, but winced in discomfort.

"Hey, let me help you."

He closed the laptop and leapt to her side so she could use his arm as leverage.

"What are you doing here?" she asked.

"Where else would I be?" mumbled Evan, noting the confusion on her face.

"What time is it?"

"Almost eight in the morning."

She looked up and down at him then around the room.

"Did you stay here last night?"

"Of course I did. You almost got hit by a truck, Nia. I wasn't going to leave you." Evan clenched his jaw. His tone sounded harsher than he intended. But it bothered him that she would expect less from him in the role as her new lover.

"I was going to call my friend Lianne. But I guess I fell asleep," she explained, sounding apologetic.

That annoyed him even more. She thought he only stayed out of obligation, because no one else was there. He cleared his throat, biting his tongue. Now was not the time to think about his bruised ego.

"Are you in pain? Do you need anything? The nurse left some pills in case you need them."

She shook her head then grimaced.

"No, I'm just sore. Pretty minor considering what could have happened. I guess I was lucky."

They were interrupted by another nurse visit. Evan left the room so Nia could get showered and dressed in the comfortable gym clothes he had brought for her. The doctor on call arrived a short time later, officially releasing her from their care. Evan drove her home and Nia used the time to call her office and her friend Lianne. He was surprised she didn't also call Nigel St.

Clair. Or would she only do so in private, he wondered with a sharp bite of annoyance.

At her apartment, Evan got her settled on the couch. He would have preferred she stay in bed to ensure a good rest, but Nia insisted she wanted to be in the living room. It didn't seem to matter. After some orange juice and toast that Evan made quickly, she fell into a deep sleep bundled in a blanket, and with daytime television playing in the background.

He spent a few hours sitting at her dining table working until he got a call from Tony.

"Are you alone?" the agent asked right away, his tone suggesting it was essential.

Evan checked in on Nia, still resting comfortably.

"Give me a sec."

He left the apartment to stand out in the building's small hallway. It was the middle of a school day, so the area was quiet.

"What's up?" he demanded.

"We found a bug on Nia."

"What? Where?"

"It was in her bag. Her laptop power cable. It's one of those transmitters disguised as an adapter. Clever, but pretty basic stuff. It has wireless Internet transmission built in, powered by the adapter itself. So the receiver could be anywhere."

"Son of a bitch!" cursed Evan. "How did we miss it the first time?"

"We did the initial sweep early in the morning last Wednesday. She wasn't in the office yet, so she would have had the power cable with her," Tony explained. "Ice, it explains how they knew about the jewels, the delivery, and the code to the safe. They would know everything she's discussed in her office. Or anywhere her laptop was powered by the cable."

Their suspect pool was now extensive.

"Did you find any others in the building?"

"No. We're doing a second sweep now, but it looks like just Nia so far," confirmed Tony. "We'll check all the other laptop equipment tomorrow when everyone is back in the office."

"Okay, leave the device intact. We don't want to tip our man that we're on to him," Evan instructed. "But now we'll know everything they're hearing. Is there a way to trace the signal back to the receiver?"

"I'll check with Raymond and Lucas."

"Okay. Now we need to go back to the beginning and start over," Evan continued. "Our suspect list is wide open again, including whoever installed their security system. We can't afford to overlook any options at this point. She could easily have been bugged from the outside for an undetermined amount of time."

"Got it, Ice. What about Nia?"

"I've got her. All of our new information points to her being uninvolved. But, clearly, she knows something or has talked to someone that's made her a threat at this point. So, she's now an asset, and her protection is now our top priority."

"Under your cover?" the agent asked.

Evan closed his eyes.

"Yes, we continue the cover. I'll take her to Virginia through the weekend to work on my dad's collection, just as planned. She'll be safe there, and I'll have more time to find out what she knows. It still may be valuable to solving the mission."

"Look, Ice, I'm not second-guessing you. But you

could step back now. Once we tell her we know how they got into the safe and that the hit and run was deliberate, I'm sure she'll cooperate. And the rest of the team can provide round-the-clock protection. She'd never have to know you're Fortis."

It made sense. It might work. But Evan dismissed it. There was no way he was giving Nia's safety over to someone else now, not even some of the best men he'd ever worked with.

"We won't tell her anything. She's discovered something valuable, Tony, but she hasn't told anyone, not even her boss," Evan explained. "If Nia was aware the same person who has set her up for the theft is also trying to take her out, she'd never give up what she knows. Otherwise, she'd have said something already. I'm our best chance at answers."

"Got it," repeated Tony. "I'll update the team. When will you leave for Virginia?"

"Sandra had booked us on a commercial flight for tomorrow evening. But I'll have her change it to a private charter earlier in the day. I'm anxious to get her out of Boston until we know what we're dealing with and how big this thing is."

The call ended soon after, yet Evan stood outside Nia's front door for a few minutes longer. The rationale he'd provided Tony for why he needed to keep his cover was very real and valid. But there was more to his motives than he was willing to admit, even to himself.

All of the feelings and desires he had been fighting since he met Nia James were now slowly bubbling to the surface. They were raw and intense, filling him with a mix of excitement and apprehension, entwined with his need to protect her from any further threats. It was a potent combination that left Evan more unbalanced that he'd ever felt before. He didn't know what it meant or what to do with it, but there was one thing he was clear about. Nia James was his responsibility, and no one would ever harm her again under his watch.

Chapter 15

"This is crazy, Nia. You barely know this guy and he's moved you into his house," Lianne summarized over the phone. "In another state, no less."

Nia bit the inside of her cheek. She could hardly argue since it all seemed bizarre to her as well. The last two days were a complete blur of rushed decisions, and here she was.

"He hasn't moved me in," she clarified. "I'm working on his account."

"In his bedroom? That's some account," Lianne quipped.

Nia smiled.

"You know what I mean. I was already scheduled to spend a few days here to go through his collection, Lee. So it's not really a big deal."

"Yeah, well, you should be at home recuperating. I didn't even get to see you before you left."

"I know. But honestly, it's nothing. The bruising looks worse than it really is. It hardly hurts anymore,"

Nia explained. "I'd be ready to go back to work on Monday anyway."

"When will you be back in Boston?"

"I'm not sure. Tuesday? Maybe Wednesday? Evan refuses to let me do anything other than walk to the bathroom so far, so we won't get to his mother's house to start the work until Sunday."

"Okay. I want you to call me the minute you arrive home."

"I will, I promise."

They spoke for a little while longer. After they hung up, Nia sat back on the couch in Evan's living room and looked around. It was hard to believe she was here. Everything since Tuesday evening was difficult to comprehend. Those last few moments crossing the street were still hazy, except for the image of Evan running toward her, and the sound of a revving engine. Nia could only assume that instinct had kicked in causing her to dive away from the accelerating vehicle at the last second. Otherwise, there was no telling what kind of injuries she could have sustained, if she survived at all.

What Nia hadn't told anyone, was that she had a nagging feeling that it wasn't a random accident. Her talk with Nigel that afternoon was just too coincidental. Then, there was the heated conversation Chris had outside the warehouse. Had he seen her walking away? There was the very real possibly that someone at Worthington knew she was asking questions and wanted to stop her. They might want to shut her up, if they thought she knew something. Just like they had shut up Matt Flannigan. Once you've stolen jewelry worth thirty million dollars, what are two murders instead of just one?

Suddenly, Evan's suggestion that she take advantage of their planned trip to Virginia so she could recuperate for a few days seemed like a really good idea. It would give her time to think things through and decide what she would do next. If Evan thought her acceptance was out of character, he didn't say.

When she spoke with Edward after being released from the hospital on Wednesday morning, he was already aware of her accident. So it was no surprise to him that she needed to be off for a few days. He was supportive of her opportunity to leave for Virginia, but insisted she do client work only once she was fully recovered.

Originally, Adam was to accompany Nia on the business trip to provide administrative support. But with Nia out of the office for a week or so, they agreed it would be best if he stayed in Boston to help keep their other projects on track. She could bring in a local consultant for a few hours if needed.

With a sigh Nia stood up and walked across Evan's apartment in Alexandria to look outside at the tranquil view of the Potomac River, separating Virginia from the District of Columbia. Other than the impressive view, a two-bedroom condominium was not at all what she had expected.

After the lavish hotel room and mansion-like beach house on the Vineyard, Nia had imagined much of the same for his home. Particularly after the experience flying there from Boston in a private Cessna jet. Instead, his apartment was normal. It was beautifully done inside, with top-of-the-line appliances and finishes. The location and view were stunning, with a large patio and plenty of building amenities from what she could see. But it was hardly the extravagant home of a very wealthy trust-fund kid turned CEO of the international family business.

Interim CEO, anyway.

Remembering their plans for the evening, Nia checked her watch. It was time to get in the shower. After two days of coddling, Evan finally agreed to let her out of the house. They were meeting a couple of his friends for dinner. She went into the bedroom to decide what to wear.

From the moment they had arrived at the apartment on Thursday afternoon, Evan had put her things in his room. Nia hadn't objected. She wanted to be there. After their weekend together, it seemed silly to pretend otherwise. Right now, he made her feel safe and secure, and she appreciated it. Even sleeping in his arms felt good, though he padded a thick blanket around her to ensure she wasn't bruised further through the night.

Not ready to wear anything fitted against her hip, Nia laid out a long sundress made of soft, brushed linen. In the bathroom, she peeled off the yoga pants and T-shirt to look at the right side of her body in the large vanity mirror. Her skin was still marred with rough abrasions on the hip and along her upper arm near the shoulder. The large bruises were now an angry dark-blue, but definitely starting to fade. She poked the largest running down the side of her bum. It was still a little tender to the touch, but it no longer hurt to sit or walk.

Nia relaxed her arms and looked at her full body naked, still uncertain of how the hell she had gotten herself into the current situation, or what she could do to get out of it. The one thing she knew for sure was that she was *not* going be someone's victim or scapegoat. Never again.

Evan returned home from work a short time later to pick her up, driving his sleek, white Aston Martin sports car. He gently helped her get seated before they got back on the road.

"How are you feeling?" he asked.

"Pretty good, almost human," she described honestly.

"Have you been taking the painkillers?"

It was the same question he'd asked every few hours since she got out of the hospital, even though she stopped taking medication after Wednesday.

"I'm fine, Evan. Really."

He looked skeptical, but left it alone.

"Is everything okay at work?" she asked.

Today was the first time he'd left her side since the incident, and only for a few hours in the afternoon. She wondered at his ability to run a company while playing babysitter to his . . . *What? Girlfriend? Lover?*

"It was fine, just a couple of meetings I needed to attend. Though I could have joined them from home by video conference," he reminded her.

She rolled her eyes, having had this conversation a few hours ago. He had argued that it was too soon for her to be alone; she had won.

"So, tell me about your friends?" she asked, changing the subject.

"Lucas and Sam? They work together running a security company," he explained. "Luc and I met years

ago when he did some work for DaCosta. I met Sam
through him a while back."

"Are they single, married?"

"Dating, sort of," he replied with a sly smile.

"Sort of? What does that mean?" Nia asked, laughing.

He shrugged.

"It means I can't really keep track of who they're
seeing, so I don't try."

"Ahhh, I see. They're playboys."

"Lucas, definitely. He's way too pretty for his own
good."

"Prettier than you?" she teased.

Evan laughed, giving her a humble glance. She
caught a glimpse of his dimples.

"Much prettier! But Sam's too ornery to be a player.
He just has odd taste in women."

Nia was intrigued.

"In what way?"

"I don't know. I've only met a couple of his dates,
and both struck me as not very bright. I think he
prefers them that way so he doesn't have to take them
too seriously. But you'll see for yourself soon enough."

She shrugged, thinking it was going to be an interesting evening.

"What about you, what's your usual type, Evan?"
she asked, suddenly wondering if she would be like the
other women he'd introduced to his friends.

He gave her an assessing look.

"That's not a fair question, Nia."

"Why? I won't be offended. I met your ex-fiancée,
remember. And we had nothing in common, looks-
wise anyway."

Evan paused in thought before answering in a quiet voice.

"I'd say I'm attracted to many types of women, physically. But I've mostly dated the more understated, causal types. Low maintenance."

Classy, demure like Mikayla Stone-Clement, the woman he loved and wanted to marry. Nia refused to look away or feel hurt by his words. She'd asked the question and he was being honest.

"But I think that's because I was gone a lot, always traveling overseas. I thought that I was being smart to date that type of woman. Low maintenance, so she'd be content to wait for me, put up with my long absences. Which is ridiculous. And probably why my engagement to Mikayla would never have worked. Every woman wants her boyfriend or husband to be there for her."

She didn't know exactly what he was trying to say.

"In my head, women like you, Nia, were not in my best interest."

"What?" she scoffed. "What's that's supposed to mean?"

"Seriously. It may be primitive and chauvinistic but what can I say? Women that look like you have men chasing after you left, right, and center. Why on earth would you settle for a man who was never around? Seemed like a dumb choice and a recipe for disaster."

Nia just looked at him, speechless. Did he really believe that?

"You're basically saying that a woman's ability to be committed and faithful is dependent on how she looks or dresses?" Nia demanded, incredulously.

"Those weren't exactly my words. But, look, I'm just explaining to you what my type used to be and why," he added, obviously aware of how it sounded. "Clearly, I've evolved a little since then."

"Oh great. All the way from Neanderthal to early Homo sapiens. Good to know." He just laughed in response. "Explain to me your evolved thinking?"

"It's simple. I decided to go after what I want, not what I think I need."

"Are you saying you dated women you didn't want before because it was safe?"

"Of course I was attracted to them on some level. I loved Mikayla. I still do and probably always will. But now I realize that the things I love about her make a great friend, not necessarily a girlfriend or a wife," he said, and glanced at her sheepishly, with a shrug. "Perhaps it was a little safe."

"And the part about women who look like me?" Nia probed.

"You know what I mean."

They pulled up to the valet area of a casual steak restaurant.

"Not really, but I assume you mean *not* understated." she mumbled, trying really hard not to feel insulted. "High maintenance?"

Evan handed over the keys to an attendant and then helped her out of the car.

"No, Nia, you are definitely not understated," he finally replied, pulling her into a gentle embrace. "You're bold, way too sexy for my sanity, and so stunningly gorgeous that it hurts my eyes."

He kissed her, slow and deep.

"And not at all high maintenance. Now, stop asking silly questions," he added before taking her hand to walk into the restaurant.

His friends were already at the table when they arrived. And as Evan suggested, there were two women with them. Lucas Johnson and Sam Mackenzie stood to meet her, then introduced their dates, Cierra and Angel respectively, both very beautiful girls, if not a little young. Nia resolved to sit back and listen to the conversation and observe Evan in his regular environment.

The first thing she noticed was that all three men were built like warriors. Lucas was the smallest, yet still an inch or so north of six feet with lean, hard muscles clearly visible through his golf shirt. Nia had thought Evan was big, but Sam was just massive. He was at least a couple of inches taller, with hulking shoulders and arms the size of tree trunks. All together, they were an impressive group, if not a little scary.

Evan's description of Lucas was very accurate. With his rich brown skin and a trimmed goatee, he was very handsome in a boyish, fun way that suggested he preferred naughty over nice. He was also charming and funny, constantly teasing both his friends. Nia could see that he and Evan were very close.

Sam was an odd one. With his sun-bronzed pale skin, sky blue eyes, and golden brown hair, he was also quite attractive, but in a fierce, bad-ass way. While he certainly wasn't as easygoing as Lucas, Nia picked up on his sarcastic, dry humor right away, accentuated by his deep Scottish accent. That was mostly because she could relate to it. And something about him also reminded her of Evan. Maybe the serious intensity that seemed at the core of his personality?

"How are you feeling, Nia? Evan mentioned you had an accident recently?" Sam asked her as the others were deciding which dessert to order after their main course.

"I'm doing okay. Not quite one hundred percent, but close."

"Good. I hope he's taking care of you?"

She looked over at Evan who was debating something with Lucas.

"Yeah, he's been great."

Sam nodded, and the conversation swung in another direction while the group ordered and enjoyed a collection of cakes.

"We're going to the bathroom, Nia," stated Cierra, Lucas's date sometime later. "Come along."

Nia smiled at Evan and joined the other women. Though she had no need to use the facilities other than to refresh her lip gloss, it would have been rude not to go. On the way back, she was stopped by a light hand on her shoulder.

"Nia James?"

She turned around to find the last person she expected to see outside of Bloomfield, Michigan. The medium-height blonde looked very much the same as she did eleven years ago when they were both sophomores in high school.

"Hailey," Nia stated flatly.

"Oh my God, Nia! What are you doing here, in Alexandria of all places! I can't believe it's you!"

Nia allowed a hug, only because she wasn't sure how to avoid it.

"How are you, Nia? Last I heard, you had moved to Boston," stated Hailey.

"I did. I'm just staying with a friend here for a few days. How about you? Do you live around here?" she replied.

"Yeah for about six years now. Daddy transferred to one of the military bases nearby."

Nia nodded. While the two women had been close friends at one point as teenagers, they had little in common now. And even less that Nia wanted to get caught up on.

"Well . . ." started Nia, intending to politely end the conversation, but the other woman cut her off.

"You look so good, Nia. You always did, but I'm so glad you're doing well," Hailey added, her smile fading a little. "I know it wasn't possible after what had happened, but I wish we could have stayed in touch. I really missed you when you left school."

Nia didn't know what to say.

"To this day, I still wish I had known enough to say something sooner. You were my best friend and . . ." Her eyes got misty forcing Nia to look down. "Anyway, it's old history now. But I want you to know that I never once believed the accusations. I just didn't know what to do about it."

Nia shrugged.

"We were young, Hailey. You weren't responsible—"

"Sweetheart, is everything okay?" interrupted Evan as he approached the two women and slid a protective arm across Nia's lower back.

"It's fine, Evan. This is Hailey Stamford. We went to school together back in Michigan," Nia introduced. "Hailey, this is Evan DaCosta."

The two shook hands.

"It was good to see you, Hailey," Nia finally stated, turning way.

"You too, Nia."

She and Evan walked back to the table where his friends were getting their things ready to leave.

"Sorry, I didn't mean to keep you all waiting," Nia explained.

"No worries, you didn't. Is everything okay?" Evan replied.

She nodded and gave him a reassuring smile. When it came to her life in Bloomfield, Michigan, it was all years behind her, and better left in the past.

Chapter 16

Evan looked over at Nia. They were driving back to his apartment, and she was laughing about something Lucas had said over dinner. Smiling back, he was listening to her comments, but his mind was elsewhere.

It was humbling to admit to Nia that his thinking and decisions about women had been so misguided and juvenile. After the breakup with Mikayla over three years ago, he had continued that pattern. He'd date women whom he liked, respected, and had fun with, but could easily walk away from for the next assignment. Now, after some soul searching, Evan realized that he had been looking for the same arrangement his parents had; what he had seen as a reliable union that would allow him to do his job without distraction. Unfortunately, it was also devoid of true passion.

Up until very recently, he hadn't even understood what was missing. He was very familiar with lust and sexual attraction. The cure was usually sex. But this obsessive, clawing hunger he felt for Nia just keep building, only enhanced by their intimacy. She filled his thoughts during the day and occupied his dreams at night. It was out of control and it seemed to be getting worse.

Maybe his decisions about women weren't so crazy after all, he mused. If he had felt this way about any woman while still in the CIA, Evan would have been incapable of doing his job.

"How are things at work? Are they surviving without you for a few days?" he asked as they walked into his apartment.

She shrugged, biting the side of her cheek.

"I'm not sure, to be honest."

He walked into the kitchen and grabbed two bottles of water out of the fridge.

"Why, what's going on?" he asked casually, handing her one.

"Thanks," she mumbled. "It's nothing. We have something under review in the office, and it hasn't been finalized yet."

Evan remained silent, sensing she was on the verge of opening up.

"It's complicated," she finally said. "And you're a client, so it's not really appropriate for me to say too much."

He nodded, moving to the couch. Nia followed and he helped her to sit down.

"Does it have anything to do with my collection?" he asked.

"No! Not at all."

"Okay, so then there's no conflict of interest. If you want to talk about it, I promise I won't hold anything against your firm."

She let out a deep breath, toying with the lid of the plastic bottle.

"Something happened recently and we're going through an investigation," Nia revealed.

"Like an audit?" he asked casually.

"Yeah, I guess. They think I might be involved."

She stopped there.

"Are you?"

Nia looked up at him in surprise.

"No! Of course not!"

"It's okay if you are. Everyone makes mistakes, Nia."

"This wasn't a mistake, Evan. It's way beyond a mistake and I had nothing to do with it," she vehemently stated.

He shrugged.

"Then I'm sure the auditors will figure it out."

"Maybe. But I think I know who did it," she quietly added. "I'm just not sure what to do about it."

Evan's heart started pounding with anticipation, but he maintained his casual posture.

"Why don't you just tell the auditors? Or your boss?" he suggested.

"I will, once I'm sure. I don't want it to look like I'm pointing fingers, you know?"

"Nia, the truth will come out eventually. It always does. If you think you know something, you should put it out there. It will just help them discover the truth faster."

"Maybe," she whispered.

Finally, he had the confirmation he needed. She did know something incriminating, something that made her a target. With the team closing in on finding the broker, Walsh, it was only a matter of time before the dots connected. Or until Nia was ready to tell them what she knew.

They were silent for a few moments, and it became

obvious that Nia wasn't going to say anything more about the robbery investigation. Evan changed the subject to another that seemed odd to him.

"Your friend from high school. It must have been a nice surprise to run into her. Do you guys keep in touch?"

"Hailey? No. I haven't seen her since tenth grade."

"Why? Did she move away?" he probed.

"No, I did. It was a private school in the suburbs, but I went back to live with my mom in the city."

"Private school? You? Miss *I'm going out with you in spite of your money'* James? How can that be?"

Nia pursed her lips and slapped his leg in protest.

"It was a scholarship, okay?" she shot back. "Remember I said I lived with my aunt for a while? Well, it was during the academic year. Her house was close enough for me to take the bus to the school campus."

"Interesting," he noted. "I didn't think that was something you and I would have in common."

"Don't forget being an only child."

"Yeah, there is that," agreed Evan, brushing her hair off her shoulders. She had it down tonight, flowing in thick waves, the way he liked it most.

"What sort of scholarship?"

"Academic and music," Nia replied with a sigh, her eyelids drooping slightly.

He could tell she was running out of steam.

"Come, let's get you into the bath so you can take a relaxing soak."

"I don't need a soak, I'm fine," she protested.

"Yes, you do. I know you think you're almost recovered, but it's going to take more time," Evan insisted. "I have some Epsom salts. It will help with the swelling."

Nia allowed him to lead her to the en suite bath in his bedroom. He pulled out his cell phone and used it to turn on some music through the built-in sound system.

"Hmm, that's nice. Joshua Redman?"

"Yeah," he confirmed, a little surprised at her quick knowledge of contemporary jazz.

"He's one of my favorites. I didn't peg you as being into this kind of music," she added in a sleepy voice.

Evan turned on the tap in the bath, adjusting the temperature so it was warm and soothing.

"What kind did you think?" he asked, sitting on a stool beside the tub and pulling her to him.

"I don't know."

She gave him a speculative once-over while he remained focused on removing her long, flowing dress. Once the spaghetti straps were slipped off her shoulders, the whole thing slithered to the floor.

"Classic hip-hop. Like Tupac, Biggie Smalls, or A Tribe Called Quest. Maybe Method Man?"

He tried not to notice how exquisite her silky body looked in only lingerie. Instead, he focused on the scrapes along her hip, or the dark bruise on her bum. Seeing her injuries for the first time brought back all those feelings of rage and helplessness he had felt while standing in the emergency room. He took a deep breath, then gently caressed one of the abrasions, hating the feel of rough scabbing on her honey skin.

"Well? Am I right?"

He looked up at her eager expression. She was easily the most beautiful woman he'd ever known. Whether in her tailored suits and killer heels, or wearing next to nothing. Blood-red lipstick or bare pink lips, Nia stirred him on every level.

"I listen to lots of different stuff, but who doesn't like classic hip-hop."

"I'm partial to Eminem myself," she confessed with a grin.

"Well, I guess you have to be," teased Evan.

She shrugged.

"It's a Detroit thing."

He left her briefly to add the bath salts to the water.

"Okay, you're all set."

Nia was putting her hair into a loose bun with a hair elastic. Then she undid her bra, revealing those incredible breasts. Round and generous, their chocolaty tips beckoned him. He clenched his jaw, holding on to his resolve. She was still injured. It was way too soon to touch her. He was still undercover, on a mission.

"Aren't you going to join me?" she asked, slipping off the thong panties.

Evan went from semi-aroused to rock hard in a snap. *Jesus Christ,* she was sexy. He watched as she walked slowly to the tub and eased in. Steaming water sloshed over her body, caressing her skin as she lay back against the rim. She moaned with pleasure.

"I'm not sure that's a good idea," he announced, shoving his hands into the front pockets of his slacks. "You soak, then we'll get you into bed early."

"Evan, I'm fine. Really. Please join me?"

It was a big tub, plenty of room for them both. Maybe he could just hold her, relax with her. Nothing more.

"Okay. Just for a bit."

Nia grinned, and he knew he was in trouble. It didn't help that she watched him undress with her feline brown eyes twinkling with unabashed appreciation. Or that his jutting erection was impossible to hide or ignore. But Evan did his best to maintain his willpower and stick to the plan. They'd relax together for a few minutes. Anything more was out of the question.

She moved over a bit so that he could sit down in the water, then she cuddled to his side with her head on his chest and one of her legs draped over his. Evan sighed, content.

They lay like that for long minutes. Bass and saxophone notes surrounded them.

"A music scholarship, huh," he finally commented in a lazy voice. "Do you play an instrument?"

Nia ran her hand down the center of his chest and over his stomach. It was both tingling and arousing.

"The piano mostly. The guitar, too."

"Is that when you decided you wanted to be a songwriter?"

He remembered the comment from one of their early conversations.

"It seemed like a great choice at the time. But what do I know at eleven or twelve years old?"

He smiled, eyes still closed.

"I wanted to be fighter pilot. I even got my pilot's license."

"Really? Do you actually fly a plane?"

"Helicopters mostly. It comes in handy with business travel."

"Fighter pilot, huh? That's pretty sexy," she mumbled.

"Well, I was nine, so that wasn't my objective. But now I realize it would have been an added perk."

"I don't know. You're pretty sexy as it is. A career like that would just be too much."

"You think I'm sexy, huh."

"Maybe. A little. Not as pretty as Lucas, but you can't have everything."

Evan felt ridiculously pleased with her words. God, civilian life had turned him into a complete wimp.

Nia's fingers continued exploring, roving slowly over his torso, lulling him into deeper relaxation. Until they dipped lower, below his belly button and into dangerous territory. She kissed his neck, stroking the skin with the tip of her tongue.

"Nia, sweetheart," he protested.

"I'm fine, I promise," she whispered seductively.

He swallowed, struggling to resist what she was offering. If she was feeling better, then slow, gentle sex might be okay. The problem was, Evan couldn't trust himself to stick to that plan either. When it came to Nia, he seemed incapable of maintaining his control. Touching her, tasting her, being inside her turned him into something wild and primitive, too lost in her to keep his cool.

But he looked down at her soft body, sweet and sexy through the water, and thought of what she needed. Evan was going to give her slow and gentle, even if it killed him.

He trailed his hand along her shoulder and down her arm, threading his fingers through hers.

"Promise me you'll tell me if you feel any discomfort, okay?"

She looked up at him.

"I promise."

He brushed his hand under her chin, lifting her face higher so he could kiss her. She tasted hot and sweet. Nia's tongue entwined with his. Sharp bolts of electricity speared down his spine, right down to his balls. *Wow,* she did things to him! He pulled her closer until she was lying on top of him, her legs spread to straddle him around the hips.

Evan trailed his lips down her neck, pulling her body higher by the arms until her breast was aligned with his mouth. He blew on the sensitive globe as rivulets of water tricked from the soft flesh. Her puckered nipples tightened further. Nia moaned. He feasted on the image and slid his hands down her back to cup the plump curves of her rear. *Perfection,* he thought.

"Comfortable?" he asked.

"Very," Nia answered, now resting her hands on the edge of the tub behind his shoulders.

"Good."

He took one of her nipples into his mouth, swirling his tongue around it in tiny circles. Her hips bucked, brushing sensually against his lower stomach. He continued the teasing attention for long moments before moving to the other breast. Nia was panting with the kittenish moans that he loved so much. It made his cock throb hard with need.

Wanting more, Evan brushed his fingers down the valley between her cheeks then up between her thighs. He lightly toyed with the entrance to her tight passage, stroking over the swollen feminine flesh. Even in the cooling water, Nia was slick and creamy for him. Her cries become deeper, more urgent, her body quivered and tightened. Evan grimaced, holding back his own deep groan in an attempt to dampen his escalating excitement. It wasn't working. He was going to die slowly from wanting her.

Finally, he slid his middle finger into her sheath, curving the tip to touch that magically erogenous zone within her silken walls.

"Evan, yes!"

Yeah!

He stroked into her again and again, focused completely on her pleasure spot, loving the feel of her taut body climbing, building toward the peak of climax. As Nia reached the apex and quivered in orgasm, Evan savored the intense experience. She pulsed hard around his finger and sobbed into his neck. His heart galloped. His mind filled with fantasies of how she would feel throbbing around him while he plunged himself into her deep and bareback. Taking her, owning her until he shot his seed deep into her core. Embedding himself so completely, it would grow life.

Dazed by his heightened arousal and insane thoughts, Evan ran his fingers through Nia's hair, urging her to lift her head. Their eyes met, and she released a deep breath, her lips stretching into a sensual smile. His heart bloomed, spreading radiating heat through his chest.

"Wow," she mumbled. "That was spectacular."

Her enthusiasm was infectious. He chuckled, his ego swelling to epic proportions.

"Come on, let's get you out of here before you start to get chilled."

He climbed out of the bath and grabbed a large, fluffy towel from the shelf nearby. Nia stepped out after him, and he dried her off thoroughly before wrapping the plush cotton around her body like a sarong. Taking down another, he wrapped it around his waist. They walked together into the bedroom. He laid her on her back in the bed, making sure she didn't show any signs of discomfort.

"Still good?" he asked, unwrapping her body.

She nodded. He tossed away his towel and reached for a condom in the side table.

"Let me," offered Nia, taking the packet from his hand.

She sat up, tore the foil with her teeth, and rolled it on him with slow, torturous strokes. Evan leaned down and kissed her with urgent depth. She was so responsive, taking the lead to stroke his tongue, then retreating as he sucked hers. Her fingers roamed his back, scoring his flesh with her nails. His need for her was overwhelming.

"Nia," he prayed, lowering her back to the bed and wrapping her legs around his back.

With one sure thrust, he was buried in her silky, tight depth. They both gasped. Evan felt so wildly primed, he struggled to catch his breath, hold back, take his time. *Slow and gentle,* he tried to remember. He pulled back to plunge deep again. He was panting now, it was so unbearably good. Everything about her was surrounding him. Her scent, her taste was imprinted on his soul.

"Sweetheart," he moaned.

"Yes," she answered.

He stroked. She matched his gait. Again and again, until the burn of orgasm shot down his spine, holding him in the vise of its tight grip with wave after wave of pure ecstasy. The blooming heat in his chest now radiated through his whole body. It spread hot and burning, permeating every cell, leaving him vulnerable to the force, yet powered by the intensity.

Afterward, Evan tucked a dozing Nia under the covers and went into the bathroom to clean up. His body was buzzing with nervous energy, his mind racing. He took a quick hot shower, then went back in the room to pull on ball shorts. Standing over the bed, he watched Nia sleep for a while. She looked peaceful and satisfied.

Frustrated with the tangle of thoughts in his head, Evan turned to go into his living room. He would have gone for a run, but he would not leave Nia alone. And it was too late to arrange a security watch, like he had for the brief time he'd been gone that afternoon. Instead, he took out his cell phone and went out on the back deck, just in case Nia woke up.

He called Lucas.

"Hey, do you have a minute?" he asked his friend.

"Yeah, what's up?"

"Nia finally talked. A little anyway."

"What did she say?" Lucas demanded.

"What we already suspected. That she might know who's behind the theft, but wants to be sure before she tells anyone."

"She told you about the heist?"

"No, only that there was something being investigated at work. She's worried about my opinion of Worthington as a new client."

"Hmm."

"What?" Evan demanded.

Both men were silent for a few moments. Evan knew he wasn't going to like what Lucas had to say. But that's why he had called.

"Look, I wasn't a big fan of this approach to begin with," his friend started. "I get the need for it in the world of spy games, but it feels wrong within the private sector."

Evan scratched at the scruff on his cheeks.

"Yeah, I have to agree. It hasn't really worked out the way I had planned, Luc," he was man enough to admit. "I was so used to seeing my real life as a cover overseas that I hadn't considered how complicated it could get here, at home. That my family and friends would need to be part of the façade. Shit! I'm even starting to forget what's real and what's not."

"When are you going to tell her who you really are?"

There it was. The million-dollar question.

"I don't know," he answered honestly.

"Ice, we're close to wrapping this thing up. The noose is tightening on the insider. You don't have much time, man," urged Lucas. "Walk away. End the relationship so she'll never know. You can finish the mission in the background."

"No!"

There was another awkward pause.

"Evan, I saw the way you looked at her, man. You either tell her yourself and explain so she understands. Or, forget it."

Damn it, he wished Lucas would keep his opinions to himself. Especially when they were right.

"I'll do it when we get back to Boston," Evan finally committed. "In the meantime, I need some research."

"On what? I'm still working the IP address trace from the wireless bug on Nia's laptop power cable."

Evan nodded, glad Tony had passed on the ask.

"Any luck yet?"

"I'm getting there. It's supposed to be untraceable, but there's always a crack somewhere," Lucas replied smugly. "What do you need?"

"Any information on a woman named Hailey

Stamford. She went to high school with Nia up to grade ten. I have a gut feeling that she has something to do with whatever happened that year, and the sealed juvenile record."

"Sure, I'll send you what I find."

Chapter 17

Evan and Nia stayed in Alexandria until Wednesday afternoon.

He took her to his parents' home in McLean on Sunday afternoon for the first time to see his dad's collection. As they drove up to the estate, Evan saw it though her eyes. It was a sprawling Georgian-style brick home on over three acres of land. They had moved there when he was a young child and he'd lived there until after college. Yet, with seven bedrooms and several entertainment spaces, it still seemed like more space than a family of three could ever need.

Inside, they were greeted by their longtime housekeeper, Agnes. She hugged Evan and shook Nia's hands warmly. With Evan's mom away in Brazil visiting his grandparents, the house was otherwise empty. They took a few minutes to eat the lunch that Agnes had thoughtfully prepared, then Evan gave Nia a tour of the house.

Most of the paintings on the walls were his mom's, though Evan pointed out the small number that he'd inherited as part of the collection, including the Etienne Blanc watercolor. In his dad's office at the back of the house, there were also a number of items left to him, including the antique humidor, various art pieces, and vintage military items.

The rest of the things were in storage on the lower level, over one hundred and twenty in total.

"What do you think?" Evan asked as they walked through the large space, peeling back the protective drop sheets along the way.

"It's fantastic," she gasped. "Your dad had incredible taste, Evan. There are some major pieces of contemporary art here. The sculptures are wonderful."

Evan looked around. It'd been years since he'd seen the collection and there were significantly more items amassed than he remembered. When he was home, his dad often talked about the newest thing he'd discovered, or an artist that had captured his attention. Santos DaCosta showed a passion for art and beautiful things that he rarely showed for anything else. While Evan didn't understand the fascination, he was intrigued by it. His mom, on the other hand, had always rolled her eyes at Dad's constant buying, calling him an eccentric hoarder. Evan now wondered if she was a little resentful of the attention he gave all these inanimate objects.

Now, watching Nia's professional reaction to his father's hobby, it felt good to know the old man had been onto something.

"How long do you think you'll need to document everything?" he asked, peeling back the blanket over another stack of framed paintings.

"Two more days, maybe? But I'll need to work all day on it."

"Do you need any help? I have someone who does handyman work around the house for my mom. He can help you with whatever you need."

She looked about to turn down the offer, so Evan continued the persuasion. It wasn't an option.

"I know you're feeling better, Nia. But there are a lot of big, heavy things here. Lance can help when you need him. Otherwise he'll be working on a couple of other projects in the house. Deal?"

"All right, you make a good point," she finally agreed.

"Good. I'll drop you here on Monday and Tuesday for the day. I'll have Agnes take care of your meals so you'll have nothing to distract you."

With the plan confirmed, Evan left Nia at the estate over the next two days. Though there was no sign that the threat to Nia had followed them out of Boston, he still felt better knowing that Lance Campbell, one of the Fortis agents, was there to protect her. He was a former U.S. Army Ranger, and one of the best men on the team at protective detail and close contact combat. No one would get close to this house on his watch.

Evan used the time to work on the mission at the Fortis headquarters just south of Alexandria. The fact that Nia had been bugged in her office without them being aware of it had set them back significantly. Knowledge of the safe's security code was now open to anyone who had enough access to Nia's office to plant the bugged power cord. The team shifted their focus from Nia's contact with Nigel St. Clair to re-examining everyone with access to the Worthington premises. It eliminated the security company that had installed their security system over a year ago, before Nia started with the company, but it still left a long list of potentials, including Matt Flannigan when he worked the day shift.

While Evan worked with a small team of analysts at the office to comb through the Worthington personnel data, Raymond, Michael, and Tony continued the search in Boston for any hint of the elusive broker known only as Walsh.

For those two evenings, he and Nia sat in the large gourmet kitchen at the house in McLean to eat the elaborate meals Agnes left for them. Then he took Nia back to his apartment where they walked along the water before heading inside to watch television or a movie. These were the few hours in the day when Evan was able to dial down his analytical vigilance enough to relax, just a little.

"That's ridiculous. *You're* ridiculous!" Nia insisted.

It was Tuesday evening, the last night in Virginia before they returned to Boston. They were relaxed on the couch in Evan's apartment debating what movie to watch. Nia wanted to see the latest superhero release while Evan suggested a comedy. Somehow they ended up in the heated debate about which alien hero would win a fight against the other.

"You don't know what you're talking about."

"Fine, then enlighten me. How could Thor possibly beat Superman in a fight?" Nia demanded. "With his little hammer, a little rain?"

"Easy. First, he's not an alien, he's a god. And, he's just as strong as Superman, stronger even."

"So you say."

"I do say and I'm right."

She rolled her eyes.

"And," continued Evan, "he can control the elements. God of thunder and all that."

"Well, none of that compares to the ability to fly, or X-ray vision."

"Like I said, you don't know what you're talking about," he insisted.

She was reclined against his chest with her legs stretched out on the length of the sofa.

"Since you're too stubborn to see reason, I'm not going to argue with you anymore. I, on the other hand, can be very accommodating. I agree to a comedy if I get to choose which one," suggested Nia.

She could feel his chest rumble with amusement, and smiled to herself.

"That's not very accommodating at all, Nia. Just manipulative."

"Oh, I'm manipulative, am I?" she shot back with mock indignation.

"Yes, and a little bossy I might add. After all, I've invited you into my home, fed you and entertained you. The least you could do is let me pick the movie."

"What?" she demanded, sitting up to face him. "Fed me? Entertained me?"

"Did I stutter?" he drawled in a lazy tone.

"Agnes did all the cooking!"

"Hey, I provided the food, didn't I? That's what a man does, baby."

He pulled her into his lap and took hold of her booty in his hands. She knew he was just randomly pushing her buttons, trying to get her riled up. It was working.

"Sure, and if it were up to you, we'd eat it raw."

"Hmm," mumbled Evan, clearly distracted by the sensuality of their new position. "Potato, *potahto.*"

He pulled her forward and bit the side of her neck, stroking it with his tongue. It was her turn to be distracted. She could barely remember the point of their silly banter.

"And I think I did all the entertaining," she added,

her eyes closed so she could focus on the sensations he was creating.

Evan pulled her hips closer to his until his burgeoning erection was nestled between her thighs.

"You got that right, sweetheart," he growled. "Forget the comedy. Let's make our own movie instead."

Suddenly, he changed their position so that she was sitting alone on the couch and he was standing in front of her.

"Don't move," he commanded, before striding out of the room.

Nia slipped her feet under her so she was kneeling. She was tingling with a mix of curiosity and anticipation, wondering what he was up to. He really was an unusual mix of intense seriousness and playful humor. Nia had sensed the intensity from their first meeting, and it was one of the things she had found attractive about him. He seemed solid, focused, dependable.

The playfulness was a surprise, and a side of him that was apparent more and more over the last few days. And now, sitting still on his plush leather sofa, in his high-rise condo, Nia acknowledged that she liked Evan DaCosta. A lot. And his big, hard body wasn't so bad either.

As though reading her mind, he returned to the room, now only wearing his jeans, naked from the waist up, with a thick, cozy blanket in his arms. He walked leisurely across the room, stopping only to turn on the gas fireplace. Every move caused his golden skin to ripple over thick, hard muscle. The well-fitted jeans were worn in and molded to the power of his thighs, leaving little to the imagination. When he reached her, he dropped the blanket on the ground and placed a couple of condoms on the coffee table. Nia swallowed.

"Now, where were we?" he asked with a cocky grin that created deep dimples.

She shrugged, feeling saucy and provocative.

"Hmm, something about creating our own movie? But you were gone so long that I can't remember."

His smile broadened.

"I guess I'll have to jog your memory."

Nia rose on her knees as she reached up and pulled the elastic out of her hair, allowing the thick length to fall to her shoulders with wavy abandon. His eyes brightened and she giggled on the inside.

"Yes, please. Remind me," she urged.

He unbuttoned the waist of his jeans and slowly lowered the zipper. The outline of his hard erection was clearly evident. Nia bit her bottom lip, anxious to see if he would continue stripping for her. Damn, it was an erotic thought.

"Don't stop now," she protested when he seemed to pause. "It was just coming back to me."

He flashed a big grin, looking boyish and proud. She cocked her eyebrow, as though to say she was waiting. He quickly finished the job, pushing down his pants then stepping out of them. Standing in just his black cotton athletic briefs, he looked like something out of her imagination. The perfect mix of bulk strength and masculine grace. It definitely was not the body of a wealthy, indulgent playboy. Then again, very little about Evan fit that mold.

Nia reached forward to trail her fingers over the square slabs of his chest down the deep valley between his abdominals.

"You forgot something," she murmured, toying with the edge of his underwear.

"We both have lead roles in this scene," Evan explained. "It's your turn."

She met his eyes, noting that intensity had replaced his playfulness.

"Like I said, I can be very accommodating, Evan."

Nia reached down and pulled off her T-shirt, leaving her only in a pink push-up bra.

"That's a good start, but you haven't quite caught up yet," he stated, his voice now a few tones deeper.

Held by the anticipation in his eyes, she stepped off the couch to stand in front of him. Then, mimicking his pace, stepped out of her jeans.

"My memory just came back. What kind of movie did you have I mind?" Nia repeated her playful path down his body until she reached the edge of his underwear again. "A sweet romance? Or . . . ?"

She circled her thumb over the wide head of his penis.

"Or?" he prompted in a tight voice.

"Of something a little more . . . blue?"

His hard flesh pulsed under her touch. *Yummy!*

"I'm as romantic as the next guy, but blue is my favorite color," whispered Evan.

Nia smiled slow and sexy. At that moment, this man, sexy and strong, wealthy and powerful, was completely under her control. Sure, his body would likely respond to any half-naked woman with her hand in his pants. But after the last two days, she knew it was more than that. Evan wanted *her.* In every situation, his body responded to her with very little provocation. And hers did the same. It was the first honest and real connection she'd ever felt with a man, simple and uncluttered by expectations. It was worth enjoying, regardless of what the future brought.

Still teasing his stiff, sensitive flesh, she leaned forward
to kiss his chest. He stroked a hand over the top of her
head, and delved his fingers into her hair. Nia brushed
her mouth over his nipple. It was hard and sensitive.
Evan groaned, gripping her thick locks tighter. She
spent some time savoring the feel of his pebbled skin
on her tongue, tasting and teasing him as he gasped
with each brush.

"Nia."

She smiled again to herself, looking forward to the
experience she had in store for him.

Slowly, Nia lowered to sit at the edge of the couch
then onto her knees. She looked up at Evan through
hooded eyes while brushing her hand along the length
of his erection.

"Jesus, Nia," he groaned.

Biting at her bottom lip, she pulled down his briefs
until they fell to the ground. And there he was, with his
granite hard body completely naked to her. She ran her
fingers over his legs, loving the power and strength they
revealed. Nia stopped at a knot of puckered scar tissue
on the left leg, just above the knee. It was obviously the
result of a major injury fairly recently, and she was eager
to ask about the details. Evan groaned as she gently
kissed the damaged spot.

Looking up at him again, she worked her hands up
his thighs to take hold of his solid erection. Evan
sucked in a deep breath, and his whole body stiffened.
He felt like polished stone wrapped in warm satin. God,
he was perfection. She wrapped both palms around the
thick thrust and stroked up and down.

"Sweetheart," he gasped, massaging her scalp.

Nia played with him for long moments, enjoying the
way his flesh pulsed under her hands and the string of

throaty gasps he uttered. Then she leaned forward and wrapped her mouth wide over the broad tip.

"Yeah! God, yeah," he muttered, his body tightening with mounting tension.

She lowered over him, sucking on his flesh until he was deep in her throat. He was big, stretching her mouth, filling her up. Her breast tingled and she pulsed in her panties. *Yummy!* She stroked him out slowly, sucking on his head repeatedly. His flesh seemed to get harder, longer.

"Nia, stop," he pleaded, even as he stroked into her mouth with small thrusts. "I won't last."

Massaging his base with both hands, she sucked him deep again, then started an undulating rhythm meant to drive him crazy.

"No, Nia . . ."

She peered up at him, loving the look of pained excitement on his face. His jaw was clenched tight and the muscles in his arms bulged at the effort to hold back.

"No," he mumbled again, attempting to pull back.

"Yes," Nia whispered, brushing her lips over his head, caressing it with her tongue, then licking the drop of dew that seeped from the tip.

"*Christ,* you're killing me," he moaned.

Her response was to suck him deep again, restarting her rhythm, now faster, gripping his girth tighter. She felt the moment he gave in to the need and lost himself in the sensations. With deep, throaty grunts, he matched her pace with measured thrusts. He stroked her hair and cheeks gently, lovingly. Nia became wrapped up in the moment, in tune and completely turned on by his building urgency. She dripped with her own arousal.

"Nia, baby," he gasped, slowing his movements. "So good . . ."

He was almost still in orgasm, only quivering as his hot cream shot into the back of her throat. Nia stroked his pulsing length, licking and sucking everything he gave her until he shuddered deeply.

With a low sigh, Evan reached down and pulled her into his arms, kissing her slow and deep. The next moment, she was sitting in his lap with her back to him.

"That was spectacular," he whispered, kissing along the side of her neck.

She giggled.

"I'm glad you enjoyed it."

He snorted.

"That doesn't even come close to describing how good it was, Nia. I think my eyes rolled into the back of my head."

She chuckled again, but it turned into a moan as he cupped her breasts over her bra with his large hands. Then he was undoing the clasp at her back and peeling it off her body.

"So incredible. You make me crazy," he mumbled, kneading and stroking her full mounds. "I can't get enough of you."

He thrust his lengthening erection against her bottom, showing her the words were meant literally. Nia was still hot, wet, and eager. She rotated her hips, anxious for his touch. Evan obliged, sliding one of his hands down her body and into her panties, thrusting deep into her well. Swollen and ready, she almost came on the spot. He cursed, gently biting her neck.

"Evan," she panted urgently, shivering at the edge of the abyss.

"Wait for me," he whispered, taking a moment to slide on protection.

"Yes," she panted as he brushed aside her panties and drove into her, deep and hard.

They both groaned loudly, way past the stage of controlled politeness. It was fast and frenzied, intensely erotic. Nia came first, her body racked with endless ripples of ecstasy. It was all-consuming, rocking her to the core, leaving her stripped bare of all barriers. Then, as she was gasping for air, Evan reached his own height, holding her tight as he rocked wildly into her depths. Their rough, ragged breathing echoed loudly in the room while the sweat cooled on their skin.

Eventually, they were sitting in front of the fireplace, on the thick blanket naked with Nia nestled between his legs, her back against his chest. She was lightly stroking his skin and eventually traced around the puckered spot just a couple of inches above his left knee.

"I've been meaning to ask you about this," she admitted in a soft voice. "Someone mentioned you'd been injured recently? At the charity event, I think?"

Evan remembered the conversation with Mikayla's mom, Elaine.

"Yeah, it was last September," he confirmed.

"What happened?"

"I was shot," Evan simply stated.

"What?" She turned a little to look up at him. "How?"

"Just at the wrong place at the wrong time, really."

"Where?"

Evan stuck to the official story since the mission in Azerbaijan was still classified.

"In Saudia Arabia. We were negotiating some work in the region. There was a small attack to a government building nearby, and I got hit in the cross fire."

"My God, Evan! You could have been killed!" she gasped, her eyes wide with disbelief.

"Maybe. But it was just one of those fluke things, really. I've been all over Europe and the Middle East, and I have never been in any danger before."

He was tempted to cross his fingers as he told the lie. For ten years in the CIA, danger had been the first line in his job description. He did everything from infiltrating the most dangerous and deadly criminal organizations to protecting VIPs under every imaginable kind of physical threat. All while the safety of lives, regions, and countries were dependent on his every decision and action.

"Well, thank God you're not in that role anymore, right? Now you're just a boring executive chained to a desk," she teased, relaxing back against him again.

"Interim boring executive," he corrected. She giggled.

Chapter 18

They flew back to Boston on Wednesday afternoon.

Evan looked over at Nia as they drove to her place from the airport. She looked tense and preoccupied.

"Everything okay?" he asked.

"I don't know," she stated, always honest. "It feels weird to be back. It was nice to be away from the office, just working on your collection."

"You're worried about the audit."

She sighed. They hadn't spoken about it again since she first opened up on Friday night.

"A little. But I thought about what you said. I have to tell what I know, even if no one believes me. I've been a scapegoat for other people before, and I refuse to allow it to happen again."

She spoke in a low tone, looking down at her hands. Something in her words tugged at his heart.

"What do you mean?" he asked.

"Nothing. It was a long time ago."

"Something that happened in Detroit?" he risked asking.

She gave him a sharp, guarded look but Evan kept his expression neutral, demonstrating only mild curiosity. Nia looked out the passenger window without responding.

"Is it something to do with your family? Why you're not close to them?" he continued softly.

"Yeah," she finally replied. "But it's not important."

He shrugged.

"You're going to tell the auditors what you know?" Evan asked, needing to confirm her intention.

"No, I don't think they'll be believe anything I say. But I'll tell my boss, Edward. He can decide what to do with the information."

"Good," he replied with encouragement. "I'm sure you'll feel better after."

They drove the rest of the way to her place in silence.

At her apartment, Evan waited until later in the evening while Nia was in the shower to call in to give the team an update. Raymond put him on speaker-phone.

"She's ready to talk," he said simply. "But only to Worthington."

"Makes sense, Ice," Raymond replied. "She sent him a text message while you guys were at the airport. Edward's flying in to meet with her tomorrow for lunch, at a restaurant a couple of blocks from the office."

"Good. She doesn't want to do it in the office," concluded Evan. "I'll stay with her here tonight, then I'll be back at the hotel after I drop her at work in the morning. Tony, I want you on site at Worthington before she arrives, then stuck to her all day. She's back in town and meeting her boss out of the office. If anyone in the office is watching her, they're going to be worried about this meeting."

With an initial plan in place, they disconnected the

call. For extra precaution, Evan left the voice and video surveillance running in her apartment. Then, he joined Nia in her bedroom. She still seemed pre-occupied and withdrawn, making it natural for them to simply fall asleep with Evan spooning her body against his.

Thursday morning, he dropped her off at the gallery as planned, then went back to the control center at the Harbor Hotel. Tony reported back from his spot in a surveillance car behind the gallery, while the rest of the team spent another morning still combing through information and systematically listening to the taps they'd acquired over the last week of voice surveillance.

"Maybe we're going about this all wrong," Michael finally said a few hours later.

Evan walked over to where the young agent was sitting behind a computer screen.

"What do you mean?"

"We're listening to find something incriminating, a clue, some evidence. But only someone who doesn't know they're being bugged would say anything of value, right? Nia was smart enough not to use her work phone, but it never occurred to her that her cell phone conversations would matter because she didn't consider that she might be bugged. Why would she?"

Evan nodded, slapping the agents back.

"We need to look at the person who's doing the least talking," added Evan, getting the meaning right away. "That's the person who's aware of the security cameras. And since he's added his own listening device, he'd never say anything of value in the building."

"I'll start looking at cell phone activity again over the last month or so," Raymond stated, jumping on the line of thinking. "Whoever's racking up the most minutes during work hours goes to the top of the list. Then we can cross-reference with all the variables."

"I'm going to join Tony for Nia's meeting with Worthington," Evan added. "Call me if you find anything."

The two agents got busy, moving in this new direction. Evan took out his cell phone to call Tony.

"Is she still on with Worthington for lunch?" Evan asked right away.

"Seems so. I confirmed with him when he landed in Boston a couple of hours ago. No change that I'm aware of," Tony confirmed.

"Okay, I'm heading back to you," advised Evan. "I want to be near after the meeting in case she gives up what we need to finish this out."

"Sure thing, Ice."

"And Tony, stay close and alert. Our target may already be aware of the meeting. This will be their last chance to shut it down. I'll be there for backup if needed."

"Got it."

Evan hung up, and went to his room to change into comfortable dark clothes and a baseball hat. He re-attached his back gun holster, checked his Glock, and secured it to his back. Then he added a slim, deadly knife to a sheath around his ankle. Fifteen minutes later, Evan was in his car back to the vicinity of the gallery, parked in an underground lot a block north. According to Edward, Nia was meeting him at twelve-thirty at a deli two blocks south of the office. It was ten minutes after twelve. To Evan's calculations, she would be getting ready to leave now, and should walk out of the building within the next five to ten minutes.

Evan crossed the street in front of the parking lot

and entered the north entrance of the alley that ran behind the gallery. He crept along the narrow pathway, passing the rear doors to the various businesses along the block, cautiously approaching the loading dock for Worthington. His plan was to wait there for Nia to pass. Then he would partner with Tony to provide hidden security as a backup to ensure she made it to and from the meeting without incident.

Evan knew that he could have sent either Michael or Raymond into the field. There was always the chance that if he needed to engage with a threat, his cover could be blown. But it was a risk he was prepared to take. The alternative was unpalatable. There was no way he would stay hidden in the hotel room while Nia was at risk on the street. He was the leader of the team, but also the best-trained operative they had. If anything was going to go down, it was his responsibility to lead from the front.

He was in front of the warehouse loading docks, hidden behind a dumpster, when something in the shadows right near the street caught his eye. Evan froze, watchful. It couldn't be Tony, who should be trailing Nia from the other direction. This was someone else, a professional doing a pretty good job of hiding. Evan thought of the gun at his back and the knife at his ankle, ready to use either if needed. And he waited silently, breathing deep, cool as ice.

Three minutes later, Nia entered his field of vision, heading to her destination by walking down the sidewalk and passing the entrance to the alley. Her determined gait and curvaceous figure draped in an ivory suit was easily recognizable. Evan had watched her get dressed in the outfit only a few hours earlier, and had fantasized about peeling it off later.

The shadow moved swiftly. Evan was faster. He was running toward the potential threat, intent on taking him down, but Tony got there first. The agent grabbed Nia around the waist to pull her out of reach, farther into the alley and out of sight from the street. He then swung around in a flash to kick the stranger square in the chest. Nia screamed in surprise, breaking out of Tony's hold and backing away from the scene. She bumped into the wall of the alley, then watched in shock as the man scrambled to his feet, knife drawn.

Evan flattened to the wall, staying hidden to maintain the element of surprise, but close enough to step in quickly if needed. Tony faced his opponent in a wide stance, positioned in front of Nia to provide her complete protection. Evan silently prayed that she didn't move or try to run. They had no way of knowing how many hit men had been sent or where else they were positioned.

The attacker lunged at Tony, aiming for the gut with a wide swipe of his knife. The agent easily evaded the attack, remaining in front of Nia. She seemed frozen, with her eyes wide, trying to comprehend what was happening. Evan stayed still, biding his time, looking for the opening that Tony would give if needed.

The two men danced around each other. The assailant attacked harder. Tony ducked, ramming his shoulder into the other man's chest, but taking a slash in the left arm as a result. Nia screamed, pressing herself against the wall. Evan waited, unwilling to give up the element of surprise until absolutely necessary. Tony managed to throw the assailant off with enough force to create space, then rammed a right fist across the side of his face. Blood sprayed. Another fierce jab in the nose and the attacker went down, knocked out.

"Oh my God!" Nia muttered, then covered her mouth. She looked around, clearly struggling to know what to do. Tony was still watching the assassin closely, ensuring the man didn't move, but he reached back with his hand open, trying to keep Nia calm. She recoiled from his touch with alarm.

"Nia. Nia, listen to me. I'm with Fortis," Evan heard him say. "I'm here for your protection."

"What? What do you mean? Who is that?"

She stepped away from Tony and started backing up, out of the alley and onto the sidewalk.

"Nia, you need to stay here," Tony instructed, turning his head to stop her from exposing herself to any other unknown danger.

Evan saw the assassin roll slightly to lift his torso, then the hint of a dark, long metal barrel. He didn't need to think. Instinct and training had him lunging forward into a low slide.

"Gun!" he yelled, knowing that Tony would immediately use his body to shield Nia as they were trained to do.

Within seconds, Evan had his legs wrapped around the guy's shoulders like a vise, trapping his arms so he was immobilized. But the guy was strong and determined. The weapon was still aimed at Nia, so Evan wrapped his forearms around the assailant's head. A quick twist, and there was a loud snap. The unknown assassin went limp. The gun fell out of his hand to skid on the ground.

Evan threw aside the body and stood up to find Tony and Nia staring at him. At first, there was only fear and shock on her face. Then her eyes changed. Recognition caused then to widen.

"Evan?" She took a step toward him, then stopped as

though sensing something wasn't right. "What are you doing here? What's going on? What did you do?"

She looked back and forth between the dead assassin and the man she was sleeping with. Evan felt the moment Nia realized he was more than a potential client and her lover. He knew he should say something to her. Anything to explain things, assure her that she was now safe.

But he just couldn't lie anymore. He couldn't look her in the face and rattle off some made-up story to explain how he just killed a man with his bare hands. Adrenaline was racing through his veins and he was on autopilot. She was an asset at risk and that needed to be secured. Evan turned away and took out his phone to call the team.

His silence to her said everything.

"We've had an attempted hit beside the gallery. I need the area locked down and a cleanup, now," he explained to Michael abruptly.

He then turned back to Tony, who was still covering Nia with his body. She was staring at the floor.

"Take her back to control with my car," Evan continued, tossing over the keys to the Bentley. "In the garage in front of the north end of the alley, level two, northwest corner. I'll wait here for the team and the police."

"You got it, Ice."

"And get that arm taken care of as soon as possible."

"It's nothing, just a scratch," Tony dismissed, taking a moment to inspect the injury, now dripping blood down his arm.

Nia raised her eyes at that point, looking at Evan as though she'd never seen him before. The disgust on her face was intense. But he turned away, squatting to start a search of her assailant. All that mattered now was that they get her safe and secured. That was the job.

"Nia, you need to come with me," urged Tony.

"I'm not going anywhere!" she yelled.

From the corner of his eye, Evan saw Tony try to take hold of her arm but she moved it out of his reach and backed away.

"Don't touch me."

Clenching his jaw with frustration and concern, Evan stood up and walked over to her. There wasn't time to be subtle.

"Nia, look at me." She stopped moving but refused to meet his eyes. "Someone just tried to kill you. Do you understand what I'm saying? We don't know if there are any others. You're not safe here. Tony will take care of you. Please."

Her shoulders straightened and she lifted her head with that arrogant, stubborn tilt he recognized.

"Who the hell are you?" she demanded, finally meeting his eyes again. He felt singed by their anger.

"You know who I am, Nia. Go with Tony, now. We can talk later."

"We have absolutely nothing to talk about," she whispered before stepping past him to follow Tony's lead back through the alley up to the next block.

Evan wished he could take the opportunity to tell Nia what she wanted to know, explain the situation. But time was essential and could not be wasted on selfish pursuits. A trained assassin just tried to kill her. There could very easily be more than one in the area. They needed to lock down the immediate area, and do a full sweep for any other threats. Until they knew differently, they had to assume that she was still in imminent danger, and millions of dollars in stolen jewels were finally in reach of the search. While the trail was still hot, every minute counted.

After the job was done, there would be plenty of time to explain this to Nia. And maybe, just maybe she'd understand.

Or so Evan told himself.

Chapter 19

Nia followed the man named Tony through the alley and into a big underground parking lot on the other side of the street. He moved quickly, staying in front of her, occasionally stopping if something looked concerning. Once they reached Evan's car, he drove out of the lot at a speed significantly above the limit. They went straight to the Boston Harbor Hotel. Tony drove past the main entrance and continued around to the back, stopping at the service bay.

There, another man was waiting. He opened Nia's passenger door to help her out. She immediately recognized him as one of the investigators.

"Hi, Ms. James, Michael Thorpe," he stated.

"Of course," she mumbled, still confused about what the hell was going on.

Michael tossed a package into the car. It looked like a small stack of bandages.

"Ice thought you might need them," he told Tony.

The car engine revved behind her, and she turned to watch as it sped away.

"Where's he going?"

"To help secure the scene," Michael explained. "Come, let's get you upstairs and cleaned up."

Nia looked down at herself, noticing the dark brownish-red smears and spots across the front of her cream suit. It took several moments to realize what it was. Blood.

"Nia." She looked at the tall, bulky man. He still seemed so young, no more than twenty-five. Something about him reminded her of the recruitment commercials for the U.S. Marine Corps.

"We need to get you inside," he explained, still polite but now more insistent.

"Okay."

They went through a series of hallways until they reached the service elevator, riding it up to an upper-level floor. They were safely inside Evan's hotel room a few moments later.

Nia looked around, thinking about the last time she was there. Two weeks ago? It was surreal. The space looked the same. Elegant and sophisticated old-world Boston luxury. Except now she saw it for what it was. A stage, a sham. Was anything real?

"The incident with the truck. It wasn't an accident, was it?" she asked softly.

Michael was getting her a bottle of water out of the fridge. He handed it to her.

"No, we don't believe it was."

Nia nodded, accepting the drink.

"Why don't you go and change out of those clothes?" he urged. "There's a robe in the bathroom. Then we can have a talk."

She started across the room, then suddenly remembered something.

"Edward. I was supposed to meet him for lunch."
God, everything was so crazy!

"We've already provided Mr. Worthington with an
update. He'll be here shortly as well. You can talk to
him then."

Nia nodded, then continued into the bathroom,
shutting the door and locking it. She stood with her
back against the door, just struggling to breathe. The
magnitude of what had just happened fell over her
like a dark, heavy cloak. The relevance of everything in
the last two weeks of her life was now completely in
question.

She didn't even know where to begin.

Was Evan DaCosta real? Who was he? Was that even
his name?

The pain that ripped through her was so sharp that
she bent over.

No. She couldn't deal with that now. Not here in the
hotel room, with Fortis agents just outside the door.
There was no way that any of them were going to see
her break.

Nia took a deep breath in, and straightened her
back, blinking back the tears that were pooled in
her eyes. There were other things more important
than *him*. Life-and-death things. Her job. Catching a
multimillion-dollar jewel thief who just tried to kill her.
Those were the things she needed to focus on.

She turned to look at herself in the large mirror
above the marble-topped vanity, placing her purse on
top. The smears of blood looked gruesome against the
creamy fabric. She couldn't help wonder if it came
from Tony or her attacker. Or both. Either way, the suit
was ruined, joining the one she had been wearing
during the attempted hit and run.

Never mind her retirement fund, she thought. The summer auction better work out the way everyone hoped, because she now needed the bonus money just to replenish her wardrobe. Nia laughed drily, shaking her head. At least, she still had her sense of humor. Or maybe she was just in shock.

With a final look at herself, she kicked off her heels, peeled off her clothes, and washed her face with the boutique soap on the counter. Under the current circumstances, the dramatic liquid eyeliner and bold red lipstick seemed ridiculous. She then pulled on one of the large, silver-gray robes hanging on the back of the door. It was way too big for her frame, but thick, luxurious, and warm.

Nia picked up her things and placed them neatly on the counter before she went back out into the living area, with her purse. The suite was empty, but there was a rolling table near the dining room laden with several plates. It then occurred to her that it was still Thursday afternoon and someone had ordered lunch. Such an ordinary thing yet it seemed completely out of place in light of what was going on.

Uncertain of what was to happen next, Nia put her bag on the table and took out her phone. She needed to let the team know that she wasn't going to be back. There were meetings to be cancelled, a long list of tasks they would need to manage. And how long was she expected to stay away, sequestered in this gilded jail? How was she going to get home wearing just a robe? A million thoughts raced through her brain as she starting dialing the main number for Worthington.

"Nia," Michael stated as he came back in the room from a connected door. "Please don't make any phone calls yet."

She paused.

"Why? I have to tell the office that I'm delayed. I have meetings booked in my schedule," she explained.

"It's been taken care of," he stated, stopping in front of her.

"How's it taken care of, exactly?" demanded Nia, now fed up with the cloak-and-dagger dance. "Look, Michael. I understand you have a job to do, but I need to know exactly what's going on. Why am I here and what do you want from me?"

"Mr. Worthington is on his way up to the room now, Nia. We just want to talk to you about whatever it is you know about the robbery," he explained patiently.

"Fine. Then what? Am I being forced to stay here or will I be able to go home?"

"You won't be forced to do anything, Nia."

The statement came from the front door of the hotel room, from the man she used to know as Evan DaCosta. He was followed by the two other men she now knew worked with him, then Edward Worthington.

Her boss rushed forward, taking her by the shoulders. His face was filled with concern and relief.

"God, Nia. I was so worried about you. Are you all right?" he asked, taking in the robe and bare feet.

"I'm fine. My clothes got ruined during the . . . the incident," she assured him, struggling to find the right words.

"Oh, thank goodness!" the older man exclaimed.

He looked even more tired and stressed than the last time they met. Nia suddenly felt compassion for all that he had been through, and only hoped she did know something that could help.

"Nia, why don't you have a seat so we can get started."

It was *Evan* again, sounding polite and in control.

The other men moved around the room until she felt surrounded by warriors.

"I'd rather stand, thank you," she retorted, refusing to look at him.

"As you wish," he conceded, walking forward. "Then let's get to the point. You had arranged to meet with Mr. Worthington to give him some information about the theft from the gallery. Can you tell us what that is?"

His words were polite, respectful, even cajoling, but his tone was hard as ice. Had he always sounded so cold?

"Sure I can. Once you've given me some information about what just happened."

"Nia," Edward started.

"No, Edward. Someone just tried to kill me. And it wasn't the first time. So, while I recognize they've been hired to recover the jewelry, and I'll do whatever I can to help, I would also like to stay alive."

Her boss closed his mouth and nodded. He then looked over to *Evan* expectantly.

"Mr. DaCosta, Nia's right. Her safety should be the first concern."

"I can assure you that Nia's protection is our top priority, Mr. Worthington. Unfortunately, until we identify exactly who's been involved in the theft, she remains at risk. Which is why it's essential that we find out what she knows as soon as possible," he clarified. "What I can tell you is that the attacker appears to have acted alone. He's a professional but only civilian-trained. We are now in the process of confirming his identity in order to figure out who hired him."

Nia bit the side of her cheek. This was all her fault. If she had just told Edward or the investigators what she suspected from the beginning, maybe they wouldn't be here now.

"All right, then. Where do you want me to start?" she inquired, still refusing to look at him.

"Wherever you think is important," Michael stated, stepping forward to stand near her side. "You had told Raymond and me that you didn't know if anyone at Worthington could be involved. But that appears to have changed?"

She nodded.

"Yes, but I didn't have any proof. I still don't. It's just a theory, really."

"Based on the reaction you've gotten, I would say you're pretty damn close," Tony inserted, the knife wound on his arm now wrapped with a white bandage.

"Yeah, I guess," Nia acknowledged, suddenly physically and mentally exhausted. She lowered herself into one of the dining chairs.

"Tell us your theory, Nia," Michael urged, sitting down beside her.

"Well, it was obvious someone from the company was involved, right? I really had no clue who it could be until my stepbrother gave me some more information."

"Your stepbrother?" urged Michael.

"Yeah. I asked him to see if there was any word on the street about the heist," she admitted, recognizing how shady it sounded. "He knows people who know people."

"St. Clair."

The statement came from *him,* now standing near the windows with his back to them.

"Yes." Of course they would know about Nigel. They probably knew everything there was to know about her.

"What was the information?" continued Michael.

"That Matt Finnegan was connected in the company. That's how they stole the diamonds."

Michael looked up at the other men on their team. She could tell that the information was significant.

"When was that?" he asked. "When you spoke to him last Tuesday?"

"Yes," she confirmed. "But how did you know that?"

She looked around the room. All the men were suddenly looking elsewhere, except for *him*. Nia met his eyes, and a fresh wave of hot anger coursed through her veins.

"You've been listening to my calls, tracking me?" she accused.

"Nia," intervened Edward. "They've had surveillance on the whole office with my permission. It was necessary."

"Unfortunately, we weren't the ones listening to you at that time, Nia," Michael added. "Your office had a bug."

"Oh my God! Of course!" she exclaimed, covering her face. "That's how they knew everything, Edward! We had talked about changing the safe combination right there at my desk."

"I'm afraid so," her boss agreed.

"Who do you think was working with Flannigan, Nia?" Michael asked, bringing them back to the main objective.

"I think it's Chris Morton," she whispered. "He was friends with Matt, and he knew we were collecting the items for the summer auction. It was only a matter of time until they were in the safe."

They looked back at her, clearly underwhelmed by her information.

"You already knew all that," she finally added.

"We did," Michael confirmed. "Is there anything else you learned about Morton from St. Clair?"

"No. Nigel didn't know who it was. I figured out myself after I talked to Chris after Memorial Day."

"Last Tuesday?" Evan prompted, but Nia ignored him.

"What did you talk to him about?" Michael asked.

"About Matt and his murder," she explained to the young agent. "We talked about how to get in contact with Matt's girlfriend to send flowers or something. Then, later, I went into the warehouse and he was standing outside the back door, talking on his cell phone. He said: 'Matt's girlfriend must have it, but don't worry. I'll find her. I'll get the stuff back. I just need a little more time.'"

Michael and Evan exchanged looks.

"Did Morton know you overheard him?" Michael asked.

"I don't think so. I left before he came back inside."

"Did he say what he'd get back?" continued Michael. "Anything else?"

"No. I didn't stay to hear anything else," she confessed. "It's weak, I know. Which is why I didn't say anything. I knew I was high on the suspect list, and it felt like throwing accusations around would only make me look guiltier. And I didn't know who I could trust."

The last statement was directed at Edward.

"Nia, I knew from the beginning that you didn't have anything to do with it," her boss assured her.

"Ice," stated the agent named Raymond as he walked over to *him*. "Lucas and Sam will be available for a debrief in five."

Nia looked over at the man she'd slept with for over almost two weeks. *Ice*. That's also what Tony had called him during the attack. Seeing him now, standing with his legs spread wide and arms folded across his powerful chest. Unapologetic and unyielding. The name was fitting.

Now with Raymond's announcement, even more made sense. Lucas and Sam. He said they ran a security company together. Then she'd spent a couple of hours with them over dinner, thinking she was meeting the close friends of the man she was seeing. They had known the whole time that she was nothing more than a job to him. Just another string in a loose knit of deceptions and half-truths.

She looked away, feeling nauseous.

"Okay, let's get on it, team. We have a limited amount of time before our culprit realizes the attack on Nia was unsuccessful," stated *Ice*.

The other agents started moving toward the door to the connected suite.

"Wait, what happens now?" Nia demanded, standing up.

Michael turned back to her.

"Now we close in. Something that you've uncovered is the missing link so we just need to connect the dots," he told her.

"What about me? Should I be doing something?" she asked, looking back and forth between her boss and the young agent.

"All you need to do is stay here and relax. Have something to eat," Michael advised. "Mr. Worthington has told the office that you've been called away for an urgent client negotiation. So you cannot contact anyone there for any reason."

She nodded with acceptance.

"Can I call anyone else? I had plans to meet my

friend Lianne after work. I need to let her know I won't be able to make it."

Michael looked over at Ice, who was still in the room. The other man nodded.

"Okay, only her. We might need someone to get some clothes and things from your apartment. Could she do that?" asked Michael.

"Yes. She has my spare key."

"Good. Then have her pack a bag for you with enough stuff for a few days and bring it here. One of us will meet her in the lobby."

"Can I tell her what's going on?" she questioned. "I don't know how else to explain being stuck in a hotel room, watched by a security team under lock and key. I promise she won't say anything to anyone else. Lianne is a professional therapist. She knows how to keep a secret."

Michael looked at Ice again for approval and got the brief nod.

Nia let out a sigh of relief and turned away from the men.

"Mr. Worthington, if you have a moment, you can join our debriefing meeting for an overview of what we have planned next," stated Ice, then he and Michael joined the others in the next room.

"Are you okay?"

She turned back to her boss, the only other person still in the room.

"I don't know, to be honest. This is all too much," Nia admitted.

"Do you need anything?" he asked, clearly and genuinely concerned.

"No. I just want this whole thing over and resolved," she mumbled. "Do you think we'll still be able to get the pieces back whole?"

"Fortis seems to think so. So we'll just have to keep our fingers crossed. If not, we'll have to cross that bridge when we get there."

She nodded looking down at her bare feet. But something else was also bothering her and she could not hold back the question.

"Edward, did you know about Evan DaCosta's role in all this?"

"What do you mean? I just met him today as the lead partner," he replied. "Most of my conversations have been with one of the other partners in Virginia, Lucas Johnson. Why?"

"Nothing," she dismissed with a wave of her hand. There would be plenty of time to explain everything later.

Then it occurred to her that the DaCosta account might also be sham, a contract not worth the paper it was typed on. Nia covered her mouth as she thought back to the first moment she met Evan DaCosta, and every tender and intimate moment they had shared since, until the magnitude of his deception almost choked her.

Thankfully, Edward departed within a few minutes, leaving her alone to call her best friend and explain what had become of her life.

Chapter 20

Chris Morton had disappeared. By two-thirty that afternoon, their surveillance of the Worthington gallery and office showed he had left the premises with no word of where he was going and had not been seen since.

Raymond's analysis of cell phone usage provided another link. Morton's work phone had almost no personal calls, while his cell activity during the day was higher than normal, and mostly to one number. It was another cell phone with no contact information attached. A disposable cell phone.

Fortis finally had their inside man for the heist. To recover the jewels, they only had to tie all the other evidence back to Chris Morton.

The first thing to consider was Matt Flannigan's girlfriend, Jennifer Coombs. Morton's phone records also revealed several attempts to reach Coombs in the week after Matt's murder. It aligned with the conversation Nia had overheard, and it prompted Evan to send Tony to stake her out, while Raymond pulled everything they could find on her actions since her boyfriend was killed. While the team agreed it was unlikely that

Flannigan would have left the money or the jewels behind when he was skipping town, they still needed to know what Morton was trying to get back. It was too loose a thread not to tie off.

The second thing still missing was the money trail. While Morton's local bank account was overdrawn, Raymond couldn't find any suspicious transactions, or any sign of an off-shore account. That suggested he either still had possession of the goods, or he had been paid in cash.

As for the dead assailant, a federal database search of his fingerprints showed he was a hired gun, known to operate locally, and loosely associated with organized crime activities. The cell phone found on his body only led to other untraceable phones, with no connection back to Morton.

"I think we still need to use our carrot," Michael stated.

It was late on Thursday, and the team was finally able to regroup. Evan had asked Carlos, the hotel concierge, to order in the best pizza in town, and they were now devouring four boxes of deep dish, cheese- and meat-laden pies in the control room.

"Our plan from last week? With Nia?" Evan asked between chews.

"Yeah. We need to root out the broker," the young agent continued. "We know he operates out of hotels, according to Spencer. So let's go hire him."

"Shit!" muttered Raymond. "Carlos."

The other two looked at him.

"If you want something at a hotel, something you can't find yourself, who do you call?" he prompted.

"The concierge," Evan stated, wiping sloppy tomato sauce off his fingers with a napkin. "Makes sense."

"What are we going to ask for?" Michael asked. "It has to be something expensive, worth the effort. Illegal, but not something that will make anyone skittish, right? What were you going to plant with Nia last week, Ice?"

"Rare Cuban cigars," replied Evan, realizing how much had changed in just a few days. "I told her that there was an antique humidor in my dad's collection that I wanted to keep. I was going to stock it with Cohiba Esplendidos."

"Nice. Black market, but innocent," Michael added with an approving grin.

"Yeah, but it won't get much attention if we're going after Walsh directly," Evan advised.

"And we should stay away from jewelry or art. Anything that could be easily associated with the auction world," recommended Raymond.

"Scotch," Evan stated suddenly. "George Clement is obsessed with it. At the event at the Vineyard, he talked about the most expensive bottles worth over one hundred thousand dollars."

"You're shitting me!" Michael exclaimed.

"I shit you not, my friend," Evan shot back with a quick smile.

"A hundred g's for a few glasses of whiskey?"

Raymond was back at the computer, his now clean hands flying across the keys.

"How about one worth over ten thousand dollars," he suggested to the team, looking at the info pulled up on the screen. "There are a few bottles of a rare fifty-five-year-old Macallan in the city. Sounds like the kind of gig that our Walsh would be into."

"We'll ask for one at a discount, like half price. If they take the order, we'll know Walsh and whoever he works with will steal it."

"And if they actually deliver the bottle, we have them for possession of stolen goods, and enough to squeeze out some intel on Walsh, then from Walsh on the buyer."

The men looked at each other, letting the idea marinate, searching for holes.

"Boys, it looks like we have a plan. We'll start with our friend Carlos downstairs. Then we'll fan out from there. There's probably twenty luxury hotels in downtown Boston."

"Thirty-two to be exact," Raymond threw in with a grin. "I'll start making room reservations."

The team continued to fine-tune the strategy while finishing the pizza.

Evan should have been elated. After only sixteen days, he was on the verge of wrapping up his first mission with Fortis. After eight months of recovery and change, he finally felt back in his comfort zone, doing what he was good at. The leadership and orchestration of a complicated investigation felt familiar, and there was the eager anticipation of the safe and secure recovery of the assets. That day should have been a good one.

It wasn't. It was hell.

He was focused, composed, and committed to getting the job done. But only because he had to be. The alternative was not an option. If he stopped to think about the woman in the other room, vulnerable and betrayed, he wouldn't be able to leave her side regardless of how angry she was at him. So, he stayed at the helm of his operation, holding on to the sense that his actions had been worth it. The ends had justified the means, and with enough time and discussion, once the whole thing was over, Nia would eventually accept that.

Lianne Bloom arrived at the hotel before six o'clock that evening with a bag packed from Nia's apartment.

Though the sound was turned off, the security feed from the living area of his hotel suite was still connected, displayed on one of the computer screens in the control room. Evan tried not to be distracted, but caught the occasional glimpse of the two women as they moved around the space.

Nia had changed into yoga pants and a T-shirt soon after her friend arrived. Then they had sat in the living room talking. From her gestures and agitated movements, Evan was fairly certain he was the topic of some of the conversation, and not in a good way.

It was almost midnight when the local Fortis team packed it in for the day, leaving Raymond to monitor the progress of the investigation through the night. Evan went back into his suite where Nia was now alone. Lianne had left a couple of hours earlier. He knew she was in the bedroom, and tapped on the door. There was no answer, but the light was definitely on. He tried the door handle. It was locked.

"Nia," he called softly, knocking again.

"Go away, Evan."

"Open the door, Nia. I want to give you an update on the investigation."

He heard movement, then the door opened barely more than a crack.

"Fine. But in the future, I'd appreciate if you would send Michael or someone else," she demanded in a cool voice.

"Look, I know you're upset—"

"Upset? Upset doesn't even begin to describe how I feel, *Ice.*"

He clenched his teeth at the name.

"I get it. You have every right to be angry, but let's just talk—"

"Are you serious right now? You want to talk? I don't even know who you are, so unless you're going to tell me what's happened with Chris and the situation at Worthington, we have nothing to discuss."

Evan took a deep breath. After the day she'd had, he expected this reaction. He'd be patient with her, give her time and she'd come around.

"Okay. Open the door and I'll tell you what we know."

"No, you can tell me from right where you are."

His patience slipped. He felt the need to see her, be close to her, reconnect even through her anger. How was he going to fix things if she refused to even be in the same room with him?

"I'm not talking to you like this, so either you let me in now or you can wait until tomorrow to find out where we are."

It took a few seconds, but the door swung open and she walked to the other side of the room next to the window. It was a small victory but he took it, following her inside.

"I'm waiting," she snapped, arms folded across her chest.

Evan clenched his teeth at her tone, but spent a few minutes telling her the latest information about Morton's disappearance. They would find him, and it wouldn't be long before the whole thing was wrapped up.

"Do you know where Chris is?" she asked quietly.

"No, not yet. Which is why we need you to stay here for the time being. We have to assume that Morton was behind the attempt today and the hit and run last week. Which means he's dangerous and capable of anything."

Nia nodded with understanding. Silence filled the space for several moments. Evan used the opportunity to drink in her presence. She had changed into an oversized cotton nightshirt that fell to her midthigh. It felt like forever since he had held her, kissed her, seen her laugh, yet it was only that morning. The idea that he might never do so again was now unimaginable.

"Nia, let me explain this whole thing," he finally implored.

"I'm not an idiot, *Ice*. I kind of put the whole thing together myself. I've had hours to work it out. So please save both of us the trouble," she countered. "You had a job to do, and you accomplished your goal."

"It wasn't like that," he protested, stepping forward.

"It was exactly like that and you know it."

"Nia."

She cut him off with the slice of her hand through the air.

"I'm curious; how did you think this conversation was going to go? I mean, you must have known it would come to this eventually," she reasoned, sounding detached and analytical. "Or maybe not. Maybe, the plan was to just end things once you got what you needed from me. Say thanks for the good times and just move on."

Evan hung his head, ashamed that she was able to sum up one of the exit strategies so succinctly.

"I was going to tell you," he claimed.

"What?" She laughed, a dry humorless rumble. "Why? What could you have possibly hoped to achieve, *Ice*?"

"My name is Evan. Evan DaCosta," he finally snapped.

"Thanks for the confirmation. Good to know."

She turned away, shaking her head sarcastically.

"I wanted you to understand why things started the

way they did between us," he finally explained. "But it doesn't change anything else, Nia. Not really."

She turned back to him, the look on her face incredulous.

"You can't be serious," Nia whispered. "It changes everything."

Evan closed the gap between them, ignoring her look of alarm as he stepped in front of her. He wanted so badly to touch her, remove this invisible barrier between them.

"No it doesn't," he insisted.

"Damn it! You slept with me to find out if I'm a thief!" she yelled, poking him in his chest.

"That's not what happened and you know it, Nia!"

"That's exactly what it was. So own it, *Evan*. Pat yourself on the back for a job well done. Mission accomplished. But don't patronize me by watering it down," she jeered.

"You have no clue what you're talking about. There were plenty of ways to get information out of you without sex, Nia. And I'm very good at all of them," Evan shot back.

"Great, so it was just a perk? Something to keep you entertained on the job?"

"Stop it," he demanded, gripping her shoulders and giving her a small shake.

"Let go of me!" she screamed, pulling back.

Evan released her immediately and turned away. His heart was racing as he struggled to get it together. His throat tightened up from the growing lump squeezing against his windpipe.

"I screwed up," he whispered. "I wanted you. Yes, I had a job to do. I needed to get close, find out if you were involved. But the minute I saw you, I wanted you. It was never part of the plan, Nia."

The seconds ticked away as he waited for her to say something. Anything.

"So you took what you wanted, regardless of the lies you had to tell me."

"What lies? Yes, I withheld some details related to the case, but everything else was true. Everything important was real," he emphasized, turning back to face her.

"Really? Like taking over your dad's company?" she snapped back with disbelief.

"True. It's temporary until I confirm a new CEO, then I'll take a place on the board," he explained.

"Your contract with me to sell the collection you inherited."

"Absolutely."

"And your job overseas? You want me to believe that while selling defense contracts, you also learned how to kill a professional hit man by snapping his neck?"

That one was complicated.

"That's what my résumé says and what my mother knows. Anything different doesn't exist."

"Wow, no secrets there," Nia retorted, throwing her hands up.

"Christ, Nia!" he cursed, bowing his head with frustration.

"Don't try to manipulate me, Evan," she shot back, refusing to bend even a little. "Nothing important was real. It was all built on a stack of deceit."

"No," he countered. "For the first time in my life, it was all real. Don't you see, the job was a lie, but you and I were true."

She closed her eyes as though blocking him out. He was starting to see that he wasn't getting through to her.

What if he couldn't? What if whatever they had shared was damaged for good? Evan tried to swallow, but he couldn't. The lump was too big.

"What do you want from me?" she whispered, sounding tired.

He wanted to go back to that morning, when he woke up with her tucked warm against his body. He wanted to walk along the river each night in Virginia. He wanted her to feel about him the way he felt about her. Evan wanted more than just a mission, but it was too much to ask right now.

"You," he stated simply. "I want you."

Nia raised her head and met his eyes. Hers were dark with anger, glittering bright. They pulled him to her, making him desperate to remove the pain and hurt from their depths. Hungry to recapture their physical connection, he brushed the back of his finger over the curve of her cheek. Electricity shot down his spine, warm and familiar. It was too soon, too much to want, but he bent his head to taste her lips.

After all the day's events, the tenuous hold he had maintained on his control snapped. Intense need took over his body. Her life had been threatened and Evan had killed a man to protect her. And for the first time since he had met Nia James, she was looking at the real man, not the cover so carefully crafted. The look in her eyes clearly said she didn't like what she saw. Evan couldn't accept that. Not when he was finally ready to acknowledge that his feelings for her went deeper than he ever imagined. Too deep for him to just walk away.

This kiss should have been gently persuasive, an attempt to rekindle things between them. But as always, his need for her clouded his judgment and destroyed his resolve. He delved into the sweetness of her mouth, greedy to taste her wetness. God, she was delicious. Everything about her touched him, even her passionate anger.

"No. Evan, I can't," she whispered, pulling away from his lips.

But her hands gripped his arms as though she needed his strength. He slid his mouth down her neck, nipping at the pulsing vein along its length. Nia shivered, gasped. It drove him crazy. Hot, white need sizzled into his groin. He bit her neck harder relishing her groan.

The hold she had over him was frightening, uncontrollable, addictive. He now craved her like a drug, and was willing to do anything to have her. Evan hardly remembered his existence before this feeling. He struggled to contemplate life without it, without her.

Something in the back of his mind said he was pushing her. Despite the way her back curved, and her breathing hitched just so, she wasn't ready for this. He should back away, give her time to process everything. But she felt too good and he was a selfish bastard. If this physical connection was the only way to reach her, reinforce how incredible they were together, then he'd be a fool to give it up.

Evan placed his mouth over hers again, his tongue stroking hers suggestively. Nia raked her fingers across the width of his back. He reached down, pulling up the nightshirt. Then, he slid his hands under the fabric of her underwear to cup her naked bottom. His jutting erection now pulsed between them. She swirled her hips in his grasp, teasing the base of his shaft. He was so hungry for her that his knees went weak. The last thin strings of his control dissolved with blind, urgent desire.

Evan backed up a few steps, taking her with him until

the back of his legs met the bed frame and he could sit at the edge. With little effort, he pulled her up on top of him so her knees straddled his hips. His mouth never left hers, still tasting, stroking and thrusting into the recesses with his tongue. She was now fully engaged in the moment with him, mimicking his movements with teasing play. Driving him crazy, stripping away his ability to think beyond the need to be in her and consumed by her heat.

Evan fumbled with the button at his waist, shoving down his zipper. The metallic scrape was lost in the music of their impassioned cries. Released and insistent, the rigid length of his cock brushed along the damp silk of her panties, probing against the thin barrier. Nia moaned into his mouth, sucking on his tongue. He took hold of the thin strip of elastic at her hip, easily tearing the panties from her body.

Driven by pure animal craving, Evan thrust deep into her slippery sheath, burying himself to the hilt. A deep, guttural moan escaped his throat. It was magic. Pure, pristine heaven like he'd never experienced before. She gasped, running her fingers along the back of his head. He stroked into her again and she met his thrust with an enticing flex of her hips. The world dimmed around him.

"Nia," he growled.

"Yes," she begged.

Their rhythm increased, perfectly in sync, faster, harder. It was too good, better than anything before. Perfect. Complete. It was everything life was supposed to be.

Evan wanted to tell her all the feelings racing through his heart, confess the depths of commitment, give her his soul. But he couldn't find the words to convey the truth. Instead, he could only chant her name over and over again, communicating to her through the power of his body.

"Come with me," he whispered as the gripping climax surged through his body. She peaked seconds later, gripping his length in her silken depths until Evan was weak from the intensity.

They both came down slowly, falling into their familiar pattern of tender touches and lazy sighs. It all seemed so right. Until Evan pulled Nia close and he felt himself slip away from the caress of her body. He felt naked, bare. Unprotected.

Evan looked up at Nia, ready to tell her his lapse. Her face said she had already realized what he had done.

He kissed her gently, pressed his forehead to hers.

"Christ, Nia. I didn't mean for that to happen," he whispered urgently. "It shouldn't have happened like that, and it's never happened before. I should have worn a condom, but I was just so caught up in the moment."

Nia shook her head from side to side.

"Stop, Evan. Just stop."

She pulled away slipping out of his arms and off the bed.

"You should go," she demanded, turning to walk to the attached bathroom.

"Nia wait, please," he pleaded, jumping off the bed to follow her.

"Just leave," she demanded as she swung back to face him, meeting his eyes dead on. "You can't have me, Evan. And this is the closest you'll ever get."

He took her arm, gently trying to pull her back toward him, but Nia twisted out of his grip. Stubborn denial screamed in his head, pushing him to lay everything on the line.

"Baby, no. I've fallen in love with you, Nia." She froze, staring back at him with wide eyes, and Evan was desperate enough to believe she was hearing him. "Please, just give me a chance."

She slapped him, hard, straight across the face. Her expression was one of disgust and disbelief before she walked into the bathroom and slammed the door shut.

Chapter 21

Evan managed to stay away from her all day Friday. He slept on the couch in the hotel suite, and transferred his clothes and toiletries to the other hotel room.

The team put their plan in action, starting with Evan visiting the concierge at the Boston Harbor Hotel.

"Good morning, Mr. DaCosta. What can I help you with?" asked Carlos as Evan strolled up to his desk in the lobby.

"Hi, Carlos. Thanks again for the pizza last night. My friends were singing your praises for the rest of the evening."

"My pleasure, my pleasure," replied the older man with a pleased smile.

"Listen, maybe you can help me with something else," Evan added, stepping closer and lowering his voice.

"Anything."

"I need to get a gift for a very eccentric business associate. I'm hoping to get my hands on something rare and impressive."

"Okay, okay," Carlos replied with enthusiasm. "What were you thinking?"

"He has a weakness for scotch whiskey. But only the best will do. Something he can't get himself, if you know what I mean."

"Sure, of course. I have a contact who runs an exclusive liquor store in Cambridge. Perhaps he will know where you can buy a bottle. I'll give him a call."

"No, Carlos. I'm looking for something more . . . rare." Evan whispered the last word right next to the man's ear. "A specific bottle that can't be bought in a store. There would be a fee, of course."

Carlos stepped back, his smile a little less bright.

"Ahh, I understand you now, Mr. DaCosta," he replied with a few nods. "Unfortunately, I don't think I can be of assistance in that endeavor. But I'm happy to call my friend for you. Perhaps there is something else that would be suitable."

"Come on, Carlos. You're a well-connected man. I'm sure you can send me in the right direction," Evan cajoled with an easy smile. He pulled a couple of folded hundred-dollar bills out of the inside pocket of his jacket. "I have my heart set on making a good impression with this particular associate."

"Well, perhaps you can try the concierge at the Four Seasons Hotel or the Ritz-Carlton. Their contacts may be more, appropriate, than mine," Carlos finally stated in a low tone. The bills were now resting comfortably in his pants pocket.

"Thank you, Carlos. You're a good man," Evan told him with a pat on the shoulder.

"Glad I could be of assistance, Mr. DaCosta. Will you need your car this morning?"

"I do, indeed."

Evan walked casually across the lobby, then called Raymond while standing outside waiting for the leased Bentley to arrive.

"Did you get all that?" he asked.

"Yup, we have you booked in rooms at both hotels, for three-day stays," Raymond confirmed. "The Ritz is the closest. Michael's headed there now to scope out the place."

"Good, tell him I'll be there in five minutes."

By midafternoon, Evan and Michael had visited six hotels in downtown Boston before they found Craig Kelsey, a young and eager concierge at the Opal Hotel who seemed connected to the right people, and willing to procure a rare bottle of scotch for half the retail price. Kelsey promised to let Evan know within twenty-four hours if the deal was possible, by leaving a voice-mail message in his hotel room. Evan then set up a redirect so any calls would go to his cell-phone voice-mail. Now they just had to wait.

Back at the Fortis control center, the team continued the efforts to track down Chris Morton, including keeping a close eye on the surveillance from Worthington, and Emma Sterling in particular. Edward Worthington had told all the employees that Morton would be out of the office for a few days. If Sterling were involved in any way, she had to be getting nervous.

From the surveillance feed into the living room of the adjoining hotel suite at the Harbor, Evan also kept an eye on Nia. She dressed in slacks and a cardigan then drank two cups of coffee while watching morning television. Through Michael, Evan gave her the green light to go back to work, only letting the rest of the office know she would work remotely for a few days. Sometime midmorning, Tony brought her laptop from the office, with a new, clean power cord. She worked at the dining table for several hours.

As she had requested, Michael provided an update on the investigation later in the afternoon. Chris Morton was still on the run and they were watching Matt's girlfriend, Jennifer Coombs, in case he contacted her. They were getting closer to the broker, Walsh.

Nia looked disappointed, but she smiled at his agent. Michael must have said something clever, so she laughed, throwing back her head with genuine amusement. Evan ground his teeth and resisted the urge to punch the young agent in the nose when he returned to the control room.

But Evan still left her alone. She needed time, and he didn't trust himself to give it to her unless there was a wall between them.

Then he got a call from Lucas later in the evening that changed everything.

"Raymond says you look like hell," his friend stated out of the gate.

"Raymond should mind his own business," Evan snapped back. He knew his unusually short temper had raised a few eyebrows on the team.

"I have some info for you," continued Lucas, ignoring Evan's tone.

"About what."

"Nia."

Evan stood up from the chair he was in and walked to the back of the hotel room.

"Go on," he urged in a lower volume.

"The name you gave me, Hailey Stamford. I didn't

get much other than confirmation that she had attended
the same private school as Nia. Average kid, nothing
noteworthy. Her father's a general in the Marines, and
they relocated to D.C."

"That's what Nia told me, so what's the news?" Evan
probed.

"Well, I finally got the files from Nia's sealed records.
And a friend of mine sent some additional court
records. It's not good, Evan."

"What are you talking about? We already know it was
a robbery charge that was dropped."

"There's more, much more, and Hailey Stamford
was at the center of it," Lucas revealed.

"Tell me."

His friend paused. Evan heard the ping from his cell
phone notifying him of a new e-mail message.

"It's better you read it, Evan. I just sent you everything I have."

Evan swallowed, struggling past the now ever-present
lump in his throat. With Lucas's voice devoid of any
humor, it had to be pretty bad.

"Call me if you need to," added Lucas before they
disconnected the call.

Tony was still on stakeout watching Coombs at her
parents' house. But, looking around the hotel room, it
was obvious that Raymond and Michael could use some
downtime. Evan had been pushing them all hard for
the last eighteen hours, and there was unlikely to be any
additional developments that night. He announced
that they could all take a break, and suggested they
go out for dinner on him. With raised eyebrows and
surprised expressions, the men filed out of the room to
enjoy a dinner in the hotel restaurant. Once alone,

Evan checked on Nia through the surveillance feed, but she was outside of his view.

With a deep sigh, he logged into his e-mail on one of the laptops, opened the file Lucas sent, and started reading.

It was worse than anything he could have imagined.

Some of it they had already known. October of her sophmore year, Nia James was arrested and charged with burglary after a party at a classmate's house. The stolen items, diamond earrings, were found in her purse. Four months later, the charges were dropped. What they hadn't known was why. Now Lucas's research filled in the blanks.

The diamond earrings belonged to Lorraine Strom. Her sixteen-year-old son, Colby, had a nasty habit of getting in trouble. Everything from drugs to alcohol, and two incidents of statutory rape. All for which he managed to escape any real punishment.

Colby had a friend, Kyle Stamford. Under the influence of drugs at a parent-free party, the boys decided that Nia James should be their entertainment. While Colby held her down, Kyle filmed the action. After the assault, Colby planted the earrings on Nia when she threatened to tell the police.

It took four months for the truth to come out. During that time, Nia spent over two weeks in a juvenile detention center before her aunt posted bail. Her scholarship was revoked and she was expelled from the private school, returning to Detroit and missing the rest of her school year. Nia was bound for a longer detention sentence until Hailey Stamford, Nia's best friend for over three years, found the video on her brother's computer.

Evan felt nauseous. Literally, sick to his stomach. The words on the screen blurred until he lowered his head between his knees in an effort to regain his composure. His breathing was labored as he sucked in huge gulps of air. But the anger kept building until he was ready to explode. He stood up swiftly, knocking back his chair and crashing it onto the floor.

Nia. His Nia. Only fifteen and attacked by two sick boys. Fifteen!

He wanted to destroy something, smash everything around him until the pain receded. Instead, he let out a low, wounded bellow, with his fist clenched tight. It didn't help. Rage was consuming him, coursing through his veins with swift urgency. Evan paced, he sat down, covered his face with his hands, then paced again. Eventually, he found himself outside, on the small balcony of the room. The June night was warm, laden with moisture from the harbor. He breathed in deeply, desperate to regain his normally dependable composure.

Nia.

Suddenly, so much made sense. Everything about her demonstrated an incredible amount of strength, resilience, and self-reliance. That's what he had seen in her that day as she walked in front of his car, bold, confident, and unabashed. Except he had been too arrogant and jaded to recognize it.

Evan saw it clearly now. He also understood what she had given to him over those days they were together. After everything she had experienced as a young girl, she'd given herself with abandon. Only to discover his duplicity. He threw his head back, hating what he'd done, resenting the decisions he had made and the impossible situation they were now in. Most of all, Evan despised that he couldn't go to Nia, take her into his arms, and relieve her pain.

He stood outside for a long time, needed to feel well in control before facing anyone. The two agents had returned moments earlier, clearly relaxed and in high spirits. Evan left them to their fun and went into the other suite. It was dark and quiet. He assumed Nia was already in the bedroom, until something caught his eye in the moonlight. She was standing out on the large terrace, in one of the hotel robes and bare feet. Despite his better judgment, he was drawn to her like a moth to a flame.

She turned her head when he opened the door and stepped out. It wasn't the warmest welcome, but she didn't curse at him either, so Evan was a little encouraged. He walked across the tiled surface and joined her at the railing. They stood silent next to each other for long moments.

"Any updates?" Nia finally asked.

"No, but we're getting closer. We'll find the broker soon."

She sighed.

"I guess I'm stuck here for another day."

"It's not so bad. Room service, fluffy bed. Nice view."

"No, I guess not," she agreed. "I'm going to miss my Saturday morning appointment again."

"Your tutoring," Evan acknowledged.

Nia gave him a quick look of surprise, then stared back out into the harbor.

"I can take you there, if you'd like," he offered.

"Is there anything you don't know about me?" Nia asked.

She had meant it to be rhetorical. He didn't answer, but his body stiffened noticeably. Nia looked up at him again. Evan looked away from her glance, avoiding her eyes. Her heart started racing. There was only one thing about her that would cause someone like him to be uncomfortable with a topic.

Nia had known from the beginning that it was very likely that the investigation would search into her past, including criminal activity. Sealed records weren't impenetrable, particularly in this day and age. The minute Nia had sat down with Michael and Raymond for that first interrogation, she had prepared herself for the inevitable discussion about robbery charges at fifteen years old. Of diamond earrings, no less.

Nia just had never anticipated this conversation going like this, or that it would be with Evan.

"You know about my sealed record," she stated, not willing to ignore the giant pink elephant in the room. "Am I still under suspicion?"

"No, of course not!" he quickly retorted, shoving his hands into the front pockets of his pants. "We knew about the record from the beginning but it just took some time to get all of the details."

"God. I must have been the perfect suspect, huh? Code to the safe, criminal background," she mused with a dry laugh. "Even I was starting to think I might have done it."

Evan turned to lean his hip against the rail so he was facing her directly.

"Yeah, you looked pretty good for it, Nia," he confessed. "Too good. You're too smart to leave a trail of bread crumbs right to your doorstep."

"Or that's what's smart about it," she suggested coyly.

He smiled, though it looked strained.

"For someone who's been trying to prove her innocence from the beginning, you're doing a piss-poor job of it now."

Nia looked out at the harbor.

"I've had a lot of time to think about it, look at all angles."

"Well, with you, we still got stuck on motive."

"Isn't money always a motive?"

"I thought the same thing," he sighed, looking at her with a speculative gaze. "And then I met you, Nia James, and now I'm not so certain."

"Don't be mistaken, Evan. Money motivates me. Life is expensive, remember?"

"I can tell you from experience, you don't make a very good gold digger. I'm pretty sure weekend charity and refusing expensive gifts would get you kicked out of the club."

She looked down at her bare feet, cool against the patio tiles.

"Touché." Nia let out a deep breath. "Maybe I have a deep-seated resentment against all rich people who take whatever they want, destroying other people in the process."

The words hung in the air. She meant to make light of things, but the honesty was glaring.

"Is that how you really feel?"

"It's more wariness than hatred, actually. Resentment takes too much energy, trust me. Years of therapy taught me that."

Nia could feel his gaze against her profile. It burned with hopeless pity, as though she was broken, damaged, forever scarred. It's one of the main reasons she left

Detroit behind. Why the relationship with her family was so broken. Too many people looked at her like that, deciding she was forever branded as a victim.

She decided to tell him everything about the assault, show him that she had overcome it all and would never be a helpless victim again.

"When I think back to what happened, the worst part wasn't what Colby Strom did. It was horrible and disgusting, but I knew he was capable of it. Everyone knew he was a sick asshole. But Kyle Stamford was different," she explained. "We were friends, even dated a few times and I really liked him. At the party, I thought he wanted to go upstairs because he liked me, too."

She heard Evan let out a harsh breath.

"Turns out he wanted to be accepted more. He filmed it and let it happen, then lied to the police and said I had a crush on him and was trying to make him jealous by hooking up with his friend."

"Shit!"

Nia knew she didn't have to say more. Years ago, it had been too painful, so raw. She was incapable of saying the words out loud to anyone, except her therapist, and even that had taken months to accomplish. Now, it was just a sad story about a young girl a lifetime ago.

"I used to think it was my fault. That I led them to believe I was that kind of girl. Or that because I was poor, I wasn't worth anything other than what they took from me," she continued. "I was smart and talented, yet that one night took away my self-worth for a long time. Eventually, I figured out that I wasn't responsible. There are just bad people in the world, and you can't own their actions."

He bowed his head and clenched the rail.

"What I regret the most is what happened to Nigel."

Evan cleared his throat and straightened.

"St. Clair," he stated. "You said he's your stepbrother?"

She smiled softly.

"Not officially. But he stayed with us every summer while our parents lived together for a few years. He feels like my brother, and he was the only one there for me."

"His stint in prison," concluded Evan, as though connecting the dots for the first time.

She nodded and sighed.

"I called him after the incident. I was a mess, a little hysterical. I didn't know what to do. It never occurred to me that he do something about it," Nia explained. "I was arrested that night at my aunt's house. While I was in detention, he drove over from Boston to go after Colby. I hadn't mentioned Kyle, for some reason. Maybe because I still hadn't accepted his role in the whole thing. They picked Nigel up a few days later for attempted murder.

"It was bad. Colby almost died from the injuries and his family was filthy rich. Nigel would have done at least fifteen years if Hailey hadn't given the police the video Kyle made. My aunt got me a lawyer, and we negotiated an early release for him as part of the settlement. But it never felt like enough. How could I pay back three years of his life?"

He pulled her into his arms, clutching her close and she let him. The comfort felt good, though it shouldn't. It reminded her of Martha's Vineyard and Alexandria, where they had seemed like two ordinary people, dating and getting to know each other. Not like knights and pawns in an elaborate game.

"It's not your fault, Nia. He did what any man would do. If they are still alive, they didn't suffer enough. I would have killed them," he whispered in a chilling voice.

Nia closed her eyes, remembering the sight of Evan snapping that man's neck with strength and agility that seemed effortless. She didn't doubt his words for a second.

They retreated to their thoughts for a few moments. Their embrace loosened, with Evan brushing his hands up and down her back. Nia was thinking that it was strange that he had caused such crushing pain and sadness, yet was also able to take it away so easily. At least temporarily.

"Nia, we have to talk about last night," he stated in a low, gruff voice.

"No, Evan. I think we should just leave it. It doesn't matter."

"Of course it matters," he insisted more urgently. "Last night shouldn't have happened that way." He burying his face into her neck. "It was thoughtless of me."

"I was there too, Evan. We both participated."

Evan lifted his head, releasing her to cup her face gently in his hands.

"The truth is, I was ready," he insisted, as though he didn't hear her words. "I wanted that intimacy and everything it meant. But I should have discussed it with you first!"

She shook her head, too exhausted to think about it.

"I promise it won't happen again," he insisted. "Nothing will ever happen unless you're ready, okay?"

Nia blinked at his words, irritated by his arrogance.

"Evan, stop," she insisted. "I'm not helpless. If I wanted you to stop, we would have. I'm not a victim, incapable of making choices."

"I know that. I didn't mean to suggest anything like that!" He swore, harshly. "I'm trying to say I didn't mean to take advantage of you, or the situation."

Nia pulled back, out of his arms, and took a step back. She felt hot resentment building in her chest.

"Evan, let me explain this to you so you completely understand," she stated in low, slow voice. "You deceived me about who you were in order to do your job. You slept we me while believing I was a thief. That's unforgivable and I'm pissed off about it. I think I have every right to be."

"I know—"

"Let me finish," she insisted. "You lied to me, but I also know that you didn't take advantage of me, then or last night. I am not a victim, Evan. I am not helpless. I'm on the pill and I know the risk in what we did. Everything that happened between us was with my consent. We've known each other for two weeks, and you didn't make me any promises. So please stop acting like you had all the control because I never gave it to you."

He let out a deep breath then clenched his jaw.

"What does that mean, Nia? Where does that leave things between us?"

She shrugged.

"I can't trust you, Evan. So despite what happened last night, there is nothing between us anymore."

With no more to say, Nia politely said good night and left Evan on the terrace.

It felt like she was running away, but it was too hard to be there with him, to resist wanting more between them than was now possible. She had done that already, followed her desire, and the pain of betrayal was still too fresh to ignore.

Chapter 22

After Friday evening, she and Evan fell into a routine over the next couple of days. Since she had not canceled her tutoring session with Meghan McFarlane at the center, Nia accepted his offer to take her there. The drive to the Dorchester neighborhood community center was awkward and stilted. She looked out the window of the rugged SUV and wondered what had happened to his sleek Bentley.

"I heard you with the young girl the last time you were here," he stated as they parked the car near the building. "Is she the only one you give music lessons to?"

Nia looked over at him with a hard expression. It was a warm morning, yet he was dressed in all black, with cargo pants and a close-fitting cotton top that molded over his muscles. There was no sign of the wealthy businessman. Instead, he looked lethal and dangerous. How many more things would she discover had been happening in the shadows of her life since she met him?

He sighed.

"We had you under surveillance for the first few days, then full protection after the incident with the truck," revealed Evan. "You can ask me anything, Nia. I will answer honestly if it's within my ability to do so."

Nia pondered his response, wondering why any truthful answers would be outside of his control. She immediately thought of the gunshot wound on his leg and the explanation of being in the wrong place at the wrong time. Her gut said that was one of them.

They were walking into the building as she replied.

"Only Meghan right now. I occasionally get one or two more who want to try the program."

"You're very good," he stated.

She looked at the ground uncertain of what to say in response.

Music had always come naturally to her. The notes and melody made sense in her mind and her body learned quickly how to express it through an instrument.

From what Nia had discovered over the years, her mom, Simone James, had once been a singer with great potential in the Detroit underground music scene. But poor choices in men and broken promises had destroyed her ambition early in her career.

Her mom had once told Nia that her real father was also a musician, though the rest of the story was inconsistent. When Nia was younger, Simone claimed the mystery man was the love of her life, but later it seemed he was a band performer who had passed through town when they met at a party. Either way, Nia always felt music was the only legacy she had from her parents. Later, after the incident when she was expelled from the scholarship program, it didn't seem worth very much.

At nine o'clock, Meghan arrived for her music lesson.

Nia was getting everything ready at the piano, while Evan was planted in the hall just outside the doorway.

"Hey mister, you're back," the young girl said, looking up at him.

"I am," he stated, looking amused. "You're on time."

"Yup," replied Meghan as she strolled by him.

The lesson went well, though Nia found it hard to concentrate knowing Evan was right there listening in. Meghan had been practicing over the last two weeks and it showed in her ability to complete some of the more complicated sections of the songs. Near the end of the hour, Nia played another pop song, this time by a new boy band. Meghan giggled through the whole thing. The eleven-year-old skipped out shortly after, promising to continue working on her chords.

Nia sat behind the piano for a few moments, trying to decide if she should stay for practice. It had a become a weekly routine, thirty minutes of private indulgence where she lost herself in the rhythm of whatever songs came to mind. Or, it was an opportunity to play around with the songs in her imagination, express the music that she would never compose on paper. Occasionally, the lyrics would come also, and Nia could sing them ad-lib. She never wrote them down, either.

Today, there was an audience. She didn't want to perform. Yet her fingers trailed over the keys, almost of their own accord. There was a new melody in her head, one that had been hovering in her subconscious for days. It was a ballad, made up of simple but dramatic chords laden with emotion. The notes were in fragments now, but Nia knew the sections would merge over time.

Nia played a section, connected another, toyed with

a chorus. Her throat tightened as the feelings the notes conveyed coursed through her body. There was sadness, disappointment, and hurt in the aftermath of betrayal. The loss of something incredible that she didn't even know she wanted. A raw, lingering need that would never again be satisfied. The music left her naked and vulnerable, stripped of all protective skin. It was always that way, and often more than she could bear.

Her eyes welled up, and Nia abruptly stopped playing. She rested her clenched hands in her lap, staring at the ivory keys for long moments with familiar regret. It would have been a great song, if she were really a songwriter. But she wasn't. She was a successful manager and salesperson, with a responsible career and financial stability. That had to be enough. Anything else was a pipe dream. Her mom's life was a testament to that.

Nia closed down the piano and left the room. She was so caught up in her own thoughts that she didn't notice how withdrawn her bodyguard was during the drive back to the hotel.

For the rest of the weekend, she was left alone in the suite while Evan and the team followed the trail to the broker, Walsh.

By the time he and Nia returned from the music lesson in Dorchester, there was a cryptic voice-mail message from Craig Kelsey, the concierge at the Opal Hotel. His order would be ready for Sunday afternoon. A fifty percent deposit was required up front, then Evan would get a call within the next twenty-four hours to confirm a time for the final delivery.

Evan called Lucas.

"We have a bite on the broker," he stated immediately, and provided the details.

"What do you need?" Lucas replied.

"Three men, including Lance. We need to set up the sting at the Opal Hotel for tomorrow."

"You got it. I'll send Abe, too, and Ned can fly them in with one of the choppers. There's a helipad in South Boston. They should be there by early this evening."

"Good. Send me the coordinates. Michael and I will meet them," Evan replied. "If we do this right, we could have Walsh within a couple of days."

For the next twenty-four hours, Evan and the expanded Fortis team paid Kelsey the deposit and set the trap. Like Evan, Abe Smith was former CIA, with a specialty in interrogation techniques. Ned Bushby was a former Secret Service agent, and deadly accurate with a gun. With Michael taking over the stakeout of Coombs, Lance and Tony were the other two men in the plan.

At two-fifteen Sunday afternoon, they got the call. The package would be delivered to Evan's hotel room at the Opal in thirty minutes.

Tony, Abe, and Lance would cover the entrances to the hotel, looking for whoever would deliver the ten-thousand-dollar bottle of scotch. Ned would stay close to the concierge, Kelsey, for the hand-off to Evan, and Raymond would watch video coverage from the control center. They were all connected with tiny earpieces for communication.

Abe was the first to report in.

"I have a delivery truck pulling into the service bay through the alley," he reported, dressed as a hotel employee having a smoke break.

"Got it," Raymond confirmed. "The company's called

Gleason Courier. They're a midsize delivery company for several hotel and hospitality supply companies."

"A lone man is walking in, carrying a square package wrapped in plain brown paper," continued Abe. "He's heading in through the employee entrance. Lance, he should come through one of the service doors in about two minutes. The one next to the restaurant."

There were a few moments of silence.

"Got him," Lance whispered. "He's approaching Kelsey now. The package has been handed off."

"Abe, you detain our driver. Take him to our truck. Tony, meet them there for the discussion."

"Got it," Tony replied.

"Ned, Kelsey's heading to the elevator."

"On it," Ned replied. "I'm joining him for the ride."

"Lance, take the next ride up."

"On my way."

Evan stood tall, feet spread wide, waiting for his package to arrive. His gun was holstered in reach under his loose cotton shirt next to his spine, and his slim knife strapped to his right ankle. Even in this seemingly small-time takedown, you could never be too prepared. He took a deep breath and waited.

"The delivery is almost at the door," Abe stated.

The knock came seconds later.

"Hi, Mr. DaCosta, I have your delivery," stated Kelsey, clearly pleased with his accomplishment, and the promise of his cut of a five-thousand-dollar job.

"Excellent!" Evan stated, clapping his hands together with a big smile on his face. "Craig, right?"

"Yes, sir."

"Come in, let me have a look at it."

The young concierge paused for a moment with caution. Evan sensed his hesitation, so he walked away from the door to tap his fingers on a thick white envelope sitting on the television console nearby. Kelsey stepped inside and closed the door.

"Here you go," he said, handing over the brown box so Evan could open it.

"Macallan fifty-five-year-old scotch," Evan confirmed in a low voice. "One of the best bottles of single malt at half the price. That's quite an accomplishment, Craig."

Whatever Kelsey was going to say was interrupted by the two large men who walked into the hotel room. Ned and Lance stood in front of the door, looking very threatening, and effectively blocking his exit.

"Why don't you tell us how you made it happen?" Evan continued as he placed the box of rare liquor next to the white envelope on the console. Kelsey followed his movement, clearly still hoping he'd walk away with payment for the job.

"I have a lot of contacts, that's all," he stammered, looking at the men, then back at the envelope.

"Good. Let's talk about these contacts of yours. One in particular. I want to hear what you know about Walsh."

Kelsey's eyes opened wide with surprise. His mouth opened and closed a few times.

"Who?" he finally croaked.

"Come on, Craig. No one has time for games. Just tell us what you know about Walsh and we won't tell the police about your theft of a ten-thousand-dollar bottle of scotch. That's a felony charge, by the way."

"I didn't steal anything!" insisted Kelsey.

"No, but you certainly planned to profit off the robbery. That makes you just as guilty," Evan replied smoothly. "Don't worry, we don't want you. We know you didn't actually steal the bottle. We just want Walsh.

Tell us everything you know about him, and you can go back to work."

The young man swallowed, clearly weighing his options.

"I don't know who he is. I only have a phone number," he finally admitted. "I call it when I have a special request."

"What kind of request?" probed Evan.

"Anything I can't get through regular channels, you know," Kelsey explained.

"Like what, specifically?" pressed Evan. "Don't worry, it's just between us men."

Kelsey squeezed his eyes shut, clearly uncomfortable with saying it out loud. Evan took a step toward him, and it was like the dam burst open.

"I haven't done much, just some weed here and there. A little blow. One guy wanted a young male hooker. That's it!"

"How much do you make off the deals?"

"It depends, but usually twenty percent. Walsh takes the rest."

"And how does Walsh get his payment?" Evan continued.

"The driver picks it up. He's waiting for me downstairs right now."

Evan looked at Ned and Lance.

"What about gems, like diamonds, Kelsey? Ever been asked to get your hands on something like that?"

"No! I don't know anything about stuff like that," he denied. "I told you, I'm only getting small stuff."

"Okay, okay. What about your deliver guy? Do you know him?" Evan continued.

"No. I mean, I don't know his name or anything, but it's the same guy all the time."

"Good. Thank you, Kelsey, you've been very helpful. Now, we only need that phone number for Walsh."

The concierge swallowed hard and stammered out the numbers. Evan turned away from him. Ned and Lance stepped aside from the door.

"What about the payment?" Kelsey squeaked out.

"Sorry, Craig. I think you've already made enough off this deal."

Kelsey left the room, clearly terrified by the failed job and what would happen to him when he didn't deliver the balance of the money.

The interrogation of the courier van driver was equally successful, and with an added bonus. Abe was waiting for a nervous young man at the front of the delivery van. Once Tony arrived, they escorted the driver to their truck, and made a persuasive case for why a quick, informative chat was better than a charge of trafficking in stolen goods.

"He doesn't know Walsh either," Tony explained on the drive back to the Harbor Hotel. "And he's only paid a hundred dollars for each pickup and drop-off. There's a locker at the courier company depot that's been set up for the exchanges."

"Does the driver only deliver to the Opal? Kelsey said it's the same guy all the time," Evan told them.

"He delivers to a few hotels, any that are along his regular route. And that's where it gets good," Tony added. "He specifically remembers a pickup at the King Edward Hotel back in March that was unusual. He picked up a deposit for a job, a pretty sizeable one at that, but never got contacted again for the final delivery."

Evan and Tony exchanged meaningful looks. If the regular driver didn't do the final delivery, then it was probably something too valuable to be handled by him. Maybe something so valuable that Walsh delivered it himself?

"Raymond," Evan called into the earpiece. "I need you to do a search of the guests booked into the King Edward back in March, then cross-reference it with anyone who was back within days of the robbery. That should narrow down our potential buyers significantly. And I'll send you the phone number that Kelsey gave us for Walsh. It's a longshot, but maybe we'll be able to tie it back to Morton or someone else involved."

"Sure thing, Ice."

The investigation came together quickly after that. Within a couple of hours, Fortis had the name of their buyer.

Based on backdoor access to the hotel reservation system, they found Sean Holstein. He was a fifty-two-year-old executive at a small venture capital firm based in Staten Island, New York. The slight, sheepish-looking man visited Boston twice in the last three months, and could be seen on the hotel surveillance camera communicating with the King Edward concierge just over three weeks ago. It was the day after the Worthington heist.

Further review of the various camera feeds showed a man wearing a baseball cap and casual clothes delivering a small box to Holstein's hotel room, in exchange for a thin envelope. Unfortunately, the unknown courier was smart enough to keep his head down at all times.

By Monday afternoon, Ned was flying the Fortis chopper to Staten Island with Tony, Abe, and Lance onboard for a retrieval mission.

Evan got the call just minutes after eight o'clock that night. The Crimson Amazon and all the other stolen jewelry had been recovered intact. Holstein had put up little resistance and was now quietly in the custody of the FBI, thanks to one of Michael's contacts at the bureau.

While Raymond, Michael, and Ned shared an aggressive high five, then got down to business planning a victory celebration, Evan placed a call to Lucas. They then added Sam to the line.

"Congratulations, Ice. You've finally lost your virginity," Lucas teased.

Sam laughed and Evan managed a smile. He was exhausted, but damn it felt good.

"Tony and the others are on their way back here with the assets. Abe, Ned, and Lance should be back in Virginia in the morning," Evan told them.

"What about Morton and the broker, Walsh? We still don't know exactly who pulled off the robbery," Sam stated. "Did we get anywhere with that phone number we got?"

"No, but I'll keep the team here for the rest of the week to tie up those ends," Evan explained. "We know Holstein paid the ten grand deposit in cash, then the balance of the fee by wire transfer from a numbered account in the Cayman Islands to another online bank account. One million, nine hundred and ninety dollars to be exact, and all of which is now frozen as part of the federal investigation. In exchange for the arrest, Michael's contact with the feds will tell us where the money trail leads. Ultimately, it will lead us to Walsh, Morton, and anyone else involved."

Chapter 23

"So, that's it? You're going home today?" asked Lianne between mouthfuls of steak. "You must be so relieved."

It was Tuesday afternoon, and the two friends were eating lunch out on the hotel room terrace.

"I am," Nia confirmed. "It's been five days since I've left this room, except for my tutoring session on Saturday. I'm starting to have major cabin fever."

"There are worse places to be stuck, Nia."

"I guess. Anyway, I would like to go back to real life. There's a ton of work to catch up on."

"I still can't believe all the drama. Or that you guys got back all the jewelry so quickly," mused Lianne.

"I know, I didn't think it was possible. Thank God it was kept out of the media. That would have been disastrous, even if we got the stuff back."

"How was that possible, anyway? I thought you said the FBI got involved. Isn't it now public record?"

"I don't know. Edward said something about Fortis having connections and making arrangements. It's all very clandestine," Nia explained.

"Well, I have to say, they are a pretty incredible group of men. Like sexy, modern-day gladiators."

Nia grinned. It was an accurate description.

"You better not talk like that or Eddie's going to get jealous."

"He'll live," dismissed Lianne. "Still no sign of the guy who stole the stuff to begin with?"

"Chris? No," Nia confirmed. "It creeps me out a little bit, to be honest. Evan says he's probably long gone with the cash he was paid, crossing into Canada or maybe even to the south into Mexico."

"I wonder why he did it," Lianne mused.

"I don't know. There's some talk in the office that he liked to party pretty hard, used cocaine regularly. So, maybe he needed the money?" Nia explained. "Anyway, Edward has asked Fortis to do a security review and provide recommendations on how to improve our current systems and protocol. At least, we won't have to worry about anything like this happening again."

With their meals finished, they both sat back to relax for a bit.

"I wrote a song," Nia finally confessed.

Lianne paused with her drink halfway to her mouth.

"Really?" she replied with obvious surprise.

Nia shrugged, trying to make light of it.

"I couldn't get it out of my head, so it seemed silly not to write it down."

"Nia, that's great! How did it feel?"

"Familiar," described Nia after a reflective pause. "I haven't written anything in years, since I left Detroit. I thought it would be harder."

Lianne smiled, but didn't push. Though she was a professional therapist, Nia never went to her for advice beyond that of a best friend.

"I think it helped, though," continued Nia.

"With Evan?"

"Yeah. I've haven't been able to figure out what to do. One minute, I'm relieved about the whole Fortis thing. The thing between us, whatever it was, had gotten pretty intense. The next minute, I'm so hurt and disappointed, a little sad. He was . . . He was good to be with. We had fun."

She paused, looking into the water in her glass.

"I had fallen for him."

The words hung between them. Lianne leaned forward.

"There's nothing wrong with that, Nia," her friend explained. "People fall in love all the time."

"I know. But look where it landed me, Lee? He lied to me from the start. And I didn't see it coming. I completely fell for the whole thing. I can't let that happen to me again. I'm not ready for that kind of risk. And when I do get into a serious relationship, it won't be with someone like Evan. It has to be someone normal. Like an accountant, or an electrician. Maybe your run-of-the-mill office worker."

Lianne raised her eyebrows, suggesting Nia was being ridiculous.

"You have every right to be mad about what happened, Nia. He used you to do his job."

"It's not just his job, Lee, or how things went down on the investigation. It was his whole life. We come from two different worlds," explained Nia, shaking her head. "I'm not sure I'll ever be able to trust his motives about us, together. There's just too much standing in the way now."

"Well, he's lucky. I would have scratched his eyes out," Lianne retorted.

Nia thought of the hard slap she had given Evan across his face the day she found out about his true identity. And the words he had uttered that prompted the impulsive reaction.

"I guess that's been the other benefit to being cooped up in this hotel room. I've had a lot of time for reflection. Regardless of how I felt with Evan, or if he had any real feelings for me, the time and place was just all wrong."

"As long as you're sure, Nia," Lianne stated. "You've been through a lot. It can't hurt to take a little more time to think it through. If Evan really wants to be with you, then he'll wait."

Nia wanted to give her friend a firm response, to declare with honesty and certainty that she was over him, ready to move on. But the truth wasn't that simple. She wasn't ready for all the emotion he stirred. When they were together, Evan had made her feel and want things that were just too intense. The hurt she felt after learning the truth was even more acute, like a raw aching wound. Yes, she understood what happened and why, but it didn't make it any less painful. Why would she put herself through that again? Why would anyone want to be that vulnerable and open to disappointment? If that was love, then Nia was content to let it pass her by. She'd had enough emotional drama in the past to last a lifetime.

"Promise me you'll think about it more," added Lianne.

That evening, as Evan finally drove her back to her apartment, her friend's advice was fresh in Nia's mind. She looked over at him behind the wheel, skillfully maneuvering through the city streets. He seemed quiet and alert, often checking the mirrors. Nia wondered if there was still a reason for caution.

"Is everything okay?" she finally asked.

Evan looked over and gave her a brief smile.

"Everything's fine," he stated.

They continued in silence for another few minutes.

"Edward mentioned you guys will be doing some additional security work at Worthington. How long do you think that will take?" she finally asked.

They were entering her neighborhood.

"We'll be here for a few days. A week at the most."

Nia looked out the window. He was leaving in a few days. Then it would really be over. Nia let out a deep sigh.

"Then on to the next case, I guess," she mumbled.

He didn't reply though she felt his gaze on her face several times. Neither said any more until they were inside her apartment. Evan had her wait by the front door while he did a quick search of all the rooms.

"Is that necessary?" she asked, feeling less secure than she would like. "You said Chris was long gone."

"I said *probably*. Until we locate him, I'd prefer to be vigilant," stated Evan as he carried her bag into her bedroom. She trailed after him.

"For how long? What if you never find him?"

"We'll find him. He's not sophisticated enough to stay off the grid for long. Until then, you'll have a security detail."

He said the words casually, as though she should have known that would be the case.

"What kind of security?" Nia exclaimed.

They were now facing each other next to her bed.

"Me. I'm staying here in the short-term. We'll consider a longer solution if needed."

He walked past her, out the room and back into the living area.

"Evan, you're not staying here," she insisted, annoyed that she was forced to follow him.

"Yes, I am."

"What if I don't want you to?"

"You don't have a choice, Nia. Unless you'd prefer to go back to the hotel indefinitely," threatened Evan as he stopped in her kitchen.

"This is ridiculous, Evan! I can't live like this. I want my life back!" she shouted at him.

He clenched his fist at his side.

"What would you have me do?" he demanded. "Walk away? Leave you here unprotected? They tried to kill you twice, Nia! I'm not taking any chances."

She turned away, frustrated by the truth. How was she going to resist him, move on, forget, if he was right here with her?

"Look, I know this isn't ideal. We're doing everything we can to find Chris Morton. But until we do, I need to be here," insisted Evan.

Nia looked back at him, standing firm and strong, his arms folded stubbornly across his chest. She had no doubt she'd be physically safe. Her heart and soul were another matter.

"I'm going to unpack," she finally stated, resigning herself to the situation. "You can stay in the spare bedroom."

Maybe it will be fine, Nia told herself as she put away clothes and toiletries, sorted items for laundry. Evan was a professional, and obviously very capable of keeping his distance. He'd done a pretty good job of it since they'd talked on Friday night. He was polite and courteous, but with an icy detachment that was almost familiar to her now. Despite Lianne's suggestions that he'd wait for her to decide what she wanted, Nia now wondered if he had already moved on. Then in a few days, he'd be gone for good.

It shouldn't have hurt so much. But it did.

About an hour later, she took several fresh towels out of the linen closet and entered the second bathroom from the entrance in the hallway. The air was moist and steamy, but the room was empty. Nia placed the towels on the counter and turned to the door leading to the guest room, now slightly ajar. Her intent as she pushed it open was only to let Evan know she'd also bring fresh sheets for the bed, but the words immediately lodged in her throat. The room was almost dark, with only the lights from the bathroom spilling into the space. He was standing next to the bed with his back to her, only a towel covering the hard contours of his haunches.

She must have made a sound, because Evan turned quickly toward her.

"Nia," he whispered.

They stood there, both frozen. Her heart was beating erratically. He looked bigger, harder than she remembered. *So good.*

Their eyes met, and he took a step forward.

"Sorry," she mumbled, looking away. "I . . ."

"No. I'm sorry. I should have closed the door."

She cleared her throat. Her eyes were drawn back to him, washing over his chest, those arms, trying hard to avoid the narrow valley that ran down the eight-pack of his stomach.

"I brought some extra towels," she finally stated, turning away a little.

Nia knew she should leave. Turn around, walk away.

Firmly close the door between them. But she couldn't move. Her mind felt cloudy and her body drugged by the heat of his presence. She looked back at him, swallowing.

"I should go," she whispered.

"Don't," Evan commanded. "Stay with me."

He walked forward slowly as though he were afraid she would run away. She couldn't move.

"Please stay," he repeated, before pulling her into his arms and kissing her.

His lips were soft, gentle, coaxing. He was deliciously familiar, stirring warm desire low in her belly. It was always this way with him, no one else. Strong, pulsing, intoxicating. Too good to deny.

Nia kissed him back, pulled into the sensations he created. She stroked her tongue into his mouth, brushing and entwining his.

"Baby," he breathed hotly.

It felt like forever since they had touched, Nia was starving. She kissed him harder, deeper. Maybe a small taste would be enough, she thought wildly. Just a sample of how good they felt together, then she'd stop, move on. Just a little more time with him.

Evan groaned low and deep, wrapping his powerful arms around her like he'd never let her go. She purred, losing what was left of her willpower. He quickly unbuttoned her shirt, pushing it off her arms. Nia helped. He unsnapped her bra, she pulled it off by the straps. She removed her pants and underwear while he cupped her breasts tenderly, teasing the tips.

His towel fell to the floor, leaving them naked, pressed skin to skin. Breathing harshly, they paused, kissing sweetly, lips stroking. His hot, hard erection was pressed against her stomach. Nia was lost in the pulsing desire, wanting more, needing him, craving the completion only he could give.

"Evan," she moaned, stroking over his shoulders, clutching around his neck.

He swept one hand between them, down her stomach to brush between her lower lips. She gasped and he moaned.

"So wet," he uttered. "Jesus, Nia, I want you so much. I need you."

One more time. Just one more time and it'll be enough.

"Yes," she whispered.

He stopped moving, breathed out harshly, his body quivering with her every touch.

"I need to get protection," he explained.

"It's okay, I'm on the pill."

"Sweetheart, are you sure?"

"Yes," Nia stated.

Evan lifted her easily by the hips and wrapped her legs around his waist. He was stroking into her within seconds. His slow penetration was unbearably good, until she was filled completely with his hardness. It was so incredible, Nia forgot everything but what she needed. She tightened her legs, flexed her hips, loving the feel of his thrust.

They remained in that position, kissing, breathing, and groaning from the slow, erotic friction. Nia was dying for more, so greedy she begged with soft, kitteny cries. Evan knew her so well and understood her desires. He turned, carrying her, and gently placed her on the bed on her back. Their bodies were still connected; her thighs still gripped his waist. Their eyes met, electric in intensity. He thrust forward, deep, hard. Perfect.

"Nia, baby."

His fingers found her clit, pressing softly, twirling over the bud.

"Yes!" she screamed, her back bowed with pure pleasure.

Nia was so close. So close. He thrust deep, again and again, full, hard, pulsing. *Just one more time and it'll be enough.*

She peaked hard and with complete abandon and he followed moments later, her name chanting from his lips.

Chapter 24

Evan woke up the next morning feeling better than he had in days. It was early, only a little after six o'clock. He gently eased his arm from under Nia to roll off the bed. She stirred a little then settled back into the warm spot he'd left. He smiled, pleased that she missed his presence. Maybe that meant she was ready to put everything behind them and move forward from here, together.

He hoped so. Last night had taken him by surprise. His intention had been to ensure her safety until all the loose ends were tied up. That's all. She said there was nothing more between them, and Evan had been determined to respect that. He'd used every bit of his willpower to stay as distant as possible.

It became impossible when she looked at him with those eyes, biting her lips with desire. Despite his nickname, Evan wasn't made of ice, and he was incapable of resisting that kind of temptation. Now, as he went into the shower, he felt renewed. There were a few details to be worked out, but they hardly mattered as long as Nia was his.

After his shower, he dressed in fresh clothes and took

out his laptop from the duffel bag he had taken out of the truck the prior evening. Then he went into Nia's kitchen to make some coffee. He spent the next hour or so working between sips of hot, creamy java.

Lucas, the genius security specialist at Fortis, had designed an impenetrable network and hardware system for Worthington. While he completed the systems configuration remotely, the rest of the team in Boston would finish installing the hardware and other components today. Evan and his team had moved their control room yesterday from the hotel to an office in the gallery warehouse to complete the assignment. The other guys would remain at the Harbor Hotel in case they needed a safe place for Nia.

Evan would not take any chances with her safety. They would have eyes on her at all times until Chris Morton reappeared. As he had assured Nia, the fugitive would be found. Fortis had every surveillance option turned on, including eyes with Interpol and a few other agencies within their network. If Morton managed to leave the United States, they'd know about it. So far, there was a real concern that he was still in the state, maybe even in the city.

Evan heard Nia moving around. It was almost seven-thirty. He knew she'd want to leave for work around eight o'clock, so he completed a few additional tasks then started to pack up his things. She entered the living room when he was washing up his cup at the kitchen sink. He turned to find her putting on her shoes and walking to the front door.

"I'd like to go into the office a little early, if that's okay," she stated quietly.

Any thoughts Evan had of a warm, intimate morning welcome faded a little. Thinking she may just have been feeling awkward about things between them, Evan walked toward her, a relaxed smile on his lips.

"Sure. I'm all set," he replied.

She turned as he approached, bending to pick up her large bag left near the front door from yesterday.

"Good," she mumbled, looking down at her feet.

His smile faded as he looked at her profile and posture. She wore a simple, blue sleeveless dress in a soft, draping fabric and narrow skirt that fell to her knees. Her hair was freshly straightened, slicked into a high ponytail. In black stiletto heels and blood red lips, Nia looked incredibly stunning and completely untouchable.

He clenched his jaw, recognizing her attempt to erect a wall between them. Despite the night they had shared, so deeply intimate and unrestrained, she still didn't trust him. Disappointment pooled in his stomach, but Evan nodded his head in acceptance. It was just going to take more time, but he could be patient.

On the way to her office, he explained the arrangements for the next few days.

"You and I will ride to and from the office together. Then, Tony and I will be on-site at the gallery providing full protection at all times. You'll eat lunch in your office or in the break room, and we'll ensure you have whatever you want."

She nodded, looking out the window the whole time.

"What if I need to go to a client meeting?" she asked.

"It would be preferable if you assign any meetings outside of the office to one of your account reps. But if it's unavoidable, I'll take you."

She didn't respond, but Evan could feel her annoyance rolling off her in waves.

"It should only be for a few days, Nia."

"I hope so."

She took out her cell phone, keeping herself busy for the remainder of the drive. He left her to it.

At the gallery, Tony met them inside the front doors. Nia said a polite hello then went up the curved stairs to the offices.

"Everything all right?" Tony asked Evan as they both watched her ascend the steps.

"As good as can be expected."

"I can take the night watch if needed," Tony added.

Evan looked at him hard. Like there was any chance in hell he'd let another man stay with her through the night. The agent seemed immune to his glacial stare, and only shrugged.

"Just offering to help," the older man added before walking away.

Evan ground his teeth, annoyed with his own asinine reaction. How had a mere woman turned him into an undisciplined animal, ready to mark his territory with the littlest provocation? It was pitiful. He followed the other man through the gallery floor. As they approached Emma, the receptionist, she smiled brightly and stepped out from behind her counter. She was now aware that Evan was a partner in the security consulting firm hired to update their systems.

"Edward said you all would be working here for a few days," stated Emma. "Just let me know if you need anything. We're a little disorganized with Chris gone, but I'll help out any way I can."

"Thanks, Miss Sterling. Appreciate it," Tony replied.

Evan gave the young girl a nod and the two men entered the warehouse space. They had set up their operations in the office Morton had occupied. Raymond and Michael were already there doing an inventory of the new security equipment. They had a lot to get done. Now that Edward had explained to everyone that there was an updated security system being installed, the team was able to move around the building with full access and transparency. As an extra precaution against any leak to the media or their clients, the employees were only told that Chris had quit, with no mention of the theft and or the attempts against Nia's life.

The team worked quickly, and the new system was up and running by late afternoon. Then, they dialed into the videoconference bridge at the Fortis headquarters for a final meeting with Lucas and Sam.

"Everything looks good, boys," Lucas confirmed, reviewing the infrastructure through the network admin access they had mirrored to the Fortis headquarters. "Raymond, let me know when you've completed the full diagnostic, then we're good to go."

"We have some new info from the feds," Sam stated in his gruff Scottish bur. "Holstein claims he has more information about the diamonds and wants to make a deal."

"What kind of deal?" Evan asked. "He got caught red-handed with the goods."

"Well, he's asking for immunity before he tells them what he knows."

Evan looked at Raymond. The computer wiz was already going through Holstein's details.

"Tell the Bureau guys to give us twenty-four hours. Let's see if we can find out what he plans to share, for free," Evan suggested.

"Okay," Lucas agreed. "What about Morton? Any sign of him yet?"

"No, nothing," Evan replied. "It's like he's completely disappeared. But he has to raise his head eventually.

If we assume that the ten grand cash deposit was split at least three ways between Morton, Walsh, and the concierge at the Mayfair Hotel, Morton's cash flow will run out pretty quick."

The meeting lasted a few more minutes, then Evan's team went back to work. Edward had hired a new security team, and the plan was for Evan and Tony to train them over the next two days. Raymond and Michael would stay focused on the other aspects of the investigation.

It was after six o'clock when he met Nia at the front doors and they drove home in silence. Somehow, through the day, she'd managed to become even more withdrawn. Evan wanted to ask how her day was, have a normal conversation, but the tension emanating from her stiff posture suggested it wasn't a good idea. They were within blocks of her apartment when she finally spoke.

"I don't really have anything in my fridge to make dinner," she stated. "Maybe we should just order something in. Chinese or something?"

He gripped the wheel, suddenly extremely annoyed. That's it? That's all she was going to say? *Damn it!* Evan had promised himself he would give her time, but this was impossible to ignore.

"We can order whatever you'd like," he replied stiffly.

Another few moments went by. He pulled into a spot in front of her duplex. She started to collect her purse and laptop bag.

"Is that all you want to talk about, Nia? What we're going to eat for dinner?" he finally demanded. His tone was harsher than he intended, but Evan was at his limit.

"What else is there?"

He was about to explain exactly what else there was,

starting with a night spent naked and entwined, when a shadow near her front door caught his eye. Evan was exiting the car within seconds, his hand resting on the grip of his gun tucked into the back of his pants.

"Stay right here and don't move," he instructed firmly before he slammed the door and locked it.

As Evan strode swiftly up the walkway, the shadow moved from the doorway, to look into Nia's apartment from outside the window. The man then pressed his face close up against the glass to block out the glare from the sun. The baseball hat on his head kept his face in the shadows. Evan crept up behind him, soundlessly, and had the gun pressed to his back before the guy could flinch.

"Hands up, and don't move a hair," whispered Evan next to the prowler's ear, mindful of anyone who may be walking by. "Now, who the hell are you and what are you doing here?"

The man had followed the instructions. He was a few inches shorter than Evan, with a lean, wiry frame.

"Who the hell are *you?*" the stranger shot back, the voice heavy with attitude and little fear or concern for the weapon aimed at close range.

"I asked you first, and I won't ask again. Who are you?"

"Evan, stop," he heard Nia yelling as she ran up the walkway.

Damn it! He cursed in his head.

"Move, and you'll have a bullet in the back of your knee," Evan muttered to the man just before she arrived.

"Evan, what are you doing?" she demanded, stopping in front of them, glaring openly at Evan as he stood aggressively behind the other man "Let him go!"

"Not until one of you tells me who he is. I tried asking nicely, but this clown wants to play games."

The prowler still refused to say anything, and Nia looked at Evan like he was the criminal. He felt the pulse in his forehead start to throb.

"It's Nigel! Now, let him go!"

Evan stepped back immediately, the gun back in the waist holder before they drew any more neighborhood attention.

"He could have told me that," he grumbled, stepping away, refusing to apologize for his vigilance. "You may want to tell him it's not a good idea to creep around in the shadows."

"Nigel, are you okay? What are you doing here?" Nia asked, ignoring Evan's suggestion. She hugged the thug in a long, close embrace that became uncomfortable to watch. Yet Evan kept his eyes trained on them.

"I came to see how you're doing," Nigel St. Clair finally replied. "Who is this pit bull?"

Nigel jabbed his thumb over at where Evan was standing, as though pointing at an annoying fly. Evan ground his teeth.

"His name is Evan and he's . . . providing protection for a little while," Nia finally explained.

"Why?" demanded St. Clair with obvious concern. "Nia, what's going on? I thought you said the case was solved?"

"Okay," Evan finally interjected. "Let's take this inside."

St. Clair looked like he was going to object to the order, and Evan hoped he would. Something about his cocky attitude made Evan want to knock him on his ass. But Nia took the arm of her "stepbrother" and walked him forward toward her front door.

"Okay, what going on, little girl?" the clown asked once they were inside.

Evan left them to do a quick sweep of the house. When all was clear, he went into Nia's spare room to make a call.

"What's up, Ice?" answered Tony.

"Nigel St. Clair has just arrived at Nia's house. I want to know why he's here and anything else relevant," Evan instructed in a clipped tone.

"You got it, boss."

They disconnected and Evan went back in the living room to keep an eye on things. Nia and her new visitor were sitting on the couch. St. Clair had his arm around the back of her seat, and held one of her hands. They looked close, cozy.

The throbbing vein in his forehead was pounding against his skull.

Evan had seen the guy's pictures, so he knew what he looked like. Yet St. Clair was still more put together in person than Evan expected. With his dark blond hair, sharp green eyes, he was also better looking. Not exactly the picture of a down-and-out ex-con. Clearly he had moved on from his time inside, now making a decent living supervising in a warehouse.

Nia bowed her head at something St. Clair said, and the other man brushed her back gently with his hand. Evan saw red. He folded his arms across his chest in the effort to not break the arm attached to that hand.

The knowledge of what Nia and this man had been through and endured together was impossible to ignore. This was the man who was there for her when she needed protection at fifteen, when she was alone and vulnerable, abused in the worst way possible. This man, who would have been no more than twenty years old at the time, had sacrificed himself to enforce raw justice. Evan knew St. Clair deserved respect and gratitude, not the white-hot jealousy pounding through his veins. But the knot in his stomach only grew as he watched them together, bound by history and the worst kind of tragedy.

Nia finally stood up and walked toward Evan. He maintained his planted stance at the back of the room, his face more hardened than he knew.

"You don't need to watch us like a hawk, Evan," she snapped, giving him the eye. "I'm ordering Chinese and Nigel is staying for dinner."

They ate sometime later. Evan stayed in the back of the apartment, watchful but distant, listening to the hum of their conversation for the next couple of hours. Finally, St. Clair left for the night. Evan followed him outside, and watched as the other man got into a higher-end sedan parked down the street and drove off, engine revving high. He then secured the perimeter of the duplex again, and was headed back into the apartment when his phone rang with a call. It was from Raymond.

"Ice, the state police just found a dead body in a motel in Somerville. It was Chris Morton."

"Okay, give me a minute."

Evan locked the front door, then checked on Nia. She was in the shower.

"What are the details?" he finally asked in reply.

"He's been dead for a few days, maybe even since Thursday," Raymond explained. "It was a gunshot to the head. Same caliber as the hit on Flannigan."

"Shit! Someone took him out the same day as the attempt on Nia. They were cleaning up."

"Yeah, but who?"

Evan ran his hand over his head.

"It's whoever was listening through the bug on Nia's laptop. And if it wasn't Morton, then it has to be Walsh or whoever he hired to steal the jewels. We have to find them, Raymond."

"I'm working on it," muttered Raymond with frustration. "But I think I've found out what Holstein wants to bargain with. The bank account used for the money transfer isn't his. Not directly, anyway. I did some aggressive network intrusion in places I shouldn't, and the Cayman account traces back to a shell company also registered on the island. The same shell company owns Holstein's venture capital firm, but it's also a small subsidiary of Strom Investments."

"Strom," Evan repeated with a mix of urgency and dread.

"Yeah. They're a stock brokerage company with corporate headquarters in Detroit, but their biggest office is on Wall Street."

Evan's heart was pounding as he looked across the room as Nia walked in from her bedroom, now dressed in a soft nightshirt.

"Looking at Holstein's balance sheet, I don't think he would blow two million dollars on some jewelry that he could never sell," Raymond added. "I think he was representing the real buyer."

"Send me everything you have," Evan stated in a low voice.

Chapter 25

Evan was up long after Nia had gone to bed Wednesday night. He couldn't sleep. The implications of what Raymond had revealed were racing through his brain.

Strom Investments was founded in Bloomfield, Michigan, twenty years ago by Walter Strom. Now, his son Colby was an upstart executive in the company, managing their New York office. The same Colby Strom who had viciously attached Nia just eleven years ago.

It all made sense. Like Tony's contact Spencer had told them, people who wanted to know about jewels knew of Worthington's acquisition of the Crimson Amazon for their upcoming auction. And if Strom were keeping tabs on Nia, he definitely would have known about it. Then he set out to steal it right out from under her, and possibly ruin her career in the process.

When Evan looked at the picture of Colby he found online, it wasn't hard to imagine the resentment that was fueling him. If he had once been a good-looking boy, there were few signs of it now. Whatever Nigel St. Clair had done to him had left considerable damage to his bone structure around his nose and along his jaw. And any plastic surgery since had only left mask-like skin over a lopsided frame.

It was definitely enough to feed the rage of a narcissistic sociopath who would rape a fifteen-year-old classmate, and capture it on film. And he must have blamed Nia for the damage done to him after.

Thursday morning, Evan told Lucas what they had found.

"Who else on the team knows about the details of Nia's juvenile records?" Evan asked.

"Just you, me, and Sam," his friend replied.

"Good. I'd like to keep it that way if possible. For Nia's sake. I think we should hand over what we know to the feds and let them take down Strom. They won't need to cut a deal with Holstein. I'm sure Raymond was just scratching the surface of what that prick Strom was involved in."

"No problem, I'll send them what we have today," Lucas stated. "Now, are you ready to owe me drinks for the next month? I finally locked down the IP address for that bugged laptop power cord. The signal was bouncing around in a random rerouting pattern. But once I was able to isolate—"

"Luc, what did you find!" Evan finally interrupted, impatiently.

"The IP address for the receiver, and a location in Dorchester."

"Send it to me."

Evan had the team assembled in the Worthington warehouse a few moments later working out a plan to investigate the receiver, and the renter of the residence, a Tommy Blige with a sizeable criminal background. By noon, he, Tony, and Michael were converging on a townhouse only a few blocks from where Flannigan was

shot. Michael knocked at the front door, while Evan
and Tony entered through the unlocked rear entrance.
Apparently, the single male occupant didn't like
Michael's look, but when he turned to run out of the
house, he found the other two Fortis agents blocking
his path. There was a brief struggle in which Evan
landed a couple of satisfying blows to Blige's face. But
it was an otherwise smooth operation.

Not only did they find the receiver to Nia's bug, but
there was also an impressive amount of illegal equipment and contraband in the house to make talking
worthwhile for Blige. He gave up what he knew pretty
easily, confessing to be one of the three robbers, and responsible for the work on Worthington's surveillance to
loop the video and shut down the motion sensors.
Fortis walked away with the names of his others partners in the heist. All three were in police custody within
hours, and now under investigation for the murders of
Matt Flannigan and Chris Morton related to the stolen
property found in Blige's house. But Blige couldn't give
them Walsh.

"I still don't see where Chris Morton fits into all
this," Tony stated when they were back at Worthington
at the end of the day. "Blige confirmed Flannigan
planted the bug and gave them access to the warehouse
the night of the robbery. Then Blige and his two partners
stole the stones and delivered them to a locker in
Gleason Courier's depot. Just like the delivery driver
told us. But what about Morton? And Flannigan's girlfriend, Coombs? No one in Blige's crew even mentioned
their names."

The same thing was bothering Evan.

"Let's regroup in the morning before we pack up,"
he suggested. "With the stolen assets acquired and

everyone involved either in police custody or dead, the mission has been successfully completed. We've neutral- ized the threat to Nia."

"What about Walsh, Ice?" Michael asked. "We still don't know who he is."

"No, we don't. His operation is much bigger than the Worthington robbery. So he's the FBI's problem now. We'll give them everything we know for a head start."

Nia was out of time. She had known it was inevitable but it still took her by surprise.

She was lying next to Evan, early in the morning. Her head was on his chest and he was trailing his fin- gers over her arm. The sun was starting to rise. Time was almost up.

It was Friday, and Fortis had officially completed their mission. Chris Morton confirmed dead, the thieves were in police custody, and the investigation into the jewelry heist was almost over. With the Wor- thington security team now trained on the new system, Evan and his agents were scheduled to leave Boston today.

"Nia," Evan whispered.

She knew they had to talk. There was so much to say, yet Nia had managed to avoid any meaningful conver- sations for the last few days. They discussed the case, her work, his dad's collection, what they'd do for dinner each evening.

Then, despite promising herself that she wouldn't let it happen again, that it was pointless, she walked into his arms again last night, for one more time. It had been slow and leisurely, meant to last for as long as possible.

"Nia, we need to talk," he continued.

"I know," she acknowledged.

"Tell me what you want?" Evan asked.

How did Nia explain that she wanted this, here, now, with him in warm comfort in the aftermath of incredible sexual chemistry? If this was all there was, she'd be good, content. But she didn't want the rest of it. She didn't want the need and dependency, to lose herself in someone else, her happiness controlled by them. The risk of betrayal and pain. To be so in love with a man that he could destroy her.

But Nia knew that she couldn't have one without the other, and the cost was just too high.

"I really like you, Evan," she started, and his body stiffened immediately. "But I don't see us working out long-term."

The words seemed to hover in the air above the bed. They sounded so emotionless and final. His fingers stopped moving and he didn't respond. Seconds ticked by as she waited for him to say something, anything. Nia closed her eyes, wanting to cry. Her heart felt constricted.

"I don't understand," he finally said. "Explain it to me, Nia."

"There's nothing to explain," she replied, feeling cornered.

"You mean you don't want to."

He pulled his arm out from under her and sat up, swinging his legs off the end of the mattress. She immediately felt cold, alone.

"So, what was all this then?" he demanded, sweeping

his hand around in circles to indicate the bed and what they had done in it, repeatedly. "Why, Nia?"

"What difference does it make?"

"No more games!" snapped Evan. "Stop avoiding the issue. Just tell me why. I at least deserve that much."

She couldn't lie there anymore. Nia scrambled off the opposite side of the bed. She walked across the room, naked, to grab her robe off the hook behind the bathroom door.

"How exactly would this play out, Evan?" she questioned, sarcastically. "I say 'yes, let's be together.' What does that mean, exactly?"

"It means just that. We're together, in a relationship. We make a commitment, make plans for the future," he shot back, his face wrinkled in confusion. "It's a fairly common concept, Nia."

"Then what? Walk me through how this would go. We date long distance? For how long? Then what?" she insisted, starting to pace in front of him. "We move in together? Where would we live?"

Evan hung his head, shaking it from side to side.

"I don't know. But we'd figure it out. That's the point. We'd find a solution," he stated quietly.

She laughed, clearly not amused.

"There's only one solution, Evan. I'm supposed to leave my job, give up my career, become your Stepford robot," she spat. "I'll whittle away my time in the Virginia mansion in winter, at Martha's Vineyard in the summer. Maybe I'll start a charity, hang out with the elegant Mikayla Stone-Clement for tennis matches at the country club. Become a nice, understated wife."

"What are you talking about! I never said any of that!"

He stood up, gloriously naked and towering with frustration.

"You don't have to. I can read the tea leaves pretty well," she muttered.

Nia turned away, out of steam. Now, she just wanted the whole thing over and done with.

"Nia, none of that is true. I want you, just the way you are," he replied, his tone marginally softer. "Why would I want you to change? Become anything like you described?"

She didn't reply, standing firm with her arms crossed and back to him.

"I don't know where we'd live and frankly, I don't care," added Evan. "We can stay here, I'll commute to Alexandria by helicopter when needed. I doesn't friggin' matter, Nia."

"You're being ridiculous," she threw over her shoulder.

"I'm being ridiculous? You've got to be kidding me!"

There was a pause as they both stubbornly held their ground. Until Evan let out a bark of harsh laughter.

"This is all just smoke and mirrors, isn't it, Nia." He strode forward and took hold of her shoulders, forcing her to face him. "Where's that honesty you've always shown? Why don't you just admit that you're scared?"

She shook off his hands, attempted to walk away, but he blocked her path.

"Let me pass!"

"No, not until I hear the truth. You're afraid."

"Yes! I'm afraid!" she yelled back out of sheer frustration. "I'm scared that you'll lie to me, manipulate me. That you're pretending to be something you're not.

That I'll give up everything I have to be with you and be left with nothing when it all falls apart!"

Evan stepped back as though she had hit him. Nia covered her mouth and her eyes filled with tears. *Damn it!* She turned away before he could see them spill.

"Nia. That's not going to happen," he whispered.

She walked away, afraid he'd touch her and then she'd really fall apart.

"It already has, Evan."

"No, no. We talked about this. You know how it happened. It was my job!" She heard his sharp sigh. "We can get past this."

"I understand you were doing what you needed to, Evan. But that doesn't make it hurt any less. And I'd be a fool to give you the opportunity to hurt me again."

"I wouldn't. Damn it, Nia. I love you! Can't you see that?"

"Maybe," she whispered, turning back to him but unable to meet his eyes. "But I also know it can be a fleeting, fickle thing. It's just not enough."

"You can't be this cynical."

"Call it experience, Evan."

That seemed to knock the wind out of his sails. He brushed by her, and Nia listened to him moving around the room. She wiped the tears off her face, but they just kept coming.

"At least tell me that this meant something to you, Nia," he finally asked, his voice low and rough. "Being with you . . . Tell me you felt even a fraction of what I did."

Nia couldn't say the words. They were stuck in her throat, cutting off her breathing. She was sobbing now, her shoulders shaking from the wave of sadness that engulfed her. The bathroom door closed firmly as Evan left the room.

By the time he emerged from the bedroom a short time later, she was waiting in the kitchen much more composed. It was only a few minutes before seven o'clock yet the day already felt old and worn. He was fully dressed in his now usual black gear and carrying his duffel bag. Nia forced herself to walk forward, meeting him near the front entrance of her apartment. Neither spoke. There was nothing else to be said.

She opened the door, eyes downcast, praying the tears didn't return. He brushed his finger under her chin, lifting her face. Their eyes met briefly, hers shining, his dark and clouded. He lowered his head and kissed her, brushing his lips against hers as though to taste them for the last time.

Then Evan DaCosta was gone, striding down the hall of the duplex and out of her life.

In the aftermath of the theft, things went back to normal at Worthington fairly quickly. Eager to get things back on track, Nia tried to create a sense of stability and community within the office, rallying everyone toward the upcoming summer auction. There were a few days of gossip around Chris's mysterious death, including more rumors of drug use. Emma in particular seemed preoccupied and less cheery than usual. While Edward immediately began the search for a new operations manager, Nia suggested they involve Emma in the interview process to keep her engaged.

Despite how badly things had ended between them, Evan didn't quite disappear from her life as she had anticipated.

The day after his departure, she got a call on her cell phone. Nia was having lunch with Lianne after her tutor session, then almost choked when she saw the number. When she didn't answer, he left a voice-mail message, just to say hello, make sure she was okay.

The next week, he called again with a message offering more of the same. She answered the third call, Friday evening. It was one week after she had walked away from his commitment. They only talked briefly, stilted. He teased her about what movie she'd be watching, she criticized his bad taste in superheroes. When they hung up, Nia cried, wishing things could be different. Saturday, she stayed at the community center for several hours writing another song. It was the last day of her volunteer term before the summer programs started.

The following Tuesday, Emma called Nia from the reception desk. Someone had called into the main number looking for Chris Morton, and was waiting on the bridge.

"This is Nia James. You're looking for Chris Morton?" she asked hesitantly.

"Yeah, he left a few messages for me a couple weeks ago. He was friends with my boyfriend, Matt."

Nia took in a sharp breath, trying to think of how to reply.

"Chris isn't here. What was it regarding?" she finally asked.

"Look, I don't want to get anyone in trouble. But just tell Chris I don't want to have anything to do with what Matt was into," the woman stated. "I found the coke and I flushed it down the toilet. And if he calls me again, I'll go to the police."

Nia sat back in her chair with surprise, but Matt's girlfriend hung up the phone abruptly before she could say anything in response. The anxiously spoken words replayed in her head for a few moments until they only created other questions. Could it be that Chris had nothing to do with the robbery? That he was trying to reach Jennifer Coombs for something else completely? Is that why he was killed?

As awkward as it felt to do, Nia picked up the phone and called Evan.

Chapter 26

The dream was always the same. It started out perfect, with Nia in his bed, flushed with arousal. Sometimes she was on her back, wearing that pretty pink bra-and-panties set he really liked. The one Evan liked to peel off slowly, revealing all of her warm honey skin, one inch at a time. Other times, she'd be naked, on her stomach, her perfect, round bottom begging for his touch. She was always smiling, her brown, feline eyes sparkling.

Evan would touch her. Anywhere. Everywhere. She was firm, soft, toned, slick, and wet. It felt so real. She would gasp, lick her lips, bite the bottom one. His balls would tighten painfully, deliciously. He was breathless with the need to bury himself inside her, feel her wrapped around him with silken tightness.

He pulled her close, widening her legs so she was ready. Her eyes clung to his, penetrating his soul while her kitten-like moans begged him to take her. One sure stroke and he was there, encased deep. Home.

No!

The word sent a chill down his spine. Evan looked into her eyes, and they were clouded with pain, hurt, distrust. Suddenly, they were standing apart, still naked but distant. Her red lipstick was smudged, staining the side of her face as tears ran down her cheeks.

No!

The moan was his.

Evan gasped, suddenly awake. It was a few seconds before he realized he was at home in Virginia, in his bed alone. His throbbing erection was only one of the things still lingering from the dream. The details sometimes changed a little, but it always ended the same.

He took a moment to catch his breath, try to keep the best parts in his memory, erase the other things. Not that it mattered. He would experience it all again in a couple of days, just as he had repeatedly since he had left Boston. Since he'd left her.

No. Since she had left him.

Evan sighed, looked at the clock. Just after six o'clock. He rolled out of bed, ignoring the inconvenient morning wood. It seemed like his constant companion these days, reminding him of what he wanted but couldn't have.

He dressed in loose shorts and headed out for his daily run along the river, setting a pace guaranteed to prevent too much analytical thinking beyond a strong breathing pattern. It sounded like his team was starting with a new client today. He needed to get his shit together.

Two hours later, he walked in the Fortis headquarters about six miles south of downtown Alexandria on a four-acre private compound. Lucas was already there, in the main building sitting at his desk engrossed in something on his computer. Evan wondered if his friend and partner sometimes slept there.

"Hey," Lucas called when he saw Evan walking across

the open space in front of the offices held by the three partners. "Did you get my note?"

Evan stopped at the threshold of the spacious room enclosed in glass.

"Yeah, a senator thinks he has a leak in his office?"

Lucas nodded.

"We're meeting him at ten o'clock this morning. I'm hoping you can be lead on it. I'm taking on that security contract with Magnus Motorsports in Toronto, and Sam's got some work to do with Clement Media."

"Clement? We still do work for them?"

It was the newspaper and magazine empire built by Mikayla's father, George Clement.

"Only for George. He's not running the company anymore, not day-to-day anyway. But we conduct annual personnel audits for him, with full reviews for all the publishing houses. After that situation a few years ago, he wants to make sure there is no sign of media corruption anywhere in the company."

"Got it," Evan stated, nodding. "I can take the new assignment."

"Great. I've sent you and Sam the preliminary details. Let's meet at nine-thirty to go over it, before Senator Wolfe arrives," suggested Lucas. "By the way, do you have any plans for tonight?"

"Not really, why?"

"Cierra wants to invite you out for dinner with us," his friend said, but his mischievous grin said it was more than that.

"Why would she do that?" probed Evan.

Lucas shrugged, pretending to continue working at the computer.

"I may have mentioned that you were broken-hearted." Evan rolled his eyes. "She has a friend who has a cure for that."

"Well, tell Cierra thanks but no thanks. I don't need a cure."

"Yeah, you do. We're all sick and tired of your long face and sad eyes. It's pathetic, my friend. Quite frankly, it is so nauseating that it ruins my appetite."

"That's a real problem, Luc. You can't afford to lose any weight," Evan shot back.

"What?" Lucas demanded, standing up and looking himself up and down. "What're you talking about? Just 'cause I'm not the size of the Hulk like you and the Scotsman doesn't mean I'm skinny!"

It was a running joke between them all.

"Not skinny, just slender. Slim?" Evan added at the look of horror on his friend's face. *Serves the bastard good for trying to set me up!*

"It's lean!" insisted Lucas.

Evan just laughed, walking away. His office was at the other end of the open space, an add-on to the original office floor plan once he joined Fortis six months ago.

Despite the ribbing, Evan knew his friends were a little worried about him. His moping was very sad, ruining his own appetite. In fact, he was already down eight pounds. He wished the answer was a night out or to date other women. If it was just another ordinary relationship breakup, that would be an easy solution. Just get back on the horse, and all that. What Evan was feeling wasn't anything resembling ordinary. His life had been altered forever and there was no quick fix for that.

It was now a few days since he had last spoken with Nia. It had been a quick chat, the first time she had answered any of his calls. Now, Evan was struggling to resist phoning her again. Even just to say hello. But the day was a busy one. He quickly got wrapped up in the charge of a new mission, and managed to put her out of his mind for a few hours.

He was working a surveillance plan for the senator's office when his cell phone rang. It was Nia, and his first thought was that something was wrong.

"Nia? Hi," he stated, trying to seem casual, unaffected.

"Hi, Evan. I hope I'm not interrupting you at work," she stated politely.

"No, not at all. I'm just sitting around eating bonbons, counting my limitless cash supply," he quipped, missing the freedom to tease her.

"Ha-ha, very cute," she shot back, though he could hear the smile in her voice. "Jokes like that are only funny when poor people make them. It's called irony."

"Hey, I'm a working man. I earn a paycheck like everyone else. I'm allowed." It wasn't exactly accurate, but she didn't need to know that.

"Whatever," she dismissed.

There was a small pause.

"What's going on, Nia?" he finally asked, sitting back in his chair.

"I just got a very strange phone call that I thought I should tell you about. It was from Matt Flannigan's girlfriend."

Evan sat up straighter, caught off guard by her statement.

"Jennifer Coombs. Why was she calling you?" he asked.

"She just called the office looking for Chris."

"What did she want?"

"That's the strange part," Nia explained. "Do you remember the call I told you I overheard? Where Chris said he was trying to find her to get something back?"

"Yeah, of course."

"I think it was cocaine. She said to tell Chris that she flushed the coke down the toilet and to never call her again."

"That's everything?" he asked, now walking out of his office toward the bull pen where Raymond and the other agents on the team sat.

"That's all. She just hung up after that."

"Okay, thanks for letting me know, Nia."

"Okay. But there's one more thing."

Evan stopped midstride.

"I have some preliminary estimates for your collection," she stated.

He clenched his jaw. She only wanted to talk about business.

"I wondered how you would like to review it. I can just e-mail it to you, then you can let me know if you have any questions. The options are well outlined, in terms of how you can sell or auction them off," she continued.

Then what? His dad's art collection was the last thing that connected them.

"I'd like to review them with you if that's okay," he replied.

"Over the phone?" asked Nia.

He looked at his watch. It was twenty minutes to three.

"No, in person. Tomorrow. How about nine o'clock in the morning?"

There was silence in response.

"Evan," she finally whispered.

"In fact, I'll be in Boston this evening. We can have dinner tonight and finish off my contract tomorrow."

She paused again and Evan suddenly felt as though

he had to see her. As though if they didn't meet tonight, he might never see her again. He couldn't explain the irrational thought but his heart started beating like a drum in his chest.

"I'll pick you up at the gallery later. Let's say, at six o'clock?" he pressed.

"Aren't you in Alexandria? How can you possibly be here by then?" she questioned.

"Don't worry about it. Six o'clock, Nia."

"No." His heart stopped, painfully. "Pick me up at home. I'll be there by then."

Evan grinned, feeling the adrenaline now coursing through his veins.

"It's a date," he confirmed before disconnecting.

Evan jogged over to Raymond's desk to give him the update. The agent looked relieved to see him.

"Hey, looks like we can finally cross Chris Morton and Coombs off the list on the Worthington mission," Evan announced. "Turns out Morton was only chasing Flannigan's girlfriend for some lost drugs."

He repeated what Nia had told him about the cocaine. But Raymond just nodded and waved his hand dismissively.

"Good, but Ice, I was just about to call you. I think I have something on Walsh."

"That's great! Go ahead and send me the details," Evan replied as he turned away, already thinking about everything he needed to do to get one of the choppers in the air within the next thirty minutes. "I'm headed for an overnight trip to Boston, so I'll read it when I land."

He was back across the office floor to his office before Raymond could respond. Within another fifteen minutes, he had everything he needed for the trip. That included a packed duffel bag in his office that was always ready and stocked with two extra sets of clothes and toiletries. It was an old habit from the agency, one he was grateful he hadn't let slide.

With his bag strung across his chest, Evan found both his partners sitting in one of the smaller board-rooms, reviewing some files.

"You going somewhere?" Sam asked with a sardonic lift of his brow.

"I'm taking chopper two," he stated.

"Okay," Lucas replied simply. Fortis had two leased helicopters, ready to fly at all times to support their missions.

"Anything you care to share with us?" added Sam.

"I'm going to Boston. I'll be working there tomor-row, but I'm not exactly sure when I'll be back. Monday morning at the latest to start the senator's case on the ground," Evan explained, very aware that he sounded a little off the hinges. He didn't care.

"All right then. Go get your woman," Sam ordered, almost cracking a smile.

"Keep us posted," added Lucas, grinning like a fool, and looking a little like Evan felt. "No details or anything. I'm not into that. Just the highlights. Sam needs tips."

"Yeah, yeah, yeah," Evan chided.

His two friends continued to provoke each other as he left the building.

The hangar and landing pad were at the rear of the Fortis property. Evan had one of the machines started up and inspected by three-fifteen. He remembered the private heliport about ten minutes from Nia's place. Before takeoff, he sent a note to Sandra Blake asking her to arrange landing approval, and for a car to meet him on the ground in Boston. She acknowledged his request in less than a minute, proving that his interim CEO title at DaCosta Solutions certainly had it perks.

With everything in place, Evan lifted the powerful machine into the air to start the two and a half hour flight at top speed. Hopefully, it was enough time to figure out a game plan to convince Nia they should be together. By the time he landed the chopper, Evan had it all worked out. Nia was afraid of love, scared to trust him. So, they would date, like at the beginning, for as long as needed. He just had to remind her of how much fun they had, when they were just two people getting to know each other, before his Fortis role was uncovered. And Evan would be there for as long as it took, without expecting her to make any changes in her life. If that meant rethinking his life, then so be it.

Maybe Fortis needed an office in Boston. Or he could accept the DaCosta CEO role permanently and run the company from Massachusetts. There were plenty of feasible scenarios, with nothing to stop him from doing whatever he wanted. For once in his life, Evan was truly grateful for the financial security that made the various options possible.

Sandra came through, and there was a car and driver waiting near the landing pad. At five-fifty, Evan was on his way through South Boston with a few minutes to spare. He sent the executive assistant an e-mail to say thanks, followed by a text message to Lucas confirming his touchdown. When the driver pulled the car up to the curb in front of Nia's apartment, the lights were out suggesting he had managed to beat her to the finish line. Jogging up to the door, Evan knocked, not surprised when there was no answer. He went back to the car to wait for her arrival.

Almost fifteen minutes later, he was still waiting and was now concerned. Particularly since her cell phone and work phone rang unanswered. Nia James was punctual to a fault and he had no doubt she would have called if she were running behind schedule.

Trying to be patient, he had used the time to review the information Raymond had sent. The agent had finally discovered a connection between Walsh and a Worthington employee. Gleason Courier, the company where Walsh's delivery driver worked, had contracts with many large distributors in the hospitality industry. Their drivers would pick up large skids of supplies from these warehouses, then transport them to the Gleason depot to be assembled for customer orders.

One of these large warehouses was in Watertown. One of their shift supervisors was Nigel St. James.

With his heart racing, Evan did a location search of Nia's cell phone, with confirmation that she was still in the gallery. It was now six-twenty. His gut told him something wasn't right. He asked the driver to head into the downtown core, while he tried to call Nia's cell phone again.

He was about five minutes away from her office when he received a text from Lucas simply stating *911*. It was their code to call headquarters immediately.

"Yeah?" he asked the moment Lucas answered the phone.

"Where are you?" Lucas immediately asked.

"Downtown Boston. Nia's running late so I'm going to meet her at work. Why?"

"I have her on surveillance at the gallery, Evan."

Evan swallowed, not liking the sound of urgency in his friend's voice.

"What's going on?"

"Did you read the report from Raymond?" Lucas demanded.

"Yeah," Evan replied tightly.

"I got an alert from the new security system. Someone's entered the Worthington protected zone without the right protocols."

"Nia," Evan stated, closing his eyes against the implications.

"Yeah. And the security guard on duty, Stan, isn't responding to my calls."

"How much time do I have?" grilled Evan as he reached into his duffel bag and pulled out his gun.

"Not long, a few minutes, tops. The safe zone was meant to alert security if someone enters any of the sensitive zones in the warehouse outside of business hours, including the safe."

"I'm on my way," Evan confirmed in a chilling tone.

Chapter 27

"These look incredible," Nia gasped.

She held up one of the photos spread out on the small table in her office. Her team finally had the pictures ready for the summer auction in August. With all of the beautiful shots of the jewelry and other art pieces, it was going to be hard to pick the final ones for all the marketing collateral.

"I know," Adam added, rifling through another small stack.

"It's almost three-o'clock now, so we have an hour or so," Nia confirmed to him and Nancy. "Let's get as far as we can in selecting one for each item in the auction. We can send the extra ones to the clients. They always appreciate that. If we have time after, I'd like to start working on descriptions. I think you did a good first draft, Nancy. We're getting close."

Her two employees nodded, and they dived into the task.

For Nia, it felt great not only to know that the Crimson Amazon and other pieces were again safe and secure, but that the time line required for the auction was not impacted. The international exhibit of the rare jewelry was an ambitious plan to begin with, usually only done by the bigger players in the industry. But it was now all coming together. The first was scheduled for Independence Day weekend in New York.

By four-o'clock in the afternoon, she and the coordinators were able to finish choosing the images needed. They set aside the selected pictures from the ones Nia would send to their clients. Once the two coordinators had left, Nia sat behind her desk to call Emma at the reception area.

"Hi, Nia," the young girl replied, still not quite her usual bubbly self.

"Hey, Emma. Can you do me a favor?"

"Sure."

"I'm sending several packages out tomorrow to clients. Do we have any of those padded courier envelopes?"

"I think so. How many do you need?"

Nia counted in her head.

"Fourteen, I think?"

"All right, I'll bring them up in a few minutes."

"Thanks, Emma."

The receptionist walked into her office about ten minutes later while Nia was thinking about Evan and their plans for that evening. How on earth was he going to get here from Virginia by six o'clock? You can barely get through airport security and on a plane that fast.

"What's wrong?" asked Emma as she put the envelopes on Nia's desk.

"Huh?" Nia replied, snapping her head up with surprise. "Oh, nothing."

"Are you sure? You look worried."

"No," denied Nia, relaxing her shoulders and sitting back. "It's nothing. Just a meeting I wasn't expecting."

Emma nodded, lingering a little. "How about you, how are you doing?"

The young girl smiled but it didn't reach her eyes.

"I'm good."

"Are you sure?" probed Nia. "I know things have been a little hard for you, with Chris . . . gone."

Emma waved her hand dismissively.

"It's fine."

"Well, once we've hired a new manager, things will go back to normal. You'll see," Nia assured her.

"It doesn't matter."

"Wait, Emma," said Nia as she stood up from her desk. "Can I ask you something?"

The younger girl paused, her face sad.

"I know Matt and Chris were friends. Were they into anything dangerous together? Like doing drugs?"

Emma looked down and then away.

"I'm not trying to criticize, I promise," Nia insisted. "But if you know something, it might make you feel better to talk about it."

Emma's face crumpled, and her eyes filled with tears.

"It was harmless," she whispered. "Matt and I like to do a little blow on the weekends. That's it. Matt would always have some around. So Chris thought he could make some money on the side, supply other people. Nothing major. Just a little here and there."

"Oh, Emma," Nia whispered, expecting something like this but still surprised to hear it confirmed.

Emma wiped at her eyes and brushed her wrist across her nose.

"And now they're both dead," she ended in a whisper.

Nia rubbed her back soothingly until the young receptionist stopped crying.

"I'm okay now," she finally stated, but her voice was still a little shaky.

"You're going to be okay," Nia reassured her.

Emma nodded.

"Thanks, Nia," she added before she left to go back down to the gallery.

Nia let out a deep breath, glad that Emma had finally told someone what had been going on. Now, Evan and his team could determine if Chris had really been involved in the robbery, or not.

Then remembering her dinner plans, she got back to work.

It was hard to suppress the bubble of excitement in her stomach. But Nia tried to stay grounded. She couldn't assume that Evan was flying into Boston just to see her. In fact, it now seemed likely that he had been headed there anyway. He was probably already sitting in the airport when she called him, right?

She also tried not to think about what this evening could mean. As much as she missed Evan and wanted to see him again, nothing had really changed. He still wanted something more, and she still could not trust him with her heart.

Forcing herself to focus, Nia went back to the task at hand. It was hugely satisfying to put together the client packages, particularly for Aubrey Niknam. Just four weeks ago, there was the real possibility that Nia would have to inform Aubrey and others that the unthinkable had happened. That their valuable assets had been stolen from Worthington, despite the state-of-the-art security measure they had been promised. The appraised value would have been covered by the company's insurance but that was often much less than what it could fetch at auction. So, as Nia wrote out the courier parcels containing the beautiful photos of each item in the auction, it felt pretty satisfying.

The only hiccup was that she had miscalculated the number of shipments to be sent and was short by one envelope.

A few minutes before five-thirty, she was shutting down for the day, ready to take a taxi home in order to get there a little early. Nia packed up her laptop, grabbed the prepared packages and remaining photos. The only thing left to do was stop at Emma's desk to write up the final envelope. Then the whole stack would be ready for pickup tomorrow morning.

Downstairs, the large gallery area was empty. Though the doors closed at five o'clock each evening, the operations team typically worked for another hour to lock down the building. With Chris gone, Emma was managing on her own with some part-time help. Nia waited by the reception desk for a few minutes for Emma to return. Getting impatient after a few minutes, she went into the warehouse and looked around. The receptionist was nowhere in the immediate vicinity, and Nia was running out of time.

Checking her watch, she turned to head back into the gallery when she saw a discarded shoe near the back door that led to the alley. It looked like the one Emma had been wearing today. Nia stopped to look around. Then she took a few steps forward until her path was suddenly blocked by the man who stepped in front of her.

"Hi, Nia."

She screamed in surprise, then covered her mouth, feeling foolish once she realized who it was.

"Nigel! What are you doing here? How did you get in?"

Nia glanced around again, still searching for Emma and wondering about the discarded shoe.

"Nia, I need your help," he stated.

The serious, nervous tone of his voice made her look back at him.

"Did Emma let you back here? Do you know where she is?"

"Nia, listen to me!"

He grabbed her arm tight, causing her to stumble forward.

"Nigel. What are you doing? Let go of me!"

Her heart was now hammering in her chest as the confusion turned to fear. Something wasn't right. Nigel had never been to her work before, now here he was in the warehouse, and Emma was missing.

"Listen to me. Listen to me!" he insisted in an urgent voice. "I'm in trouble, Nia, and I need your help."

He still had a strong grip on her arm and Nia grimaced from the pain.

"You're hurting me, Nigel," she implored, looking into his eyes. They were dark green and dull. "Please, let go of me."

He released her suddenly, turning away to pace in front of her.

"I don't want to hurt you, Nia. That's the last thing I want to do. But I need you to help me."

"Help you with what, Nigel? What are you talking about?"

"I need to get out of town. Fast," he stated, still walking back and forth with agitation.

"Why?" she pleaded. "Please, Nigel. You're scaring me. Just tell me what's going on."

"I can't. You wouldn't understand, okay," he shot

back heatedly. "Just give me what I need and I'll be gone."

"I don't know what you're talking about!" she finally yelled.

"You do. You know exactly what I need, Nia."

He took a step forward, staring at her hard. There was a fierce determination on his face that she had never seen before. And suddenly, she knew.

"No," she whispered. "No, Nigel."

"Yes. I need you to give me whatever is in that safe that's untraceable," he said with chilling clarity.

She could only shake her head, now speechless.

"Loose stones, money. Anything," he continued.

"No," Nia croaked, stepping back from him. "Nigel, I don't know what's going on but I can't do this. You know I can't do this. Please! Just tell me what's going on. I'll help you, I promise. I have money. Let's go to the bank and I'll give you whatever I have. Then I can cash in some of my stock. Whatever you need. But not this."

"There's no time, Nia. This is the only way," he replied in a hard voice.

He wasn't going to back down, she realized. It was written in the hard bite of his jaw and the tight clench of his fists.

"No. I'm not going to steal anything, Nigel. Not even for you."

"You owe me, Nia," he spat. "You owe me!"

She was shaking her head back and forth while bile rose in the back of her throat.

"Nigel, please. I know what you went through . . ." Her voice broke. "I know what you did for me. But I can't do this. Don't make me do this. Please." The last word came out in a hoarse whisper.

"Sorry, Nia, but you don't get a choice."

In a flash, he had a small gun pointed right at her forehead.

Everything stopped for Nia. She was frozen. Nigel, the man who had protected her, whom she loved like a brother and lived with for over five years as roommates, was threatening her life.

"Now, you're going to open that safe for me."

She could only stare at him, unable to process a response.

"Why?" she finally whispered. "Why, Nigel?"

"Walk, Nia!" he insisted, removing the safety latch on the gun in a slow, deliberate step.

Nia stepped forward toward the large safe in the back of the room. He approached behind her to follow.

"Nigel, please. Just tell me what's happened. Why are you doing this?"

"Jesus, Nia. I kept telling you to just mind your own business and keep your head down. But you just couldn't do it, could you?" he spat, shoving her at the back of the shoulder, suggesting she should walk faster. "If you had just done what you were told, none of this would be happening. So like I said, you owe me. And I'm going to get all the compensation I deserve. Those fucking rich assholes took three years of my life, and I'm finally going to get mine."

It was really hard for her to concentrate, to make any sense of his rambling while he pushed her toward the safe with a weapon at her back. But something finally clicked.

"The robbery," she gasped. "It's the robbery, isn't it? You knew something all along, didn't you?"

He let out a dark, harsh laugh.

"Yeah, I knew something."

Nia turned suddenly to face him, too stunned to remember the gun.

"What? Why didn't you tell me? What does any of this have to do with the robbery?" she shouted. Then found herself gasping for air as Nigel grabbed her around the neck and squeezed just enough to make her panic.

"You stupid, stupid bitch. Who do you think set the whole thing up, Nia? Who do you think made it happen?" he growled into her face, his harsh breath filling her nostrils as she struggled to breathe. "I did! I had it all planned. It was flawless, my biggest job yet. And you fucked it up, Nia!"

He shoved her away, so hard that she fell backward, landing on her behind.

"Two million dollars," he yelled down at her. "I had almost two million dollars in a hidden bank account, and half of it was mine. And you led that guard dog and his goons right to me."

Nia was coughing, then she was backing away from his stiff, threatening stance, her eyes still locked on the gun in his hand. Everything he was saying was painting the worst picture she could have ever imagined.

"Nigel, how could you?"

"How could I not, Nia? It was the perfect opportunity. I had a buyer looking for the red stone, and you had access to it. It was perfect, like winning the lottery!" he screamed. "Then you had to go and fuck it up."

He suddenly leaned down and dragged her to her feet.

"Now, you're going to fix it," he spat, shoving her

toward the safe, now only a few feet away. The gun was back up and pointed at her.

Nia swallowed, frantically trying to think through her options. Somewhere in the distance, she heard her phone ringing. She had left it on the reception counter in the gallery. *Evan.* She was late to meet him at her house. Would he think she stood him up? Would he leave, go back to Virginia?

Nia stumbled forward from another push to her shoulder. They continued for another few steps in silence. It seemed to take forever, and her mind raced to find a way out of this situation. He shoved her hard again, and this time it was right up into the safe.

"Open it, Nia," Nigel demanded.

Nia turned to look at him.

"Nigel, you don't have to do this. It's not too late to stop."

"Do you think I'm stupid, Nia? I know you're trying to stall," he declared with a smug look on his face. "It's not going to work. That security guard of yours is out cold in the bathroom, and the blond chick is lying right next to him. And if anyone else shows up, I'll just shoot them. Do you understand? So, shut up and open the safe."

Nia gasped, her brain racing. Maybe she should just attack him, she thought. Put some of the kickboxing to use. Maybe she could at least knock the gun out of his hands, make a run for it.

But his grip on the weapon and the look in his eyes said he wouldn't hesitate to stop her in any way necessary.

"Okay, okay. I'll do it. Just don't hurt anyone else, Nigel. It's not worth it," Nia pleaded.

"I'm glad you finally understand."

She turned back to the safe, her fingers ready to press the buttons.

"Did you know they were going to kill me?" she whispered, suddenly turning back to him. "Was that part of you big master plan? My life for a million dollars?"

If she was going to die, she wanted to know the truth. She wanted to see just how much he had betrayed her.

He had the decency to look away.

"Of course not, Nia. I didn't mean for it to come to this," he explained. "But the other guys panicked when they heard you asking questions and trying to figure things out. So they decided to get rid of you, like that security guard, Flannigan. I didn't even know about it until it was too late."

Nia let out a sob, so heartbroken she couldn't breathe.

"But you have no one to blame but yourself, Nia," he continued with renewed frustration. "I warned you. I warned you, but you didn't listen."

"Nigel, please," she begged.

"Now open the safe! Or I swear to God, I'm going to shoot you. Somewhere soft and painful, Nia. Don't think I won't do it."

Nia swallowed, turning to face the large vault built into the wall of the building. She punched in the six-digit digital code that only she knew as part of the new system implemented by Fortis. The light on the access pad blinked red, and beeped. It didn't open.

"What did you do?" he demanded, pulling on the safe door to test it. "What did you do?"

"Nothing!" Nia insisted. "I must have made a mistake."

"Do it again. This is your last chance, Nia."

Nia punched the numbers in again, her hand shaking from nervous fear. The pad beeped red twice, then green. The safe was unlocked. She almost collapsed with relief. Nigel shoved her out of the way to swing the door open and Nia stumbled, hitting her back against the wall.

It was over, Nigel had what he wanted. And now Evan would know that she had been responsible for the robbery after all. Not once, but twice.

"I'm sorry, Nia. But I can't leave you to lead them straight to me again," he was saying, his voice sounding tired, but his aim was firm and sure. "I wish I didn't have to do this, but there is no other way. I'm not going to prison again."

Nia closed her eyes and held her breath. She was out of time.

Evan.

The deafening *pop* was the last thing Nia heard before being enveloped in black nothingness.

Chapter 28

Three minutes. That's how long it took Evan to get to the gallery. The limo driver did his best to rush through the evening traffic, shaving off crucial seconds in the route. They pulled into the alley behind the building, stopping in front of the loading bay to the warehouse. Lucas was still on the phone, talking to Evan through a wireless earpiece the whole time, providing all the details he could from his surveillance and security access.

There was a first attempt to unlock the safe, but it didn't work.

Evan jumped out of the backseat of the car before the tires stopped rolling. Gun drawn, he ran up to the building and was inside the rear entrance to the warehouse within seconds. With a sharp focus, he crept his way silently against the wall toward where he knew the safe was located.

His breathing was hard, but everything else was crystal clear.

"Nia has opened the safe," Lucas stated in his ear.

Evan heard a voice echoing through the big space.

The words were chilling. He ran faster, turned a corner, and had both people in his line of sight. His subconscious took in everything. Nia pressed against the wall next to the safe. Nigel St. Clair standing in front of the unlocked safe with a gun pointed from a straight arm. Driven by experience, training, and instinct, Evan fired one shot even as he was running full speed at them.

Nigel's gun also went off just as he screamed and dropped the weapon. Evan's bullet had torn into his shoulder. Evan ignored him as he slid up to Nia, catching her by the shoulder as she fell to the floor. The side of her skull was slick with blood, oozing against his palm as he cradled her head.

His brain froze, his breathing stopped. He was too late. Nigel had shot her.

"Nia?" he whispered hoarsely. "Nia!"

She didn't respond.

Evan gasped, looking down at the woman he loved, still, lifeless. The pain that cut through him was staggering, immobilizing. He swept his eyes over her prone form, desperate for a sign of life. Somewhere behind him, he heard Nigel moaning and sirens approaching. The local police were then finally on-site, securing the scene.

How bad is the bullet wound? Evan examined Nia again, his eyes sharper, more focused. He gently pulled her body to him, searched her other side and back. His hands shook with the effort to stay calm. He inspected the nasty gash that ran along the right side of her head, behind her ear. It was from the graze of a bullet, fired at close range.

Evan wanted to feel relieved, to have hope that she would be okay. But the wound looked deep and there was so much blood. It now coated his hands and was smeared on his clothes. It was too much. She was so still.

The ambulance arrived moments later. Evan pulled it together enough to show his credentials and give a statement. The next few hours were a blur.

His team arrived at the hospital with Lucas and Sam sometime later that evening. Nia was in surgery, and they found Evan sitting in the waiting room.

"Any news?" Sam asked as the five men surrounded his slouched form.

Evan only shook his head. The words were stuck in his throat, chocked by the giant growth lodged in his trachea.

"The police found the bullet. He had only fired the one round, and it looks like it grazed Nia before lodging in the wall."

They all absorbed the words, understanding the significance. Nia had been a hairbreadth away from certain death.

"What about Emma and the security guard?" Lucas asked.

"They'll be okay. A little bruised from the ordeal. Looks like St. Clair pistol-whipped them both when he arrived."

"I'll get us some drinks," stated Tony as the others took seats or standing positions to continue the silent vigil.

As another hour passed, Evan started pacing. The wait was excruciating. He tried to use every technique he knew to remain calm, clear his mind, empty his brain, but nothing worked. His thoughts were filled with every image of Nia. The first time he looked at her picture, noting the dark, chocolate brown eyes. The moment she passed in front of his car with traffic stopping around her. The electrical charge that shot through him when he touched her hand to shake it.

The fireworks when he kissed her that first time, out on the hotel-room terrace.

That yellow dress, draping her body with perfection, hugging every wonderful curve. The sight of it falling to the ground, revealing her naked flesh.

Her laugh, full and unabashed. The cute snort she sometimes gave.

Red lipstick, and dark lined eyes. Gorgeous firm legs, in sexy-as-hell shoes. Her hair, loose and wavy around her shoulders.

The feel of her climaxing over the thrust of his flesh. The soft moans from her throat.

He couldn't stop the thoughts, the memories, the details from clogging his mind until he couldn't think of anything but her. She was all there was for him, the only thing he knew to be truly meaningful. She was his life. And without her, he would be lost.

Evan paced some more, holding back the need to scream at the pain, destroy everything in reach, or curl into a ball like a baby.

At some point, he felt Lucas stop beside him. His friend rested an assuring hand on his shoulder, as though trying to share the burden.

"She's going to be okay, man. Nia's strong, she's a fighter. You know she won't give up."

Evan nodded. That's what he hoped.

"I can't lose her, Luc," he whispered hoarsely.

"You won't," assured Lucas.

"It would destroy me," Evan finally confessed, blinking back the wetness that filled his eyes. "She's . . ."

He couldn't say it. It was too hard. Lucas just patted

his shoulder, nodding. The two friends stood like that for long moments.

"Mr. DaCosta?

Evan turned to face the doctor.

"How is she?" Lucas asked for him. The rest of the team stepped forward like a line of giant sentinels.

"Ms. James is through surgery, and is now in stable condition. We stopped the bleeding and closed the laceration. The MRI showed no sign of traumatic brain injury. But she has more swelling than I'd like and has lost a lot of blood. The next few hours will be critical to her prognosis," the doctor explained. "We've just moved her to an observation room."

"Can I see her?" Evan asked, his hands thrust deep in his front pockets.

"Briefly. Due to her injury, it's uncertain if she'll wake up when the anesthesia wears off. She'll need as much rest as possible to allow the swelling to reduce. We'll do some additional tests once she's awake."

Evan nodded.

"Thanks, Doc," Lucas replied.

The six men followed the physician down the hall until they reached Nia's room. Only Evan went in. It was dark. The beeping heart monitor reminded him of the last time they were in that same hospital, waiting for her to awaken. It felt like so long ago, like he'd already loved her for a lifetime. And it was not nearly enough.

He walked to the side of the hospital bed to look down at her sleeping form. Her head was wrapped with a thick, white bandage, underscoring the seriousness of her condition. There was so much he wanted to say to her.

"Nia," he whispered, brushing his thumb over the

curve of her cheek. "I should never have left. You needed me and I should have been here, with you, protecting you. I'll never forgive myself. You're the most precious thing I've ever had, and I failed to keep you safe."

Evan squeezed his eyes closed, clenching his jaw tight, then bent down and brushed his lips over her forehead. Turning away with his head bent low, he took another minute to get it together. A nurse entered the room, signaling that it was time for him to leave. He lowered his head to hers again, until he was close enough to whisper in her ear.

"I'll be right here when you wake up. I'm staying for as long as you need me."

Nia heard the soft promise, somewhere in the cushioned subconsciousness of anesthesia. His other words swirled around her, creating a comforting haven in a gray void. She tried to blink, move, acknowledge his words, but the tired, sleepy darkness pulled her back down into its depth.

Her next moment of awareness was dominated by mechanical sounds. Beeping monitors, muffled alarms, and electronic voices over a dated intercom system. Nia managed to crack her eyes open. The room was dark, still, and empty except for a tall, large figure standing next to the bed, looking out the window. She tried to move, but it was too hard. Her limbs wouldn't cooperate, her mouth couldn't move. She sighed, and the figure turned. But sleepiness overtook her again until it carried her away.

"Nia? Nia, are you awake?"

She blinked at the urgent sound. Light filtered into her vision, almost too bright to handle. Nia tried to lift her hand to shield her eyes, but her arms could barely move. She moaned in surprise.

"It's okay, don't try to move," instructed the female voice.

"Lianne," she croaked through a dry throat and cracked lips.

"It's me, I'm here. Don't move, okay? I'm going to get the nurse."

Nia nodded, closing her eyes again. Why did everything take such an effort?

"Hi, Ms. James, how are you feeling?" asked a nurse as she approached the bed. This time, Nia was able to see more clearly, getting used to the light.

"Hmmm," was all she could manage in response.

"Have something to drink, Nia," Lianne offered from the other side of the bed. She had a large cup of water in her hand, a bent straw sticking out of it. Nia sipped the cool liquid as instructed. It was heaven.

"We're happy to see you awake," the nurse added as she looked at the various monitors and inspected the IV drip. "The doctor will be in shortly to have a look at you."

Nia turned to look at her friend when they were alone. Every move felt like it was through thick mud.

"What happened?" she managed to ask.

"You don't remember anything?" Lianne questioned back.

"Nigel. Shot me?"

Nia's eyes opened wide with realization.

"Yes," replied Lianne. "It was only a graze. But Evan took him down."

"Evan? How? I heard the gun go off . . ." Nia mumbled. Evan saved her? "Where is he?"

"He went to take a shower, change his clothes. Those

partners of his almost had to remove him by force," Lianne explained. "How do you feel? You've been in and out for almost twenty-four hours. We were starting to get worried."

"What? What time is it?"

"Almost four o'clock. It's Wednesday."

Nia closed her eyes shocked that she'd lost a whole day of her life.

"Are you in pain?" continued Lianne. "Does your head hurt?"

Nia suddenly noticed the numb sensation at the side of her skull. She reached up slowly, feeling the thick bandage that seemed to wrap completely around her head.

"They repaired the gash from the bullet in surgery," added Lianne. "I was so worried about you, Nia! Why do you keep getting yourself in these messes?"

It was meant to be a teasing comment, but Nia could now see the bruising under her friend's red eyes. She had been crying.

"I promise it won't happen again," Nia replied, doing her best to lighten the mood.

"Good! Because, it's just too much drama for me to handle."

Nia closed her eyes, just breathing, feeling her body, getting used to being alive and lucid.

"Do you know what happened to Nigel?" she finally asked.

"I heard that Evan shot him in the shoulder. He'll live, apparently, but he's in police custody. The official charge is armed robbery. It was all over the news."

"Oh, no! After everything we did to keep this quiet," Nia moaned.

"Well, it sounded like a good news story to me. The

reporter said the robbery was foiled by you and the private security firm Worthington had hired in advance of the much anticipated auction in August."

"Really? Wow. That's not so bad, I guess," conceded Nia.

"Not bad! It's publicity gold. They even had a follow-up piece on the Crimson Amazon, showing pictures of Lady Di wearing it with Dodi before her death. If I didn't know better, I would think you had planned the whole clever thing."

"Yeah, well, I'm not that good."

They smiled at each other.

"Drink some more water," Lianne instructed, and Nia obeyed.

Evan returned less than an hour later, wearing fresh clothes and smelling like soap and aftershave. Nia drank in the sight of him, including the tired look in his eyes.

He nodded at Lianne before looking down at Nia.

"The doctor says you're progressing well," he stated in a deep voice, stiff and formal. "That's good news."

Nia smiled tightly, confused by his aloofness. Disappointment gripped her stomach. Had she imagined his words? Was it only a dream? Wishful thinking while under drugs?

"Yes," she replied simply, tongue-tied for anything else to say.

"Good. You gave us all a scare."

"That's what I told her," Lianne threw in as she collected her things. "I'll leave you two alone. I'll check in on you later this evening, Nia."

The slim blonde leaned over and gave Nia a kiss on the cheek.

"Bye, Lianne."

Then she was alone with Evan.

"How are Emma and the security guard, Stan, doing? Are they okay?" she asked first.

"They'll be fine. The doctors checked them out last night," he told her.

"Lianne told me what happened. That you saved me from Nigel." Evan clenched his jaw but was otherwise stoic, his expression hard as ice. "How did you know? How did you get there so fast?"

"We still had admin access to the security system. You triggered an alarm when you and Nigel were still in the warehouse after six o'clock without using an authorization code. And I was already on my way to the gallery. I knew you would never leave me waiting for you without calling, unless there was a problem."

Nia blinked. He knew her so well, and she would be dead now if he didn't.

"Thank you," she said simply, sincerely.

"You don't have to thank me, Nia. You should never have been in that kind of danger," he stated through tight lips.

"Nigel is the broker that you've been looking for, isn't he?" she finally asked. "He was Walsh."

"Looks that way. Raymond thinks he styled himself after a Boston mobster named Nigel Walsh back in the seventies."

Nia closed her eyes pretending to rest. She didn't want to talk about Nigel. His betrayal was more than she could bear to think about.

"You have a few people who want to say hello. Do you feel up to a little company?" Evan asked after a few moments.

She looked at him with surprise.

"Who?"

"Looks like your whole office, really. And my team. Lucas and Sam," he stated.

"Your friends? They're here?"

"They came in last night."

Nia bit the side of her cheek, shocked and a little overwhelmed.

"Sure, I guess," she finally conceded.

"Don't worry, they all won't stay for long. I'll make sure they don't overtax you."

He turned and walked out, only to be replaced by a steady stream of her work colleagues. Adam stayed the longest, telling her about all the news coverage of the attempted robbery and his ideas about how to market the auction even more. Later, Tony, Michael, and Raymond stayed for a short while, telling her a few more things about the case. In order to avoid being charged with murder, one of the robbers had flipped on the others about the murders of Flannigan and Morton, and the attempted hit and run. He also confirmed that Morton had nothing to do with the robbery. They knew he had been friends with Flannigan, so they killed him to take the heat off themselves.

Lucas and Sam also visited for a little while, politely asking a few supportive questions, then sitting quietly while she fell asleep. When Nia woke again, several hours later, there was only Evan standing by the bed, looking out the window. He turned, hearing her movement.

"Hey. Did you have a good rest?" he asked with a soft smile.

"I think so," Nia replied with a shy smile of her own. "What are you still doing here? It must be late."

"I wanted to talk to you."

Evan sat on the edge of the mattress, close enough to touch, but still separate. He handed her some water and she willingly sipped it.

"How are you feeling? Are you hungry? Tony said you hardly ate any of your dinner. We can bring something in for you if you'd prefer."

"No, I'm fine, Evan," she declared.

"No pain?"

She couldn't lie.

"A little, but I don't want any more morphine. It makes me groggy."

"Maybe they can give you something milder," he suggested, about to stand up.

"No." She stopped him with a hand on his arm. "I'm fine. I'll take something later, if I need to sleep. Now, what did you want to talk to me about?"

"I know you must still be in shock about Nigel," he said carefully. "But there's more that you need to know."

Nia swallowed, wondering how much worse this whole thing could get.

"We've confirmed that Sean Holstein wasn't the actual buyer of the diamonds."

"What do you mean? I thought you guys recovered them from him."

Evan nodded, obviously hesitant to tell her what he needed to.

"We did. But the money used to pay for the job wasn't his. He was just representing the buyer."

"Okay. So do we know who that is?"

Evan brushed the back of his hand along the line of her cheek.

"It was Strom. Colby Strom."

It took her a full minute to understand what he was saying. And then everything crashed around her. Nia shook her head back and forth repeatedly before being able to articulate words.

"No," she whispered. "No!"

"I'm afraid so, Nia. It looks like Strom went after the Crimson Amazon because he knew it was your deal."

"Oh my god!" she gasped, her mind slowing coming to grasp with what exactly that meant.

"Nigel," she whispered finally, her eyes wide but unseeing. "Was Nigel working with him?"

"No," Evan told her quickly. "No, there is no proof St. Clair knew who the real buyer was. He was just after the money."

After a deep, low sob, she covered her mouth. Her eyes burned with tears of anger and frustration. Evan took her hand but she shook it away.

"Nia, please. It's okay. We got him," he explained. "The FBI arrested Strom yesterday. We got them both."

"No, no," she cried. After all the pain and humiliation she had fought so hard to overcome, he was violating her all over again. He was invading her life, taking what he wanted and leaving her broken in the aftermath. It was too much for her to bear. And Nigel!

"Nia, sweetheart," Evan repeated, but she couldn't look at him.

"Leave me alone," she croaked.

"No, Nia. It's okay. Just let me—"

"Leave me alone. Please!" she pleaded, her eyes clenched tight as hot tears seeped through and ran down her face and despair took over. She didn't even know when he had left.

Chapter 29

Nia did well in the hospital over the next day and a half, with no signs of injury beyond the deep gash in her skull. She was released on Friday morning and Evan drove her back to her apartment.

While she seemed to be healing well physically, he was very worried about her emotional state. The news of Colby Strom's role in the robbery on the heels of Nigel's attack was more than anyone should be expected to handle. Even a woman as strong as Nia.

He watched her move around her apartment, getting settled into a comfortable spot on the couch with a blanket and the television remote. On the surface, she seemed fine, but there was a dimness to her eyes that pulled at him. Evan wished more than anything that he didn't have to tell her about Strom, not so soon. But the news of his arrest was already circulating in the media, and Evan knew he had to be the one to tell her. It was a moment that would haunt him for a long time.

Now, two days later, there were a few other things that had to be addressed, and he couldn't put them off any longer. He joined her on the sofa, careful not to disturb her position.

"Nia, we need to discuss things now that you're out of the hospital," he started.

She looked back at him with a steadfast gaze.

"Like what?"

"You'll be off work for about four weeks, so you're going to need some help until you're better. Someone to make sure you don't experience any serious side effects from the gunshot wound."

"I'll be fine, Evan," she said simply, turning back to the television.

"Nia, I'm staying," he said simply.

She looked back at him with a puzzled look on her face.

"I've already worked it out with Luc and Sam. I can work from Boston for as long as needed, though I may have to go back to Alexandria for the day, on occasion. But I'll keep the chopper ready, just in case."

"Chopper? Helicopter?" Nia asked, blinking. "You have a helicopter?"

"Yeah, I flew it here on Tuesday. Fortis has two."

She just continued to stare at him.

"You were serious about flying helicopters," she repeated, remembering their conversation at his apartment in Virginia. It seemed so long ago. "You fly planes, too, don't you?"

"Small ones," he replied with a shrug and a slightly cocky grin. "I told you I had my pilot's license. But you're getting sidetracked, Nia."

"Sorry, go on."

"I'll stay for as long as you need me to," he finished.

There was a heavy silence as she looked down at her hand.

"Evan, this isn't going to work. We're not going to work." His heart stopped. "I . . . I just can't do this."

She closed her eyes and lay her head back on the sofa cushion.

Evan clenched his jaw and did what he knew he had to.

"Nia, there's nothing for you to do. I'm not talking about us, or our relationship. I'm just talking about you getting better. I'll only be here to help you recuperate. Okay? Will you let me do that?"

When she finally looked back at him, her eyes were so sad that Evan could barely look at them.

"You're right, Evan. I need to get better. I need to come to terms with everything that's happened and move on," she said softly. "I know I can do that. I will. But I can't do it with you here. It hurts too much."

Evan blinked at her words, and at the painful honesty behind them. He, St. Clair, and Strom had all hurt her in different but unforgivable ways. And the only way for her to heal was to move on from them all, including him.

"I'm sorry," she whispered.

He shook his head, unable to respond. Evan wanted to say that *he* was the one who was sorry, for everything she had been through and his contribution to her pain. But no words could really express how he felt about losing the opportunity to have her in his life.

They sat silently beside each other until Nia finally fell asleep. Evan took a few more minutes to indulge the simple pleasure of watching her sleep, trying to come to grips with losing the privilege. Then, when he couldn't put it off any longer, he took action. By that evening, he had arranged for his mother's housekeeper, Agnes, to fly to Boston and spend the next few weeks with Nia. He stayed in Boston for another couple of days, sleeping on the couch only long enough to ensure the two women had everything they needed. Then he flew back to Virginia to try to move on.

At first, Nia was so relieved to have Evan gone. Looking at him hurt, like a physical wound that would never heal as long as he was there. Every day after he left, she woke up feeling stronger and stronger, and a little bit more like herself. At first, she had been a little annoyed with Evan for taking control of her life by sending Agnes to stay with her, but Nia quickly came to appreciate the gesture. The older woman was a godsend; easy company, and exactly what Nia needed during her recovery.

Every day she also spent time thinking about what had happened with Evan, Nigel, and Colby. What they had done to her, and why. How she could learn from the experience and never be in the same situation again. Every day, the pain in her chest lessened until she felt ready to talk. On Friday afternoon, three weeks after being released from the hospital, she called Lianne at her office.

"Hey, Nia, how are you feeling?" her friend answered.

"I was wondering if I could see you," asked Nia. "Today, at your office. I need to talk."

"Okay, sure. But why don't I come see you?" suggested Lianne. "I was planning to stop by for a visit tomorrow anyway."

"No, that's okay. I need to get some fresh air anyway. I'll bring Agnes with me."

"All right, if you're sure. My last appointment is at four-thirty. How about five-thirty?"

"That's good. Thanks, Lee."

"Is everything okay? Is it about the robbery?"

"No, not really. But I'll tell you more, later."

Lianne ran her counseling practice out of a medical center on the other side of downtown Boston. Nia had been several times over the years they had been friends but it felt odd to do so now. She pushed open the door, labeled with a bronze plaque engraved with the title DR. L. BLOOM, PH.D.

A few minutes early, Agnes took a seat while Nia walked around the waiting room. Lianne opened the office door about five minutes later, looking professional in a white silk blouse over black slacks and black kitten-heeled pumps. Her friend smiled easily, waving her into the private space, and Nia let out a deep breath. It was going to be fine.

"So, what's going on," started Lianne once they were seated on the couch in her office.

"I needed to talk, about . . . stuff," Nia explained.

"Okay. But we can talk anytime, Nia. Why here?"

"I know. I guess I wanted your opinion as a professional, not a friend."

"It would probably be the same," her friend replied with a teasing smile.

"Maybe. I think I just need to hear it that way. You know what happened when I was fifteen. So, I spent a lot of time in therapy when I was younger. I thought I knew all the answers, about what happened. Now after Nigel and . . . everything, I feel stuck, like there's more I need to figure out."

Lianne sat back.

"What do you think has happened to make you feel stuck?"

Nia sat back also.

"Evan," she answered simply.

"What exactly?"

"In the hospital, when he told me about Colby funding the robbery, I think I just shut down. Suddenly, they all got confused in my head. Kyle, Colby, Nigel, and then Evan. They all became one big . . . nightmare . . . form," she tried to explain. "They were inseparable, combined as one large threat. And the only way to protect myself was to run."

Nia paused, wondering if the words were really explaining how she had felt.

"And how do you feel now?" Lianne asked.

"I'm able to separate things now," Nia concluded.

"What about Nigel? He was like a brother to you, right?"

"I thought so. But now I'm not sure if I ever knew who he really was. I think I just saw him as some kind of hero who came to my rescue when no one else did," Nia replied. "And I felt this huge sense of guilt and responsibility for what he went through."

"But, you weren't responsible for his actions any more than you were to blame for what Colby and Kyle did," insisted Lianne.

"I know that. Rationally, I know that. But I don't think I ever let myself believe it. And now I just feel sad for him."

"What about Colby?"

"I don't feel anything about Colby. I should feel vindicated I guess, but it doesn't matter one way or the other. I believe in karma, and I always figured his actions would catch up with him eventually," Nia explained. "I reached out to Hailey a few days ago. She told me that Kyle had joined the Marines after high school, and then was injured in Afghanistan on his second tour. He's lost both his legs."

The women looked at each other.

"So that just leaves Evan," Lianne concluded.

"I woke up a couple of day ago and I couldn't remember why I was angry at him, why I didn't trust him. Not right away. I just missed him. Then, I remembered something he had said to me about the things he had learned from his dad. A sense of justice and to protect your family and country."

"That sounds noble," Lianne replied.

Nia looked down at her hands.

"I think he was telling the truth, Lee. I think he was honest with me about who he was while we were going out. I think I know him at his core. And I do trust him." She looked up at her friend and trained therapist. "Is that crazy? He lied to me from the moment we met, and now I'm saying that I trust him."

"What do you trust him with?"

"My safety, my life, my well-being. I trust him to be honest about anything important."

"Maybe that's what's relevant, Nia. Do you think he will lie to you again?"

Nia smiled.

"I'm sure he will, if he thinks it will protect me. Or if his job requires him to."

"Well, from what I know about his career, that might not be a bad thing."

They both chuckled a little.

"So, if you trust Evan, why don't you just tell him that? What's holding you back?"

"I don't know how. I can't figure out how to take that step. I'm scared, and I'm stuck."

Lianne nodded in agreement.

"That's what Evan said the day he left Boston the first time, and he's right. I'm scared and I've used everything else to convince myself that love and relationships aren't worth the risk."

"Are you saying you're not scared anymore?" asked Lianne.

"No, I'm still scared," Nia admitted with a sad smile. "But I think I'm more terrified about being stuck in this isolated spot, walled off from any real emotions. I thought the worst feeling was to be hurt or betrayed by someone you love. The emptiness and loneliness of missing them is so much worse."

"I'll let you in on a little secret, my friend," Lianne stated, patting Nia's leg. "We're all scared to really fall in love. Maybe you just needed to find someone who made it worth the risk."

Nia smiled, feeling pounds lighter.

"So, what happens now?" asked Lianne. "What are you going to do about Evan?"

"I don't know, really. I still have some things to work out. Maybe I'll write another couple of songs," she added with a shy grin. "Turns out it's pretty therapeutic."

"Is that all it is, or is there something more?"

Nia shrugged, almost too excited to say the words out loud.

"It's only been a few weeks, but I've been thinking about how to put music back in my life. In a real way."

"Like how?" Lianne probed, her facing lighting up.

"I don't know. Maybe volunteer for an art center or music school? Write for a community-based theater? Maybe even perform some of the songs I've written. I have to look into the options, but I just know it's what I really want to do with my life."

"What about your job?"

"I can't give that up anytime soon. I still have bills to pay, shoes to buy," Nia quipped. "I think I'll be back in the office within a week or so, once I have my final follow-up at the hospital. Then the summer auction is only a few weeks away. All of that is really important to me too. But I still want music back in my life in some way."

"Nia, I can't tell you how happy it makes me to hear you say that. You deserve to be happy and fulfilled, and if songwriting or performing is what you want to do, go for it!" Lianne told her as they stood up. "I'm just hoping I get to hear something of yours soon! You could even do an open mic night. Like at that place we went Memorial Day weekend."

Nia giggled at the idea, even as a bubble of excitement settled in her chest. The friends hugged tight.

"Maybe," Nia teased when they parted. "Thank you for this, Lianne. I really needed it."

"You're welcome, anytime. And you don't need an appointment! You're my best friend and I love you. The advice will always be the same. Now, how do you feel about staying out for dinner? The pub down the street has happy hour with half-priced appetizers. "

By the end of the evening, the idea Lianne had planted was developing in Nia's head. Maybe the only way to get unstuck was to do something drastic. Take a leap so big, there was no going back. And, maybe she could kill two birds with one stone.

After a little bit of research and lots of time psyching herself up, Nia called Evan on his cell phone, suddenly anxious to hear his voice.

"Nia? Is everything okay?" he had quickly answered with concern.

"Hi, Evan. Everything is good," she replied, certain her voice was shaking. They hadn't spoken since he had left.

"How are you?" Nia asked.

He had paused before replying.

"I'm okay. How are you feeling? Agnes tells me you're getting better every day."

That had surprised her. Nia hadn't realized the housekeeper was providing updates.

"I'm feeling good, stronger."

"Good," he stated, firmly.

She took a deep breath and jumped in.

"Listen, I'm planning to be in Arlington sometime next week, and I wondered if you'd like to meet for dinner."

"Yeah, of course, Nia. When will you be here?"

Nia grinned, feeling a thousand pounds lighter.

"I'm not exactly sure yet, but can I give you a call back to confirm?"

"Sure, call me anytime."

"K, bye."

"Bye, Nia."

She hung up the phone, and covered her mouth, wanting to shout out with excitement and fear. Then Nia went back to planning her surprise. A few days later, most of the details for her trip were ironed out. She just had to catch a flight to Virginia in order to pull it off.

Chapter 30

"I wish I could be there too," declared Lianne.

It was Thursday afternoon, almost a week since they had talked in Lianne's office. Nia smiled at the wistful tone in her friend's voice over the phone.

"Next time, I promise," Nia committed. "And I'll make sure the whole thing is recorded, okay?"

"I guess that will have to do. Are you nervous?"

"I'm freaking out a little," Nia admitted. "I told you, I haven't performed in front of anyone since I was fifteen."

"Well, this is a little bit like 'go big or go home,' Nia. Are you sure you're ready for this? There are other ways to tell Evan how you feel. Less public ways," her friend suggested. It wasn't the first time Lianne had made that argument.

"I know. But I need to take the leap, throw off the shackles. This way, there will be no backing out or going back."

"How long are you staying in Arlington?" asked Lianne.

"I'm booked into the hotel until tomorrow. Then it depends on what happens with Evan, I guess."

"Would you stay if he asked you?"

"Eventually, I think. But there's so much we'd have to figure out before that. The auction's coming up, and there's still lots of work to do for it."

"It will work itself out, one way or the other," Lianne assured her.

"Thanks, Lee. I know. I better get going. Evan will be picking me up within the hour and I still need to get in the shower," Nia finally explained.

"Okay," Lianne sighed. "Good luck tonight. I'm sure you're going to be great. And don't forget to record everything!"

"I won't, I promise."

They hung up, and Nia spent a few minutes relaxing on the bed of her hotel room, thinking through the evening she had planned. She was actually going to perform her songs live, with Evan in the audience.

A secret smile played on her lips. Once the idea had formulated in her head, Nia was surprised at how easy it had been to execute. The biggest challenge had been to find a venue willing to let an amateur artist perform, relatively close to Evan's home in Alexandria. As Lianne had suggested, Nia wanted a place like Moody's in Boston that they had gone to with Eddie and Eddie's brother, Kevin. It was the perfect kind of venue, casual and intimate with great acoustics and an appreciative audience. So Nia set out to do a search for places similar in the Washington, D.C. area.

To her surprise and delight, Moody's was a small chain of clubs on the east coast, including a location in the city of Arlington, less than half an hour from Evan's place. The second hurdle was to get on their stage. While they didn't have a formal open mic opportunity, the manager, Bud, was willing to put her on during a slow night with the resident band. He just needed to listen to her perform first. Nia managed to convince the manager to let her audition by submitting a video recording. Then, with some help from Agnes, she went to the Dorchester community centre on Saturday to record a session and sent the file to the club manager that afternoon. On Monday, Bud booked her for Thursday to do three songs.

Now, the evening was here. Nia was as ready as she ever would be. Her only hesitation was with Evan. After that initial conversation last Friday, they had spoken several more times. Just short, casual conversations to confirm their plans. Each time, she could tell he wanted to ask her more about the unexpected trip to Virginia, and she wondered whether to tell him about the real reason she would be there.

At first, it seemed like fun to surprise him, watch his reaction to her onstage as she poured out everything in her heart. Now, Nia realized that she had only been buying time. The performance tonight would take her life on a new course. Once she performed these songs to Evan and the rest of the audience, she could never take back the words. Everything she wanted and felt would be completely exposed. It was what she needed to do in order to move beyond the fear that had kept her frozen. Now, onstage tonight, she was all in.

It was also the first step in living her dream, one that had lain dormant for years, only stirred by the impact of Evan in her life. It had been awakened, taken form, and was impossible to suppress. Now, she had to make a decision. Did she grasp the opportunity to pursue the aspiration of being a songwriter? Or continue safe and secure in a well-paid day job.

Loving Evan had taught her that you can't have what you really want without taking a risk, and it was worth it in the end. So tonight, she would conquer her fears and go after the two things she wanted most.

By five-thirty, Nia was ready for whatever happened next.

She wore a long dress, in softly textured cotton. It had a sexy, bustier-inspired bodice with delicate raised stitching, while the full skirt draped loosely to the floor, creating a more casual look. The butter-yellow color reminded Nia of the dress Evan had bought for her some weeks ago. She hoped he liked this one as much. Nia added chucky wedge-heeled sandals. She played with her loose hair and finished touching up her new, berry-red lipstick before heading into the living room.

A few moments later, there was a knock at her hotel room door. She opened it to find Evan standing there, looking as strong and imposing as ever. He wore dark jeans and a white cotton shirt.

"Hi," she said, finding it hard to believe it had been almost four weeks since she had last seen him. It suddenly felt like an eternity.

"Hi," he replied. "You look beautiful."

She smiled self-consciously.

"Let me just grab my purse, then we'll get going."

She was back within a minute, and they headed down to the lobby.

"Is there anything in particular you'd like to eat?" Evan asked when they were in the elevator. "There's a really great Vietnamese place down the street."

"Well, I actually have somewhere in mind," she admitted coyly.

"Okay," he replied, shrugging with an indulgent smile. "Whatever you want."

They walked outside to where his glossy white Aston Martin was parked. Nia gave him the address to Moody's and they arrived there a short drive later, parking on the street nearby. As they walked inside, Evan looked around speculatively, and she wondered if he suspected what she was up to. But there was no way he could have any clue.

The plan was for them to have a quiet dinner, just the two of them within the hour before the show started. At seven-thirty, Nia would get onstage and open for the resident band, singing her original songs while playing an acoustic guitar, borrowed from the club.

They made it until their meals arrived with polite conversation before Evan asked some of the questions she could feel in his eyes.

"You look great, Nia. How are you feeling?" he asked, his concern clear in his expression.

She smiled softly.

"I'm good, Evan. How are you?"

He shrugged and looked down at his plate briefly.

"I'm okay. But better now that you're here," he stated. "I've missed you."

Nia reached out to touch his left hand as it rested on the table.

"I missed you, too," she admitted.

He nodded, and they ate in silence for the rest of the meal.

"So what brings you to town?" he eventually asked.

It was now seven-fifteen, and she knew the other guests for her performance would be arriving soon.

"Other than dinner with you?" she teased, liking the dimples that flashed on his cheeks. "I have a few things to take care of."

"How long will you be staying?"

Nia couldn't resist.

"That depends on you."

Evan paused, recognizing the words he had told her on their first date. But he was then distracted as Raymond entered into the small club. Evan watched the agent walk across the room toward them. Raymond slapped Evan on the shoulder when he arrived, and then bent low to kiss Nia on the cheek before he sat down at the large empty table beside them.

"What're you doing here?" Evan asked, relaxing back in his chair, his expression unreadable.

Raymond looked around with a straight face.

"I've been meaning to check out this place for a while. I hear the music's pretty good."

The two men looked at each other, communicating something Nia couldn't read.

"How are you feeling, Nia? You look great," Raymond said to her.

"Thanks," she smiled. "I feel pretty good."

"No complications, huh? That's a relief," he replied, nodding. "I've heard of people getting serious head injuries, then developing completely new personalities. Or suddenly discovering they can do things they've never even tried before. Like speaking another language, or something."

Nia burst out laughing, followed by one of her snorts. Raymond raised his eyebrows, trying hard to suppress a grin. Evan looked back and forth between them, trying to see what was so funny.

"Nope," she managed to reply after a few moments, still grinning. "Still the same me as before."

"Good. I'd hate think that gorgeous ballbuster I had met was gone. Ice here needs someone to keep him in check."

Nia burst out laughing again.

"Really, Raymond? Watch your mouth," Evan shot back with annoyance, sitting forward in his chair.

"What?" Raymond claimed, blinking innocently. "It was a compliment."

"That's how I took it," Nia assured him.

Raymond winked back at her and Evan clenched his fist, working his jaw back and forth.

The others arrived in the next few minutes. First Tony and Michael, then Lucas and Sam, no women in tow this time. They all slapped Evan on the shoulders and the back of the head, kissing Nia on the cheek or forehead.

"What's going on?" Evan finally asked, turning to face the table full of his friends and team.

"We're not allowed out for the night?" Lucas replied flippantly as the others ordered drinks from the waitress.

Evan looked at Nia with narrowed eyes, but she was saved from any interrogation as Bud, the club manager, stepped on the stage to talk into the mic.

"Hello, everyone, welcome to Thursday nights at Moody's. We have a great night of entertainment planned for you. Before our resident band, The River Boys, take the stage, I'd like to bring on a special guest with us this evening, all the way from Boston. Please give a warm Arlington welcome to Nia James!"

That was it, the moment she thought would never come. Nia was about to perform live, in a club for the first time ever.

The other guests were clapping while the Fortis crew was cheering loudly. Taking a deep, calming breath, she looked at Evan briefly, but his expression didn't tell her anything. It was too late to have second thoughts, so Nia stood and walked through the maze of tables on to the front of the room. The borrowed guitar was now beside a chair in the front center of the stage.

"Hi, everyone," she began, speaking softly into the mic. "My name is Nia James. As Bud said, I live in Boston now, but I was born and raised in Detroit."

"The D. 313!" someone yelled from the audience. Everyone else laughed, and Nia smiled as she looked out at the small sea of faces. *This isn't so bad*, she thought.

"That right, the 313!" she acknowledged, settling the guitar into her lap and checking the tuning as she talked. "As a kid, I had a crazy obsession with anything early Motown. It drove my mom crazy. Anyway, soul music is a huge influence in what I write, so I'm excited to share my songs with you tonight.

"I should add that this is my first time performing in a very long time, so be kind." Several people laughed some more. "I hope you enjoy my performance."

Then Nia closed her eyes and strummed the initial cord.

The first song was the hardest. It was the one she had written in the days after believing Evan had used her as part of the Fortis investigation. The words were deep, emotional, speaking of pain and betrayal. It described a man who wore a mask, played a character in their love, but who wasn't real. It ended bleak and lonely as she walked away from the false promise of love. The final note hung in the air for a few seconds before the crowd started clapping loudly, cheering at times, with a few people standing up.

Nia looked out to find Evan. His chair was empty. Lucas caught her eyes, and gave her an encouraging smile, nodding to say it would be okay. Then Nia looked around to see Evan's back as he made his way through the tables toward the direction of the bathrooms at the back of the club. She let out a deep breath, anxious to know what he was thinking, feeling.

But the crowded quieted, and there was no time to ponder it more.

"Thank you," she told them all sincerely, smiling as the Fortis table cheered loudly again. "The next song is for Evan, the man who showed me how to get unstuck in life."

The second was lighter, with a jazzier feel. It spoke of the freedom on the other side of fear, where she realized anything was possible if you were willing to take the chance. The words described the powerful feelings of love, hope, and trust that made all dreams possible, and all desires attainable. It ended by declaring her love to the man who freed her from being held back by fear.

The audience went wild, with almost all on their feet. As she bowed her head with acknowledgment, her heart racing with the incredible feeling of accomplishment, Nia tried to find Evan in the crowd. Then, as everyone began to sit back down, she spotted him standing in the back of the club, leaning against the wall. Their eyes met, and though his expression was firm and stoic, his eyes burned with intensity. He'd heard her message loud and clear. Nia smiled, feeling one hundred pounds lighter, freer than she could remember.

She took a deep breath and spoke into the mic again.

"I have one more song for you. This one is a little different," she teased with a flirty wiggle of her eyebrows.

Then she launched into a faster rhythm with a more bluesy sound. It was sexy and seductive, using suggestive words and provocative phrases. Nia sang of wanting to be touched, needing to please, ready to explore. She described the taste, touch, smell of passion, and the crazy thirst that was never truly quenched. It was the racy, intimate blueprint to a woman's desire.

The audience was silent for a few seconds after the final note echoed around the room, until Nia felt panic start to bloom in her stomach. Then the claps started, increasing in speed and volume until everyone was up in a standing ovation. She shook her head, hardly able to believe the response. The cheering continued and her eyes filled with tears as Nia realized what this meant.

There were no more barriers or confines to who she could be or what she wanted to do. No matter what happened in the future, Nia was going to be okay. She was finally free.

Chapter 31

From the moment she walked on the stage, Evan was transfixed. The surprise of her being here in Virginia and having his friends from Fortis there with them faded pretty quickly. Nia was always beautiful. But up there, sitting with a guitar, teasing the audience, made her vivacious and enthralling. She was born for music.

Evan knew she could sing and play the piano, so he wasn't surprised by her talent. Her ability wasn't to carry a tune well, or play the guitar expertly; it was in using words to convey hair-raising emotion. The music was only the vehicle to deliver the experience. And he was in awe.

As the crowd finally settled down after her first performance, Evan was overwhelmed. He listened to Nia sing in that rich soulful voice, with such heart-wrenching passion, and every single word cut him to the quick. They were honest and painful; reminding him of all the ways he had hurt the person he cared most about in the world. By the end of it, Evan felt raw and exposed.

Unable to remain contained surrounded by his friends, he stood abruptly, pushing his way through the crowd. In the bathroom, he wiped down his face and attempted to get a grip on his frayed emotions. He was heading back to the table when Nia dedicated the second song to him, and Evan had been rooted in that spot by the rear wall for the remainder of her performance. The last two songs told him everything he'd wanted to hear, and echoed all the words in his heart.

Finally, she stepped down from the stage, walking around the tables as people stopped her to express their enjoyment. Her face glowed, and her eyes sparkled. Evan swallowed past the lump in his throat and made his way back to his woman. His friends got to her first, each hugging and kissing her cheeks, all clearly blown away by her talent. Finally, it was just the two of them standing as the club manager took the mic to thank Nia and offer an open invitation to return anytime. Evan heard it in the background but his eyes held hers, and neither was able to pull away.

He reached out for her hand. She gave it freely, then allowed him to all but drag her out of the club.

"Wait," she demanded once they were outside, laughing from the rush. "We can't just leave. We have to say bye to your friends."

He stopped in the middle of the sidewalk, pulling her into his arms.

"No we don't. I'm sure they know what comes next."

She raised a brow, still smiling widely.

"Really? And what comes next, *Ice?*" she teased, settling into his embrace so their bodies were sealed tight.

"You tell me what I've wanted to hear since I kissed you that first time," he growled low, near her ear.

"Really? Since then?" she asked, her eyes widening with surprise.

"Pretty much," he muttered in a low, husky tone.

"Hmmm. And what exactly is it that you want to

hear? That I want you?" Nia whispered back, her lips brushing his neck, causing shivers down his spine.

"I like that, but it's not it, Nia."

"No? Then what?"

"You know what," Evan countered, feeling his heart swell with anticipation.

"That I want to be with you, even if it's in Alexandria, if that's what you want?"

Evan smiled, liking that statement too.

"That's nice, I'm sure we'll work out the details. But that's not it, either," he insisted. "Tell me, Nia. I need to hear it. It's the only thing that matters."

She nuzzled under his jaw, driving him nuts with her touch.

"I love you, Evan *Iceman* DaCosta," she finally declared.

"Yeah, that's it," he whispered back before finally kissing her sweet lips. Those were the words that gave him the life he wanted, with her forever.

"By the way, it's just *Ice*," he clarified a short time later, when they came up for air.

She smiled.

"Really? I like *Iceman* better. You should think about changing it. It's a bit more superhero-ish, like Superman."

"It's *Ice*. And it's not changing."

He took her hand as they separated, walking toward the car.

"That's right, you're a Thor fan," she shot back, sarcastically.

"I'm not a fan, I just think he would beat Superman, that's all."

"All right, whatever. Maybe we should get you one of

those magic hammer thingies so you can create your own thunder and lightning."

Evan grinned, flashing deep dimples.

"Baby, you've already seen my hammer. The thunder and lightning always follow."

Her snort of laughter echoed into the night.

Don't miss the next thrilling book in the Fortis series,

Hard and Fast

Available in January 2016!

Chapter 1

Lucas Johnson strode purposefully through the entrance of an apartment building in downtown Chicago. While he looked casual and relaxed in dark blue jeans and a lightweight charcoal jacket, his eyes were sharp and alert. A pretty, full figured woman passed him in the lobby, giving him an open look of interest and appreciation. At six feet, two inches with a lean, athletic build, he was hard to miss. Lucas flashed her a broad, flirty grin and she winked back. His pretty face and disarming smile suggested a naughty playboy, not a brilliant and lethal former-government agent.

"How far are you from the target?"

The question came from Raymond Blunt through the tiny earpiece in Lucas's ear. Raymond was an agent at Fortis, the full solution security and asset protection firm owned and managed by Lucas and his two best friends Evan DaCosta and Sam Mackenzie. They had a team of twenty-two highly trained and experienced field specialists, technicians, and operations analysts with experience from all branches of elite government service.

Lucas had three men with him on the ground for

this assignment. Their objective was to shut down a small-time blackhat hacker named Timothy Pratt who had infiltrated their clients secure computer system with a complicated Trojan Horse program.

"We're inside, heading into the staircase," advised Lucas.

The other two Fortis agents were entering the building from other access points, and linked into the connected earpieces.

"Okay, the signal is coming from the fifth floor," confirmed Raymond from his position providing surveillance support from their truck parked down the street. "According to the building schematics, you're looking for the third unit on your right, from the West staircase."

Lucas was now at the base of the staircase closest to him.

"Ned, you take the East stairs," he instructed. "Lance, take the elevators and I will approach the target from my end. We'll converge on the apartment door. I'll make contact, with both of you as back-up in the wings."

"Got it," confirmed Ned Bushby. Like Lucas, he was a former Secret Service agent.

"Confirmed," added Lance Campbell, an ex-Army Ranger.

Lucas ran up the staircase, two steps at a time. The hall on the fifth floor of the building was empty, except for Lance as he exited the elevator. Ned came through the other exit door only seconds later. The three men crept swiftly and quietly to apartment 514. Ned and Lance took positions next to the door, hands hovering near the grips of their concealed pistols. Lucas gave them both a signal with his hand, and knocked.

There was no answer.

The men looked at each other. Lucas knocked again.

"There's no answer, Raymond," Lucas stated in the earpiece.

"Well, the system's on and running, so it may be an automated program," Raymond replied. He came to Fortis after twelve years with the NSA, and next to Lucas, was their top systems and security specialist.

"Do we have any activity from the target?" asked Lucas, in a whisper.

"No, no cellular phone usage since nine forty-three a.m.," Raymond confirmed. "And the phone's GPS signal is still in the apartment."

It was now almost eleven-fifteen on Friday morning. Lucas looked at his two men, putting up two fingers to indicate their plan B. He then took out a small, pointed tool from his back pocket, picking the standard residential lock in twelve seconds. The deadbolt took another ten seconds. The three men slipped into the apartment silently, guns drawn and ready for any situation. They quickly fanned out from the front entrance into the small, messy studio apartment, checking in the closets and bathroom. The abandoned food containers and discarded clothing everywhere suggested the place was well occupied, but there was nobody home. A laptop was set up on the kitchen counter.

"Raymond, we're in," Lucas confirmed. "The computer is here."

"Boss," stated Lance from the living area. "He couldn't have gone far. His cell phone and wallet are on the coffee table."

Lucas nodded. He was already turning on the laptop to assess the tech.

"Let's be out of here in ten minutes," he told Ned and Lance. "You guys see if you can find any info that can identify his motives. I'll need at least seven minutes to clone the system and shut down the Trojan."

He did a quick inspection of the equipment, a standard, off-the-shelf laptop connected to a wireless modem. The operating system was another story. Lucas quickly bypassed the secure login and accessed the system administrative functions before connecting a small jump drive to one of the USB ports. It was a sophisticated program that he had designed, meant to wirelessly transmit a cloned version of the desktop, operating system and hard drive of the target system. It also left behind a passive rootkit software that would allow Lucas and the Fortis team undetected access to the computer and connected networks.

"Raymond, I've started the clone," he advised.

"Yup, the data is coming through here," Raymond confirmed through the earpiece.

"Good, we're at forty percent transmission. It should be done in three minutes."

Lucas did a few more configurations to the programming code in the admin program, then backed out of the system, and erased all traces of his presence until not even the most elite intrusion detection specialist could sniff his activities. He put the computer back in sleep mode just as the data transfer was complete.

"Got it, Lucas," noted Raymond. "The info looks complete."

"Good. We'll be out of here in one minute." He turned to the other agents as they completed their careful search of the apartment. "Anything?"

"Nothing," Lance replied.

"I got this," added Ned, holding up a couple of empty,

used bank envelopes. "Whatever Pratt's up to, he's being paid in cash."

The team did one final sweep to ensure their presence would be undetected. Then they exited, locking the door behind them and split up to meet with Raymond at their rented truck a block down the street. Ten minutes later, they were headed out of the city back to the Fortis chopper grounded at a private heliport fifteen miles outside of the Chicago city limits.

"So, what are we dealing with here, Lucas?" asked Lance. "From what we saw, Pratt looks more like a messy college kid than a corporate hacker."

"He is a kid," added Raymond. "He just graduated from John Hopkins a year ago, with mediocre grades and an unremarkable college life. Up until January, he was doing tech support at Best Buy in Maryland."

"So what happened three months ago and why's he in Chicago trying to break into the computer network at Magnus Motorsports in Toronto?" continued Lance.

"Hactivism maybe?" asked Ned.

"I don't think so," Lucas replied. "Magnus is a relatively small player in custom race car components. Their latest project is a high-performance, fuel efficient hybrid engine. Not really something to upset any political or social groups."

"When Marco Passante hired us last year to set up a secure computer network and data back-up system, was it just the timing of their new technology, or was he worried about a particular threat?" Raymond questioned, referring to the President and owner of Magnus.

"Last summer, he suggested their technology had the potential to be revolutionary, and highly coveted in the auto industry," Lucas told them. "He talked about general concerns that his competitors would try to steal or destroy the work."

"Well, Pratt's not good enough to have built the Trojan we just shut down. He has no online portfolio or footprint to suggest he's an active hacker," Raymond added. "Looks to me like someone has set him up as a script kiddie for several months to go after information that has to be worth a big return on the investment. So either Passante had great foresight, or there is more to this client engagement than we thought."

"Raymond, my man, you've read my mind," Lucas concurred as they arrived back at the small airport in north suburban Chicago. "Once they've detected that we've shut down this attack, whoever's funding Pratt will have to find another way to get what they're looking for. Since the full Magnus network is self-contained in a local, private UPN within their building in Toronto, any additional attacks will be directed onsite. So, I need to have a more transparent conversation with our client, and re-scope this project."

They all piled out of the rented truck and began loading up their chopper.

"Question," interrupted Lance while they worked. "What the hell is a script kiddie?"

Lucas and Raymond exchanged looks of disgust.

"How do you not know this stuff?" demanded Raymond with a shake of his head.

"Because I'm not a geek," the ex-Ranger shot back.

Lucas grinned, and Raymond shrugged since neither was the least bit offended.

"A script kiddie, or a skiddie is not skilled enough to design their own programs," explained Lucas. "So, they use tools and scripts built by other hackers."

"Got it," Lance replied, looking even less interested in tech-talk than before. "So maybe Pratt's just a lackey here. Maybe we should be looking for the person that developed the program he used."

"Not necessary. I already know who designed the Trojan program," Lucas stated with a dry smile. "It's called AC12 and it's been around for a while."

The others looked at him with various degrees of surprise.

"AC12?" repeated Raymond. "Are you sure? I worked on a few instances at the NSA. It's an ugly fucker, nearly impossible to disarm without wiping your whole system clean."

There was a pregnant pause.

"I'm sure," Lucas finally confirmed. "I built it in my freshman year at MIT."

Two days later, Lucas landed at the Billy Bishop airport on the Toronto Islands in Lake Ontario. He headed straight into the city to check into his hotel, a short block away from the Magnus Motorsport shop and offices. A couple of hours later, he was unpacked in his room, and seated at a table in the hotel's lobby restaurant for dinner. He was scheduled to meet with Marco Passante first thing Monday morning.

Lucas was not a big fan of hotels. During his career as a cyber-security consultant with the Secret Service, he'd spent many nights in cold, cramped rooms around the world. Even ones as nice and fancy as the five-star Metropolitan didn't come close to the comforts of home. The only advantage they offered, hopefully, was a decent restaurant, and a selection of imported beer. Maybe, a beautiful stranger to share the bed with for a night or two. Like the woman that just walked into the room, he thought. Now there was someone who could make this trip more enjoyable. Around five feet, eight inches, slender in a tight dress, long, bare legs and stiletto heels. Since it was April and raining hard outside, Lucas concluded she was a guest at the hotel, possibly alone. Perfect circumstances and exactly his type.

He took another drink from his beer bottle, watching unobtrusively as the hostess escorted the attractive woman to a dinner table across the room from his. Her hips swayed gently with each step, and she tossed her long brown hair with confidence. He relaxed back again, patiently anticipating how the evening would unfold. If she remained alone, Lucas would invite her to join him for dinner.

"Sorry! I'm just going to steal this seat for a second," announced a feminine voice. "These boots were definitely the wrong choice for tonight."

In the chair across from him, all he could see was the flat of the woman's back. She was bent over, doing something under the table, muttering swear words like a trucker. Lucas's lips quirked and he took another sip of his beer.

"Who designs these torture devices?" she added while straightening up.

He followed her hands as she gestured to her legs encased in a pair of very high, very sexy black leather boots. They went past her knees, but the table cut off the rest of his view. Lucas had to resist leaning forward to see where they ended, but his imagination was now fully engaged.

"Definitely a man," he replied smoothly.

She finally turned in the chair to look at him. Lucas paused, caught by the intensity in her large golden brown eyes. He had the impression of creamy caramel skin, pink shiny lips and a mass of jet black dreadlocks falling well below her shoulders.

"What?" she asked, clearly confused.

"Those boots were definitely designed by a man," he stated with a wide smile.

She finally blinked, then looked back at her feet.

"You're right. Explains why I can't stand in them for more than an hour at a time," she muttered.

"I don't think they were meant for that kind of action," Lucas added, giving her a wicked grin.

The woman looked at him again, assessing him intensely. Her frank stare was strangely unnerving, but he fought the urge to look away.

"You're pretty," he finally said. It didn't sound like a compliment. "Thanks for letting me take a load off for a minute."

"Stay as long as you'd like," he offered casually, sipping his bottle again.

Her eyes narrowed, and her gaze lowered to his lips. Lucas felt the start of a low, familiar pulse in the base of his stomach. She licked those plump, pink lips, and his pulse deepened.

"I'm Lucas, by the way," he added when the silence between them stretched uncomfortably.

She blinked again, then smiled broadly. Lucas stopped breathing, while his pulse deepened to a full throb.

"Thanks Lucas, but I'm good now."

She stood, allowing him to see her full length. As Lucas rose to his feet also, he noted her height and soft curves. The boots ending a few inches above her knees where shiny, latex-covered thighs continued, topped with a crisp white men's style button-down shirt. But only her eyes kept his attention. They widened with surprise as he stepped closer, topping her by at least six inches. Her brows knitted, then she brushed past him without another word. Lucas turned to watch her walk away as the scent of sweet vanilla and brown sugar lingered softly in her wake.

"Lex! Nick's leaving," he heard, as a man from the group at the bar waved in her direction. She was swallowed into the crowd of people.

Lucas looked back at his table, wondering what had just happened. There was no way he had imagined the physical chemistry between them, or her subtle reaction. His body was still humming at a low frequency.

Lex.

In all likeliness, she was here with another guy. Someone from the private party milling around the bar. But the night was young. With any luck, he'd have a chance at round two. Particularly since the other options in the room no longer held any interest for him. Lucas sat back down and ordered another beer as his prime rib dinner arrived.

Over the next forty minutes, Lucas got several glimpses of black locs within the group of noisy men. She talked and laughed with many of them, but none seemed to have a claim on her. He finally drained his second bottle of beer, charging the tab to his room, and headed in her direction.

He was only a few steps from her position against the bar when she said something that must have been very clever, because the three guys around her peeled with laughter, one of them almost chocking on his drink. Lucas took in her bright smile and the teasing look in her eyes, wishing he could share the joke. He brushed her shoulder lightly as he leaned toward the bartender.

"Stella Artois, please. And whatever she's having," he requested, pointing to Lex's empty cocktail glass.

Lex glanced at him from the corner of her eyes. He met her gaze steadily.

"Thank you," she said softly when the fresh drink was placed in front her.

"Club soda?" Lucas quizzed.

She shrugged with one shoulder. "I'm driving."

He nodded. There was a pause. Lucas intended to wait for her to make the first move, ideally to indicate she also felt the attraction and his attention was welcomed. It was usually a pretty easy strategy at a bar. But the seconds ticked on and she just watched him with those curious eyes. He cleared his throat and caved.

"How are your feet doing?"

She smiled.

"I'll survive for a little longer, I think."

"Good. But I'm happy to help you out again if needed." His grin was meant to be charming and flirty, but her raised brows made him doubt its effectiveness.

"Really? And how exactly would you do that?"

Suggestive words sprang into his mind, like the offer of a soft bed to rest on and a long foot rub to ease any discomfort. The direction of his thoughts must have been clearly written on his face because she finally looked away. Lucas leaned forward so he could whisper near her ear.

"I'm a gentleman, so I'd do whatever you need me to do."

"I bet you're good at that," she shot back, playing with frosty condensation at the side of her glass.

"At what?" he probed, now facing her with his elbow resting on the bar. His fresh mug of Belgium draft beer remained untouched.

She rolled her eyes, suggesting he knew exactly what she was referring to. "At doing whatever a woman needs."

"I can only try my best."

Lex looked at him again.

"So, Lex, is it? Are you from Toronto?" he finally asked.

"Born and raised. But I can tell from your accent that you're American. Visiting for work, I take it?"

"That's a pretty accurate guess," he conceded.

"A man like you, alone in a downtown hotel bar on a Sunday night, and looking for company? Not hard to figure out."

"Ouch," Lucas stated with a grimace. "Pretty, and a cliché."

"Sorry, I didn't mean it as an insult, just an observation," she added, her eyes twinkled with amusement, taking the sting out of her words. "Unless of course, you have a wife and kids back in . . . where, New York?"

She took a sip from her drink.

"Alexandria, Virginia actually. Born and raised in New Jersey but I live in Virginia now," explained Lucas, lifting up his left hand as evidence. "No wife, no kids. Not even a girlfriend."

"Hey Lex, this dude bothering you?"

Lucas didn't take his eyes off Lex, but he could make out that the guy asking was back in the crowd, standing over six feet and big, almost as big as his best friend, Evan.

"Are you bothering me?" she asked with a big smile. She was enjoying the conversation. Lucas felt encouraged for the first time.

"I hope so, if you don't mind," he replied with a grin of his own.

"I'm good, Adrian, thanks," she told the other man

before facing Lucas again. "I'm leaving now, anyway. Thanks again for the drink."

"So early? We were just starting to get to know each other," Lucas protested.

"Sorry, I have to be at work early tomorrow."

Lucas followed her as they made their way through the crush of people pressing close to order drinks.

"Alright, I'll walk you to your car."

Lex gave him a funny look.

"Okay, if you insist," she conceded.

"I do. I'm a gentleman, remember."

They were silent as she handed in a coat check ticket and got back a long red rain coat that tied at the waist. He escorted her out of the restaurant.

"My car is in valet parking, so I'm just going to the front entrance. There's really no need to accompany me," she added.

Lucas looked down the long expanse of the hotel lobby, with the main doors at the opposite side. There was plenty of real-estate for more conversation.

"No biggie. It's on my way to the elevators anyway," he dismissed with a shrug.

"Giving up on the night already?" she teased with raised eyebrows. "You're walking away from a lot of potential."

"Who says I'm giving up?" Lucas shot back. His gaze said very clearly that she had all his attention.

Lex let out a short bark of laughter, her lips spread wide in a big smile. He was now certain she was enjoying their banter as much as he was.

"Exactly what is that you think you'll accomplish on this short walk?"

"Nothing. I'm just enjoying your company, that's all," he lied smoothly while he plotted the right words to say that would convince her to stay with him for more of the evening. Maybe even all night.

"Liar. You think you can talk me into sleeping with you tonight," Lex shot back, her voice still soft with humor. "And I bet you're successful with almost all the women you meet. But, unfortunately, I really have to be up early in the morning."

Her blunt assessment caused Lucas to stop his slow stroll. His expression showed a mix of surprise and intrigue. Lex stopped two paces ahead and faced him.

"And as tempting as your offer is, I'm not what you're looking for. I'm the exact opposite of what you want, Lucas."

He heard two things in her statement: She remembered his name and she was tempted. Lucas smiled, slow and sexy.

"I haven't made you an offer, Lex," he clarified.

"Not yet, but you will."

"Touché," Lucas conceded. He continued their walk, slightly slower than before, and she fell in beside him.

"What do you think I'm looking for, and why is it not you?" he finally asked, genuinely curious.

"The answer to the first question would damage your fragile ego, pretty boy. And the second is way too complicated."

Lucas snorted, not the least bit insulted.

"Try me. I'm tougher than I look, and I've got time."

She looked him up and down, her eyes lingering in some interesting places. Lucas felt like straightening his back and flexing his chest. But he resisted the juvenile urge. Nothing he did would demonstrate just how strong or lethal he really was.

"Okay. But I don't think I can handle it if you start crying," she shot back, her lips twitching with the effort to hold back a grin. "You're looking for someone fun, easy going, comfortable with a casual hook-up. A girl that's not going to have expectations beyond a night or two. A week, tops. And all on your schedule."

She wasn't asking for him to agree, and he wasn't offended. The summary was pretty accurate. Casual sexual encounters required honesty and clarity at the onset for they were bound to go disastrously and un-comfortably wrong. A complication that he never had time for.

"And that's not something you're into," guessed Lucas. "I can respect that."

"No, I prefer casual, actually" she clarified. "And I'm partial to pretty men without expectations. But I need it on my terms. My available time is limited and I don't like to waste it. And that's where it gets complicated."

They had both stopped walking, and now stood side by side in the middle of the marble tiled hotel corridor. A small number of people walked about around them, but neither noticed.

"I'm pretty sure that's not going to work for you, pretty boy."

"Let me be the judge of that. I can compromise," he replied softly, completely captivated by her frank state-ments and overall energy.

She looked back at him speculatively, her bold, golden eyes piercing into his. Lucas found himself holding his breathe, willing her to see what she needed in order to make a connection between them worth-while.

"Was that an offer?" Her expression was deadpan, but her tone was teasing.

Lucas laughed. He liked her. "I believe it was."

"Thanks, but I have to pass," she finally replied. "I

don't compromise very well. One of my less enduring qualities, I've been told."

She started walking again, much faster and determined than before, and Lucas could only fall in step. He felt much more disappointed than he cared to admit. And it was more about the end of their conversation than a spontaneous roll in bed.

"Well, there's no need to decide so quickly," he added when they reached the large revolving door at the hotel entrance. "I think I'll be here all week."

Lex turned to face him, then backed into the open section of the turning door and pushed herself out of the building, her eyes fixed on his. Lucas shoved his hands into the pocket of his jeans, experiencing a rare moment of indecision. She'd already turned down his invitation, and was walking away. It was just unmanly to chase after her further. Yet, a minute later, he was following her outside, ignoring the damp, windy night air that easily blew through the fine wool of his sweater.

The valet attendant had already taken her ticket and they stood waiting silently for her car to be bought up. He looked at her profile, then felt her look at his. Their eyes finally locked before the deep, low rumble of a powerful turbo engine vibrated around them. Lucas turned to watch the slow arrival of a late model Porche 911 Carrera, tricked out with sexy skirts, matte black sport rims, bright red brake callipers, and a slick storm gray paint job. It was a beauty.

"This is me," Lex said at his side, and he turned to find her watching the car as it rolled to a stop. Pride of ownership was written all over her face.

"Wow," was all he could say.

She laughed, throwing back her head. Lucas couldn't help laughing also.

"I was serious about my offer," he added seconds later, feeling helpless to stop her from walking away.

Her lips quirked again, and she stepped to his side, close enough to brush against his arm, but still a breath away. Lucas looked down towards her face, locked on those incredible eyes, and did what he wanted. He leaned down until his face was close to hers, then paused to gauge her reaction. Lex lowered her lashes and tilted her chin up an inch. His mouth covered hers without a plan of attack, only the irresistible need to touch her, explore the powerful attraction, and taste her flesh before she disappeared into the night.

The kiss was open-mouthed and instantly hot, giving her a glimpse of what he had to offer, and taking more than he was entitled to. Lucas was rewarded with her quick response. Lex leaned in until her soft curves pressed into his side. Her tongue met his, swirling around with arousing strokes. Lucas Johnson, elite security specialist and practiced bachelor felt his knees go weak.

His lids were still closed when she pulled back, stepping out of his reach. His breath was caught somewhere between his stomach and throat, dreading what came next.

"Nice to meet you, Lucas," she said softly.

He opened his eyes to watch her walk around her car and slide into the low driver's seat. He was still standing in the cool night air, hands buried in his front pockets as the sports car disappeared down the street.